Happy Christmas Glenda
OXOXOXOX

Praise for *The Lost Dog*

'This is the best novel I have read in a long time.' A.S. Byatt

'Reading *The Lost Dog* one is torn between contradictory urges—to race ahead, in order to find out what happens, and to linger in admiration of de Kretser's ravishing style.' *New Statesman*

'*The Lost Dog* is an uncompromisingly literary (and literate) book: ferociously intelligent, highbrow, allusive and unflinching in its probing of the question, "What relation does the individual have to history?" It is equally intransigent with its oblique, sometimes scathing answers. A book such as this, so preternaturally attuned to listening to "the patient rage of history," is marvelously layered palimpsest.' Neel Mukherjee, *Time*

'Michelle de Kretser is one of those rare writers whose work balances substance with style. Her writing is very witty, but it also goes deep, informed at every point by a benign and far-reaching intelligence . . . so engaging and thought-provoking and its subject matter so substantial that the reader notices only in passing how funny it is.' Kerryn Goldsworthy, *Sydney Morning Herald*

'A beautiful piece of writing—place your bets now for the Booker.'
Kate Saunders, *The Times*

'This is a stunning book, each sentence handcrafted with precision, each theme hauntingly explored . . . De Kretser weaves a magical web, juxtaposing continents, attitudes to literature and art, the wildness of the natural world with the empty heart of cityscapes. She highlights the fragility and selectiveness of memory and contrasts the brash soul of 21st-century living with the poetry of what we have lost. What emerges is an achingly personal perspective on history. And it is a joy to read such gloriously paced, beautifully written prose.'
Good Reading

'. . . a dazzlingly accomplished author who commands all the strokes. Her repertoire stretches from a hallucinatory sense of place to a mastery of suspense, sophisticated verbal artistry and a formidable skill in navigating those twisty paths where history and psychology entwine.' Boyd Tonkin, *Independent*

'. . . a superb stylist . . . *The Lost Dog* is written in a devastatingly pointed style, with not a hint of Jamesian circumlocution. De Kretser has a talent for sizing up a character, at once bringing them to life and puncturing their pretensions. Her hardboiled sentences invariably hit their mark. "Seeing through" is one of her strongest suits . . . a wonderfully written novel that is often funny, but, despite its sharp critical intelligence, it is not at all cynical.' James Ley, *The Age*

'Lucky readers will discover the trickery of Michelle de Kretser's *The Lost Dog* only upon finishing reading it, at which point the author reveals her astonishing sleight of hand . . . an uncannily compelling mystery.' *Washington Post*

'Michelle de Kretser's powerful imagination transmits an extraordinary energy to the narrative . . . a remarkable achievement. Fully to enjoy it requires slow and patient reading, but the effort brings ample rewards.' Francis King, *Literary Review*

'A captivating read . . . I could read this book 10 times and get a new perspective each time. It's simply riveting.' Caroline Davison, *Glasgow Evening Times*

'. . . remarkably rich and complex . . . De Kretser has a wicked, exacting, mocking eye . . . While very funny in places, *The Lost Dog* is also a subtle and understated work, gently eloquent and thought provoking . . . a tender and thoughtful book, a meditation on loss and finding, on words and wordlessness, and on memory, identity, history and modernity.' *The Dominion Post*

'Michelle de Kretser is the fastest rising star in Australia's literary firmament . . . stunningly beautiful.' *Metro*

'. . . a wonderful tale of obsession, art, death, loss, human failure and past and present loves. One of Australia's best contemporary writers.' *Harper's Bazaar*

'In many ways this book is wonderfully mysterious. The whole concept of modernity juxtaposed with animality is a puzzle that kept this reader on edge for the entire reading. *The Lost Dog* is an intelligent and insightful book that will guarantee de Kretser a loyal following.' Mary Philip, *Courier-Mail*

'Engrossing . . . De Kretser confidently marshals her reader back and forth through the book's complex flashback structure, keeping us in suspense even as we read simply for the pleasure of her prose . . . De Kretser knows when to explain and when to leave us deliciously wondering.' *Seattle Times*

'De Kretser continues to build a reputation as a stellar storyteller whose prose is inventive, assured, gloriously colourful and deeply thoughtful. *The Lost Dog* is a love story and a mystery and, at its best, possesses an accessible and seemingly effortless sophistication . . . a compelling book, simultaneously playful and utterly serious.' Patrick Allington, *Adelaide Advertiser*

'A nuanced portrait of a man in his time. The novel, like Tom, is multicultural, intelligent, challenging and, ultimately, rewarding.' *Library Journal*

'. . . rich, beautiful, shocking, affecting.' Clare Press, *Vogue*

'. . . a cerebral, enigmatic reflection on cultures and identity . . . Ruminative and roving in form . . . intense, immaculate.' *Kirkus Reviews*

'De Kretser is as piercing in her observations of a city as Don DeLillo is at his best . . . This novel is a love song to a city . . . a delight to read, revealing itself in small, gem-like scenes.' *NZ Listener*

'. . . de Kretser's trademark densely textured language, rich visual imagery and depth of description make *The Lost Dog* a delight to savour as well as a tale to ponder.' *Bookseller + Publisher*

'A remarkably good novel, a story about human lives and the infinite mystery of them.' *Next*

'. . . confident, meticulous plotting . . . strong imagination and . . . precise, evocative prose. Like *The Hamilton Case*, *The Lost Dog* opens up rich vistas with its central idea and introduces the reader to a world beyond its fictional frontiers.' Lindsay Duguid, *Sunday Times*

Praise for *The Hamilton Case*

'. . . one of the most remarkable books I've read in a long while—subtle and mysterious, both comic and eerie, and brilliantly evocative of time and place. I've never been to Sri Lanka but I feel it's become part of my interior landscape, and I so much admire Michelle de Kretser's formidable technique—her characters feel alive, and she can create a sweeping narrative which encompasses years, and yet still retain the sharp, almost hallucinatory detail. It's brilliant. (Booker judges, where were you?)' Hilary Mantel

'Multilayered and beguiling . . . The rackety lives of Sam Obeysekere and his family eloquently illustrate the fundamental messiness and illogic of the human condition . . . This novel—which also beautifully renders the sensuality of Ceylon—is a very artful and evocative plea for interpretation over explanation . . . *The Hamilton Case* does enchant, certainly, but—more important—the book admirably and resolutely sees the world as it really is.' William Boyd, *New York Times Book Review*

'I read *The Hamilton Case* in a single day, greedily, absorbed in its narrative drive, its poised voice, its rich texture, its dense sense of life.' Delia Falconer, *Sydney Morning Herald*

'Bewitching . . . an utterly captivating blend of intellectual muscle and storytelling magic.' Boyd Tonkin, *Independent*

'. . . I devoured this book. De Kretser misses nothing: she has a keen ear for dialogue and an eye for detail.' Christopher Ondaatje, *Literary Review*

'De Kretser is an elegant and accomplished storyteller . . . nevertheless, it is not the story itself that makes *The Hamilton Case* exceptional, but the means of telling it . . . [She has] the extraordinary ability to write for the senses with the kind of intuitive grace and attention to detail that can only result from extremely hard work. The result is a novel so delicious that you have to keep stopping as you read, for fear of finishing too soon.' Jane Shilling, *Sunday Telegraph* (UK)

'De Kretser positions herself as a truly international writer in theme and outlook. She deserves comparison with JM Coetzee and her countryman Michael Ondaatje.' *Courier-Mail*

MICHELLE DE KRETSER

QUESTIONS OF TRAVEL

First published in 2012

This project has been assisted by the Australian Government through the Australia Council for the Arts, its arts funding and advisory body.

Allen & Unwin
Sydney, Melbourne, Auckland, London

83 Alexander Street
Crows Nest NSW 2065
Australia
Phone: (61 2) 8425 0100
Email: info@allenandunwin.com
Web: www.allenandunwin.com

Cataloguing-in-Publication details are available from the National Library of Australia
www.trove.nla.gov.au

ISBN 978 1 74331 100 4

Internal text design by Sandy Cull, gogoGingko
Set in 10/16.5 pt Berkeley Oldstyle Book by Midland Typesetters, Australia
Printed and bound in Australia by Griffin Press

10 9 8 7 6 5 4 3 2 1

IN MEMORY OF LEAH AKIE

Under cosmopolitanism, if it comes, we shall receive no help from the earth. Trees and meadows and mountains will only be a spectacle . . .

E.M. FORSTER,
Howards End

But surely it would have been a pity
not to have seen the trees along this road,
really exaggerated in their beauty

ELIZABETH BISHOP,
'Questions of Travel'

I

Anywhere! Anywhere!

CHARLES BAUDELAIRE,
'Anywhere Out of the World'

I

WHEN LAURA WAS [illegible]

[illegible] were eight [illegible] and [illegible] Lucy [illegible] mother [illegible] had [illegible] they [illegible]

[illegible] school [illegible]

[illegible] from the [illegible] mother's [illegible] to her [illegible] well again [illegible] the connection [illegible] explain [illegible]

[illegible] There was [illegible] through [illegible] were [illegible] would [illegible] the [illegible]

LAURA, 1960S

WHEN LAURA WAS TWO, THE twins decided to kill her.

They were eight when she was born. Twenty-three months later, their mother died. Their father's aunt Hester, spry and recently back in Sydney after half a lifetime in London, came to look after the children until a suitable arrangement could be made. She stayed until Laura left school.

Look at it from the boys' point of view: their sister arrived, they stood by their mother's chair and watched an alien, encircled by her arms, fasten itself to her nipple. Their mother didn't die at once but she was never well again. *Breast cancer*. They were clever children, they made the connection. In their tent under the jacaranda, they put together a plan.

Once or twice a year, as long as she lived, Laura Fraser had the water dream. There was silky blue all around her, pale blue overhead; she glided through silence blotched with gold. Separate things ran together and were one thing. She was held and set free. It was the most wonderful dream. But on waking, Laura was always a little sad, too, prey to the sense of something ending before its time.

She had no recollection of how it had gone on that Saturday morning in 1966, her brothers out in the street with bat and ball, and Hester, who had switched off her radio just in time, summoned by a splash. No one could say how the safety catch on the swimming-pool gate had come undone; the twins, questioned, had blank, golden faces. Next door's retriever was finally deemed responsible, since a culprit, however improbable, had to be found.

To the unfolding of these events, the boys brought the quizzical detachment of a general outmanoeuvred in a skirmish. It was always instructive to see how things went. They were only children, ingenious and limited. They had no real appreciation of consequences or the relative weight of decisions. If Laura had owned a kitten, they might have drowned that instead.

The pool was filled in. For that, too, the twins blamed their sister. Their mother had taught them to swim in that pool. They could remember water beaded on her arms, the scuttle of light over turquoise tiles.

LAURA, 1970S

LONG-FACED AND AMBER-EYED, what Hester brought to mind was a benevolent goat. She had spent the first seven years of her life in India, from which misfortune her complexion, lightly polished beech, never recovered.

Every night, Laura listened while Hester read about a magic land called Narnia. By day, the child visited bedrooms. They contained only built-in robes—a profound unfairness. Still she slid open each door. Still she dreamed and hoped.

Glamour, on the other hand, was easily located. It emanated from the sky-blue travel case in which Hester kept her souvenirs of the Continent. There was a tiny Spanish doll with a lace mantilla and a gilded fan. There was a programme from *Le lac des cygnes* at the Paris Opéra, and a ticket from the train that had carried Hester over the Alps. Dijon was a *menu gastronomique*, Venice a sea-green, gold-flecked bead. An envelope held postcards of the Nativity and the Fall as depicted by Old Masters, and tucked between these arrivals and expulsions, a snapshot of Hester overexposed in white-framed dark glasses against the Greek trinity of sea, sunlight and symmetrical stone.

Laura would beg for the stories attached to these marvels. Because otherwise they merely thrilled—they were only crystals of Aeroplane Jelly: ruby red, licked from the palm, briefly sweet. Hester saw a small, plain face that pleaded and couldn't be refused. But the tales she offered it disturbed her.

As a young woman, she had settled in London. There, stenographically efficient in dove-hued blouses, she survived a firm of solicitors, a theatrical agency and two wartime ministries. Then she turned forty and went to work for a man named Nunn. On the occasion of the Coronation, Nunn smoothed his moustache, offered Hester a glass of sherry and promised her *tremendous times*. Hester expended three pages on this in her diary but not a word on the practical arrangement at which she had arrived with the mathematician from Madras who rented the flat below hers. Novelties to which he introduced her included cheating at bridge and a sour fish soup.

In Hester's girlhood it had been hinted that France was a depraved sort of place, so naturally it was to Paris that her thoughts turned when she realised, as her third Christmas in his office approached, that she was in love with Nunn. Hester imagined him making her his mistress in a room with a view of the Eiffel Tower—she imagined it at length. An accordionist played 'Under the Bridges of Paris' beneath their window; Nunn threw a pillow at him. Food was still rationed in England, so Nunn gave orders for tender steaks and velvety puddings to be placed under silver covers and left at their door. Their bed was draped in mauve silk—no, a deep, rich red. When Hester learned that her employer intended to spend the holidays with his wife's parents in Hull, she crossed the Channel anyway. Nunn might detect traces of French wickedness about her when she returned and be moved to act.

Paris, in those years still trying to crawl out from under the war, was morose and inadequately heated—scarcely different, in fact, from London. But a precedent had been set. Every year, Hester penny-pinched and went without so that she might go on spending her holidays abroad. Partly it was the enduring hope that she might yet return with something—an anecdote, a daring way with a scarf—that would draw her to Nunn's attention *in that way* at last. Partly, and increasingly as time passed, it was the dismay that pierced her at the prospect of solitary days spent in London with neither companion nor occupation (for her arrangement with the mathematician was confined to alternate Wednesdays).

When Nunn's wife finally came to her senses and died, he promptly married her nurse. Hester realised that she was fed up with England. On the voyage home to Sydney, she stood at the ship's rail late one night. The eleven volumes of her diary splashed one by one into Colombo Harbour.

Because all this had to be excluded from the stories laid before Laura, they suggested journeys undertaken in order to seek out delightful new places. Whereas really, thought Hester, her travels had been a kind of flight.

The way to crowd out her misgivings was to talk and talk. So it wasn't enough to describe the dishes on the handwritten menu from Dijon: a pear tart as wide as a wheel, snails who had carried their coffins on their backs. Hester found herself including the lilies etched on the pink glass shades of the lamp on her table, and the stag's head mounted on the wall. She described the husband and wife who, having had nothing to say to each other for forty years, inspected her throughout her meal. Where recollection had worn thin, she patched and embroidered. Laura shivered to hear of the tight little square in front of the restaurant where once the guillotine had stood: a detail Hester concocted on the spot, feeling that her narrative lacked drama and an educational aim.

So the story that made its way to Laura was always vivid, informative, and incidental to what mattered. Conjuring the glories of Athens, Hester passed over the unspeakable filth of Greek public lavatories that obscured her memory of the Acropolis, greed and incaution having led her to consume a dish of oily beans in Syntagma Square. Calling up the treasures of the Uffizi, she didn't say that she had moved blindly from one coloured rectangle to the next, picturing ways in which Nunn might compromise himself irrevocably in the filing room. Rose windows and Last Judgments dominated her description of Chartres, but when Hester had been making the rounds of that cold wonder, all her attention was concentrated on the selection of a promising effigy. Tour guides harangued, Frasers howled in their Presbyterian graves. Hester lit candles in a side chapel, knelt, offered brief, fervent prayers.

After talking about her travels, Hester was often restless. Turning the dial on her transistor late one night, she heard a woman say gravely, *Away is hard to go, but no one / Asked me to stay.*

RAVI, 1970S

THE SEA TUGGED PATIENTLY AT the land, a child plucking at a sluggish parent. That was the sound behind all other sounds. Ravi's life ran to its murmur of change.

The town, a pretty backwater, lay on the west coast of Sri Lanka, twenty-three miles from Colombo. The baroque flourish of its colonial churches threw tourists into confusion. They had come prepared for Eastern outlandishness, not third-rate copies of home.

The new airport wasn't far away. At night, the tilted lights of planes were mobile constellations, multiplying from year to year.

Ravi lived in a lane crammed with life and food. Foreigners sometimes strayed there by mistake. If they noticed the Mendises' house, they saw a box devoid of charm. But the house was built of bricks plastered over and colourwashed blue. It contained an electric table fan, a head of Nefertiti stamped on black velvet, a three-piece cane lounge suite. The roof held through ravaging rain. In the compound lived a merry brown dog called Marmite, who could sing the chorus from 'Cold, Cold Heart'. There was also a tree with mulberries as fat as caterpillars, and a row of violently orange ixoras. The lavatory was indoors and flushed.

He hated girls and sisters. How had Priya come by a copy of the *Jacaranda School Atlas*? She made a great show of studying its pages. When Ravi came to stand at her elbow, she spread her hands and leaned forward, calling, 'Mummy, Mummy! *Aiyya* is breathing on my book.'

On the veranda, their mother was singing to the baby: *John, John, the grey goose is gone*. In a classroom that resembled a stable, with a half wall and a wooden gate, Anglican nuns had taught Carmel to sing. Her husband could play the guitar, and there was the radio, of course, but music in that house meant singing. The older children sang *Why can't my goose* and *Christmas is coming, The goose is getting fat*. Geese, like God, were taken on trust and for the same reason: they must exist somewhere, there were so many songs about them. Carmel broke off to nibble Varunika's tiny nose. Then it was *Five golden rings, Four calling birds* . . . She had sung it to each of her children, standing them up on her knee.

The baby was beneath Ravi's attention. But he was only ten months older than Priya. The two fought or played with ferocious concentration. In cramped rooms, they exercised childhood's talent for finding secret places.

There were games with the neighbours' children. Brandishing a stick to signify authority, *Kang kang buuru!* chanted the leader. *Chin chin noru!* came the chorus. 'Will you do what I say?' 'Yes!' 'Run, run, run and bring me . . .' When it was Ravi's turn, he would request objects that struck him as magical: a square white stone, a green feather. But Priya set daring tasks, ordering her subjects to pluck a mango from a tall tree, or to pull the tail of the chained monkey who performed for tourists, his face savage and full of sorrow.

Long after a shower was installed in the house, the children went on making a game of well baths, each icy bucketful eliciting screams of joyful fear. The bathroom and lavatory, the last rooms in the house to be built, were not completed until Ravi was almost four. Perhaps a memory of this work, an odour of damp cement, a sense of walls rising, his parents' preoccupation with the shaping of domestic space, ran under a game the boy devised when he was older. Accompanied by Priya, he would roam the town looking at houses. When he hissed, 'Here!', the children would stand and stare. Priya liked to speculate about the people who lived in the house: she assigned names and ages to the children, she sought Ravi's opinion on whether their mother was stern or smiling, she dithered over the dishes they preferred. Ravi bore her babyish chatter in silence and contempt. He cared nothing for the lives enclosed within a set of walls and was excited only by the character of *the house itself*. A circular porch lent this one a jovial air, a double row of openwork bricks rendered another spiteful, while a third, *an upstairs house* situated deep in a treed garden, exuded a sinister charm. Ravi's imagination worked to penetrate the enigma of each dwelling: the brilliance and dark within, the disposition of rooms, the dusty places where dead flies collected.

This game, at once deeply satisfying to both children and the source of bitter quarrels, continued throughout the long Christmas holidays one year.

LAURA, 1970S

A SUMMER CAME WHEN, HAVING twirled up the seat to adjust its height, Laura would photograph herself in the booth at Central Station. There were weeks when all her pocket money, changed into twenty-cent coins, disappeared that way. The result was always the same: a gloomy adolescent skulking under a bush of hair.

One day she pulled back the pleated curtain and emerged from the booth to see Cameron. Her brother had his back to her and was using one of the payphones, listening with one palm on the tiled wall. His head drew all the light in that dim place. The receiver, pressed to it, had the black potential of a gun.

Laura dodged back into the booth. Why had Cameron left his office to use a public phone? When she heard the whirr that signalled the delivery of her photos, she peered out. He had vanished.

The way home lay past gardens that were gatherings of green decay. Rain might fall, caressing and warm, hardly different from the thick, damp heat that preceded it. Now and then a cloudburst encouraged delirium. Timetables and commuters were thrown into chaos, traffic lights blacked out, the broken bodies of umbrellas littered the streets. Sydney quite forgot that it was Western and efficient. It squinted over its brown back at Africa, at India; an old, old memory of wholeness stirred.

After the storm, pavements showed a heightened brilliance of blossom. Here and there, a stone face wore a cockroach veil.

When there was a scorcher, afternoon tightened around the streets in a blinding bandage. On the nature strips, the nerve had gone from the grass. But in the park the light was necklaces and pendants looping through trees. Laura lifted an arm from the elbow like an Ancient Egyptian; admiring her pretty hands, with their pointed fingers, her thoughts were bright and dark as leaves. Half-naked children were to be seen darting through a shimmer. Laura would have liked to join them beside the fountain, but an elf shouted, 'What's Vince gunna do for a face when the camel wants its bum back?' and Laura recognised that she was no longer a child. She walked on, badly frightened. She had just realised—which is to say, *felt*—that she was going to die. The elf, too, was doomed, along with Vince and all that shrieking crew. The broad-faced European woman stealing municipal begonias would die, and those two snooty girls flicking their flat hair at each other. All the teachers at school and everyone in Fleetwood Mac. No one on earth would be spared. The galloping gaucho, the indigo Tuareg on his dune: inside each, the skeleton smiled. The dead strolled through the suburbs, through the city, their numbers uncountable and always on the rise. How could anyone, knowing this, select the correct concourse at Central, or deal with the yellow fat on a chop while not disdaining the multitudes that starved? The gravel slurred under Laura's shoe, the planet groaned as it turned. Behind her, screams revived and fell like sirens.

•

Her brothers, paid to apply the rack and the screw, Hamish in finance, Cameron in commercial law, rented a flat in Rushcutters Bay. Donald Fraser, the medical director of a hospital, often dined out. So Laura and Hester watched TV with plates on their laps. There were evenings when they sat on and on, homework and washing-up neglected. By the time the sound of a car could be heard in the drive, it was a point of honour not to move. It was not that Donald criticised *Dallas* or fish fingers. But he stood there, jingling his keys, before retreating to his room.

Wielding his electric toothbrush in the ensuite, Donald Fraser was reliving the moment when he had looked in on his daughter and his aunt. One was a glazed wooden goat, the other . . . he rinsed and spat, traversed by pity for the female morsel he had engendered. His daughter's eyes were coins of a lowly bronze denomination. Crossing a room, she caused him to fear that she would collide with the furniture. He couldn't conceive of the absence of beauty in a woman as anything other than a misfortune and had no doubt that he was responsible for Laura's affliction. Long before her birth, mirrors had presented him with lips as coarsely suggestive as a double entendre. He pressed a hand towel to them. Yet they excited women. For context is all. It was a mouth that would constitute an invitation on an attractive girl; on his poor child, it was an obscenity from which her father flinched.

She was the repository of all that was massive and defective in Donald's lineage. He had escaped the worst of it. Even so, as he peered over the towel, he fell far short of his own ideal. Beautiful young women—*stunners*—were therefore necessary to him. His wife had been one. Her radiant fairness had passed to the boys, adulterated by the Fraser motif of thickly turned limb. But it was the girl who had suffered the full force of the paternal theme. *The runt had copped the brunt.* At her birth, Donald had thought of a piglet he had dissected as a boy. Loving his sons, he showed them no quarter. Laura, whom he didn't like to touch, raked in money, extravagant presents, indulgence in all things except the failure in which she had played no part.

Donald put the thought of his daughter from him by recalling the image of a succulent oncologist who was driven to adjust her goldilocks if ever they met in the lift. But her smile contained a pink expanse of gum. So he had pretended not to understand when she 'accidentally' called his extension. Emboldened before the bathroom mirror by this proof of standards, he dared to let the towel fall.

In the rumpus room, they were eating Tim Tams straight from the packet. An ad break interrupted a Ewing machination—something involving a secret and a lie. It must have been the reason Hester chose that moment to confide that she hadn't always been the last after a run of boys. A sister had contracted diphtheria in India at the age of three. Pinafored Hester, lingering outside a window, heard her mother say that the child's throat seemed to be lined with grey velvet. 'That was the infected membrane,' said Hester to Laura. 'Dr Norris had ridden through a cyclone to reach us but he was too late. Ruth choked and died.'

Yuk! thought Laura. The unfairness of being saddled with *an old bag* as companion had recently begun to oppress. Thankfully, the Ewings had returned to cavort and divert. Hester went on holding half a Tim Tam. Eventually, she placed it on her saucer and drew a hanky from her sleeve. Laura thought, If you cry, I'll have to kill you. She waited, sliding her eyes sideways and holding a cushion like a shield. The whole hanky thing was disgusting, too—what was wrong with a Kleenex?

Hester was in the grip of a senseless thought: *Death runs in our family*. For a long time, the space occupied by Ruth had remained visible; the child Hester had to step off a path or choose a different chair. A Ruth-shaped form, something like a mist but less definite, still moved now and then along a passage or across a window. Back teeth together! said Hester to Hester. It was the only salve known to her childhood: offered when a funny bone collided with a cupboard, when a sister died. Over the years that followed, the command lost its power; it survived in the present as a joke. It wasn't that Hester regretted the shift, exactly. But the saying belonged to a world that was imperfect and solid: how had it grown as light as mockery? She wiped her ringless fingers—carefully, one by one.

Ravi, 1970s

ON THAT DAY IN 1779 when Captain Cook died in Kealakekua Bay, an Italian apothecary arrived in Galle on a ship registered in Rotterdam to the Dutch East India Company. One of these men was already famous and the other would die in obscurity, but each had his part in a great global enterprise that ran on greed, curiosity and the human reluctance to stay still.

Ravi's pedigree reached back through two hundred years to the Italian adventurer; on his mother's side, which didn't count. Of his father's ancestors, however, he knew almost nothing. No tales circulated of them, for they lacked exoticism and hence the glamour from which legends are made.

Mindful of his wife's European heritage, Suresh Mendis had once brought home a sideboard inset with speckled mirrors and a portrait of Edward VII. It was solidly constructed from teak, but two of its clawed feet had been sawn off and one of its drawers was stuck. Suresh told his wife that he had acquired it from a colleague who was emigrating and had *let it go for next to nothing*. Suspicion fluttered in Carmel, but this was in the first year of their marriage, and they hadn't yet learned to look on each other's wishes as flaws.

Propped on bricks, the sideboard was placed on the back veranda to await repair. There it stayed and became, in fact, a useful receptacle for the odds and ends that every household accumulates: a pot of glue, string, receipts, a saucepan without a handle, a cracked dish that might yet serve for the dog's rice. 'Look in the sideboard,' the Mendises would advise each other when they had searched everywhere else for an elusive object.

It was here that Ravi came to stand when his father went into hospital with pains in his stomach and failed to return. The sideboard, ever further advanced in decrepitude, one of its mirrors shattered by a cricket ball, a second monsoon-warped drawer now as unyielding as the first, had nevertheless endured. Ravi was just tall enough to lay his head on the battered board, beside a blurred whitish ring left by a glass. Marmite, believing this stance to signal a new game, trotted up and remained beside him, gently wagging her tail.

Laura, 1980s

SHE NOTICED AN ANT SCURRYING about the bathroom basin. Overcome with tenderness—for where could it go? on what could it subsist?—Laura resolved to pick it up in a tissue and deposit it outdoors. But her need to pee was urgent. Satisfying it, she grew dreamy and remained seated far longer than necessary. She turned on the tap to wash her hands and recalled the ant too late, as it was swept away.

Afterwards Laura thought, Perhaps suffering isn't a sign that God is absent or indifferent or cruel. Perhaps all the horrible things happen because he just gets distracted.

She was sixteen, a metaphysical age. The Absent-Minded Almighty: having created him in her image, she felt quite protective of him and worshipped him tenderly until the phase passed.

Ravi, 1980s

'HISTORY IS ONLY A BYPRODUCT of geography.' It was Brother Ignatius's greeting to every new class, the gambit unchanged in thirty-one years. Then very deliberately, with the air of a curator about to reveal a precious artefact, he would manipulate a cord that unrolled a map of the world.

Much creased, nicked here and there, the map brought an unsettling dimension to the room. At once, the gazes of all the boys flew to their island, a dull green jewel fallen from India's careless ear. It was so small! But no one is insignificant to himself. And in a niche high above the classroom door lay a flat water bottle, its bright red plastic dull with dust, that had been flung up there to avenge a long-forgotten insult; and bedbugs moved in the wooden chairs that the pupils treated at the end of each term, carrying them outside and spraying them with Shelltox. Remembering this, the boys shifted in their seats, certain that the backs of their knees itched. The tips of their fingers grazed words gouged out with dividers and inked into their desks, and they recalled scraping the lids smooth with razor blades, after which they had applied a rag dipped in shoe polish to the wood.

There was the matter of the Indian Ocean. These children were well acquainted with its fidgety expanse. There remained the problem of how to match it to a blue space labelled *Indian Ocean*. Ravi, studying the map, saw that what he knew of existence, the reality he experienced as boundless and full of incident, had been reduced by the mapmaker to a trifle. If the island were to slide into a crack in the ocean and be lost forever, the map would scarcely change. He was visited by the same sensation that came when a wave pulled free from beneath his feet. Things tottered and plunged.

Brother Ignatius was pointing out the conjunction of trade routes, ocean currents and deep-water harbours that had brought the Phoenicians to their island—and, in time, everyone else. It was vanity that led men to overestimate the force of history, he said, for history was a human affair. But, 'Geography is destiny. It is old. It is iron.'

Old. Iron. They were not so much words as emanations from the reverend brother's core.

When Brother Ignatius smiled—rather, when his thin mauve lips slipped sideways—boys trembled with fear. He could be glimpsed around the town on a high black bicycle, very early in the morning or at dusk, when the uncertain light, the silent glide of the bicycle and the figure in white drapery lent these sightings the quality of apparitions.

Without the benefit of notes, Brother Ignatius spoke of the Zuiderzee, the Nullarbor, the Malay archipelago, evoking places he had never seen in such living detail that now and then, in years to come, a man arriving somewhere for the first time would be made uneasy by a persistent impression of familiarity, until, if he were fortunate, he would recall a lesson half attended to on a morning he could barely retrieve from the rubble of days under which it lay.

When the reverend brother turned to the blackboard, there were boys who flicked each other with rubber bands or stared out of the window. The shadow of a great tree lying on the grass contained pieces of light, coins in a dark hand. But Ravi's thoughts answered to the irrigation systems of vanished kingdoms, to the complexities that attend the siting of cities, to the almost-freshwater Baltic Sea.

Brother Ignatius was a tea bush: born upcountry, a Tamil tea-plucker's Eurasian bastard, the lowest of the low. Condemned to toil on the plains, he said, 'Hills are God's gift to our imagination.' And, 'Who can say what lies on the other side of a hill?'

Ravi waited until Priya was out. He knew where she hid her atlas. His thumbnail traced journeys across continents. He went for a walk across the world.

When the time came to choose between subjects, he didn't want to give up geography.

Carmel Mendis, now in the purple stage of mourning, donned an uncrushable lilac dress and set out to address the problem at its source. Her hair was opulently pinned and curled, for Carmel had trained as a hairdresser before her marriage. Ushered into Brother Ignatius's presence, she remained undaunted. He was imbued with the awful grandeur of the Roman Church. But she had brought children into the world.

'My son is going into the science stream,' she announced.

Brother Ignatius looked at his palms, which were paler than you might expect from the rest of him. 'Junior science students are encouraged to study an arts subject if they wish.'

Carmel was obliged to speak of a son's duty to his mother.

For what could a tea bush, abandoned at birth and reared by priests, know of that sacred bond? A Rodi woman had told Carmel's fortune and assured her that she would not want for anything in old age. Carmel knew this meant that her son would be a surgeon. Her eyes, which were large and still brilliant, remained on Brother Ignatius to remind him of origins and limits.

The next time Ravi mentioned going on with geography, the reverend brother's lips shot sideways, and he assured his star pupil that there was not much future in it.

LAURA, 1980S

DRIVING HOME FROM A WEEKEND in the Blue Mountains, Hamish misjudged the speed at which he could take a bend. Speaking of it years later, Laura said, 'It should have been terrible, shouldn't it? It was, for Cameron.'

At the funeral, her brother had the lopsided appearance of a badly pruned tree. Looking at him, Laura knew how much she had been spared of grief. Flint-eyed throughout the service, she was handing around a plate of chicken sandwiches to people in dark clothes when she began to cry. It was a purely selfish emotion. She was crying for the loss of a family romance she knew only from a photograph. It showed the twins, aged five, leaning into their mother.

When everyone had gone away, Cameron appeared in her bedroom. 'What are *you* snivelling for? It's not as if Hamish liked you.' Laura beheld him magnified, a long figure with light about his head. 'Back teeth together!' cried Cameron. He reached for her wrist and administered an expert Chinese burn. Then he began to laugh. It came out like vomit, in lumps.

Ravi, 1980s

A MRS ANRADO, KNOWN TO the Mendises from church, was having an extension added to her house. She intended to rent rooms to foreigners, and was urging Carmel Mendis to do the same.

Ravi couldn't stand the Anrado woman. Pointing out walls that could be knocked through, she was all advice and teeth. The neighbour's daughter came to play, and Mrs Anrado asked Ravi, in front of everyone, if the squint-eyed brat was his girlfriend. How Priya crowed! Mrs Anrado was informing the children's mother that toast would have to be provided, tourists expected it. And the mulberry would have to go.

For weeks, every conversation led to plumbing and foreign notions of breakfast. Then Carmel Mendis arranged an interview with her bank. Afterwards, whenever Mrs Anrado was mentioned, Carmel's face tightened. The idea of strangers traipsing through one's home!

LAURA, 1980S

THE HOUSE IN BELLEVUE HILL was elevated, split-level, sluiced with light. The terrace dropped to scaly red roofs and a segment of harbour. When Hester left for a flat in Randwick, she mourned the loss of the jacaranda and that different, restless blue. But in low-ceilinged rooms her movements grew expansive. She remembered coming home from dances as a young woman: how spacious life had seemed when she took off her girdle.

Before leaving Bellevue Hill, Hester threw away her sky-blue travel case. Spreading its contents over her bed one last time, she was struck afresh by the fraudulence of souvenirs that suggested pleasure while commemorating flight. The green Venetian bead rolled silently away and came to rest in a corner of the room. There it remained, exquisite and unseen, a solid drop of light-flecked water.

Laura, 1980s

AT SCHOOL THEY HAD SAID, Laura is creative. Into that capacious adjective, oddity, uncompromising plainness, a minor talent—in short, much that was inconvenient—could be bundled. Laura had acquiesced, wanting them to be right. Also, she so admired Miss Garnault, the head of Art: the Split Enz badge on her lapel, the bottle-red hair gelled into spikes.

Laura's misfortune was the ease with which she drew, doublings of the world flowing with incurable accuracy from her hand. It was these nudes and streetscapes and bowls of pears, all flawless and false, that had carried her along to art school. But in that corner of the brain where truth persists, however starved of light, dwelled the knowledge that no one in all the vacant centuries to come would ever stand before work she had brought into the world and know the undoing that came when the wind shivered through a sloping paddock of grass. Or when a fragment of song—*that* song, the one you had bought the cassette for—wafted into the street from a passing car. With the revelation that arrived when the turned page showed the altarpiece at Isenheim, Laura didn't presume to compare. A sentence was often in her mind: *An eye is not a photocopier*. It kept bobbing to the surface of her thoughts that year: a corpse insufficiently weighted.

In an act of quiet desperation, she had perpetrated a perfect copy of *Organised Line to Yellow*, on which she pasted, here and there, extracts from the more savage evaluations of Sam Atyeo's painting. She propped her canvas on a table draped in canary-yellow nylon, and laid on this altar an array of factory-fresh yellow offerings: a china rose, a plastic banana, a string of wooden beads, a rubber duck. Filching from Degas, she called it *What a Horrible Thing Is this Yellow*.

When it was completed, the feeble wit and flagrant ineptitude of this assemblage overwhelmed Laura. Nevertheless, she entered it for the Hallam Prize. Nevertheless, it was declared a *wittily iconoclastic appraisal of Australian modernism* and included on the shortlist of six.

The annual Hallam Prize, open to all undergraduates at the college, was endowed by a former student who had inherited a largish deposit of opals near Lightning Ridge. It offered the use of a Paris studio for twelve months, an almost-generous stipend and tuition at the Beaux-Arts. Miss Cora Hallam had long since fled her native land for historic stones and up-to-date plumbing in St Germain but remained mindful of those condemned to vacuous ease.

On Laura's Walkman, Bowie sang of modern love. She crossed a park on wings and never saw the two-tone flare of the magpie who decided, at the last moment, that she wasn't worth swooping. Nor did she offer her customary salute to the man who sucked sherry from a paper bag, for her thoughts, as cinematically black and white as the birds overhead, were of Belmondo and cobblestones, and herself advancing down a leafless avenue in a slanted hat. Paris was surely her reward for irregular verbs committed to memory, for the existentialist struggle of persisting to the last page of *La nausée*.

Luckily she glanced down just in time to sidestep the small corpse lying on yellow wattle blossom and wet black leaves.

In a corner cafe, her friend Tracy Lacey was waiting at a metal-bordered table that was genuine Fifties laminex. Tracy, too, was a finalist for the Hallam, with a video that involved a housewife in a robe of steel wool taking a hatchet to Superman. It was uncomfortable viewing, for this *radical deconstruction of androcentric hegemony* was quite as horrible as Laura's jaundiced gaffe.

So here were the girls, meeting to celebrate their good fortune with ciggies and cappuccinos.

The announcement of the winner was still a fortnight away, but Laura knew that the Hallam would go to a final-year student called Steve Kirkpatrick for *Mr Truong in a Red Chair*. She accepted this as right and just, yet being human hoped. Hope beat its wings under her breastbone. It went so far as to insinuate that men with trenchcoats and ageless bone structure would speak to her of post-structuralism on terraces hedged with potted shrubs, while a waiter wrapped in a long white apron plied her with *fines*.

To suppress these ravings, she asked whether Tracy ever looked up when walking down a street and imagined rooms that hadn't yet been built. 'Apartments with people cooking and watching TV where now there's just air.'

Much of what Laura Fraser said was best ignored. Yet how Tracy loved her friend, for Laura was a darl and tried so hard and looked so . . . *unusual* was the kind way to think of it. And Tracy was all heart. And joyful choirs were making merry in those crimson chambers. Surely even Laura might hear their carolling?

But Laura had the lid off the powder-blue Bessemer bowl and

was intent on sugar—with a figure like hers! So Tracy had to lean forward and hiss, 'Guess what, guess what!'

Dull Laura Fraser hadn't a clue.

'You have to *swear* you won't tell anyone. Ant'll kill me if word gets around.'

Ant was Tracy's latest, this guy in Admin who looked exactly like Mel Gibson. But a bit shorter.

Laura swore the required oath.

'Guess who's won the Hallam!'

For a soaring moment, Laura imagined . . .

'*Mais oui!*' cried Tracy. '*Moi, moi!* They gave Ant the judges' report to photocopy.'

Boulevards and Belmondo were fast fading to black. It was hard to breathe, the air was so choked with debris from the collapse of flying buttresses. A lightning protest in Laura's brain declared, I could have had Paris until the announcement if. Fourteen days of sophisticated depravity in garrets overlooking the Seine trembled and were reduced to dust. For the last time, Laura lit another Gauloise and said, 'Is it not the case that your refusal to place the metaphysics of presence under erasure is always already an aporia?'

Ashamed of such selfishness, she offered congratulations without delay.

'Thanks, darl,' said Tracy. 'You'll have to visit me. In Paree.' She wore her hair combed back and up, and tied at the nape with a floppy pink chiffon bow. Under her black quiff, her face was a white pumpkin. But the profile sliced.

'In any city with decent licensing laws, we'd be calling for Bolly. But while we wait for civilisation to arrive, let's go crazy and have another round of cappuccinos—*n'est-ce pas, Mademoiselle Lacey?*'

How Laura's tongue clattered and clacked, like that wooden noise-maker she had rattled as a child.

'God, you make me laugh, darl! Mine's a skinny.' And when Laura returned with it, 'I wouldn't be surprised if the *Herald* did an interview. The Hallam's never gone to someone in first year.' Tracy fingered the ironic pink rag at her neck and observed, 'I'm a break with tradition.'

Laura, reminded of another who would have hoped, and with far greater cause, murmured, 'Steve.'

'I still can't believe they shortlisted him.' Tracy's profile stood out as clearly as if stamped on the silver light of Paree. 'I mean, he's technically quite good'—for she was magnanimous in victory—'but where's the concept in that painting?'

The words *truth* and *beauty* occurred to Laura, but after six months at art school she knew better than to utter them. The aroma of ham and tomato jaffles, however, proved irresistible.

As she chewed, the image of the dead mouse over which she had stepped returned to her. The eyeless head had resembled a mask. It was astonishing how a true thing might be taken for an imitation of itself.

Tracy Lacey, gazing on through drifting veils of Camel, was savouring the satisfaction of a woman who has denied herself food. That was the great thing about Laura, the comparison was always in your favour. Tracy was quite overcome with tenderness for her friend. Her complexion was after all rather gorgeous, peaches and cheese.

Here Tracy looked closer, because something in Laura's face, bent over buttery crusts, suggested despondency. At first she couldn't imagine why, on this gold and blue day with such news bestowed upon her, Laura Fraser should be glum. For herself, electric eels were slithering along her veins.

When enlightenment arrived, 'Oh darl!' she exclaimed and ground out her ciggie. 'I'm really going to miss you too, you know.'

A damp, greenish seed clung to Laura's chin, where tomato had spurted when she sliced open her jaffle. But Tracy scarcely noticed it, being sincerely moved.

In her share house in Newtown, when she should have been working on a project or researching an essay, Laura was to be found reading fiction. She read dreamily, compulsively, pausing only to pop in a square of Cadbury's or knock the hair from her eyes with her wrist. Novels, dutifully taken apart at school for Themes, had reasserted their wholeness, like time-lapse films of decay reversed. Now she read them as if they were guidebooks, looking for directions on which way to turn.

But she was so alone at humid midnight, trying to pummel her pillow into coolness! While still at school, Laura had realised that she could enjoy rather more success than far prettier girls by making it clear to their bumbling, flesh-fed brothers that she was willing to sleep with them. When she tumbled to that little ploy, There's *that* taken care of, Laura thought. Many a pleasant hour followed. But it turned out to be no more than a kind of competence, not so different from the facility with which she drew. In both cases, a degree of victory only heightened awareness of all that remained out of reach.

The numbers on her old clock radio clicked over again, and there Laura Fraser lay, thoughts scraping like the lemon-scented gum outside her window: a modern girl in the grip of antique cravings. The next novel waited beside her bed. Passing a bookshop that afternoon, she had spotted one of those brilliant little manuals called something like *The Children's Barthes*. Paree flared, quivered, threatened: it was a marble-topped table feathered with grey. But a merciful rush of dun-coloured patriotism came to Laura's aid. By the time it receded, she was leaving the shop with a secondhand copy of *For Love Alone*.

Laura picked this up now and opened it with the tips of her fingers. She approached Sydney gingerly in fiction. Was it really up to literature, even the Australian kind? She always feared that it might be like watching someone she cared for, but whose ability she doubted, thrust on stage by an ambitious and deluded parent. What if the performance came over as provincial and amateurish, or blustering and self-important? Sydney was *always already*: rakish, stinking, damp, radiant, too much with her. She turned a few pages. Multihued ballpoint warned from the margins: *Irony. Opinion of Australia.*

Downstairs, the phone began to shrill. It stood in the hallway, just outside Cassie and Phil's door, but they were at band practice and wouldn't be home before two. Tim's room lay between Laura's and the head of the stairs, but Tim held himself aloof from domestic activity; he was an artist, he had explained. So Laura heaved herself out of bed. She took the stairs at a gallop—as the young do, upright and unafraid.

There was silence at the other end of the line. Then the click as the caller broke the connection.

It wasn't the first time it had happened.

Laura switched on the jug for a hot chocky. But then—she checked in the sink and behind the couch—there were no mugs to be found. Tim lived on Vegemite toast and milky tea, and one by one every mug in the house would vanish into his room until someone banged on his door and demanded. Laura got dressed and went out into the night instead.

Above her, stars were conducting their long migrations. Hefty eucalypts filled tiny yards: broccoli jammed into bud vases. The trees must have been planted in the optimistic Sixties, when minds expanded and it had seemed that everything else must follow. When Laura tried to peer past one, a veranda showed its wrought-iron teeth. She ambled on, trailing her fingers against a sandstone wall, crumbling grains that had known the weight of an ocean. Oh, sea-invaded Sydney! The Pacific never tired of rubbing up the city, a lively blue hand slipping in to grope. It made you want to shout or sing—or swig the stars. But what came out of Laura Fraser's mouth was a giant burp. She was passing an open window at the time. The two on the other side muffled their merriment in a pillow, and enjoyed each other more fiercely thereafter.

She had been walking for a while when a lone car slowed and flashed its lights. Recalled from her trance, Laura remembered that she was female and veered closer to a fence as if its hard brown arms might save her. Over the accelerator's screech he called, 'You're too fucken ugly, love!' The harbour smell was reaching south to tickle scentless roses.

Laura had been choosing back streets, but instinct now led her towards thoroughfares and lights. Soon she was approaching the place where Glebe Point Road ran into Broadway. It was a junction Laura associated with vivid occurrence. Once there had been a motorcyclist face down in the road and a shriek of sirens. And quite recently, a gust of wind had presented her with a sheet of paper on which someone had copied out the lyrics to 'Message in a Bottle' with the chords written in above.

Tonight in the op shop, lights blazed scarily for no one. Drawing closer, Laura saw a big window peopled with frozen brides. They modelled beaded sheaths, dresses that frothed, skirts that belled, empire waists, sweetheart necklines, a bolero, a veil. A cream-embroidered caftan proclaimed that the Seventies were over. Taffeta and lace, rayon and silk proliferated in a bank of dressing-tables at the rear of the display.

At first, what fascinated and appalled was the approximation of life: the mannequins were spooky, multiple, sci-fi. But it was their setting that gradually pressed its claim. The brides posed among the varnished sideboards and satin-skirted standard lamps, tile-topped tables and brown corduroy armchairs of yesteryear. Smack in the middle, posing on a china cabinet that held an orange telephone and a lidless willow-patterned tureen, was a small plush dog of the breed that flourishes in the rear windows of cars. As Laura looked on, its head began to nod; a draught must have crept into the shop. There the little dog sat, assenting to the triumph of time and tawdriness over dreams—secondhand dreams it was true, somewhat threadbare, but impulses towards an ideal, all the same.

RAVI, 1980s

HE HAD BECOME FRIENDS WITH a boy named Mohan Dabrera. A mild rivalry served to intensify their awareness of each other. They sat next to each other in class and snorted at each other's jokes. Now and then, overcome by comradely feeling, one or the other would kick or strike his friend.

Dabrera, a short boy with a large head, had a worldly air. His father, an importer of catering equipment, had contacts at the hotels that lined the beach. Dabrera liked to boast of their buffet lunches. But he was essentially harmless. He invited Ravi home one Sunday and let him listen to The Police on the Walkman bought for him by his father on a business trip abroad.

These Sunday afternoon visits soon became a fixture. In Dabrera's bedroom, which stood at the end of a long, gloomy passage, the boys listened to music; a shelf held a collection of pre-recorded cassettes. Snacks were served to them, and cold glasses of Coke. The ceiling fan wheezed as it turned, while the boys practised card tricks. Sometimes they played Mastermind. Mostly they talked, Ravi cradled in a tangerine beanbag, Dabrera reclining on his bed.

They were at that stage of adolescence which sets great store by purity, Dabrera shedding his ceremonial air to lose himself in fervent homilies on the theme. He revealed that he took a cold shower-bath three or four times a day. To do less was *caddish*. Where had he picked up the distinctive word? It studded the boys' exchanges, for like all zealots they were much exercised by what they denounced. They would analyse anything that caught their attention: a classmate's remark, a line in an advertising jingle. Then: *Caddish!* They would shout it, jubilant. Entire categories were damned, tourists for instance, a species Dabrera had studied at first hand, who went about with practically nothing on, and didn't wash their feet at night before climbing into bed.

Carmel Mendis cried, 'What will you do when you catch dengue fever and die?' But Ravi had discovered something thrilling: he could ignore his mother. He went on setting up his bed on the back veranda. When he woke at night, the moon returned his stare. He vowed to do stupendous things. But then he felt thoroughly disgusted with life. Because Priya often teased him, poking fun at his mannerisms and turns of phrase, he lost himself in an elaborate story that culminated when she begged for his forgiveness. He assured her that she had it. Then he had her hanged.

Sometimes, taking Marmite with him on her chain, he slipped out into the street. Feelings of wonder and tenderness for all living things would overcome him. There was also the great mystery of selfhood. It was amazing that he was he, Ravi Mendis, with all that he thought and felt accessible to him alone. How terrible that the intricate web of his consciousness could never be experienced by, say, the one-eyed man who called periodically at the house to buy old newspapers. Or for that matter by Sting. Ravi held out his hands: there, at those ten fingertips, he ended. The sea sighed as it stretched in its bed. Marmite licked his knee.

There came an afternoon in July when Dabrera's feelings were tuned to an excruciating pitch. His face was strained, and his voice, habitually sonorous, disintegrated into childish piping as he swore Ravi to secrecy. Then he announced that their form teacher, Brother Francis, masturbated with the aid of a mango skin. Dabrera always avoided slang, preferring to say masturbation, penis, and so on; the formality lent his disapproval a redoubtable force. Swaying back and forth on his short legs, he refused to reveal how he had learned about the mango skin, saying only, 'Trust me, our so-called reverend brothers are a filthy lot.' And—a scatter of fine spittle accompanying his climax—'It's all just unspeakably *caddish*.'

Dabrera often required Ravi to accept his claims without question. But his loftiness grated this time. Perhaps Ravi had tired of his role as guest, with treats portioned out like devilled cashews—gratitude is rarely an emotion that keeps. Or perhaps it was just the irritability that spurted in him these days, causing him to take offence at the least little thing.

He said, 'I don't believe you.'

It was one of those suspended moments. It might have ended in a blow or—the vision that came to Ravi was at once precise and highly peculiar—a caress. But Dabrera only stood on tiptoe and fumbled along the top of his almirah. Then he held out a copy of *Playboy*. He had found it the previous week, he said, hidden in his father's desk.

'Can't you see?' Dabrera's voice shot up the scale again. 'It's much worse than you think. No one—*no one*—is above caddishness. It's all around. There's nowhere safe.' He crossed the room. 'Move over.' He settled himself into the beanbag and said, 'Look at it, will you.'

Side by side, neither sitting nor exactly sprawling, they looked. Ravi turned the pages, sometimes quite fast. Now and then the movement brought his arm into contact with Dabrera's shoulder. In the distance, or it might have been just outside the window, a crow cried, Ah-ah-ah.

Light was starting to fade, rubbed from the sky with a dirty eraser, when Ravi left. He walked down an avenue of crotons, away from the large, silent house. The only other person he had ever seen there was the grey-haired servant who brought them their nibbles and drinks. Dabrera was an only child, and Ravi had never met his parents. He had the impression that Mrs Dabrera was sickly; the long, dim passage suggested hankies soaked in cologne. But now and then, an angry female voice rose behind 'Roxanne'. The servant's face was always frightened and exhausted. Ravi began to walk faster and, eventually, to run.

On and on he sped, and a piano hurled the notes of an arpeggio after him like stones. He passed a broad, dark banyan tree and a green where cricket was played. Still he fled, running past the rest house, running past people and open-fronted stalls.

He reached a street lined with souvenir shops and places where tourists went to eat. He dashed across, and into a lane. Here, after the brassy streetlights, shadows surged to meet him. Blinded, he ran into a pale shape.

Brother Ignatius said, 'Always rushing to get on, Mendis.'

The shock of the collision caused the emotions of the afternoon to swarm up in Ravi. His thoughts flashed in all directions. Dabrera hissed, *They're a filthy lot.* But why was Brother Ignatius on foot, where was his bicycle? Confusion and embarrassment mingled in Ravi and filled him with rage.

Mrs Anrado's guesthouse stood halfway down the lane. A group of foreigners came strolling out of the darkness, young people in bright, loose clothes, one girl with a temple flower in a wave of yellow hair. She was saying, 'I don't care if it's Bali and Phuket. I just want to go somewhere cheap and with great food.'

On a great surge of courage, Ravi turned to Brother Ignatius. 'Geography is destiny? You don't know anything!' If he stopped for a second, he knew he would be lost. He shouted, 'People like that—' But he didn't know how to say what he meant.

'Pray for them, child. Going here and there, far from home.'

Now Ravi was close to tears. Again he yelled, 'You don't know anything!' Then he ran away.

At school it was easy enough to avoid Brother Ignatius. But what furtive purpose had taken him to a lane that led only to hippies and fields? Then anger would rescue Ravi from the swirl of shame and helplessness stirred by the memory, and he would conclude that the reverend brother was just a dirty fool.

As if by agreement, Dabrera and Ravi greeted each other in class with the flawless civility of mutual mistrust. By the middle of the week, Dabrera had been granted permission to exchange his desk for one on the far side of the room; a note from his mother claimed that the light from the window was weakening his eyes. In any case, there would have been no more afternoons at his house. In the north, Tamil guerrillas slaughtered fifteen Sinhalese soldiers in an ambush. Very soon the retaliations began, and Dabrera was missing when school resumed. His classmates learned that his mother was a Tamil. In Colombo, a mob had set her parents' house on fire and hacked the old people to death. Dabrera's mother would no longer let him leave the house. Ravi pictured him, a prisoner in a bedroom with The Police in his ears. When his jailer wasn't screaming orders, she couldn't stop crying. Ravi remembered the servant's frightened face.

Another awful thing was that Marmite settled down on the veranda, gave a mighty thump of her tail and died. Priya wrapped the old dog in a towel and placed her in her grave. She had once shrouded her dolls in handkerchiefs and buried them in the same spot under the mulberry, then as now rounding on Ravi when he tried to help.

Eventually, there came the news that the Dabreras had been granted asylum in Norway. Then someone else said Denmark—at any rate, somewhere where they could be certain of being cold.

LAURA, 1980S

AT THE END OF HER first year at art school, Laura looked carefully at all her work. Then she withdrew her enrolment. A few days later, in a video shop, she ran into one of her teachers—a lovely, sexy man!—and told him of her decision. Charlie McKenzie nodded. 'Smart girl.' She ended the summer in his bed.

Self-conscious under his gaze, Laura drew a red quilt over her stomach, her heavy breasts. He went away from her on bare feet and returned with a book. 'No need to hide.' Laura inspected the dimpled thighs and pear-shaped torso of Rembrandt's Hendrickje and was not reassured.

Charlie was a squat-bodied man with a tiny, hooded penis scarcely larger than Laura's thumb. But he was imaginative and unhurried. There was a dollop of Maori in his ancestral mix, making him a prize in certain quarters. At parties, Laura Fraser thrilled to the novel sensation of being envied.

Quite soon, there were other women. But Laura couldn't learn to share. When she said so, Charlie remained a friend, now and then still meeting her in bed. She was restful, he once remarked.

Laura would have wished for a gaudier assessment. By that time she was in her final year of English at university, yearning for irrevocable acts and large, sincere, nineteenth-century fictions.

On a blustery October morning, Hester sneezed. Six days later she was dead.

Laura left a message at the law firm where Cameron was a partner. He didn't return her call. Donald Fraser had remarried the previous year. He and his wife, a brisk anaesthetist, were doing something medical and crucial in Boston when Hester died. They sent a wreath. The card read, *A great innings!* That would be the anaesthetist, thought Laura, she was from Melbourne.

With Charlie's help, Laura packed up her great-aunt's flat. A chest of drawers yielded a photograph album with matt black pages. Two sepia children posed in buttoned boots: *Hester and Ruth* said an inscription in an upright hand. The album couldn't be given to the Salvos or thrown into a bin, but how many photos could Laura keep? The day passed in decisions that were betrayals. Charlie, returning to the room with a mug of instant in each hand, found Laura stricken. She had come upon a toffee tin containing every birthday card she had given Hester: 'I missed 1984.' Charlie tried to console her, but like most people, Laura dispensed self-reproach in inverse proportion to the damage done.

Hester's ancient transistor still lay beside her bed. A death notice, a funeral: these are formal, they have a shape. But what is to be done with the spreading sadness of a radio in a perforated leather case? Laura slipped the strap over her wrist and held the trannie to her ear. On winter afternoons Hester had sat like that, listening to the footy. She had spent two years in Ballarat as a girl and retained a life-long fervour for Australian Rules. When the enemy had a free kick, she would cross her fingers and hiss maledictions. The twins had imitated and mocked, chanting, 'Chewie on your boot! Chewie on your boot!' if ever they found Hester in a tricky manoeuvre such as the separation of whites from yolks.

One last relic pierced afresh: it was a charcoal portrait of Hester. Laura was responsible—how she hated it now. The drawing was as exact as a coffin: all that had escaped was everything vital. 'It's so lifelike!' Hester had exclaimed. But the lifelike is not life.

At her bridge club, Hester had flexed an old talent at discreet intervals; a blue bankbook revealed a surprising sum. She had left her father's gold watch to a man in London with fourteen letters in his name; everything else went to Laura. The anaesthetist would report, eventually, that her husband considered the will insulting.

And so, like a heroine, Laura came into an inheritance. There was only one thing to do. She set out to see the world.

LAURA, 1980s

LAURA HAD READ WIDELY TO ready herself for adventure: travellers' tales, histories, guidebooks. They warned of pickpockets, rabid dogs, unboiled water, children's eyes in which the incautious might drown. But no one mentioned the sheer tedium of being a tourist. Dreaming of travel, Laura had pictured a swift slideshow of scenes. But oh, the long, blank hours that linked! They were spent waiting for buses, trains, ferries, flights, waiting to cash traveller's cheques, waiting for the museum to open, waiting to make a booking or a call. Once, Laura waited to buy stamps while the clerks read her postcards with frank interest, passing them from hand to hand. It was like being trapped in a particularly irritating Zen koan: *In order to advance, the traveller must stay still.*

She came to savour the brief minutes at the end of every journey when travel was over but arrival remained prospective. The bus bumped into the station, the plane slipped into its bay. People rose, straightened their clothes, looked around for their belongings. Their involvement with each other held but was already infiltrated by change. Soon they would scatter, individual and purposeful as seeds.

In Bali, the plane door opened and there was the smell of the tropics, a moist coupling of fragrance and stench. Laura crossed the tarmac, stunned by a marvel: This is Asia and I am in it.

Dusk brought jetlag and large, velvety black butterflies. One startled her by having a face. Then she saw that it was a bat.

She couldn't wait to write to Charlie, to describe and enthuse.

There were Australian voices in the street, bars that advertised Foster's, surfers with eyes like blue fish.

It was nothing like home.

A man staying in the same losmen in Ubud addressed Laura at breakfast. He had been spending his holidays in Bali since 1971, he announced. 'Of course it's not the same these days. Legian was a fishing village. Have you seen it now?'

Hairy and resolute as a character from Tolkien, he moved without invitation to Laura's table. His name was Darrell; he was *in concrete in Alice*, he said. It was easy to picture him on a municipal plinth scanning the spinifex for wear and tear—but that was quite wrong, the beard marked him plainly as a garden gnome. The gnome squeezed lime juice over the sunset flesh of a papaw, saying, 'This place used to be paradise. It's ruined now.'

For the next twenty minutes, he spoke, in statements indistinguishable from accusations, of the forested acres felled since he had first come to the island, the multiplication of hotels, the destruction of reefs, the corruption of values, the poisoning of water and air.

What was totally infuriating was that not everything he said could be dismissed.

Laura had just finished a postcard to Charlie. There was a little cartoon of herself overflowing a flowery sarong, recumbent under a palm tree. *Miss you, heaps of love*. Dull lies were all that came as soon as she held a pen. That didn't matter because the real letter, a long one, was being composed in Laura's head. Among other things, it told Charlie about the affection the Balinese lavished on the very young. *We'd call it spoiling a child. When did we decide that love was a curdling agent?*

Darrell was saying, 'Take Kuta. You've been there, of course.'

There was no denying it.

'Rip-offs and tacky nightclubs and pissed footballers everywhere you turn. Burgers and *bananasheks* on the menus. The whole place shut down by ten when I was first here. You could hear a pin drop. Even Ubud's not the same these days.' He inventoried changes, all of them for the worse.

Near the entrance to the losmen, a bowl held the daily offering of flowers and cooked rice. The more distant view was of terraced fields. Laura's eyes followed a frieze of men and women labouring in the mud, watched by the sun's ancient face. Her letter continued: *A factory might save them from breaking their backs. But this gnome I know would have something to say about pollution. Anyway, who'd want to take a photo of a factory?*

Darrell leaned in. 'First time?' It was less a question than a diagnosis. When she confirmed it, he brightened. 'No worries. Reality'll soon set in.'

Reality/concrete: they were the same, Laura realised, something grey that spread and trapped.

A waterfall in a forest was mourning its lost life as a cloud. Under the lament, a whisper reached Laura: *What are you doing here?*

She shook her head and raised her camera. But the question remained.

She blamed it on Darrell. How dare he assume that she was a green girl? Stuffed into the back of a bemo, with something alive and unhappy fastened up in wicker and wedged into her ribs, Laura added to her phantom letter. It noted that ugliness, typically attributed to the modern by *orientalising foreigners*, was present equally in age-old elements. It cited the toddler with ulcerated sores along his legs, the man bowed with exhaustion between the shafts of a laden cart, the fly-wreathed filth by the wayside, the savage, stick-figure dogs. Nor did it neglect what progress had brought: the ominous flutter of discarded plastic bags, the traffic-choked road designed for the passage of beasts, the pink-kneed Dutchman across from Laura whose T-shirt, suitably illustrated, bore the legend *Bali—Land of Tits*. She alighted at her destination bone-rattled, filmed with dust, refreshed.

What she couldn't know was that Darrell was only a prefiguration. Across the world, the world-weary were waiting. Time after time, Laura would learn that she had missed the moment; to be a tourist was always to arrive too late. Paradise was lost: prosperity had intervened, or politics. The earthquake had finished off Naples. Giuliani had wrecked New York. Immigrants ruined wherever they squatted. France—well, France had always been blighted by the necessary evil of the French. But if only Laura had seen Bangkok before the smog/Hong Kong before the Chinese/Switzerland before the Alps/the planet before the Flood.

A girl called Corinne befriended Laura. They stood before a famous temple where tour buses exhaled. A sign declared in multiple tongues that menstruating women were not welcome. That morning, the girls had risen before dawn and been jolted on a bus for three hours. Corinne, who stepped lightly and stood perfectly straight, placed her hands on her hips. 'Fucking priests. The same shit everywhere.' In Montreal, Corinne had been educated by Ursulines; she owed them her spine and her contempt. She travelled with only a child's brown suitcase and was dressed always in creaseless white. Her cotton dress, bound with a temple sash, was a patch of light moving through dim, sacred interiors, along stairs, pausing to examine stonework. In the noon haze of a courtyard, she seemed to float. Laura, heaving along behind, wondered uneasily when and where she might change her tampon. Corinne appeared on a high brick outcrop, balanced on one leg, her joined palms raised. A volcano, not extinct, was propped above the temple. Laura pictured the punitive spurt, people fleeing and dogs, the lava nipping her guilty heels.

Mica glittered on a black beach where a gnome clad in a breastplate of fur placed himself in her way. Stupid Laura Fraser forgot the quiver of scorn she had prepared. Instead of letting fly with, *Do you imagine you're not a tourist?* and *Hasn't anyone ever told you that describing a complex culture as paradise is deeply patronising?*, she gushed, 'Isn't this the most beautiful place? Aren't we lucky to be here?'

Out of dull dreams, she opened her eyes and found that she was wide awake. Above the paddies, a cloudy crystal ball. Outside her window, one of her countrymen throwing up. A drum sounded somewhere, faint and insistent. How many Balinese would visit Australia to spend up on bargains and vomit in the streets? *What are you doing here?* Now she knew that the whisper had nothing to do with Darrell. It merely pursued everyone who left home.

•

Her guidebook had guided: *Stay in family-run losmens. Your money goes directly to locals, not to the multinationals who own the big hotels.* So Laura stayed with Balinese families and talked to their children in Useful Vocabulary. Corinne, who had studied anthropology, spoke of the benefits of cross-cultural encounters. 'In the measure one learns from the Balinese people, our Western egotism erodes. Have you remarked their faces? So full of joy!' Then she asked how much Laura was paying for her room. Laura named the sum—a few Australian dollars. Corinne was dismayed. 'But it is bourgeois to pay what they ask! That I can tell you without error. To respect their culture, you must not give more than half.'

On Laura's last evening on the island, Wayan, the owner of the losmen, inserted a tape of gamelan music into a cassette recorder and placed lanterns around the yard. His barefoot daughters began dancing, costumed in sarongs tucked up under their arms. Nimble as fish, their hands darted and curved. The smallest child wearied of the performance, broke off mid-step and went away; she reappeared from the shadows later to pick up the dance. On a woven mat beside Laura and Corinne, the children's grandmother had nodded off. When the tape came to an end, only the two visitors applauded.

The next morning, when the last strap on her backpack was fastened, Laura looked around her room. Quite soon, it would be swept clean. Someone else, pillowed on fresh linen, would dream in her bed. The clouds would still press on the hilltops, the children's voices would sound like rain. But the quilted green view would keep no trace of her gaze. The life of the place would flow on as if it had never known Laura Fraser. She dismissed the thought—it was plainly nonsense.

When she had settled her bill, Laura followed Wayan into the family's living quarters for farewells. A patch of colour sang in the dimness there. It was a cardboard box, decorated with purple and yellow tulips, that had once held Kleenex. Laura had thrown it away the previous day. Now it displayed its pretty pattern on a shelf.

Laura made a to-do of getting out her notebook and speaking to the children. In a flurry of shame, she wrote down their names and the family's address. Corinne appeared, yawning in a white cotton nightie. She had already explained that she wouldn't be staying in touch: 'To travel is to say goodbye.'

The rest of the day, vexatious with fumes and delays, barely registered with Laura. She was light-headed with schemes: she would write to every guidebook and tourist office recommending the losmen, she would pay for the education of the youngest girl. She would send the family . . . something marvellous and transforming, a new motorbike or an electric jug. She had taken photos of everyone: she would post them copies, for a start.

But in India, Laura's canisters of film disappeared from her pack while it was strapped to the roof of a bus. Months later, in London, the losmen children rose from an address in her notebook; it wasn't too late, she could still send them little gifts. While hesitating over what to buy, she decided to enclose a letter, explaining the absence of photos, describing her adventures. So much had receded that loomed large when she was staying with the family: the old lady's cataracts, Wayan's plans for expanding the business, the children's progress at school. The letter would enquire about all these things. She embarked on it at once and covered three pages with barely a pause. Then came a knock at her door or some other distraction. Laura had every intention of finishing the letter, buying the presents, posting the package. But she never did.

LAURA, 1980S

SHE CLIMBED INTO AN AUTORICKSHAW outside the bus station in Pondicherry and gave the driver the name of the guesthouse she had chosen.

'Oh yes, madam. Number eleven.'

Thinking he had misunderstood, Laura repeated the name.

'Yes, madam,' he said over his shoulder. 'Number eleven, Lonely Planet.'

Laura consulted the map in the travellers' bible. The guesthouse was the eleventh item in the key.

In a gloomy coffee house in Thanjavur, she ordered prudently milkless tea. Courting couples had sought refuge in the adjoining booths, where they nestled with decorum.

A waiter making passes at Laura's table with a filthy rag enquired where madam was from. When she told him, 'Dean Jones,' he murmured.

Laura had arrived in India not knowing this deity and had quickly been enlightened. 'David Boon,' she replied.

'Merv Hughes.'

'Allan Border.' And politely added, 'Kapil Dev.'

'Kapil Dev!' he repeated, eyes aglow.

The ritual satisfied, he asked how long she was staying in Thanjavur.

She was leaving the next day, said Laura. 'I'm going on to Madurai. And to Kanyakumari after that.'

'Then Kovalam and Trivandrum,' he supplied. 'And backwater boat trip and Alleppey and Cochin.'

'But how do you know?' cried Laura. She had spent pleasurable hours putting together her itinerary from guidebooks and maps.

He was equally astonished. 'All the tourists are going there, madam.'

On an afternoon in spring, she rested against fallen marble near a Moghul tomb. There were birds, stretches of grass, the names of God carved between chipped tiles of celestial blue. Families were picnicking under trees, while a group of young people photographed one another beside fragments of masonry, or climbed a flight of steps that ended in air. Then they, too, settled down to eat.

Laura had come to this place some miles outside Delhi in the company of two young men, students encountered at the Red Fort. What was irritating was that she could find no reference to the tomb in her guidebook, although this one was the superior kind devoted to culture and art. The omission might mean that she had arrived, at last, at one of tourism's blank spaces. But how annoying not to have any information about the ruins. Again she checked the index. Her new friends were no help. One said that the tomb housed the bones of a prince, while the other insisted that they were those of a saint. Was the prince worshipped as a saint? wondered Laura.

The boys neither accepted nor rejected her hypothesis. Aziz had a famous picture of Che Guevara on his T-shirt, Sanjay a photo of Michael Jackson. To tell the truth, they were both hungry, for the journey to the tomb on a scooter borrowed from Sanjay's uncle had been a lengthy one, and they gazed with longing at the picnickers around them. Each felt obscurely that Laura, a Westerner and a female, should have provided their party with food; each recognised, too, that this was unreasonable. On the grass, the group of young people laughed and pinched one another's arms. The scent of pakoras teased.

Aziz began to recite snatches of Urdu poetry. A translation followed: exalted stuff, nightingales and tears. Laura boiled the lament down to a preoccupation of her own, India's smells and sights, the spiced food, the languorous air having worked on her like light, rousing touches. She remembered the sexy temple carvings of the south. She had loitered, inspecting them through dark glasses.

In India, the single men she met backpacking conformed to one of two types. There were those, frequently unbathed, who were blissful with prayer or other addictions. Only the other day, a dhoti-clad boy, scabbed and with shaven head, had waylaid Laura to announce his dissatisfaction with the natives. 'You heard them lads going on about the cricket on the telly? All *lovely-jubbly* and *jolly fine shot*. Pretending like they're English, innit?' Then he told Laura that she could have sex with him. When she declined the opportunity, he produced his trump: 'I do Tantric. Goes on, innit?' Laura's infinite letter to Charlie wondered if it would be a kindness to explain that the prospect of it *going on* only lowered his meagre chances.

For the second kind of man, visiting the subcontinent was a strenuous sport played with set jaw against touts, germs, rip-offs, beggars, officials, in the end an all-India game, which he would one day recall, point by triumphant point, in the tranquillity of suburban conversation. Laura was unable to summon the effort such men required; nor did they appear to care overmuch for her. Tanned, several pounds lighter and hung with silver from the markets of Yogyakarta, she remained large and quite plain.

But here, where royalty or holiness had rotted, seeking out her company were these two. In a teashop they frequented, it was the boys' habit to detail their exploits, each one—both virgins, of course—striving to outdo his friend in the number and nature of his conquests. They had gone there as usual after arranging the excursion with Laura, brimful of hope and graphic speculation. Now they stared at this big foreign girl, and one pictured her hair spread on a pillow, and the other ventured no further than loosening it from its combs. What was she thinking of, this huge stranger? She must be mad to have come out here with them! Soon it would be dark. Their stomachs growled.

Mosquitoes sang. The sun crashed into the plains. They returned to the city as they had come, all three straddling the scooter. Laura, in the middle, leaned into Sanjay's shoulder blades; her nipples lengthened. On a quiet stretch of road, she slid her hand down from his waist. His response was instantaneous, but he kept heroically to his course. As the lights of roadside stalls approached, he gently but authoritatively disengaged her hold.

Outside her hostel, Laura thanked them. They waggled their heads—what *did* Indians mean by that? Assent, forgiveness, denial, rebuke?—and Aziz said, 'It has been a most enjoyable outing.' She watched the night drink them up.

The following morning, when Laura came out into the street, Sanjay was waiting under the sign that advertised *Three-Bedded Rooms*.

In the neutral tone a guide might adopt, he observed, 'In India there are many hotels.'

In the decrepit one to which he led her, she pretty much ripped off his clothes.

A sneeze might last longer! When she suggested something he might try, he scrambled down from her and into his clothes. 'My uncle will be angry if I am late,' he said, backing away from Laura on her rented nylon sheet. 'He is a very angry man.'

But he was there, waiting for her, the next morning. Laura moved to a single room and spent six days longer in Delhi than she had intended.

LAURA, 1980S

SHE LOOKED AT A BRIDGE, and what she saw wasn't balustrade and arch but the embodiment of a sonnet. As for the monuments, they were iconic from tea towels. Then came a red-purple tree, magisterial in a park. Laura had never seen another like it and she recognised it at once—copper beeches were always turning up in novels. That was what it meant to be Australian: you came to London for the first time and discovered what you already knew.

But that was in the first floating, glassy days. Underneath, it was all strange. The trees were large green buildings locked up in squares. And why had they called it Paddington? It was nothing like Paddo in Sydney. That went for Edgeware Road, too. It was equally amazing to find Indian shops run by Indians, unlike at home, where Indians were few, and the same racks of bright, flimsy garments and clumsily carved pantheons were presided over by flowerchildren who had faded on the stem. 'Hoxton! Isn't that a little off-piste?' exclaimed a rotund voice, and Laura knew herself incurably alien. English in the mouths of the English was a dream language, an affair of allusion and code.

She couldn't get used to the washing arrangements. No showers! But doing things differently was the point of leaving home. Willingly she scrubbed the tub before and after. Then her landlady, a sweet-faced Christadelphian called Blanche, asked her not to bathe every day. 'It uses hot water, you see.'

It was June. Each blade of grass stood up polished and green.

Laura came out of the National Gallery. She told the first friendly face, 'I am twenty-five years old.' What she meant was something like, I've missed twenty-five years of looking at those pictures. It was a straightforward sentiment, but all she could do, trembling a little, was repeat herself. Passers-by saw one of London's mad, a large girl talking to a lion.

Blanche's house was the latest in a succession of rooms Laura had rented in Bermondsey, Stamford Hill, Hackney, the blighted boroughs to which the exchange rate sentenced her. From tower blocks, those modern wrecks worked by the twentieth century's Unenlightenment, pit bulls and other monsters came and went. Once in a while, at the foot of a thundering flyover or mirror-glass cliff, she would observe a pink-eyed ancient frozen to the spot, as if engaged in a last attempt to drag a remembered map clear of the architectural felony that had obliterated it.

The ravages of monetarism were abroad, too: boarded-up shops, purse-snatchers, bulging job centres, bag-children asleep in doorways, cardboard suburbs erected and dismantled with the night.

Leaving the British Museum, Laura detected a distinctive vowel. Suddenly homesick, she accosted it. Phillip was elderly, forty-six at least. In archetypal tweed, he was a sausage in its skin. He admitted to his provenance but informed Laura at once and superfluously that Wollongong had been a long time ago. But as the day drooped in Finsbury, where she had after some labour drawn an orgasm from him, he spoke dreamily of *a really fresh lamington*.

On learning where Laura lived, he said, 'You can't live there. We tried.' He recited, 'Scrubber, mugger, junkie, thief. When we heard Toby's new counting-out rhyme, we knew we had to get clear.'

He offered this splayed on Toby's bed, for Toby had been dispatched to boarding school. On a chest of drawers, a silver dog grinned in a silver frame: Toby's Weimaraner, run over at Easter. So unfortunate, but in the midst of life.

Exhausted by his exertions, he began to snore.

Autumn in Sydney was a chameleon season that borrowed from summer and winter. Here, shapeless August ended, and things took on a distinctive edge. There were afternoons of sidelit trees. Laura trod on wet grass, followed a gravel path where chestnuts gleamed. It was necessary to visit the parks, not only for the leaves, but because she needed to escape into calm, expensive districts, away from the shitty smears on the pavements, the litter, the mean-eyed children, the shops selling only ugly or necessary things.

Hurrying home past Electrical Goods in glum November, she turned her head. A bank of screens was showing men and women astride a wall or clambering across fallen barricades to embrace. At the reporter's elbow, a boy's round face stared into the camera. Multiple and diminished, history flashed before Laura's gaze. She had missed it. She might have been in Berlin, could easily still go: Europe, to a mind that judged on an Australian scale, was an undersized place. But what had all that happiness to do with her? At home, memory thickened all occasions, however news-unworthy. Here, she would never look at a cinema and see the scene of her first kiss, never pass a stand of stiff-winged dark trees that had invaded the dreams of five-year-old Laura. She realised, That's why ghosts return. She walked on, because the wind was gritty as well as cutting, but the face of the German boy went with her. It showed a peculiar mixture of satisfaction tinged with alarm—it was the face of someone who has just bitten into a hot potato.

Phillip's card remained in her purse. From time to time, Laura took it out and looked at it. But she never called the number at University College. Put it down to the silver photograph, and to *we*. After she left him, he would have answered the phone. Nothing much, he might have said, or one of the other phrases that had reached Laura now and then as she lay in Charlie McKenzie's bed.

Before Blanche inherited the house in Hackney, she had lived on a commune in Wales. A magnet fixed one of her poems to the fridge. *Once there was a rainbow valley, / Gentle people living free* . . . A photo showed children in multicoloured crocheted ponchos standing in mud.

Christmas was coming. Blanche had spent up big on chickpeas, and Laura was invited to the feast. Phillip's advice about moving had gone unheeded. Laura might experience a genuine frisson for the corpse discovered, after seven months and the rats had passed, in its council flat; might sincerely curse the vandalised telephone booth or the privatised, non-arriving bus. But where the fear of being trapped forever by these things was lacking, so too was the compulsion to *get clear*.

The sun, if it showed itself at all, entered Laura's room in the late afternoon. It lit up the scratches on the furniture, and the nylon fibres, each ending in a tiny ball, that quivered up from the peach-coloured spread. Even along the river or in the stripped parks, the low winter sun was baleful. Suspended in blueish vapours, it showed as round and red as the eye on a surveillance camera. It stayed half an hour, as if that were all it could bear to record of earthly iniquity. If Laura was present when it slid through her window, a headache threatened along her hairline. But as long as the corners of the room remained in shadow, she could almost believe it was a painting: a minor effort by a would-be Sickert, in which wall-paper and wardrobe mirror offered the same creepy green. Was that why people went on leaving home to struggle with luggage and exchange rates? Not for the shot at novelty or adventure, profit or escape, but in the hope that their lives would be lifted into art?

The problem was that the mirror always held her, too: untrans-formed in the foreground of the scene.

Laura made up her mind to find work when Hester's money ran out: to dig in, stay. The galleries were full of pictures; when she dared, she was looking at them one by one. Perhaps the point was also to stay away. There was the memory of all those times when she had rushed to question travellers returned from the magic land called *overseas*. They would assure her that it was great for a while but. *A while* was elastic and corresponded to the length of time they had been away. Laura learned that Australia was the best place to bring up kids, no question. Everything was so much easier here. It was simply wonderful how away confirmed that home was best. Photographs were produced as evidence that travel had occurred, for the travellers themselves were unchanged. Souvenirs, strategi-cally deployed around the house, proclaimed the sophistication and broadness of outlook that familiarity with foreign cultures conferred. And that was all of *overseas* that anyone needed.

Ravi, 1980s

AT THE FAREWELL PARTY FOR the de Mels, the young people were sitting out on the veranda. A vein of lightning opened, and sky showed bright and thin—it was the skin of a balloon seen from the inside. Then the power failed. In the commotion, Ravi drew Roshi de Mel around the side of the house and kissed her. She was sixteen and a district swimming champion. He kept a newspaper photograph of her in her swimsuit hidden in his old Bible, among the prayer cards and images of saints.

By this time, with the de Mels leaving for Canada in a week, there was a sense of crisis to the affair, which had not progressed beyond the play of glances and an exchange of boldly confessional letters.

The de Mel girls, a quartet of sisters, were all forward and long-limbed. Roshi returned Ravi's kiss open-mouthed and pressed herself against him. Early evening drizzle had left a vegetable scent in the air. Ravi had an impression of ripeness and branching. It was answered by a bloom of light on his lids. He opened his eyes and saw a bodiless head suspended beyond the trees.

Recently, the Mendises had attended a family wedding near Galle. All those cousins were cheerful and mean. One by one, they had spoken with satisfaction of a lane where each driveway contained a body with a dark circle in the forehead. The day after the ceremony, when the oldest cousin had sobered enough to drive the Mendises back to the station, they chanced on a little procession of soldiers herding a group of insurgents along the road. 'Don't look!' ordered Carmel. One of the prisoners was a girl, not much older than Ravi, wearing a printed cotton dress. She was plain and thick-browed, and her eyes moved sideways as the car passed. She was pushed on.

When Ravi tried to remember the girl's face, all he could see was a brown button. But she was involved in the fear that opened inside him in the de Mels' garden. The apparition, oddly lit and drawing closer, was entirely suited to the times: unnatural, out of joint. Then he recognised Dudley, a poor relation of the de Mels, a moonstruck idiot with a large, lolling head. He had come trotting up from the rear of the house with a lighted candle held under his chin. Roshi swivelled and, placing her hands on her hips, began to abuse him. Squealing with delight, the idiot brushed past. From the house, a voice called, 'Roshi! Roshi! Where are you hiding, darling?' The girl seized Ravi's hand and crushed it. Then she was gone.

Candles had been set around the room where everyone was gathered, and a kerosene lamp glowed. Christmas flies delirious with light littered every surface with iridescent wings. They dragged their maimed bodies here and there, then died.

Aloysius de Mel, Roshi's father, was saying, '. . . our *bothal karaya*'s nephew. Young fellow, twenty years old. The JVP cut his throat after a falling-out, and left the body tied to a lamppost with a notice saying not to touch it. But the father went and cut down his son. In the middle of the funeral, the JVP showed up and killed the whole lot. All the mourners, ten, fifteen people.'

There were the standard murmurs. But reaction to the tale was muted. In the first place, there was nothing unusual about what had happened to the bottle-man's relatives. For months, rumour and journalists had been reporting far worse. War and peace, anarchy and government were no longer discrete colours but had run together and changed hue. Besides, the de Mels' ties to the country had already begun to fray. The gathering felt that it was less than tactful of Aloysius to dwell on woes that no longer touched him.

This vague resentment prompted Carmel Mendis to say, 'The JVP is finished now. The universities are reopening. My son will be able to carry on with his studies at last.'

She might have said more but desisted. When people left the country, there were always clothes and household items that they were unable to sell and gave away at the last minute. Carmel coveted a mirror with a bevelled border that hung on the de Mels' wall. It was etched with clumps of grass and a pair of swans. On entering the room, she had checked at once to see if it was still hanging there from its chain. Months had been known to pass with no sign of her widow's pension because the government claimed to have run out of money. Arrears were paid, eventually; meanwhile the Mendises lived on lentils and vegetables, supplemented now and then with tinned mackerel or an egg. To buy food meant standing in line for hours, and Carmel was down to a single pair of shoes that pinched. But a lady never left the house in rubber slippers.

All this was rendered bearable because of the mirror. It took shape in Carmel's thoughts as soon as she woke. Throughout the day it remained there, gathering light at the back of her mind.

When Aloysius held forth, he would angle his neck forward and lift his chin. With his bald head, he had quite the air of a reckless tortoise. 'Wijeweera has been finished off, correct. But his supporters are all over the place. Security forces are going into the villages and killing people left, right and centre.' He evoked this bloodletting with great satisfaction, for it proved the wisdom of his decision to leave.

Discussion broke out about the circumstances of Wijeweera's death in custody. The latest theory was that the insurgent leader had been taken to a crematorium, shot in the leg and burned alive. Not that anyone really gave two hoots. They were all pleased that the man was dead. It was this impression of the lifting of a pall that lent the party its festive sheen. Even the envy that attended every farewell was tempered by the sense that brighter days lay ahead. At one point or another in the evening, the conviction that the de Mels were making an atrocious blunder thrilled through each of their guests.

Leaning against a wall, Ravi was following the turns of the conversation in a swirl of boredom and disgust. He considered Wijeweera a vicious lunatic, but the relish in Aloysius's voice sickened him. In fact they all sickened him: the politicians, the Tamil Tigers, the insurgents, the older people in the room. The sole function of their opinions was to cage them off from thought. What was more, their talk was always of death, when anyone could see that what mattered was life. He could hardly bear to think about his own. Here he was, stuck at home with the future on hold, obliged to coach lacklustre schoolboys in physics and maths. He was seized by an urge to shout and overturn furniture. How wonderfully alive Roshi was, he thought, remembering how she had let fly at her idiot cousin. A little havoc wouldn't upset her at all.

She was going around the room with a platter of food. When she reached him, she whispered, 'Come to the back of St Mary's at seven tomorrow night.'

Ravi heard *the back of seminary* and was confused. 'Where?'

Priya arrived at his elbow to ask, 'What are you two lovebirds cooing about?' She considered Roshi not at all pretty. Those big tombstone teeth! But an aunt living abroad supplied the de Mel girls with clothes, so here was Roshi parading herself in imported jeans and a sequined T-shirt, while Priya had to get by with a purple rag that everyone would recognise as having belonged to her mother. After leaving school, Priya had held a secretarial position with a tour operator. But tourists were so few now that most of the staff had been sacked. For the first time, Priya would have nothing new to wear to church on Christmas morning. Gloomily, she picked out the largest stuffed chilli on Roshi's plate.

Roshi gave her ponytail a shake and laughed in Priya's face. But Ravi said, 'I was just asking Roshi what will happen to Dudley when they go.'

'He's going to a place for people like that,' answered the girl. 'He'll be happy there. He's always happy, anyway, the fool.' Then her voice changed. 'Some people have been saying why don't we take him to Vancouver. Can you imagine? Damn cheek.'

Just then, although scarcely an hour had passed, the lights came on. Everyone looked around in shock.

Roshi said, 'It's a home run by the church.' She looked at Ravi intently as she spoke and stressed the last two words.

Anusha, the youngest de Mel girl, came thrusting into the group. Ravi's little sister, Varunika, tagged along—the two were great friends. Anusha wanted everyone at the party to sign her autograph album. Priya read aloud as she wrote: *Remember me by the river, / Remember me on the lake, / Remember me on your wedding day / And send me a piece of your cake.* At this threat of matrimony, Varunika and Anusha exchanged a look. They started giggling and couldn't stop.

Carmel could stand it no longer. She followed Roshi into the kitchen and said, 'Darling, has Mummy sold her swan mirror?'

'Auntie Sunila's taking it,' answered the girl. She stared boldly into Carmel's face, finding Ravi's handsome nose and rectangular brow. But the eyes, with that sunken look, were like nothing Roshi had ever seen.

The following evening, Ravi set out far too early for his rendezvous with Roshi. Not wishing to loiter, for aimless young men attracted the interest of the police, he walked with a purposeful stride while in fact turning left or right at random. He marvelled at the freedom Roshi enjoyed. Anything might happen to her as she roamed the streets after dark. Yet the careless tilt she gave to everything was integral to her charm.

At one point, he found himself outside the house where his friend Dabrera had lived. In those days, the wrought-iron gates had always stood open. Now they were shut and reinforced with metal sheets. There was an intercom in the gatepost, and the wall had been raised above head-height and set with broken glass. The whole place was in darkness and seemed deserted, but that was true of most houses. People had got into the habit of barricading themselves indoors as soon as it began to get dark.

The caretaker, drunk but pious, was singing 'Holy, holy, holy' in his hut. Lying entwined with Ravi in the side porch of St Mary's, Roshi sucked his finger and positioned it as she pleased. Her bushy hair gave off a pleasant reek of brine. Soon she turned her mouth away from his and nipped his arm.

Fastening her strong paw around him, she said, 'Hurry up! Mummy will be wild if I'm late.'

He had no difficulty doing as she asked.

Roshi was already astride her bicycle when she dismounted and let it fall. She clung to Ravi and said, 'I'm so frightened of going to Canada.'

'Nearer, my God, to Thee, nearer to Thee,' came the caretaker's unsteady bass.

For a few minutes, they exchanged all kinds of vows. Then Roshi sped off, having rejected Ravi's pleas to let him pedal her home.

It was typical Christmas weather, windy and cool. Ravi was a box of birds. He knew he would never see Roshi again; also that everything they had said to each other was entirely sincere. A star wobbled at the bend in the road, and he thought she was coming back for a last exchange of kisses. But the cyclist passed without a word, and the sky winked Ravi on his way.

In the weeks that followed Roshi's departure, his mood plummeted. He spent days dreaming of cities where everything was new and clean. Gleaming buildings stood out against a fresh-washed sky. Ravi saw himself crossing an expanse of pastel carpet to enter a glass lift. Effortlessly vertical, it bore him aloft.

It was the old human dream of *the good place*: one where horizons were wider, or at least less tightly jammed between sky and sea. It was associated in Ravi's mind with the hotels that lined the beach. He could just recall the coconut palms they had replaced. Of the construction of the hotels, he remembered nothing. They had simply arrived, glamorous as spaceships and equally remote.

He fell into the habit of walking this stretch of beach. The hotels were deserted, many of them shuttered and barred like the businesses in the town that had catered to foreigners. The addition of politics turned paradise into hell; there was nothing in between. At the height of the insurgency, tourists had been flown out of the country. Ravi wondered where they went now: Phuket, perhaps, or Bali—anywhere cheap and with great food. Islands encouraged nursery wishes; on maps, they were miniatures that charmed.

One evening Ravi walked all the way to the end of the beach. Where the shore narrowed stood a hotel that had just been built when the flow of tourists trickled dry. The opulent fittings planned for it had never arrived; the developer hanged himself from a hook where a chandelier should have impressed.

The gate was padlocked but not sealed off since there was nothing to steal. In the inky-blue interval that preceded nightfall, the building's imperfections disappeared. By day, the windows were wounds; now Ravi couldn't detect the absence of glass. Set in greenery that had darkened first, the walls glimmered white, their stains camouflaged as shadows. There was the suggestion of a ship about the structure, its long balconies taking on the air of decks. Ravi could see it slipping its moorings one night, kitchens, bedrooms, conference suites gently lurching over the waves, a parched pool drinking its fill.

Then the light dimmed, or he heard a dog howl, or the moon slid out from behind a cloud to show him her scars. In any case the scene stirred and changed. The hotel now had the look of something very old, a secret the sea had clasped for a long time in its damp bed before it had risen and crawled back to shore. The hair lifted along Ravi's arms. He tried to call up his vision of *the good place*, but its forms, so compelling by day, had melted. There was nothing for it but to return by the way he had come, although he didn't like turning his back on the hotel.

On his way home, he met a face he hadn't seen for some years. It belonged to a man who had once kept a little shop where cheap household goods were sold. Ravi expected to pass him with a nod, but the man stopped. They talked for a while, and Ravi learned that the shopkeeper was home from Dubai, where he worked as a cleaner. The money he made had sent his sons to a private school, paid for his father's heart surgery, bought his sister a respectable groom. He offered Ravi a duty-free Dunhill and said, 'Don't go.'

LAURA, 1990S

WHEN IT BECAME PLAIN THAT January intended to go on forever, a ticket from a bucket shop carried Laura over clotted skies. Two hours from London, a sunlit planet waited. There was trudging and happiness. There were little glasses of dark *digestivi*, bitter with herbs. There were angels in the architecture, and cypresses and tombs, and strangers with known faces: they had floated free of seventeenth-century paintings. It was true that to try crossing the street was to be plunged into terror. And there was that day she saw a girl lean from a pillion to detach a bag from a negligent arm. But for the space of a whole morning, street led to street and brought nothing that didn't please. She had to look at everything. She had to eat gnocchi on Thursday because when in Rome. In every direction, buildings were ochre, burnt orange, the rosy-red of crushed berries. Even vertical new suburbs risked lemon and olive and a rather poisonous blue-pink.

Cats stalked over tawny rooftops to enquire at the window of Laura's *pensione*. From the far side of the world, a pragmatic continent declared that it would be only kindness to destroy these ragged regiments—humanely, of course. But scraps of bread and Parma ham made their way to Laura's sill in defiance of antipodean common sense.

In a piazza named for a superseded god, a toddler pointed: *Gatto!* Then, as a pink coat passed, *Rosa!* So it went, each fresh sighting calling forth an elated affirmation. Car! Spoon! When the child's eye fell on the tourist eking out a latte at the adjoining table, he glared. But they were not so different, really, each marvelling at the wonders of the world.

A sunless afternoon brought the pitiless arches of the Colosseum. Out-of-place figures, shivering in synthetics, came slipping out. They offered carvings, and beads hefty as sorrows. One elongated, knife-thin form, a Giacometti sculpted from ebony, knelt to release a white bird at Laura's feet. Together they watched it whirr heavenwards, a soaring no less full of hope for being mechanical. They could only try to replicate it later in a room at the end of a bus line, far from the relics of emperors and saints.

Afterwards, Laura stood at a terminus in a road where rubbish blew. Posters advertised a band in an enigmatic, attractive script. The people passing had cheap coats, and eyes full of calculations. But unlike Laura they were hurrying home. The stout African waiting for the bus, her hair bound in a gaudy cloth, was privy to knowledge enjoyed equally by the apricot-complexioned rich admiring each other on the via Condotti. It was the reason tourists read travel guides like missals. If they chose the correct street, dined on a particular terrace, went through a crucial door, everything would be different. Laura felt in her bag for her guidebook; she needed to check that it hadn't been left behind, along with the starburst of joy, in the room with the exposed wiring and the single, cold-water tap.

Recently she had dreamed of owning a chart, white lines on blue paper, with a telephone number at the bottom: 85148. All she had to do was to follow the diagram or, in the worst-case scenario, call the number. Then she would possess the city at last, its monuments and litter. Rome, like paradise, would gather her in.

She was armed with a railway pass. The windows of meandering *diretti* framed towns and towers on rounded hills. They were teasingly familiar, touched with déjà vu. After a while, Laura realised that she was looking at the bland, pretty vistas with which the minor masters of the Quattrocento filled in their backgrounds. At any moment there would be a Crucifixion on a bald, middle-distant hill.

La Spezia came, and the mincing sea that drowned Shelley.

France brought Mediterranean ports and hotel rooms with a view of dank light wells where night arrived at half-past three. On the wall, turquoise roses as large as frisbees bloomed on baleful trellises. Sometimes there was carpet there instead—the same brown *moquette* that exerted a squelching suction underfoot.

The richly pink walls that in Rome had summoned berries now looked to Laura like boiled beetroot. It was just as well that along with a change of jeans and the sturdy merino jumpers of home, her backpack held a small library, even if the feeble wattage she encountered everywhere was opposed to books. A shuttered villa flanked by cypress candles might have been only hostile if it hadn't called up the brittle modern heroines, bravely rouged, of doomed Katherine Mansfield. Laura could only envy their predicaments, the nerves that caused them to suffer and bound them to webs of human intrigue, as she grasped a paperback with woolly paws in a marble park. In every direction, leafless perspectives delivered lectures on fearful symmetry. The trees had been hacked about by someone who preferred statues. Trees and statues alike stood frozen in the wind that had set off in Russia and rushed straight down the Rhone Valley. Why did people in novels come to the south of France for winter? Laura lifted her eyes to the hills and found them blue with cold.

Well muffled, she walked about the steep streets behind the seafront as the long evening descended, waiting for the hour when she might decently dine. Windows opening on to the street allowed her to catch the crash of cutlery or game-show laughter. She came to a square and looked up at the balconies, each with its crocheted iron. Here and there, where a lamp had been lit in the room behind, a tense chair showed or a mirror in a golden frame. But no one opened the glass doors and stepped out among the empty window boxes to say, 'But who are you, *mademoiselle*? You simply must come up and join us!'

In a sinister boulevard lined with bars and ugly shops, lonely North Africans hissed. Stranded in jackets, dreadfully checked, over shiny-kneed trousers, they lacked consequence. They might have been characters plucked from a story of family and politics and consigned to a footnote—even the jut of their cheekbones was mournful. At the going down of the sun they were to be observed gazing south from sea-view parks, restrained by balustrades from darkening water.

When the youth hostels weren't closed against winter, they were situated as far as possible from stations, shops, markets, bars, anything that might conceivably interest the young; a *pension* was in any case more Mansfield. But a fit of economy, backed by deep boredom with her own thoughts, drove Laura at last to a bunk in a dorm. During and long after dinner, she drank *vin ordinaire* with Daniel, Alissa, Masuko, Piotr, Kelly and a Belgian. Grievances and baguettes were sliced up and shared. Everyone had a story about trains that ran late or simply stopped between stations, and all were agreed in their opinion of the French. The hostel had only two long rooms for sleeping. Daniel and Alissa had spread the contents of their packs in the first room to show how things stood. At midnight, Alissa, one of those girls with emphatic eyes, was ready to go to bed, but Daniel and Kelly were on to politics. Every time Kelly used her Swiss Army knife or a tube of mayonnaise to designate injustice—'Say this is Gaza here, right?'—Piotr's gaze rested on whatever she had touched. So Alissa was driven back on the Belgian. His face was a wedge of cheese, but Alissa was determined now to stay and fascinate. She undid the knot of her hair, releasing a torrent of light, and saw herself at thirty: rare, mysterious, wrapped in a cloak, the latest door softly closing behind her on the sound of masculine tears. She spoke a confident French sprinkled with literally translated idioms and didn't hesitate now to confess to itchy feet: '*J'ai les pieds qui grattent.*' She meant it kindly, as a warning: Do not imagine your devotion can conquer my need for freedom. '*Un eczéma?*' suggested the Belgian. He moved smoothly into the first of his long, bitter tales about a race called the Ongleesh.

In fine, cold rain, Laura and Masuko walked the two kilometres to the nearest bus stop. The new day was still black; they hadn't bothered with bed. Their flashlights went ahead, pausing on coiled dog turds coloured a bold orange. Masuko, considerably widened by her backpack, sported a beret and a perm. In Japan, curly hair designated a free spirit, Laura learned. She, too, wore an angled beret. There was nothing more useful to the French, marking the tourist below. An architecture student, Masuko was on her way to see Le Corbusier's Unité d'Habitation. Why not go there together? she proposed. She held strong opinions on subjects that rarely crossed Laura's mind, declaring, 'I hate the revolution of 1848,' and 'Upholstery was put on earth by enemy aliens.' Now, 'The only tolerable utopia is a shabby one,' she flung into the first stirrings of dawn. The idea of *a shabby utopia* almost persuaded Laura, but she didn't want to double back to Marseille. Also, she was on a pilgrimage of her own. In the bakery opposite the bus stop, the young women bought warm, greasy *pains au chocolat*, and Laura Fraser, stuffing her face, showed the paperback she carried in her coat. She wanted to visit Saint-Jean-de-Luz because Patrick White had written one novel in the town and drawn on it for another. Masuko had never heard of White or *The Aunt's Story*, but remarked, as they boarded the bus, that she had no time at all for Mishima: 'A very arrogant man.' At the station, they waved from opposite platforms. Encouragement, regret and undying friendship can only be expressed for so long in mime; it was a relief when Laura's train pulled in. Travel was only really tolerable when solitary. Two was a group barricaded behind *we*. It offered conversation and someone to blame for disappointments, but the dream of transcending tourism wasn't available—there was always another foreigner in a foolish hat.

A magical morning in Madrid brought the white annihilation of snow. The olives were wonderful, purple and full-flavoured. But in a bar all the profiles were Picassos, the line of the forehead continuous with the bridge of the nose. Fairy-light-entwined among the bottles, the Virgin's plaster robe shone Aryan blue. Laura left without ordering, and from every radio along the street, Madonna II declared that it was *just like a prayer*; a song that had pursued Laura across the globe, fanning out from the bus station in Tamil Nadu where it had first emerged in tinsel tinkles from someone else's Walkman.

She escaped to Cintra, where her passport was pinched on a Romantic stair. The upset this caused was undeniable. Laura remembered France, her solitary *plats du jour* in out-of-season cafes where there were always postcards fading to yellow above the bar. She felt too exhausted to continue. It was senseless, this shuttling between stations and the provincial masterpieces that disgraced the walls of overheated museums. Such pleasures as she took were transient and casual: touristic, in a word. And on top of everything, she had a cold.

But in Lisbon she racketed over the hills in tin trams. Glass caskets done up with iron were fixed to every wall: the opera boxes of the street. Laura could just see herself up there on this or that balcony, conducting a scandal on a worn velvet seat. There were grilled sardines, a mosaic promenade, tiles painted with ships and insouciant whales. And everywhere, Rome's grandstanding Baroque transformed for lack of funds into something altogether more humanly decayed. Even the young had an old-fangled air. Boys were neat in navy blue, their girls restrained in crisp white. They held hands as they walked but didn't caress, although now and then embracing with fervent self-control at the descent of all-forgiving dusk.

It was a backward city, a European capital folded in a pleat of time unknown to Golden Arches. It returned Laura to childhood and to India, which is to say unmodern places. This was the effect of food cooked in the street, the care with which even modest purchases were wrapped, the dim shops with their diffident displays, the heavy spectacles on fine-boned faces. Yet ships sailing from this harbour had once shrunk and expanded the world, mapping its modern configuration. Somewhere in that rage for profit and cartography, the outline of Australia had been waiting to take shape.

Laura's bed and breakfast occupied the fourth floor of an apartment block. Names she had seen in Goa—da Costa, Oliveira, Gomes—converted the list of residents posted in the lobby into a genealogy of empire. Here, the Age of Europe had begun—when she realised that, her view of Australia shifted. Her birthplace had always seemed singular: solitary and distinctive. Now Laura saw it hooked into histories that ran back and forth across the globe, so that it hung in its watery corner with the stretched, starfish look of a map produced by a radical projection.

She emerged from a cinema one evening to find herself in a road transformed by rain into gleaming black glass. Her fellow spectators ignored her as they dispersed, already starting to process the American scenes they had all received into alien words. Every light in the city was shining. *What are you doing here?* This was travel, marvellous and sad.

She stayed three weeks. She would never come back. For the rest of her life, *Lisbon* would summon a season: sealed, sufficient unto itself as a fruit. Even details would return: an armoire, carved and overlarge, where linen was stored; the spectacular dandruff of the foreign-exchange teller at the bank. Smells came back, and the taste of warm codfish patties, and the metal props buttressing a tree whose branches roofed a square. Who can explain the sympathy that runs swift as a hound and as stubbornly between people and places? It involves memory, prejudice, accidents of weather. (Although in fact, Laura would later confuse certain things; the armoire, for instance, didn't belong to Lisbon at all but to a dark, waxed corridor, inset with rectangles of light, in a convent on the Ligurian coast.)

In her last week in Lisbon, shaken from her siesta by the rumble of a tram, Laura wondered if she had lived here long ago. For an entire afternoon, she considered staying for the rest of time. She imagined meals, routines, the room she would have, its curtains, the elderly neighbour who carried his Pomeranian up the stairs when the little dog grew frail. But then she realised that the whole continent was breathing down her neck. Where was there to go but out to sea? Along the green Tagus, where she walked in the evening, the ghosts of caravels canvassed the failing day. Laura consulted the special offers of travel agents and totted up sums on the last page of her notebook; briefly, she shared the lust of conquistadors for a new world.

But the considerations that had spurred them on reined her in: gold, questions of territory. Laura's money was running out. Her mother, born through no fault of her own in Cornwall, had bestowed on her daughter the right to live and work in the United Kingdom. The Americas, north and south, told a different story.

Somewhat out of breath, Laura arrived at the summit of an icing-white tower. There she farewelled the city while vulgarly consuming a custard tart. When she dusted her hands of crumbs, it produced a flutter of sparrows. Far below, the Atlantic approached, slow as a slattern, to smear its grey rags along the shore.

Ravi, 1990s

WITH A PLASTIC BAG HELD over his head, he ran through sheets of rain. The wind was at his back. Here and there in the darkness, light streamed from a lamp. Trees bending at the waist gave the impression that the whole campus was fleeing at his approach.

He was in luck. The bus had been held up by a group of female students clambering aboard. Ravi squeezed in beside a girl in a damp blue dress. He had noticed her on campus, distributing leaflets about violence against women. She was in her final year of history, she said. Her complexion, the same dark gold as the uptilted eyes, was lightly pocked.

The bus lurched, throwing them together, and she spoke to Ravi about fate. She told him that her name was Malini, adding that it meant *a maker of garlands*. Her mother had chosen it because the horoscope cast at her daughter's birth had seen flowers in the child's destiny. Then it had warned that she would grow up as bright as a boy.

Malini de Zilva was not exactly a pretty girl, but there was a magnetic quality to her pull. In the days that followed, she blossomed in Ravi's mind: golden-skinned, her head lightly balanced on its stalk.

Quite soon, they were married. Six months later, Hiran was born, the day after his mother turned twenty-four.

Laura, 1990s

LAURA WAS MAKING FRIENDS, THE London phone numbers in her notebook were mounting. Piece by piece, she was assembling a city of her own. She joined a library and found a pool where she could swim. Good coffee, sold even in the airport in Sydney, even in malls in far, far suburbs of brick veneer, continued elusive in London. But Laura acquired a favourite cinema, a GP she could trust. She walked and walked, or rode a borrowed bicycle. She listened and inspected. Kilburn. Twickenham. She could place them now, and not only on a map. She knew what they *meant*.

Strangeness still sprang. The English voices came through a door as she climbed to a party. Laura froze in pretty sandals on the landing. How happy they sounded and inhuman, gathered in a room like that.

An unpromising alley behind Paddington yielded a genius called Sharon, who preserved the luxuriance of Laura's hair while laying into it with blades. The result was sinuous and faintly sinister. Her lips, coloured a violent ruby, were a declaration. Men noticed it. Somewhere along the way she had learned to dress, shedding her jeans and shapeless tops for styles that flattered and draped. There was now a queenliness to her volume. The bloom that would have begun to wilt in Sydney was ancestrally suited to England's damp cold. She was firm-fleshed, the flesh rose-flushed and fine-grained.

Like all her friends, Laura Fraser had spent the Eighties in black to express her nonconformity. Now she found herself starved of colour. Oxfam yielded a shirt in mulberry and plum. The following week there was a kameez: eau-de-nil cotton paisley-printed in emerald and pink.

A girl who was going home to Brisbane passed on a slate-blue coat. Laura wore it on a weekend jaunt to Paris, where she bought a cheap, perfectly cut dress in a satisfying French blue.

It wasn't a fairytale transformation. But there were those who saw the large white girl with pointed fingers and thought of a fairytale character, a goose perhaps or a duck. She looked motherly, capable of malice, sacrificial.

Work meant waitressing in a pub in Clerkenwell staffed by Australians and New Zealanders. A couple who often lunched there told Laura that they were looking for a house-sitter while they visited their daughter in the States. Laura realised that she was tired of Mapledene Road. To reach the kitchen, it was necessary to cross a room in which, at unpredictable but frequent intervals, Blanche's friends sat cross-legged and chanted under rugs. Laura had never determined whether this rite was Christadelphian or a legacy from the commune in Wales.

Word got around. One thing led to another. 'You Australians are so marvellously reliable,' exclaimed yet another householder. Laura was now sufficiently fluent in the native tongue to decode this as *worthy* and *dull*. That was okay. She moved around London, stuccoed terrace to mansion flat to loft conversion, reliably walking dogs, feeding fish, watering plants. When stranded, she was always welcome to the couch in a flat shared by three cheerful girls from Auckland.

When she could, Laura travelled. She went to Antwerp, Istanbul, Vienna, Fes. She went to New York for six days. Manhattan confounded all her expectations, which were of the future, the sensation of *zip*, the latest thing. But the streetscape was old-fashioned and moving, an unforeseen effect of all those modernist grids. There was such innocence in their hymning of a century that had been enchanted, then.

Groups of tourists from the former Eastern bloc had appeared in London. Their jeans bagged at the knees, their hair was big and terrible, gold lurked behind their lips. But what was striking was the reverence they brought to looking. Unlike the polite Americans from the north and the operatic ones from the south, unlike the suave French and the tall Dutch, these visitors were not encountered in department stores or cafes. Too poor to buy most of what was for sale, they haunted monuments, window displays, churches. There were drifts of them in parks. What were they looking for? A fountain in which a sparrow had drowned? A statue of The Leader?

Middle-aged, with thick waists and packed lunches, they brought to mind long, hard winters enlivened only by a really tremendous new variety of turnip and the latest steel production figures—so Laura mocked silently, unnerved by their effect. In fact, these strangers made her think of pilgrims—of journeys that begin in yearning and end in bliss. They were serious, appreciative and archaic: travellers for whom the link between travel and holiness still held. Very soon their numbers increased, and they disappeared into the general motley of London. What one noticed then were the fur-clad Russians. Laura bristled with the native-born at their rudeness in queues.

There was another report from icy Sarajevo on the news. As soon as the visiting British cabinet minister began to talk, Laura muted the sound. She had made a donation to an Oxfam campaign to raise money for women raped in the war. Her sympathy was engaged, her interest limited. The conflict was too tangled, the country too obscure, its heroes elusive, its villains possessed of forbidding names.

She remembered a recent documentary that had featured a political prisoner released after seventeen years in a Moroccan jail. His cell had been so cramped that he would spend the rest of his days in a wheelchair. Listening to him, Laura had felt pity, aversion, guilt. Reports from unhappy places clung like a shadow, now lengthening, now reduced, always there. It invaded the other story, the familiar, enjoyable one, about weekend getaways and splurging in Tower Records and investigating spices under the gently smiling guidance of Madhur Jaffrey.

On TV, the camera panned to demonstrate desolation. UN soldiers stood guard against a backdrop of fresh ruins, one shifting on the spot in his boots. Helmeted, armed, padded against winter and snipers, he had the impersonal air of such men. But his feet, unable to forget they were human, continued to protest.

Laura scarfed up and went out. A dumpbin in Stanfords displayed a new guidebook to London. She had heard of the publisher—Ramsay—but in a vague way.

A man and a woman were talking behind the counter. Laura asked what they thought of the book.

'It's Australian. But good.'

Thus Laura learned that her accent had altered.

As Australianly as possible, she enquired, 'Like Lonely Planet?'

'Not to be compared, if you believe the Ramsay rep. Same difference if you ask me.' The man shrugged. 'We've had good feedback.'

The other bookseller said, 'I hated it myself.'

They looked at her.

'It gave me such a shock, reading about beggars in London. I know it's true. But seeing it printed in a guidebook. I mean, I've been to India and Marrakesh, and there used to be those scary gypsy children in Paris, but you never think of it being like that here, do you?' Lilac-shadowed eyes implored in English porcelain. 'Then you read something in a book and realise foreigners look at us just like we look at them and . . .' But the chasm revealed by this crack was too dizzying to explore.

Ravi, 1990s

RAVI AND MALINI WERE LIVING with Carmel Mendis when their son was born. Although Ravi had majored in maths, he had taken extra units in computer science, and his ambitions, as formless and changeable as clouds, now revolved around the new growth area of information technology. But success found its way to graduates with connections. Ravi was unnetworked. His letters to employers turned to pleas and still went unanswered. Having thoughtlessly acquired a wife and child, he couldn't afford to train as a teacher and was obliged to pick up his old work of coaching school students. He wasn't the only young man on the beach at sunset, gazing westward as the day drowned.

The beach, like the sea, could turn grubby. Tourism had revived with astonishing swiftness, and it was a town where foreign men came for boys. Strolling languid-hipped where the little waves rushed his ankles, Ravi knew himself the object of appraisal. He swaggered a little under this weight—at night, pushed a fraction deeper into his wife's greedy mouth.

•

When his old school received a donation of ten secondhand PCs, Ravi was hired to train a handful of teachers in the rudiments of word-processing. He returned to spaces and smells so instantly familiar that changes, great and small, burst on him like assailants.

In the classroom where the training took place after school, the red water bottle had gone from its niche. Brother Francis had lost his hair and acquired the habit of scratching his head. Part of the Science block roof had collapsed, and the new section of tiling appeared lurid and false. And the great tree had gone, cut down to make way for an auditorium. The grounds now contained only a few shrubs which, chosen to thrive in shade, were being slowly murdered by the sun.

Instructing men who had once known so much more than he did was uncomfortable. Ravi had looked on his teachers, whatever their individual traits, as uniformly wise. Now he realised that their wits were as varied as their faces. He wondered how many seemingly self-evident truths would crumble over the course of his life. What a wasteful process! And when everything else had worn away, would the last vista have any more substance than the painted cardboard it had replaced? Ravi felt weary in anticipation of all the adjustments to come, and sad.

Passing an open door, he saw Brother Ignatius's map, fully extended, on the wall of an empty classroom. Ravi went in and examined it—the cord that rolled it up or down had disappeared. So even that was different! The map, hanging there limply on view, seemed as unremarkable as a desk or blackboard, robbed of its former flourish.

The sea was a few streets distant from the school. Three windows on the upper floor held wide bands of bright or deep blue. Boys going to and from classes barely noticed this. But some remembered it for the rest of their days.

•

There were many more lay teachers than in Ravi's day, more lady teachers, too. But Ravi looked in vain for Brother Ignatius. It would have been easy to enquire after him, but the old authority of the reverend brothers kept Ravi from a question he feared would be personal and rude.

One afternoon he arrived early, before the final bell had sounded. He lingered near the gate, smoking a cigarette to pass the time. A man dressed in white, who was chatting to the security guard, spotted Ravi and crossed the road. It was Sirisena, the school servant. At interval, boys tipped him to fetch paper cones of boiled gram and other treats from the little shops at the junction.

He began at once to remind Ravi of this service, saying, 'So many times I brought buns and *achcharu* for master.' His head jerked, as if dodging a blow.

Ravi resigned himself to the inevitable. The coins seemed to melt into Sirisena's hand. But his eyes, veined and mournful, went to the pocket of Ravi's shirt.

Shaking a cigarette from the pack, Ravi asked after Brother Ignatius.

'He's gone away.' The cigarette, too, having vanished with greased efficiency, Sirisena informed Ravi that the reverend brother had left the school from one day to the next and gone to work in a refugee camp in the east.

'When was this?'

'Two, three years now.' A bold, contemptuous look came over the servant's face, and he spoke of a woman in the camp. Only he didn't say 'woman'. As he came out with the obscenity, his head twitched again. Ravi could remember mimicking the tic, staggering around the playground with his head tucked into his shoulder, tongue lolling. Boys had held on to each other, weak with laughter.

What amazed him now was the chalk-white cleanliness of the servant's sarong and shirt. By what daily miracle of labour and resolve did this man emerge immaculate from his slum?

The bell announced the end of school. It obscured Sirisena's next remark. But a phrase reached Ravi: 'Tamil dog'.

Between Carmel and her daughter-in-law trouble simmered and seethed. The girl had her own notions about everything and a father who drank. Worse still, she wasn't a Catholic. She wasn't even a Buddhist, declaring as if it were something to be proud of that she was *not interested in religion*. Her father had studied abroad when he was young, and Malini had been raised in unorthodox ways. One of the outrages of which Carmel suspected her was birth control.

The blue house bulged with people and discontent. Varunika was boarding with a relative in Colombo, where she had recently completed her training as a nurse. But Priya, who now worked on reception at one of the beachside hotels, was living at home. With the arrival of her brother's family, she had been obliged to exchange her room for the one Ravi had occupied as a boy. Intended for storage, it had no door but only a curtain. Priya worked shifts, and her sleep was often disturbed: the baby screamed, people came and went from the house making no effort to lower their voices.

For several years now, Carmel had been running a hairdressing salon in the front room. She was always up and down past Priya's curtain, fetching or discarding basins of water. Priya lay in bed, staring at the nail in the wall from which her work sari was suspended, folded over a hanger. There was not enough space for an almirah. And just think how much she contributed to the household expenses!

The Mendises had always spoken English at home. Now Ravi snapped at his mother in Sinhalese, saying that none of her objections to his marriage mattered. Carmel's blood boiled. 'Think of your father!' she cried, and raised her chin at the framed photograph, entwined with nylon roses, in which her husband stood only three colleagues away from a deputy cabinet minister. Her grandson lay on his mat, and his eyes travelled all about as if to swallow the room.

A wealthy relative of Ravi's father lived in the town, one of those connections by marriage that are roundabout yet persuasive. This man, a D.S. Basnayake, had once been prominent in local politics. Retired now, he was writing a history of the municipality in which he and his ancestors figured decisively. Being rich, he wished to be modern, and had bought himself a computer with no idea how to use it.

Carmel learned this when she called on the Basnayakes, as she did three times a year. Her feelings towards the old couple were complicated. Although prosperous, they were Buddhists, therefore damned. And there was a sharper spur to her pity. A few years earlier, the Basnayakes' son, a senior government official, had suddenly started denouncing ministerial corruption and so on. His mother had confided that he was the target of a sorcery which had curdled his brain. Whatever the case, he was arrested and jailed. The charges against him, wholly spurious, were dropped after long months, and he came out of prison. A week later he killed himself, leaving no explanation.

Day and night, a light shone below his photo. It showed the dead man at the height of his power and good fortune, but the eyes were already moths stuck in wax. Under the influence of this ominous image, Carmel offered up Ravi at once. 'He knows everything about these machines. Spare parts, everything.' The old lady stuck out her lips and looked at her husband. It occurred to Carmel that the couple might not wish to be exposed to sons. 'My daughter-in-law can help you also,' she said quickly. 'A very clever girl, varsity trained.'

So Malini now spent six mornings a week with the Basnayakes. Ravi guided her for the first few hours, but with the help of the notes he had made for the reverend brothers, she was soon transferring the old man's papers on to his computer. She had a low opinion of his work: 'Boasts and statistics.' When Ravi asked whether history was ever anything else, she laughed. What frustrated her was this: Mr Basnayake appeared to think that word-processing was a kind of magic that would automatically transform his disjointed jottings into a coherent chronicle. Instead of working to impose order on his chaotic material, he could think only of the glorious day when it would be published. Who would launch the book—a local dignitary or an eminent historian? Where would the party take place? What food would be served at it? The guest list alone would require weeks of forethought, diplomacy and ruthlessness. Malini started to relate all this scornfully, but soon began to laugh and had to hold a pillow over her face in order not to wake the baby. One of the things that charmed Ravi about her was her willingness to be amused. But she hated, as she loved, without humour.

She said that the Basnayakes' house was a morgue. At the rear were vast, treed grounds where no one walked. Chained dogs barked there. As for the Basnayakes, when they visited their daughter in Cleveland once a year, they insisted that their cook accompany them—even though she spent the flight terrified, with an airline blanket over her head—because the old man wouldn't touch American food. The old woman, having nothing better to do, interrupted Malini constantly with her grieving, repetitive stories.

Once, when Malini picked up a bottle of pills for her as a favour, she frowned at the receipt and openly counted the change.

Cows grazed on the Basnayakes' front lawn. They owed their existence to the old people, who followed the pious tradition of buying a beast destined for the abattoir so that it might live out its natural life. Each year, on their dead son's birthday, the herd increased.

Ravi noticed that for all her grumbling, Malini set out each day readily enough. Her wages soothed the Mendis household, antipathies and grudges submerged under the inflow of cash.

LAURA, 1990S

SHE WAS LEADING AN IMPROVISED, peripatetic, rather hectic life. There was the illusion of flight and the safety of tether. Days passed like a sequence of swiftly dealt cards. She was happy, she would have said.

But there is always time for the worry-worm to tunnel through, especially around 3 a.m. On a futon in Clapham, Laura thought, I'm growing old. Her days were so various that she hadn't seen them piling up. She had always pictured a life shaped by books or art hovering there, in the distance. But now her thirtieth birthday was no longer unimaginable. She couldn't go on waitressing forever. The brilliance of Doc Martens notwithstanding, her calves ached.

Not for the first time, she considered going home. There were days when she could have wept for the blue fern-leaf of that harbour. But Charlie's last letter had introduced a girl called Fee. She made surrealist—or possibly socialist: his scrunched writing!—sculptures from dirty crockery. With Charlie she would have no shortage of raw material, thought Laura, uncharacteristically sour. He had noted, in a marginal scrawl, that their child would be born in May.

There came the memory—slipping in like a blade—of the Balinese family to whom she had never written. Laura told herself that they would have long forgotten her. This failed to cauterise because it missed the wound: namely, that she was unable to forget them.

At length, the late-night swirl of remorse, indecision and creeping, unfocused fear drove her to the bottle of valerian. Waiting for it to take effect, I need to do something about a career, she thought.

The community centre was offering an evening course in word-processing for beginners. Fluorescently illuminated, Laura clutched a mouse and tried to keep her green cursor from sliding off the screen.

She was the youngest person in the room. Everyone else my age already knows how to do this, realised Laura. She heard the *whoosh* of the technological future as it rushed past.

But the course progressed and so did she. Soon she was cutting and pasting text, copying documents, experimenting with formats, getting the hang of keyboard shortcuts. She recalled typing classes at school. All that fiddling with Tipp-Ex and ribbons! Here words ran across her screen or were removed with the same untrammelled ease.

The classes were held in a red-brick school. Laura's seat was by the window. She looked out into the night and was rewarded by the reflected sight of fifteen humans contained in a big lighted box and mesmerised by small ones.

The white-haired man at the adjoining work station looked her way just then. Their glances appeared to meet in the window, although his was doubly veiled by glass. Laura risked a smile that wasn't returned.

During the break halfway through the class, she noticed him looking at a jam jar that held a quarter-inch of damp, stained sugar into which other people had been sticking their spoons. Laura said, 'Hang on.' She grabbed an unopened packet from the shelf in the kitchenette.

He was already scraping the brownish contents of the jar into his polystyrene cup. 'This is ample.'

'Oh. Okay.'

He held out the box of Liptons. Laura wanted Nescafé but didn't wish to seem rude.

Sipping brown water, they stood a little apart.

She had seen his daughter, a girl of barely twenty, accompanied by a small boy, greet him after class. All three wore coats that seemed too large yet inadequate against merciless March.

On an impulse Laura told him her name, adding, 'I'm from Australia.'

He considered this. Then asked if she knew the Nullarbor.

'Not really. I'm from Sydney.'

He remained silent, which muddled her into asking if he'd been to Australia.

He had not. He added, 'I would like to see the Nullarbor.'

Why?

His rather elegant hand traced an arc: oh, you know. 'There is nothing like it in my country.'

So then she could ask where that was without fear of sounding racist.

'Sri Lanka.'

'Oh!' cried Laura. 'I really, really wanted to go there when I was in India. But there was a lot of unrest. People said it wasn't safe. This was a few years back?'

He didn't respond.

'Have things settled down since? Politics, I mean.' She could hear her hateful, bright chatter but was powerless to strangle it.

He appeared to reflect. Then he shrugged. He had drunk his tea but went on holding his cup in both hands, as though it might still yield warmth.

How long had he been in England?

'Two months. Before, we were in Germany for six, seven months. Stuttgart.'

She kept her eyes from his heartbreaking maroon jumper with the too-long sleeves. 'Winter must have been a shock.'

People were leaving the kitchen. He held out his hand for her cup and binned it along with his. He said, 'It is the winter in people's hearts that is hard to bear.'

The girl and her son were waiting when the class ended. At the sight of his grandfather, a smile splashed all over the child's face.

It was not that the Sri Lankan man avoided her, exactly. But he never chose the monitor next to hers, and during their tea break he visited the lavatory, or stood at the window with his maroon back to the room.

Arriving for her last-but-one class, Laura saw a thin, bespectacled figure herding his flock between walls of institutional beige. The girl's black plait, hanging down over her collar to her hips, was the thickness of Laura's not inconsiderable wrist.

Mother and child turned into a room where—Laura glanced at the sign taped to the door—Beginners English was conducted. A teacher was already writing on a whiteboard. Laura smiled at the old man as she caught up with him, expecting no more in return. But he quickened his step to walk beside her to their classroom around the corner.

They were the first to arrive. She asked, as they unwound scarves, if his daughter was enjoying her classes.

He replied indirectly, saying that the Catholic aid agency responsible for bringing the family to Europe was paying for English lessons. As he already spoke the language, he had elected to study word-processing instead.

'And your grandson, how's he finding it?' Laura was struck by a thought. 'Are there other children in that class? I thought it was all adults.'

He replied that the boy was learning English at school. 'He goes with his mother to her classes but sits quietly and draws.' He said, 'That is a child who loves to draw.'

'I used to be like that,' confided Laura.

When he next spoke, he said, 'She is my wife. The boy is her son.'

'Oh. I see.'

For a while, each contemplated her manifest lie. Laura Fraser was pretty shocked, in her puritan young soul, by the disparity in age.

He had pushed up the sleeves of his jumper. Below blue flannel cuffs, his wrist bones were white-tufted. She pictured them roving the girl's sweet flesh.

But he was more than a match for her brutality. 'Soldiers came to my wife's village when she was twelve. One of them fathered the boy.'

The following week, at the end of their final class, Laura went up to the child. He had taken an instinctive half-step behind his mother at the approach of this large stranger. But huge black eyes peered when Laura said, 'I've brought you a present.'

She had taken some trouble with the parcel, wrapping it first in midnight-blue tissue scattered with glitter and stars. The whole was finished with clear cellophane and done up with silver string.

The child looked up at his mother, then accepted the celestial object with both hands.

There were flat golden flowers in the girl's lobes. Her tiny face, adorned with luxuriant sideburns, was so dark that the scarlet bindi on her forehead stood out like a jewel. Beaming, she recited, 'Thank-you-we-are-nice-to-meet-you-please-don't-trouble.'

The child was transfixed by a rainbow in a tin.

'Goodbye,' said Laura. 'And all the very best.'

At the bend in the passage, she glanced back at them. All three—the man, the girl and her son—stood watching her. Laura bowed her head.

Ravi, 1990s

HIS SON'S EARS APPEARED REMARKABLE to Ravi: so perfectly curled!

Malini was pushing her face into the baby's neck. Ravi heard, 'Who did a lovely big fart? Such a stinky fart! Who did a big fart?'

With his fingernail, he drew a heart transfixed with an arrow on his wife's leg. Every morning, Malini dotted her shins with Nivea from a blue tin and rubbed in the precious moisturiser. But parallel white tracks still appeared whenever she scratched her legs.

Husband and wife went for walks together and talked about everything. Sometimes they would buy a sweepstake ticket from one of the small boys who roamed the streets selling hope. But their great treat was to buy ice-cream cones, which they would eat strolling around the cricket ground or along the beach. Sooner or later, their route would take them past a giant banyan tree. It stood in a patch of waste ground by the side of the road, but was encroaching on the asphalt; the edge of the road had cracked and tilted up. Ravi had always disliked the banyan. It drank light through its roots, and its dark armpits spread. But Malini liked to linger there, in the tree's deep shade.

Long afterwards, when Ravi tried to picture happiness, it was those evenings that came. Folded into them were older memories: his feet planted next to his father's in damp yellow sand, or the smell of candle wax as he puffed his cheeks over an iced cake. All the happy moments were connected, like bright rooms opening on to one another. Yet the young couple's conversation, as they planned how they would live, was often grave.

There was the question of whether they should try to emigrate. The insurgency had ended, but the war for and against a Tamil homeland dragged on. There were assassinations, retaliations, disappearances, suicide bombers; the killing had been going on for years. One night, a little further down the coast, the incoming tide had brought what seemed to be a collection of colossal turds. The sun, creeping up on the array, revealed bodies from which the heads and limbs had been removed.

Ravi was the kind of person whose heart contracted at the sight of a frog-shape mashed into the road. But dailiness normalises everything, even slaughter. And Ravi was young—what he feared wasn't extinction but exclusion. He was haunted by the sense that he was witnessing the birth of a new world. A digital revolution was gathering speed. He ached to be part of it. Soon it would transform the way everyone lived, he told Malini; its power, located everywhere and nowhere, would exceed armies. He used a word that had become fashionable: *global*.

Malini said, 'Who'll be left if we all emigrate? Only idiots and brutes.'

Her attachment to the country was a blind thing, tunnelling up through the years. Her father, once a journalist of some renown, had taken her all over the island when she was a child. She had seen Jaffna and the great blue harbour at Trincomalee. From a beach where spindly casuarinas grew, she had waded into the sea. 'For miles. The water never came over my arms.'

Her father had shown her the chain of tiny islands at the northern tip of the country that linked it to India. In Islamic legend it was known as Adam's Bridge. 'But then Daddy told me that Hindus call it Rama's Bridge. That was so typical of him. He was always trying to teach me that everyone has their own version of events.'

Ravi thought of his father-in-law: a wall topped with broken glass. It had been a long time since a newspaper had employed him. In Welikade jail in 1983, psychopaths kept under lock and key had been excited with stimulants, provided with weapons and turned loose on the Tamil political prisoners. Malini's father, tipped off by a warder, arrived in time to see what they had achieved. After that, his drinking was never less than daily and fabulous. He had been known to strike his wife, igniting Malini's fury. But Ravi, walking in on an argument that ended when the old man picked up a slipper and hurled it at the girl, sensed that this was the parent who mattered; the knotted force of Malini's rage suggested its origin in foiled love. By contrast, her attitude towards her mother, a soft-armed woman with a secretive smile, was at once protective and laced with contempt.

Snooping among his wife's belongings, Ravi had found an old exercise book. Between stiff red cardboard covers, it contained verses she had copied out, exhortations, lists of Hit Parade songs, sporadic diary-like jottings. He read, *Friendship is a china bowl / Costly, rich and rare. / Once it's broken, can't be mended / The crack is always there.* Someone, identified only as T, was 'an open door leading nowhere'. On her sixteenth birthday, there was an entry in red ink and capital letters: I RESOLVE NOT TO LIVE MY LIFE IN VAIN.

One evening, under a luminous green sky, she told him about the earth's shadow. The phenomenon was easily observed on the east coast, where, a few minutes before the sun went down, an ominous band showed on the horizon. It was nothing less than the shadow of the whole planet cast up on the atmosphere. As the sun sank, the shadow crept higher, then gradually faded away. Its ascent was thrilling and frightening. Almost no one noticed it. 'That's the way with people, you have to point out what's under their eyes.' Ravi felt accused, although Malini's tone was offhand and her thoughts had already skipped on. Why, she wondered, was 'nightfall' the standard expression? Night didn't fall. She had seen it rising above the earth.

LAURA, 1990s

WALKING A TERRIER IN HAMPSTEAD, she noticed an open window on the upper floor of a house. There was a video camera between sash and sill.

The window was closed and curtained in the days that followed. Then the camera appeared again. After a while, she worked it out: it was there on Saturdays, and only briefly. If she walked back the same way half an hour later, it was gone.

On a mid-week morning, as the terrier sniffed around the gate of the house, a young man came out of the garage. He wore a blue and grey striped shirt over a blue and green chequered one. Seeing Laura there at the gate, he smiled.

Laura barely hesitated. She would be gone from Hampstead in three days, the little puzzle forever unsolved. And then, one advantage of being colonial was that brazenness was expected and overlooked, if not forgiven.

So she spoke; and boldly, Australianly unlatched the gate; and proceeded to her involvement with Theo Newman.

•

Inside the house, a first glance suggested nothing more sinister than deep pockets and cultivated taste. Laura followed Theo to a scrubbed oak table where she sat on a vinyl chair. An empty bottle stood on the draining board beside a glass with a ruby sediment. The radio, like radios across the planet, was playing Nirvana in tribute to freshly dead Kurt Cobain. There was a view of an apple tree knee-deep in grass, of a granite woman with apple blossom in her hair.

Coffee arrived in translucent porcelain and chunky stoneware with an unpleasantly gritty base.

Theo noticed her noticing and touched first cup, then mug: 'Mutti. Me.'

The terrier chose that moment to dance ragefully about the stranger's feet. Fed expensive poison from a tin, he was dyspeptic and irascible. Theo scooped up the dog, one long hand about the muzzle, and expertly massaged his ears.

On a Saturday half a century after a German child arrived in London, her son stood at the window of her bedroom for nine minutes. He had just watched life shiver from her face. That first morning, drinking coffee in the kitchen with Laura and trying to describe what had passed through his mind as he contemplated the hateful, ordinary street, Theo spoke of *the bald light* and *the blank day*.

Since then, at the same time every Saturday, Theo Newman set up a camera at his mother's window and recorded whatever passed in the next nine minutes. 'It's one of my projects. They're pointless and vital.' Five years of tapes were stored, unviewed, under the dead woman's bed.

Theo had inherited her house, its contents and half her money. As it turned out, there wasn't a whole heap of money: Anna Newman had failed to fill out the life insurance forms, and had spent with an open hand. Her stockbroker son-in-law saw to the investment of what remained. When it was not enough, Theo sold a Meissen dessert service, a Biedermeier secretaire.

His sister was ensconced in a home county with the stockbroker, their three children and a lurcher. 'She has vanished into the known, poor Gaby.' Then, rubbing his ivory forehead, he pondered the case. 'There *is* the dog . . . A retriever would have left no room for hope.'

He told Laura that he was working on a DPhil about nostalgia in the twentieth-century European novel. 'I'm calling it *The Backward Gaze*. Proust, Lampedusa, Thomas Mann . . .' A hand can design an arabesque that suggests everything/nothing.

His study, a large room, was dim. At the window, a venetian blind was suspended between curtains of heavy blue stuff. Theo, speaking of *fictions of longing*, tilted plastic slats. Now light and the apparatus of scholarship could dazzle: photocopies, floppy disks, cardboard folders, a desktop umbilically linked to an inkjet printer, books stubbled yellow with Post-its or Dewey Decimal-stamped on the spine. Many of these objects wore a light coating of dust. But Laura was looking at an orange portable TV on a marquetry escritoire. It stood next to a telephone table with angled gilt legs and a handsome marble veneer.

Months passed before Laura noticed that questions about Theo's research usually brought only a fresh revelation about his supervisor, Dr Gebhardt. This libellous saga, of which Theo never tired, opened in the impetuous, cobblestone-hurling years of Dr Gebhardt's youth when the chief cause of broken necks in Paris was slipping in seminal fluid in the Sorbonne amphitheatres.

Laura learned that Dr Gebhardt had stripped to the skin in one of Lacan's seminars while keeping up a forceful chant of *Woman is the profane illumination!* Thereafter idolised by the great man, she still referred to him, not unkindly, as Shorty. Theo also claimed that Dr Gebhardt's father, once Idi Amin's preferred arms dealer, had later founded the planet's first Buddhist fur emporium—the demand in Hollywood was strong. His widow lived on in a nursing home in Bournemouth, turned out of her flat because Dr Gebhardt needed somewhere to store her collection of shoes.

Theo's face—bloodless, long-nosed, prominently boned—was pure Northern Gothic. Dark brows contradicted grey eyes that went back and back. Laura placed him in the company of angels, gorgeously robed at the edge of the canvas, and burdened him with a lute.

When they met he was almost twenty-seven, three years younger than Laura. He drank a bottle of wine every night; more if he had company. 'I'm a steady drinker. But not, I think, a drunk.'

He was not; or not exactly; or at any rate, not yet. Wine—in those days, he never drank anything else—turned Theo garrulous. Then he was inclined to hold forth. But when Laura first knew him his talk ran in unexpected directions, its course not yet grooved.

In a pub one night with Laura and other friends, Theo was expounding his theory that a dystopian fairytale could be glimpsed in the Holocaust. The journeys in cattle trucks were a version of the arduous expeditions undertaken by the heroes of tales. As for the camps, they resembled those brutal, fantastic kingdoms ruled by ogres where the contravention of arbitrary laws brought death. Uniformed witches tended the ovens. Impossible tasks—a lumpish sack that had to be made up into a bed or an order that required the starving to stand to attention for hours—were variants on ropes woven from ashes and fortunes spun from straw.

The discussion looped around the table and back to its beginning: a bestselling Holocaust memoir recently revealed as a fake. A girl with soft lips in a hard face wondered aloud why the writer had lied. 'The lure of squillions, I guess.'

'Not money.' Theo's finger circled the base of his glass. 'The fulfilment of a wish. The currency of childhood is wishing. Money's only what grown-ups put in its place.'

'So you're saying . . . what? That when this woman was a child she wished she'd been in a concentration camp?'

'She wished what everyone wishes. To be loved unconditionally. So you could say she wished for a happy ending. A fairytale ending. Like surviving the Holocaust.'

Laura rose and crossed to the bar. When Theo's mother was sixteen, a ghost had come looking for her. It was Cousin Ernst: toothless, rheumatic, twenty-eight years old. He had come to tell Anna that everyone in her family was dead: not only her mother and father and sisters, but the grandparents, the uncles, the second wives, the babies bayoneted first in front of their parents. Ernst said that the forest floor had moved for days. How could Theo, knowing all this, talk of an enchanted wood of shining Polish birches? It was monstrous. It was spotted with brilliance.

He accepted the thick Australian claret Laura offered, then ran a finger down her pimpled arm. 'Someone's walking on your grave.'

Theo loved men. He loved the *unrepentantly heter*, men who had wives or girlfriends, men who didn't love him in return. His current Beloveds were an old college friend, now an actor in a long-running soap, and a neighbour with whom Theo engaged in guerrilla gardening. They planted tomato seedlings in telephone booths—that kind of thing. He dined, a frequent guest, at these men's tables. Their women confided in him. He was godfather to the actor's younger son.

For sex, there were strangers met on dance floors and so on.

'Nothing doing there,' said Laura to Laura, sternly. But it was far too late.

In the pub in Clerkenwell, it tickled Englishmen to ask, 'Do you know the difference between Australia and yoghurt?' Or rather: Orstraylia and yog-urt. They were *hilarious*, spluttering into their warm beer.

There was another kind of man, whose methods were more refined. At parties, he would stand between Laura and the door asking, Which is your favourite Tarkovsky? Have you read *Discipline and Punish*? Whom do you rate more highly, Borges or Kundera? At confessional moments, angry names broke from him: Bellow, Roth. His brow might as well have been stamped 'Frightened Early & Often'. Laura dressed him in a clean shirt rolled up at the elbows and placed him behind a desk in a room with no shadows. The luckless, passing one by one before him, wept hot, useless tears over their cancelled lives: they had mispronounced Coetzee or chosen Warhol over Duchamp.

On that first morning in Hampstead, 'Australia,' admitted Laura and readied herself. 'How lucky you are!' said Theo Newman. He quoted an Australian poem: *To sit around in shorts at evening / on the plank verandah.*

He told her that when he was a boy, hours had disappeared into a daydream that would rise like a cloud from an old book. The frontispiece showed a fanciful map, ornamented with monsters and putti, where lost souls gathered at the edge of the world. Curled in the red chair on the landing at the top of the house, the child Theo lost himself in the map's invitation to imagine. The southern hemisphere boasted a ship in full rigging. It was sailing to Australia. 'I was the boy on the bowsprit.' He did battle with tempests and monsters. Dolphins were his familiars. At last, the shuffle of surf and a shining bay.

Laura pictured it, the boy's limbs whiter than eucalypts folded into the red chair. Theo spoke of looking up from his book to a little window with a curved top, and how the rain skittering across the glass was spray stinging his face. His recollection of detail struck Laura from the first. Theo Newman kept the past in a brass-bound chest, drew out memories like ropes of pearls.

In the early days, he would say, 'Tell me what it's like in Sydney.' Laura said that the rain fell in sheets there and so did the light. She spoke of the train ride between Edgecliff and the city: the stretch where the track ran over Woolloomooloo, and the jacarandas were already flowering there in the dip, answering the summons of a blue bay. Once she said that Sydney was a pointillist painting of leisure and democracy. Take any fine Sunday afternoon, everyone picnicking half naked by the water, the dogs frolicking and the sails: you could almost see the dots.

But it was dangerous to linger on those summers: the houses shut against the heat all day, then flung open at both ends so the southerly could walk through. So sometimes Laura said things like, 'Have I mentioned that they can't spell "boulevard" in Sydney?' Or, 'It's the kind of place where you see orange lipstick worn non-ironically.' But even as she mocked, her mind tilted back to an evening when every open door she passed showed a corridor leading to a lighted room, where two women, an old one and a younger one, were watching TV. Why should this now pierce as if Laura had swallowed glass?

•

In the house she bought in Hampstead, Anna Newman had set about re-creating the villa in Charlottenburg from which the Kindertransport had plucked her, aged six, in 1939. There was a photograph of her taken on arrival in London: a solid, braided child with careful eyes. Fostered by Quakers, she had grown up English, secular, scientific. She specialised in neurology, acquired a husband, discarded him after the birth of their son.

Remembering and misremembering the vanished rooms of childhood, Anna might have confused Turkish and Persian, mistaken beech for walnut, substituted pistachio for eau-de-nil. There was certainly an excess of painted wood and fruit stands about the place: like anyone making up for losses, Anna had put too much in. From a table crowded with frames, Laura selected a large photograph that showed the room in which it stood. The picture had been taken on Anna's last birthday. The mantelpiece was visible in the background, and a shepherdess who had simpered since 1783. She still clasped her flowery crook, but now Darth Vader had insinuated himself between her skirts and her porcelain suitor. Laura looked from the plastic doll to the photo. It showed part of a Hepplewhite chair. In fact there were two in the room, she saw, with a milk crate between them. Laura glanced around. On one wall, paintings of plump-cheeked children, their eyes glistening with tears, flanked a tiny watercolour by Klee. Below them, propped on a credenza beside a bust of Mozart, was a sooty rectangle stamped with a golden nude. Laura's finger stroked the marble, the velvet. *Mutti*, said Theo's voice. *Me.*

As a child, Laura had loved those puzzles that ask, What is wrong with this picture? The image in question would appear perfectly banal until careful scrutiny revealed a single-bladed scissor or a sunrise in the west. It was not so much the spotting of the anomaly that satisfied as the sly intrusion of the anarchic into the everyday. This slippery enjoyment was what Laura had missed in those mathematical riddles which, requiring the calculation of the next number in a sequence, insisted on the merely inevitable.

As she came to know the house in Hampstead, Laura might surprise Bambi prancing over a cushion on one of the Hepplewhites, or realise that the palm in the bay window sprang from a synthetically Grecian urn. She might notice an aluminium saucepan with a coloured lid among the copper-bottoms and the Le Creuset. Whereupon, What is wrong with this picture? she would think, amused.

Laura Fraser belonged to an age and a place where an amazing thing was taken for granted: for the first time in history, ordinary people could raid the past and the planet to decorate their homes. Her eye was accustomed to ecumenical style, to African masks hanging beside industrial signage, to a witty postmodern aesthetic that refused to distinguish between designer and detritus, kitsch and cool. She wandered around Theo's house counting venetian blinds and orange TVs. In the garage—Theo had sold the Renault long ago—were things like gilded sconces and a macramé wall-hanging draped over a stack of mirror tiles. 'You can pick them up for pennies,' said Theo of two cheerful polyurethane cherubs that served as bases for lamps. You could pick up white plastic roses, bedsteads covered with buttoned vinyl, biscuit tins that featured Van Gogh paintings, pictures of weeping children, oval plastic buckles decorated with Pre-Raphaelite images that had adorned a type of wide, stretchy belt popular in the 1970s. You could pick up anything untouched by retro glamour and find a place for it among the Tyrolean cupboards and the Dresden.

The rooms that Laura knew in Theo's house were the public ones on the ground floor; she was never invited upstairs.

•

When she told Theo about dropping out of art school, he replied that he wasn't surprised. Art's first imperative was to make. An artist was someone who reimagined the world through new objects. 'But technologists do that better than anyone else today. And they do it *more*. There's so much radically new stuff coming into the world that we're overwhelmed by change. What you were suffering from was the exhaustion of excess.'

The exhaustion of talent, more likely, thought Laura. What mattered, however, was that like a magic mirror, Theo gave her back to herself in a kindly form.

'These days, new is for technology,' he was saying. 'Art makes do with now. The only tense it has is the present.'

She almost told him about a little plush dog in Sydney who nodded now-now-now.

But all these disclosures and exchanges lay in the future. That first day, Laura merely walked through Theo's house with him, already hungry for his presence. On shadowy cherrywood heights, white roses gleamed like ghosts.

Ravi, 1990s

THE BASNAYAKES' INFLUENCE PROCURED RAVI a temporary post at the hospital, where a cautious expansion of the computer system had thrown everything into disarray. The clerical staff, inadequately trained, blamed Ravi for every difficulty they encountered or created. That was only natural. He was an outsider and an exponent of change.

Ravi had to concede that the new system was not entirely suited to the needs of the hospital, which were predictably contradictory. There was always an exception or quirk for which technology failed to account. But it annoyed him also that the clerks would go on swearing they had read the instructions he had prepared when it was plain that they hadn't. Why did people hold on to lies like that? He remembered visiting the dentist as a child and insisting that he always brushed his teeth after meals, the fabrication so taking hold of his mind that he was convinced by it and furious with the dentist for his scepticism.

Malini, who had turned up to walk home with Ravi, shifted the baby onto her other hip and signed a petition that was being passed around by an orderly. Later the same evening, she announced that she wanted to go to Colombo to attend a rally protesting the tear-gassing of garment workers by the police.

'Are you mad?' enquired Carmel. 'Are you asking to be killed or worse?'

Carmel Mendis was in the habit of picking up her cup of tea, then lowering it again without drinking; she would repeat the gesture five or six times until the liquid was stone cold. It drove her daughter-in-law wild. When her mother's back was turned, Priya gave a flawless imitation of the performance with the cup, the maddening way Carmel would set it down and fold her lips or pluck at the shoulders of her dress. The two young women snickered together. Later their talk turned grave, Priya confiding the details of a quarrel with a girl at work. Ravi came home to find them on the veranda, slapping at mosquitoes. They looked at him as if they had never seen him before.

In the afternoons, Malini helped Carmel in her hairdressing salon. It was frequented mainly by old ladies of limited means who, as the flood of obsolescence rose around them, clutched here and there at scraps that passed for style. Malini was tender with them, massaging a damp, ancient scalp for long minutes while an old woman sat with head tilted back over the bowl at a stiffly cautious angle. Sometimes, a tear oozed from a wrinkled lid, acknowledging the pleasure and rarity of being touched.

More and more often, a coin slid from a claw into Malini's hand. She never failed to pass on these tips to Carmel, but her mother-in-law began finding fault with her over trivial things. She accused Malini of heating the water for too long. There were conflicts over shampoo, too. It was sometimes sold in sachets since many people couldn't afford a whole bottle, and several of Carmel's customers would bring along the kind they preferred. When this happened, Carmel never used the whole sachet. At the end of the afternoon, she would salvage the little plastic packet from the wastepaper basket and squeeze out the dregs into a container. These leftovers served for other clients; indeed, for Carmel herself. It was a simple procedure and Carmel had explained it simply, yet Malini would squeeze a sachet dry before throwing it away. When confronted, she talked about honesty—the nerve!

Priya, who had been regretting her recent confidential impulse, seized the chance to support her mother now against Malini. She was in love with a married man and tended to snap at everyone else. The affair was conducted in the honeymoon suite at the hotel where Priya and her lover both worked. She lost herself briefly in reliving the moment when his mouth closed on her nipple, and the sea murmured at their window like a bride.

It was unfortunate that Malini broke into this reverie by wondering aloud why foreigners were so keen on taking pictures of everything. 'Taking, taking, always taking.' She was sick of tourists, she said: when they came with their money and their diseases, when politics kept them away. Priya chose to interpret this as an oblique attack on the way she earned her living. Afterwards, each went about with a shut face. Thunderclouds of silent allegation hung between them for days.

Malini said, 'You like people much more than I do. That's why you can ignore them.'

It was quite true. Time and again, Ravi watched his wife blunder into the web of human feeling and get stuck. She was right; it was all she knew. That people might be attached to absurdity or injustice or falsehood was a fact she acknowledged but couldn't grasp. Ravi, having no wish to rearrange the world, was on far easier terms with it. One day, when he refused to be roused by yet another politician's malice, they came close to a serious row. Malini hissed that she had been quite wrong, Ravi's acceptance of every kind of folly or vice was not a symptom of tolerance, after all, but a profoundly cruel assessment: 'You expect no better of people.' The quarrel was taking place in their bedroom, and it was the desire to keep it from Carmel, hovering on the other side of the wall, that prevented it from escalating. To the world—which they still confused with their families—they presented a solid façade.

LAURA, 1990S

THIS BUSINESS OF ONE SENTENCE after another, of thought moving steadily forward: it was goosestepping under another name, grumbled Theo. 'Something important altered forever in this century. Progress became the status quo. We fetishise it.' He topped up Laura's glass, refilled his own. 'So these days, taking your time, resisting change, is the radical response.'

All this had spiralled out from a meeting with his supervisor that afternoon. An adherent of graphology, Dr Gebhardt insisted on handwritten drafts of her students' work. With the spread of personal computers, there had been complaints. Theo had arrived in Dr Gebhardt's office to find her poring over the latest communiqué from the dean—his photocopied signature told of an arrested mirror stage allied to misogyny and sexual dysfunction. All Dr Gebhardt could spare Theo was a terse injunction to *just get on and write*.

Laura suggested that Dr Gebhardt had a point—after all, Theo was running late with the next chapter of his thesis. He countered with his grey stare. How, it asked, was it possible not to be diverted by a cousin's venture into beekeeping, by the tensions of a friend's research into medieval verse forms, by the potassium salts with which a neighbour was treating a twitch in her eye? Twice a month, Theo went to Fulham to take fish and chips to a bedridden letterset printer whom he had met in 1986 at a post-Chernobyl rally. He knew that the postman's stepdaughter was bulimic, he knew the name of the village in the Punjab where the Sikhs who kept the off-licence had been born. And there were his projects, his Beloveds, his collections. Had Laura seen his latest mass-market art coup? 'A quid in Oxfam. *For the lot*. I'm very tempted to hang them over my bed.' Four saucer-eyed children with shaggy Sixties hair clutched toys, drooped wistfully in individual frames.

On Laura's birthday, Theo gave her one of Anna's books: an octavo volume in blue wrappers, an essay by Virginia Woolf about Walter Sickert, a Hogarth Press first edition. The package, wrapped in paper of the same blue, was bound with a string of creamy pearls: 'From my own faux-oyster bed.'

Laura wasn't the only woman who eyed Theo with studied negligence. Most didn't last. But Bea Morley did. Laura found her way to friendship with Bea, a bedrock attachment that would last all her days. They had met at one of the Sunday evening gatherings Theo liked to host. Other regulars included a woman who was writing a book about surfing, and a guitarist whose hairline was receding faster than his hopes of fame. Sometimes an organic farmer turned up, sometimes a couple from Peru. An electronic engineer liked to take over the kitchen and stir-fry noodles for everyone. Like all drinkers, Theo was fundamentally uninterested in food. Friends knew to arrive with mezze or a roast chicken or the ingredients for mushroom pasta. Pizzas were ordered or an array of curries. Someone might show up with a dish of baked apples and a carton of cream.

Treats circulated, Es, handmade chocolates, smoky Polish vodka, spliffs, a platter of Stilton and figs. Theo had a video of 'Nostalgija', the Croatian entry in a recent Eurovision Song Contest. He would play and replay it over everyone's protests. His laugh was the kind that always surprises. He would place his hands over his face and *hoot*.

Currents crossed and sometimes sparked, conversations, ideas, causes, needs. Once there was a chunky boy, barely twenty, with red hair and the face of a pampered pug. When he left the room, Theo rose and followed him. They didn't come back.

Laura fell into an affair with a financial analyst. He was on secondment to Bea's firm, a black-eyed, experienced man. Things went on very nicely for some weeks. Then he returned to his family in São Paulo.

'I feel shitty,' sang Theo. 'I feel shitty, I feel shitty and witty and GAY!'

Ravi, 1990s

AT NOON, IN THE MONSOONAL off-season, fishermen slept in the shade cast by their sails. One man had a coil of smoke at his feet, a grey cat from whom he was never parted. Beyond the lagoon, in the sea-lit distance, the horizon went on and on. It was as steely and thin as a wire—the kind that garrottes.

Observing this scene along with Ravi was a boy with hair that matched the sand and eyes the colour of the sea. Soon they fell into conversation. Protein-reared, the stranger had long-muscled limbs covered with golden hairs where netted light quivered. His name was Mikael, he said, he had recently graduated in computer science in Stockholm. In October he was going to Silicon Valley, where he had been hired by Hitachi to work on storage software.

They talked about this for a while. Then the Swedish boy asked if Ravi would take a photo of him. It was a simple point-and-shoot camera, but Ravi fussed over everything, stepping back and sideways, then adjusting his subject's position in order to maximise the charm of the backdrop with its coconut trees and bundled nets. It wasn't the first time he had taken a photo of a tourist, and he always drew out the process. An unconscious yet almost frantic wish was at work in him on such occasions: the simple, terrible human need to be taken into account.

Mikael and he left the lagoon together. As they approached the tourist strip, Mikael suggested lunch. Ravi declined; he couldn't be sure who was to pay.

Five minutes after saying goodbye, he hurried back. Mikael had paused to look at a painted devil mask in the window of a shop. They spoke briefly, and the Swedish boy took a notebook and pen from his daypack, and handed them to Ravi.

Below his address, Ravi added: *Do not let sadness be associated with your name!*

For months, the post brought a spurt of hope. The memory of the moment when he had decided to go back to Mikael remained forceful: a zigzag of lightning, cartoonish and brilliant, had blazed across Ravi's mind. The postscript, quite uncharacteristic of him in its boldness, had flowed from the same inspired source. The impression that he had merely been obeying the dictates of a higher power was so strong that he never doubted the outcome. In fact, waiting for the offer of employment at Hitachi to arrive, Ravi was almost bored. It was a phenomenon familiar to him from his schooldays. Whenever he had been thoroughly prepared for an exam, he had felt a great lassitude on opening his paper and reading the questions. How tedious to have to go through the business of writing down his answers! Then, as now, he had felt assured of success. But first the idols of patience and routine had to be placated.

He said nothing to Malini, just as he would not have boasted, as a schoolboy, of the high mark he knew he would receive. But there was a nightmare in which a neighbour's servant, a filthy creature who might have been fifteen or twenty-seven, came running to say there was a phone call for Ravi. Holding a black receiver that smelled of other people's breath, he heard, *No connection. No connection.*

More time passed, and he no longer thought about Silicon Valley every day. And yet he had imagined it in such detail, his mind erecting vast white buildings ribboned with tinted glass. There had been low, landscaped shrubs, and saplings dreaming of fullness and tied to stakes.

LAURA, 1990S

BEA MORLEY INVITED LAURA TO spend a weekend in Berkshire with her parents. Bea had spoken of a cottage; Laura, stirred by poetic thoughts of thatch, was confronted with a substantial stone house. At breakfast, the jam spoon had been a present from Queen Anne to a Morley godchild now going to pieces under the churchyard yew. The cottage also sheltered candlesticks, pillow slips, engravings and so on passed down through generations. But what really struck Laura was a quite worthless object: a broken brick that served to prop open the back door. As she toed it into place with her wellington, Bea remarked that they really should get a proper doorstop, it was just that they no longer noticed the brick. It had been there forever, as long as she could remember. Her father, coming into the scullery, said much longer than that, he could remember it as a small boy. He picked it up, and they all looked at it. It was locally made, said David Morley, the blueish-black colour came from the manganese in the region's soil. He was a metallurgist, interested in minerals and materials. He pointed out faint creases and pockings in the brick, signs of insufficient control over its firing and hence of considerable age. It was smaller, too, than a modern brick—and by the way, did they know that bricks no longer contained clay but only sand and cement with pigment thrown in? Then Bea fetched a book, a local history. It confirmed that an Elizabethan manor house had stood on the far side of the cow pasture until a fire destroyed it in 1698. She examined the lump of brick: could it be Elizabethan, salvaged from the ruin? Maybe, said her father, it was very old anyway. He returned it to its place, and the two young women left the house to walk in polished September air, and the brick wasn't mentioned again.

But it weighed on Laura's thoughts. Blue-blooded jam spoons and their like remained within families through time and space, were transmitted by inheritance, accompanied their owners through displacement and change. That was to be expected: such objects were cherished, if only for their associations. Somewhere in her father's house lurked a pair of Victorian fire dogs, relics of the sizeable cargo shipped over oceans by Frasers for the embellishment of their stolen acres. But a broken brick! It was more matter than artefact. No one would think of packing it up to carry with them. Nor would it have survived in a house swept clean for a change of owners. Its neglected presence pointed to the persistence of Morleys in that one place. Her own people struck Laura, by comparison, as a vigorous, shallow-rooted plant still adapting itself to alien soil. The Frasers were undeniably modern, however. What was the modern age if not movement, travel, change?

She remembered Theo once saying that the twentieth century was best represented by an unwilling traveller. 'I mean, think of the millions of soldiers mobilised by wars. And all the people made homeless because of them. Now the world is full of people who don't belong where they end up and long for the places where they did.'

•

That was what Laura looked forward to, evenings alone with Theo, the coils and flows of their talk. They were comfortable in two old leather armchairs, Theo's long legs propped on a hideous corduroy pouf. The Dr Gebhardt epic would continue. Her groundbreaking study of *Hegel, Disco and Rhizomatic Hermeneutics* was in fact the work of a graduate student, subsequently dispatched to an entry-level appointment in Tierra del Fuego with no provision for sabbatical. He disappeared there in mysterious circumstances—all that was known was that he had wept on receiving a letter from Dr Gebhardt the previous day. After a costly investigation smuggled into the faculty's budget under Research, this suggestive document fell at last into the dean's hands. But Dr Gebhardt's menaces were so thoroughly encrypted in references to *Horizontverschmelzung*, text-as-paradigm and even—boldly!—to eumeneis elenchoi that nothing could be proved.

But as the evening deepened, and the level in the third bottle sank, it was always of childhood that Theo spoke, recounting pleasures and dreads, tea in the garden with the scent of mignonette borders, a sinister china mandarin that adorned his mother's workbox, where it nodded its wobbly head. There were scenes to which he returned obsessively, enlarging on earlier versions. Daydreaming of adventure, safe under the window at the top of the house, was one such recurring tale. Another involved a different window, this one in his bedroom. It opened straight into the branches of a pear tree. In spring there was an abundance of blossom. The child was told to be careful of bees. But he would stand at his open window listening to the bees at their busy work. 'I thought of it as the sound of love. A patient, devoted murmur.'

There came a spring when blossoms and bees were few; and one day the great silver tree was gone, cut down. The child blamed himself. He had not listened hard enough to the bees, he had failed in the loving concentration that keeps things steady and whole.

Laura asked if the apple tree outside the kitchen had been planted to replace the lost pear.

'I've never eaten such pears as came from that tree. Perhaps there aren't any left in the world.' Theo's hands made a shape. 'Solid, narrow. A *sculpted* look.'

It was an old-fashioned upbringing, Laura thought. There was a rocking-horse with a rolling eye, and a holiday beside a lake where the boats were shaped like swans. There were violin lessons and Sunday pony rides and wet afternoons spent with jigsaws or paints.

She once asked, 'Weren't you allowed to watch TV?'

He frowned. 'It wasn't important.'

Laura's notion of how the English reared their young was vague. Largely gleaned from books about children who tracked down smugglers or held midnight feasts at boarding school, it bolstered her Australian conviction that the old world was a backward sort of place.

As soon as Laura showed signs of getting ready to go home, Theo would beg. 'Why are you going? It's still early. Stay.' She, poor fool, would have to run for the last Tube. The next day she would slop soup, suppress yawns as she scribbled down orders. But Theo had declared, 'You're necessary.' It was quite true. As long as she stayed, he went on drinking. Laura saw and didn't see this.

There are paintings of flowers or fruit whose sheer lusciousness suggests the invisible, lengthening worm. Theo was like that: at that stage of ripeness where his attractive surface held an intimation of decay. So it was possible to speak to him of fear. It was possible to speak of the queasy sensation, running under the drift of Laura's days, that her life was dribbling away unused. 'I suppose I'm talking about a career.' Because the only professional progress she had made since the course in word-processing had been to exchange the pub in Clerkenwell for a restaurant in Islington, which had smaller servings and larger tips.

It was true that she was prized as a house-sitter these days. She picked and chose among clients who lived within a restricted circumference and who would be away for at least a month. Even so, Fitzrovia, Balham, Primrose Hill. Even so, Shepherd's Bush, Camden Town, Holland Park. It seemed to Laura that she was always packing up. And recently she had minded a flat for a physicist summoned to a bedside in Johannesburg and worried about an elderly cat. A day or so after moving on to Highgate, Laura missed a favourite shirt. The physicist said, 'Yes, I wondered when you would call.'

'Oh, you've found my shirt,' said Laura, pleased.

'Shirt?' said the physicist. '*Shirt?* It's my bin-liner that's at issue. There was a black plastic liner in the kitchen bin when I entrusted you with my belongings.' She spoke distinctly, enunciating with rageful care. 'When I came back, the bin was empty. What I want to know is, when do you intend to make good your theft?'

Laura told Theo that she had had it up to *here*—the edge of one palm slicing at the throat—with other people's houses. She was tired of the box at the post office, tired of tending leafless gardens that flowered for other eyes, tired of public phones. 'I want people to call *me*.' She wanted a telephone number. She wanted a teapot. 'I'm fed up with other people's teapots,' she wailed.

She pulled a face as she spoke, deprecating her need. But there was nothing comic about the fierceness with which she coveted the teapot in the window of a shop in Camden that sold North African wares. It was a small metal pot with a hinged lid, shapely and inexpensive, enamelled in cheerful red. 'But I can't lug a teapot around London. I need a place of my own. I need *proper* work.'

Bea Morley's firm had upgraded her laptop. Bea passed on the old one—ancient, it dated from three years back—to her friend. Every few weeks, Laura would use it to compose an application for a job that seemed congenial and that might be assumed, if she remained optimistic, to be not incompatible with an Australian degree in English literature. To letters expressing her desire to assist a publisher or work in a bookshop or even, fuelled by the insomniac elixir of lunacy and despair, to help an ex-SAS officer compose his memoirs (*Must be under thirty-five and willing to live in. Send full-body photo*), she received no reply.

She attended an information evening about a career in librarianship and a workshop on proofreading. These experiences discouraged her from working in a library or reading proofs.

Who should alight in London but Tracy Lacey, now in possession of a hedge fund-managing husband, a Grad Dip in Museum Studies and an assistant directorship at a university gallery in Melbourne. *Je regrette*, darl, Tracy couldn't stay long, in her deconstructed hair and PVC and linen shift, being en route to guest curate an Australian show at the Guggenheim.

'But I couldn't resist a stopover in London—not with you here, darl.' And there was Paree to patronise as well. Her flight to Roissy left that evening, she informed Laura. 'I don't know why I bother, I'm so over Europe these days. The work they show here—darl, it wouldn't get past the door at home. I always say Melbourne's the new New York. But you know what I'm like when it comes to Paree! Gary says I'm such a softie. As if he wasn't the one crying buckets at the airport! His men's dream group has really opened up his feminine side.'

Having on sight declared Laura *gorgeous*, Tracy was examining her old friend with a connoisseur's eye. So she might have appraised a painting, acquired as a kindness, that she had seen at once was second-rate but which she didn't quite like to let pass. The type of thing she might hang in a dark corner in case it came good over time.

What could Laura Fraser, tucking into reckless tortellini in cream, deploy against the triple assault of Gary, the Guggenheim and the new New York? It would have been nobler to refuse the contest. But she was human and imperfect. Tentatively, she offered Theo. In such a spirit Abraham might have led forth his son, each step a betrayal.

But Tracy Lacey was as magnanimous as her maker. She interrupted only to address a Do you *mind*? to the man at the adjoining table who was showing signs of lighting up.

Buoyed by victory and a Caesar salad (no egg no anchovy no dressing, *merci*), 'He sounds gorgeous, darl,' she conceded. 'Do you have a piccie?' While thinking, One of those plutonic things—no thanks! Mind you, it was just like Laura Fraser to end up a fag-hag.

A few weeks later, a card arrived from the old New York. Steve Kirkpatrick—did Laura remember him from art school?—had hanged himself in his studio. Tracy felt terrible. But it was Steve's own fault that no one wanted to show him. If only he had progressed his aesthetic. Laura would find it hard to believe, but he had never read Kristeva: Tracy knew it for a fact.

Ravi, 1990s

THE NEIGHBOUR'S DAUGHTER CAME TO Carmel's door to announce a phone call for Ravi. She peered at him through her glasses and touched her hair. A long time ago, when they were children, a lady had referred to Anoma as Ravi's girlfriend. Now he had a son and a frightening wife, but Anoma knew that Ravi was conscious of their older, deeper bond. Standing at the door, he had looked first surprised, then happy—that meant *recognition*. So what did it matter that Anoma's younger sister had married first?

How ridiculous, thought Ravi, as he dashed up the lane, that he had always pictured the summons to Silicon Valley as a letter: modern news arrived by phone. He had time to wonder how the Swedish boy had known the right number to call. Was there some kind of tracking software, known only to Californians, that had enabled it? In any case, a magical event requires an element of mystery. He seized the receiver and heard a familiar voice. It was his old professor, known to all his students as Frog-Face. He informed Ravi, without preamble, that an assistant lectureship in maths was coming up. Ravi stood there, breathing hard. He would be well advised to apply, Frog-Face said.

The young family moved to a rooming house above a bicycle-repair shop just outside Colombo, conveniently close to the university where Ravi would be working. The street door gave on to a stair that led up to the lobby of the rooming house; the cheaper rooms, such as Ravi and Malini could afford, opened off this communal space. There was a gathering of rattan-bottomed chairs there, and a huge old black-and-white TV in a wood-veneer case. The vertical hold tended to slip, but of an evening all the tenants gathered in front of it anyway. They would smoke and gossip and watch tele-dramas. If the Mendises shut their door against the noise, the room quickly grew stifling. But life in the rooming house was companionable, and Malini was content: she had escaped her mother-in-law at last.

There was a morning when Ravi woke very early. He saw his wife and child asleep, and thought, Who are these people? He grappled with feelings of suffocation and fear.

RAVI, 1990s

HIRAN PRESSED HIS FACE INTO Ravi's shoulder and rubbed. The child had returned from a visit to his mother's family with something that had once belonged to her, a toy that was already old when she was young. He couldn't wait to show Ravi this treasure: a small viewfinder fashioned in Germany from yellow plastic to resemble a TV.

A few days before this, a Tamil Tiger had driven a truck filled with explosives into the Central Bank. Ravi was called to the phone at work. On the other end of the line, Malini was frantic: her father had mentioned that he would be in Colombo that day. She had been trying to ring her mother but there was no answer. Confused reports told of hundreds of casualties; Malini was sure that her father lay among the dead.

It wasn't until the evening that news of her parents came. Her father had woken with pains in his legs and decided to stay in bed. Later, he had gone out on the veranda and applied himself to the analysis of a bottle of arrack. Then it was his wife's turn to lie in bed, ignoring the phone, with the sheet pulled over her head.

Learning that her father was safe, Malini began to cry. She had been so sure he had died—slowly, under twisted concrete—that she had to see him. She set out the next day, accompanied by Hiran.

Examining the viewfinder, Ravi marvelled at the mobility of *things*. By what elaborate journeys had the little souvenir waltzed over continents and oceans and ended up in his hand? Hiran showed his father how to place his eye to the peephole at the back of the toy and work a lever to produce a succession of three-dimensional images: a plumy fountain in a rose garden, swimmers at a lido, a mountain with its feet in a roofscape of blue slate. But it was the scenes featuring the interior of a bathhouse that held the child enthralled. There were dark green palms and a pale green pool surrounded by columns and mirrors. Archways repeated themselves endlessly. The watery, indoor light lent these pictures a remarkable quality: they appeared at once outdated and not-yet-seen. They were dreams and premonitions, scenes penetrated by the past and the future, irredeemably spooky.

Hiran loved the viewfinder to the point of preferring it to the TV in the lobby, but he avoided it after dark. It had to be placed in the suitcase that contained the family's spare clothes, and the case padlocked, before he would lie down to sleep.

Sometimes he woke crying. There had been *a devil with long ears*.

Malini learned that her best friend at school, shopping in the Fort when the truck exploded, had lost her sight in the blast.

At the time of these events, Malini was working for an international aid organisation dedicated to improving the status of women. The NGO ran village clinics, microfinance schemes, adult literacy classes, that kind of thing. Malini volunteered her services at first, but after a while was paid for a few hours of work each week. She was quick, clever, brimming with *push*. Her responsibilities and salary expanded. Ravi informed his mother of these developments with pride. But occasionally he recalled the first time he had taken Malini to Mr and Mrs Basnayake's house. Ravi had been examining their computer when his wife rose, crossed to the vase of orchids below the photograph of their dead son and set about rearranging the flowers. The old people stared as if watching the first flames reach the roof. Malini smiled: 'That's better.' Neither justification nor apology, it merely stated a fact. At moments of marital wear and tear, Ravi imagined her going about her rounds, the open-mouthed villagers contemplating their improved lives.

Ravi, 1990s

HE HAD BECOME FRIENDS WITH another assistant lecturer in his department. Nimal Corea's father owned a printing business, and Nimal was familiar with phototypesetting. Investigating website markup, he had realised its resemblance to the typesetting code. Now Ravi and he were working together on building the university's website. It was a matter of fierce principle that this should be accomplished without assistance from the specialists in Computer Science.

The Maths department had only one computer with a dial-up connection to the internet; the two young men tended it like an altar. During the day, the phone line was always busy, so they took to working on the website at night. When the power failed, as it often did, they stretched out on the concrete floor, and didn't wake until the lights came on again.

A new word entered Ravi's vocabulary: 'yahoo'.

Half mad from lack of sleep, he was in a state of exaltation known to pioneers and priests. He fanned himself with a newspaper—the fragrance of drains arrived, compounded by the cannabis with which Nimal was always well supplied. Mosquitoes were holding a banquet on Ravi's ankles, but hyperlinks were irresistible: as *all-at-once* as a conjuror's bouquet. Screens opened and vanished before him, dissolving and multiplying like dreams.

It was called surfing the net. Ravi tried to describe it to Malini, the way one electronic landscape gave way to another, the thrilling suspension between surface and depth. It was magical: a string of typed words made wishes appear on the screen. Place had come undone, said Ravi. He spoke of flight and speed.

Five or six years later, when dial-up and Mosaic were dim monuments of digital prehistory, he would recall how slow it had really been. He was waiting to cross a road in Bondi, and the woman jogging on the spot next to him kept hitting the pedestrian button. Her request had been electronically registered the first time, and the lights weren't going to change faster whatever she did, but the heel of her hand continued to punch. Ravi remembered waiting for the upload all those years ago, jiggling his mouse, circling it on its mat, humanly reluctant to relinquish control to mere technology.

Eager to experience these modern marvels, Malini visited Ravi at work one evening. Nimal was there, perched in a spiral of smoke. A childhood accident had left him with a withered arm; he was chubby, bulge-eyed, gifted. Watching his friend build the site, the almost wasteful elegance of his ingenuity, Ravi felt the scrape of envy. His own mind was an iron: it smoothed. It could improve on what Nimal, who worked fast and with a degree of disdain for the immaculate, had produced. But Ravi was aware of belatedness: of his painstaking ability grafted onto another man's casual flair.

Early on, Nimal had linked into the wealth of pornography on the net: its unfree flow. His good hand trembled on the mouse, but he had no credit card and no prospect of obtaining one. However, he had discovered Jennifer Ringley, an American student who had set up a webcam in her room to document her life. JenniCam refreshed every three minutes. There were dull hours of Jennifer holding forth about herself, but Nimal had once watched her masturbating. She had promised to strip for the camera, an event both men anticipated keenly. What if it coincided with their teaching duties or a blackout? Jennifer had said that she wanted to give everyone a really open, honest view into her life. It was appalling and riveting: Jennifer Ringley was a new kind of person. Every tyrant in history had dreamed of spying on hidden lives—but that dream required subjects who wanted to hide. It shrivelled before a pudgy eighteen-year-old, exposed on camera to the world, *who didn't care in the least*.

Now Ravi saw Nimal's huge eyes, reddened by ganja and fatigue, linger on Malini's breasts. To distract her, Ravi spoke hurriedly. 'You're you and anyone you can imagine. There is the same as here.' He felt the insufficiency of words as he guided Malini through portals and loitered with her in chat rooms, trying to demonstrate this disembodied travel. Webcams showed them a fishtank in San Francisco; in a basement in Cambridge, coffee dripped into a pot. The world had shrunk, said Ravi, and at the same time it was tentacular and unconstrained. From New York to Negombo, life would be digital and linked. What mattered weren't computers but the possibilities they unleashed. He declared, 'The internet will free people from *this*.' The sweep of his hand took in damp-stained walls, the large brutality of politics, the petty humiliations of making do.

He said, 'Soon everyone will be a tourist.'

Malini was typing words into a search engine: *human rights sri lanka*.

In bed that night she spoke of a forensic scientist who had identified the remains found in a mass grave in a wildlife park. She said, 'Bodies are always local.'

But their embraces were Venetian: fluidly magnificent. Melting inside her, Ravi was assailed by images: of streaming and connection, of data and bodies. There was HTML, there was DNA. Things flowed together on his mind's screen.

The NGO was involved in a rope-making enterprise in a village in the south. Malini returned from it with the story of an eight-year-old raped nightly by her father while her mother was working in Geneva as a nanny.

'Everyone knows what's going on.'

'Why don't they report it?'

'The father's a constable. His brother's a sergeant. For all I know, he's in on it as well. We'll have to do something.'

'But what? It's terrible, but what can we do?'

'I meant the NGO.' She said, 'No one expects you to do anything.'

At the onset of a storm, Carmel Mendis would go from room to room in her house hanging towels over mirrors to keep them from attracting lightning. It was the kind of thing that Malini couldn't stand. She had nothing but scorn for her mother-in-law's superstitions and pieties: the palm-leaf cross, the plastic crucifix on which Christ hung glowing and green.

But Malini harboured fetishes of her own. Ravi learned this when a bracelet of hers disappeared. It was a childish thing made of bright and dark blue plastic beads—Malini rarely wore it, but left it here and there, and now it was lost. She was panic-stricken at first, then inconsolable. Ravi, not understanding, said he would buy her a replacement. But the bracelet was charged with magic and luck.

I'll never get to the end of her, Ravi thought, and was filled with joy. This led to further confusion, for although he remained grave, Malini sensed his happiness and believed him indifferent to her grief.

LAURA, 1990S

THEO OFTEN SAID THAT HE favoured the beaten track. 'Europe's what I am, for better or worse. There's nowhere I want to go that can't be reached on a train.'

'Australia!'

'A dream place. Best left to the imagination.'

'India?' For there, in plain view on his shelves, was a small library of large volumes about the subcontinent.

'That was Mutti. She was such a proto-hippy. She dragged Gaby and me to Mexico as well. Everything was wonderful, and we didn't understand any of it.' He took down one of the Indian books, turned pages, held out a photograph of a dancer crowned with seven cobra heads. 'This man. The beliefs that move him, that got him here—I'd always just be gawking.' He rubbed his wide forehead, trying to explain.

'Isn't that the point? Discovering things?'

'There's no past in tourism. It's one thing after another. There's no time for time to accrue.'

He also said, 'I hope for the moment when *what I know* turns strange.'

But one of Theo's great qualities was that he never tried to diminish by belittling where a friend enthused. So he studied maps with Laura, argued about destinations, passed on tips about bargain fares.

He turned up one afternoon at a house Laura was minding in Belsize Park. It had rained all morning; Theo had walked under dripping trees. When she opened the door, Laura thought calmly, He has come for me. That was because the fresh smell of rain had entered the house—the connection made sense to her, if to no one else. Inside, Theo glanced around—it was a contemporary, impersonal, chic kind of house with polished concrete and slabs of light—and said, 'How relentlessly interesting.' His hair was damp, Laura saw, and his shoes. He told her that he had run into a friend he hadn't seen for a while. Meera Bryden was the brand-new editor of the *Wayfarer*, glossiest of travel glossies. 'Of course she wants to revamp it all. So I said I knew just the person she should be begging to write for her.' He handed Laura a card. 'She'd like you to call.'

'Darling Theo!' said Meera. 'He's coming to supper tomorrow. Why don't you join us? I'm dying to meet you. And do bring something you'd like me to read.'

Laura rang the restaurant where she worked and claimed that she had the flu. She set up her laptop and sat down. Theo had said, 'Meera won't mind where you write about. India. Sydney. All those stories you've told me about places you've been—pick any one.' The latest issue of the *Wayfarer* lay beside Laura. She opened it at random and read: *Africa is adventure. That was what I discovered on my epic overland journey*. A blackened stone spire rose in her mind like a warning finger. She was thinking of a story she hadn't told Theo, and would never tell anyone, about a man she had met in Strasbourg. An airline's mid-week special had lured her there the previous year. She took a room in the sort of hotel that can reliably be found near a railway station, and went out to look at the city—her guidebook promised a famous cathedral and, in it, a famous clock. Later, wandering around, still unnerved by what she had seen, Laura spotted a shop that sold *confiture de bière*. Beer jam! Why hadn't that occurred to Australia? No need to stop at jam, either: beer bread, beer sausages, beer pasta . . . Clouds were advancing, lengthening like strands of greasy wool combed out. They rushed over her, darkening the city. It should have been frightening, but the clouds moved on quickly—they were people hurrying home, hectic and smug. Night fell. Laura walked along a canal full of upside-down houses. She went into a bar and stood at the counter drinking wine. The French were addressing each other in precise, declarative sentences. A man remarked that he was suffering from *un flux nasale*. This was so plainly superior to a runny nose that Laura turned her head away to smile.

She met the eyes of a man sitting alone at a table, with one hand curved around a beer. His nails were trim and shaped like spades. Quite soon, Laura and Émile were walking along a moon-chilled street. A high, blank wall ran down one side. Where it ended, there was a tree like a candelabra; its branches, innocent of leaves, bore upturned, waxy flowers.

In her hotel room, Laura scarcely had time to set the scene by switching off the overhead light in favour of the bulb above the basin in the corner. Some hours later, Émile was getting dressed when he asked the kind of perfunctory question a resident asks a tourist. Laura answered that her first sight of the cathedral, at the far end of a street, had terrified her. 'I had this awful feeling I was looking at something that had gone wrong—the scene of a disaster. The cathedral's so dirty and so huge and so crowded around with other buildings. There's no perspective.' What her mind was showing her, as she spoke, was something that couldn't be looked at—it could only be encountered. Walking away, she had glanced back at the side of the cathedral. She saw the wing of a giant bat that had crashed and turned to stone where it died.

Émile listened attentively. Then he told her that when he was nineteen, he had left home forever. There was a flight to Marseille, another to Grenoble. It was late when the plane touched down. The uncle who had arranged his papers and paid his fare drove Émile through darkness punctured by headlights to an apartment on the outskirts of the city. The next day he woke to the rapturous thought that he had arrived in France at last. He had analysed its revolutions, memorised its poems, listed its principal exports. He hastened to the window and threw back the shutters. Then he screamed.

It was explained to him, when he was led back into the room, that what he had seen was a mountain. The high-rise that housed him was wedged against its stony black flank. If he were to lean from the window, he might touch it—that is, if someone hung on to his feet. 'But I couldn't forget. My first sight of *la belle France*: a catastrophe that blocked the sun.'

At this point, Émile and Laura found themselves with nothing to say to each other. What they had done in the bed with the dip in the middle was timeless. But now the past had shown up. It was a tree whose roots split the dusty grey carpet; its branches brushed the walls. They held bright, harsh-voiced parrots and a soldier planting a *tricolore* in a mound of corpses and a boy who slept with *The Three Musketeers* beside his pillow.

In London the night deepened, and Laura worked on her story for Meera Bryden. She was still exhilarated by the effortlessness of writing on screen—skaters must know that swift swoop and glide. But as her work took shape, her enthusiasm ebbed. The traceless erasure of mistakes, first thoughts, alternatives masked the fallible labour that paper preserved. By the time she had finished writing, she no longer trusted her processed words. Unblemished but unfresh, they put her in mind of supermarket apples. She raised her linked hands above her head and stretched; she was thinking of Émile. His hands had smelled faintly of pepper. He rocked inside her, and in the depths of the hotel room, the door of the wardrobe sprang open; a misshapen wire hanger dangled. It was only now, remembering that night, that Laura realised this: the stories they exchanged had had nothing in common. One was about place, the other about time. She had told a traveller's tale about the jolt delivered by strangeness, while Émile had described the first step on the road to disenchantment—it was really a story about the end of childhood. Relating it, he had looked serious and kind. But afterwards he put on his jacket hastily, as if distancing himself from a blunder, and left at once.

'Don't fret,' said Theo. 'Meera'll love your story—and you. She's completely sweet. And she's gone and married this fabulous man.'

Lewis Bryden said, 'Orstraylia? I had the most marvellous time jackarooing there. All that marvellous Outback. It seemed so much more real than Sydney and Melbourne. I mean, what is the point of Orstraylian cities? They're just so secondhand.' To Laura, he added kindly, 'But I believe the whole country's come on awfully well. There was that marvellously good film about the schoolgirl murderers. Darling, what was it called? With Kate Winslet.'

He carried on like that throughout the evening. His jaw was regulation issue, his profile designed for the screen. But something in the way his head sat on his polo-neck suggested that it would come away without a fuss. So time passed happily while Lewis held forth—Laura was watching him pace about with his head tucked under his arm.

The Brydens hadn't been married long. Lewis found reasons to touch his plump, sexy wife: leaning across the table to stroke her fingers, resting his palm on her haunch as she changed his plate. When Meera, describing email to their guests, said that Lewis and she were addicted to it, his smirk insisted on the kind of messages they exchanged.

Theo, leaning on Laura's arm as they walked to the Tube, exclaimed rather thickly, 'Lucky, lucky Meera!'

He had added to his collection of Beloveds, Laura saw.

As they started down the stairs to their platform, he swayed. A Fraser instinct for self-protection, a vicious, vital mechanism, kicked in. For a second, Laura saw her pretty hand shoot out and the long length of Theo broken on concrete. She grasped him, steadied him, of course.

The surface of their relations remained the same after that evening at the Brydens. But something invisible and crucial had changed. It cleared a space for observation. Laura noticed that Theo no longer pleaded when friends tried to leave the house in Hampstead. Now he said, '*Must* you be so fucking dreary?' He spoke lightly and mockingly and meant it. More often than not, Laura gave in to his pleasant, edged hostility. She was a good sport—wasn't that the Australian way? The following day would be sour with resentment. Her muscles cried that she earned her living on her feet while Theo sat at a desk like a child.

The junk he brought home was spreading. The bedsteads from the garage had found their way indoors to rest against a desk. The heavy curtains in the dining room had vanished, replaced with orange venetian blinds on which a printed sunset flared. Mirror tiles had conquered a wall in the hallway, swirly mauve and silver paper was crawling over the downstairs loo. Throughout the house, tiny rubber dinosaurs paraded on ledges. Shaggy hot-pink or teal rugs, shorn from sci-fi sheep, had settled on carpets. Everywhere, the milk crates had multiplied.

A child in buttoned boots rose from an Indian grave and ran through the depths of the mantelpiece mirror. Laura heard Hester say, *Ruth choked and died—her throat was lined with grey velvet.* That memory misdirected. It led Laura to think of the ugly modern house rising within Anna Newman's walls as an infection rather than as something struggling to be itself.

The two shapely armchairs that cradled conversation had been joined by a third, a giant recliner striped in nubbly brown and fawn. He had found it on a pavement, said Theo. Imagine that, Laura replied.

Ravi, 1990s

HE WAS LOOKING AT A photocopy of a sheet of ruled paper torn from an exercise book. A witness statement, Malini said. 'This woman saw the bodies behind the temple. They took all the men there and hit them with rifle butts. She said she couldn't forget the sound of the skulls splitting open—it was just like coconuts falling on the ground.'

It was the kind of information that came Malini's way as she visited villages around the country. Ravi shuddered at her tales but managed to forget them quite soon. Some of these things had happened in the late Eighties; a long time ago in his view.

Malini was folding the paper, her face triumphant. The centre of him stirred.

Sex made her talkative. After lovemaking, she embarked on stories of death squads and abductions, which was one reason why Ravi didn't always listen to what she said. Their bed was a site of ecstasy and education. From the first afternoon in a friend's borrowed room, she had been shameless: experimental, bold.

A rotund baby, Hiran was lengthening into a scrap of a child. They fed him *anamalu* plantains to fatten him, but he remained a wisp; barely there.

Ravi heard, *Kang kang buuru! Chin chin noru!* From the window, he looked down at the street. Several small children, including his son, were playing on a patch of waste ground near the rooming house. A neighbour looked after Hiran when Malini was at work, and he had become inseparable from her brood. 'Run, run, run . . .' shouted a fat little boy who seemed to be bossing everyone about. Hiran scampered after the rest, his arms swinging stiffly with his fingers pointing down. These days he ran everywhere—the quick patter of his steps was one of the background noises to life in the rooming house.

Ravi lit a cigarette and remained at his post. A different game started up below. The children ran around until one shouted, 'Bomb!' At once, the others threw themselves to the ground, where they lay spreadeagled and very still. After a little while, they got up and ran around again. Ravi couldn't see the point of this game. But there were days when the children played it nonstop.

Malini didn't get on with one of her colleagues, a woman called Deepti Pieris. The origin of their quarrel was blurred. It had something to do with education—Deepti sent her children to an international school—or the position of a desk. Before it erupted, Malini had been drawn to Deepti, a confident, careless person. They had even unearthed an old connection. As a junior reporter on the social pages of his newspaper, Malini's father had been present when Deepti's aunt made her entrance at a ball. An architect had designed her dress. The inner layer was made of dark, coarse silk, the outer of an improbably fine net; at the last minute, hundreds of fireflies had been inserted between the two and the opening stitched shut. Malini's father had never forgotten it: the stunned faces all turned the same way, the girl encased in living light. His photographer, an excitable Eurasian, had swooned.

Recently, Deepti had let slip the name of her brother-in-law: a thug who owned a tyre factory. When some of his workers had agitated for strike action, two strangers paid a visit to the most outspoken. When they left, the man had a broken back. 'Deepti tells everyone that her brother-in-law paid for the man to be examined by his own specialist,' said Malini to Ravi. 'As if we don't know who put him in hospital in the first place.' That was the kind of story she brought home about Deepti now.

On top of everything, the Pieris woman had a temper. Only that morning, she had flown into a rage with the teaboy and threatened to have him dismissed. Afterwards, she had gone around the office all sweetness, pressing slices of chocolate cake on everyone, laughing and talking too loudly. 'She's a typical bully. Suddenly she realises she's gone too far and tries to win people to her side.'

Ravi was of the opinion that thugs and chocolate cake were secondary to the case. The underlying cause of Malini's hostility was that she had liked Deepti at first. After the matter of the school or the desk, she felt she had been deceived. Her father was mixed up in the whole thing—Malini was as finicky as a cat where he was concerned. The tale of the firefly dress, something that had shone in her childhood, had been handled by Deepti and was tarnished. Ravi said all this to his wife, but in a tactful, long-winded way, and added that whatever the Pieris woman had done, she wasn't responsible for her brother-in-law.

Malini was looking thoughtful. Ravi realised that she hadn't heard a word. She said, 'You know, now I think Deepti really did feel bad about the teaboy. All that fuss with the cake. He was the one she really wanted to give it to, in fact.'

A diptych:

The first panel shows their wedding night, when at Malini's suggestion, he gently dipped his fingers in her. When he withdrew them, they were strung with a luminous gossamer that thickened here and there into a silver node. For a long time afterwards, whenever he heard *worldwide web*, what Ravi saw was that glistening mesh.

The second scene dates from the last year of their marriage, a night when Hiran was keeping each outward breath pinched in his nose for a few seconds as he lay sleeping in an angle of their room behind a curtain improvised from a cloth slung over a nylon cord. It was a rhythm that created tension, Ravi's own breath suspended as he strained to hear each faint exhalation. Meanwhile, Malini was whispering of a woman who had taken delivery of a small parcel, opened a jeweller's velvet case and found her husband's eyeballs nestled on ivory satin. He was a journalist and had been missing for weeks.

Ravi's voice came out far too loudly. 'Be careful,' it said.

LAURA, 1990s

BEA'S COUSIN VIVIENNE, WHO LIVED in Naples, was returning to England because her father was ill. The thing was, she didn't want to give up her apartment or the students with whom she was paid to converse in English.

Bea reported all this idly to Laura. Yet an idea fanned open in the two women's minds at the same time. It was a Sunday morning in May, and they were drinking coffee in a blue-vaulted room, the courtyard of Bea's garden flat. There was a yellow rose and a creamy one against a wall. The hillside scent of thyme spiralled from a tub where a bay tree also grew. In twenty minutes Laura would have to leave for the lunch shift in Islington. A sense of fate—the future fixed in a shining stroke—excited and frightened her. She looked into Bea's face and saw that she was in the grip of the same shivery thrill.

Laura said that she couldn't possibly do it, she had never taught English to foreigners, she had no idea how to set about such a thing.

A soft golden moustache was sometimes to be seen above Bea Morley's lip. She stroked it now, summoning the brisk, encouraging tone she favoured when addressing an underperforming minion across a desk. 'Of course you can do it. It's only *talking*.' Bea was a great fixer. If the thought passed across her mind that in the absence of Laura, Theo might have more frequent recourse to her, she batted it away.

Fate, magic, outcomes that seemed ordained—they hadn't yet finished with Laura.

Weeks had passed since dinner with the Brydens, and she had heard no more about writing for the *Wayfarer.* She didn't like to pump Theo, now a regular visitor to their flat.

Two nights before she left for Naples, she was with him when the phone rang. He said, 'That's for you.'

Meera Bryden was so sorry she hadn't been in touch sooner, a million things had come up, she had no idea why she had ever agreed to edit this magazine, she must have been bonkers. But she had loved Laura's piece about the cathedral in Strasbourg. Had she said how utterly chilling she found it? And so original. She loved it, really, and was so sorry she couldn't run it, they had done the city's famous Christmas market last year. But now it appeared that Laura was going to Naples, how clever of her, the Mezzogiorno was *the* coming destination. Meera would love to run a feature on Puglia or Sicily—something a trifle less cerebral than Laura's Strasbourg piece, a touch more sensual? At the magazine they had been thinking about food, the simple, earthy dishes of the south, people adored reading about eating in exotic locations and you could run such glorious photos. Was Laura by any chance tempted . . . ?

Theo insisted on accompanying her to Heathrow. When Laura's flight was called, he produced a parcel from his pack. 'Not to be opened before Naples.'

She tore at it as soon as her seatbelt was fastened. The steward, touching the back of each row of seats as he passed down the aisle on a last check before takeoff, paused when he spotted the passenger cradling something red. He realised that she was crying quietly over a teapot. The things people brought on board! That spout could very well put out an eye.

Laura, 1990s

THE LAST BAG FROM THE London flight was claimed in Naples, and Laura was left alone. The carousel looped past again, a melancholy rubber stream. She might have stayed there forever, or taken the first flight back, but a uniformed figure approached. Officials spoke into walkie-talkies; Laura filled out forms; it was foolish, she was telling herself, to think in terms of *signs*. Then a panel in the wall slid open like magic: a man in overalls emerged. He handed Laura her case. It had been retrieved from the tarmac where it had fallen, unnoticed, from a trailer.

By the time the airport bus pulled in, Naples stood in a brownish, benzene dusk. What had Laura expected? Arias, gunfire, the ghosts of centurions perhaps, certainly her pocket explored by the expert hand. Circles of traffic tightened and hummed. *Just a short walk*, said the letter Vivienne had sent with a map. But there were two men beside Laura, one offering a Discman, the other a mobile phone. She shook them off and began to make her way through the crowd, between folding tables on which were set out socks, combs, pocketknives, cheap, useful things. A shadow came whispering of hashish and a hotel. Laura walked faster, tried to look purposeful and knowing. An enormous square had been dug up and barriers erected around the excavations. She had to cross it—but how? An iron hand seized her arm: it had prevented her from stepping in front of a bus. Laura thanked, wanted to cry, fled into a narrow street. The evening had deepened. Large spots of rain came padding. A bouquet of umbrellas materialised, thrust at her by a dark man. There were few streetlights and no pavement. She put up the hood of her jacket. A cat cried thinly under a parked car. The rain slanted and steadied. Laura's shoes were sodden, then her feet. Her wheeled case lurched over flagstones, always one heavy step behind, a club-footed stalker from an evil dream. A shining electric eye flew straight at her—she flattened herself against hard-hearted stone. The Vespa sped past, spraying laughter. Then there was a shrine enclosing a rouged and solid Infant: a trashy brooch pinned to a wet, black façade. Its neon illuminated the name of a piazza that Laura spent minutes failing to find on her map. She went on past the sound of someone coughing. There was always another square or another crossroad, there was always a scooter coming fast out of the dark.

A photograph of Sophia Loren adorned the window of a pizzeria. To enter would require courage, because the restaurant was crowded and Laura was wet. She trudged on, and came to a door, flush with the street, that swung noiselessly back. There was fragrance and gilt: a seraglio or a church. Laura turned a corner and before her, like a vision, a flight of shallow steps led to an archway surmounted by a bell. She knew that she was lost. She knew that she loved this place.

Laura had time and occasion enough, during the months that followed, when she was lonely, when the temperature and her spirits dipped, to marvel at her sympathy with the city. It was inexplicable. Naples was indefensible: a callous city, a raddled *grande dame* with filth under her nails.

Vivienne's flat, reached across a courtyard filled with motorbikes and cars, was on the fourth floor of a former *palazzo*. A mechanic's workshop gave on to the street. Ghost voices slipped under the noise of revving. *Since you consult only your emotions, Vanessa, I must urge you to consider the nature of Salvatore's relations with our grandmother.* Between advice about spare keys and plumbing, Vivienne's letter had mentioned a whispering wall. *It just means Signora Florescu's watching one of her soaps. Her living room's bang up against mine, and she watches telly at all hours with the sound turned right up. She's from Romania or one of those places—harmless and quite mad.*

Bea Morley came for a visit, and it was plain to Laura that her friend was appalled. She could be formidable, tall Bea. She pushed her long fair fringe away from her face and stalked about the streets saying little and sucking in her cheeks. Her mood was catching. Wishing to convey the city's attractions, Laura found herself enumerating flaws. The traffic didn't stop for pedestrians, the post office had run out of stamps, she had lost her sunglasses to a pickpocket, damp afternoons brought the scent of drains, the traffic didn't stop for red lights, there were battalions of stray dogs, she had lost her keys to a pickpocket, rubbish lay rotting on the pavements, the traffic didn't stop for ambulances, the headlines were proclaiming another Mafia murder, and the window in Vivienne's bathroom was stuck.

On Bea's last morning, they walked past newsstands patchworked with images of a dead woman. Bea had described the hillock of flowers outside Kensington Palace. 'You couldn't joke about it. People you'd have sworn were sane took offence. But the funeral was brilliant—about the time they were getting to the abbey, I drove from Notting Hill to Battersea in only fifteen minutes. I must say I wouldn't mind a royal shuffling off every week.'

They were on their way to a collection of pictures housed in a monastery. Afterwards, Laura opened a door at the foot of a flight of stairs. They went through into a cloister. It was lush with overgrown oranges, loquats, figs. Weather, working at the walls, had turned them a creamy yellow—the colour of fading gardenias, said Laura. The leaves of the orange trees were as glossy and distinct as if cut from green tin. That evening, on the station platform, surrounded by shouts, clanking, an aria oozing from the tannoy, the squeak of sneakered feet, Bea said that she would always remember the cloister. 'A wonderful place.' She couldn't understand why Laura kept complaining about Naples. 'You're so lucky to live here,' said Bea.

Other cities—Venice, Rome, Florence—offered riches to the casual eye. Naples chose secrets and revelations. Laura learned to follow the dingy street, to descend the unpromising stair. There would be a vaulted ceiling, or a family feasting on melons under a pergola, there would be the trace of a fresco or a damaged stone face. A dull thoroughfare brought a red-robed saint with an arrow in her breast—Laura turned her head and saw the painting propped in the window of a bank. So it was to be a day bracketed by Caravaggios: she had sat before another in the cold blast of a church that morning. There was no end, it seemed, to these stagings of discovery. Wrong turnings took Laura to an industrial zone near the port; every truck, slow with freight, coughed in her face. Then came a row of grimy archways and, waiting in the depths of each one, the sea. It was polluted and shining. Laura remembered the treasure hunts of childhood: mysteries, astonishments, gifts that weren't delivered but earned.

•

Donald Fraser, passing through London that Easter, had amazed his wife, his daughter and himself by presenting Laura with a digital camera. Over the years, he had sent Laura cheques at enigmatic intervals for inscrutable sums: £27, say, followed, five weeks later, by £1143. What calculation they represented not even Donald could have said; an impulse would, over two or three days, become an imperative before which he meekly gave way. On the latest occasion, he had gone into a duty-free shop at Changi Airport intending to buy himself a camera. He went on believing this until the moment when the sales assistant asked to see his boarding pass; as he handed it over, Donald realised that he was going to give the camera to his daughter. He had seen Laura four or five times in ten years, usually in London, once in Geneva. Now came the lacerating thought of his child far from reach and defenceless in the grinding world. Lines from a poem learned as a boy roamed about his brain: *'Come back! Come back!' he cried in grief, / 'Across this stormy water . . .'* He was a scientist, a rational man. But he had buried one of his tall sons. At the duty-free counter, stalked by air-freshener and electronic pop, Donald felt the weight of that coffin on his shoulder. It brought the conviction, lunatic and absolute, that a digital camera would keep his girl safe.

Jetlag, diagnosed the anaesthetist when he confessed. She remarked that she had some very nice perfume samples that even Laura would love. But Donald—although he took the hint and bought his wife a pint of Obsession on the London leg of their flight—held to his intent.

Reunited with his child in a hotel in Kensington, he was overcome by a familiar distaste. Distance diminished and enhanced his last-born. She shrank in memory, an illusion instantly dispelled by the sight of her too, too solid flesh. Her hair was cunningly piled and fastened with opalescent combs, but as she bent her head over the duty-free bag, Donald saw that it was threaded with grey. It was, at first, a sign that made no sense. A full five seconds passed before he grasped that the runt was no longer young. And by some runtish trick of transference it was the desertion of Donald's own full-bodied prime that she thus contrived to convey. She was smiling at him, and delight placed a girlish mask over her face. But the finger hooked across the camera displayed a ridged nail. A trapped thing in Donald's chest was hurling itself against its cage.

That year the camera was often in Laura's hands, a weighty silver charm. In Naples, she applied a pearly coral polish to her toenails and photographed the unflattering result. She photographed her red teapot and a yellow dish of blue plums. From day to day, she recorded the changing, textured splatters of pigeon shit on the crinkled tiles under the kitchen window. There was a compulsive quality to all this. Laura photographed Vivienne's Indian quilt: lilac flowers on a cucumber-green ground. She photographed the dancing bronze god on the TV, the mirrorwork cushion on a chair. Meera Bryden sent her to Sicily to write about the island's sweets. Oh, Palermo, capital of ice cream and murder! In streets end-stopped by a stony mountain, Laura Fraser breakfasted on cannoli. She photographed them first, along with sweet, pistachio-flavoured couscous. There were almond biscuits, cassata, and a pig's blood and chocolate pudding—but she couldn't photograph the pudding, it was out of season.

Images uploaded and viewed on a laptop had a particular luminosity: colours fresh from the brush, radiant and wet. Rather shyly, Laura emailed Donald Fraser a few photos of Vivienne's flat. There was no reply. Messages came in from Theo, from friends here and there on the planet, from the *Wayfarer*, from strangers offering get-rich schemes or sex. A new form of suspense had come into the world: everywhere, the profits of telephone companies increased as more and more people dialled up and watched a screen, waiting to see if an electronic mailbox filled with a sequence of coloured squares.

In Lincoln, Vivienne Morley's father recovered from surgery, grew strong. But Vivienne had fallen in love—deeply, life-changingly—with a girl called Gin. She was to have returned to Naples at the end of the year but now wondered if Laura would like to stay until the following summer. Laura's emailed reply carried a photo of an ecstatic bronze dance.

An anniversary came, the first day of Laura's thirty-fourth year. Birthdays are a time of reckoning and wishes. Laura spent hers writing about marzipan and a cake called the Triumph of Gluttony. 'Luna Rossa', played on an accordion, was persecuting diners at the end of the street. Long after she shut down her laptop, Laura's thoughts were still of transience and sugar. She ate a pastry cloud stuffed with cinnamon-scented ricotta. Then she ate another. On waking, she had photographed the view from her bedroom: a concrete wall on a dank day. Why had she bothered? She owned three rings, a silver band, a lump of amber, a round red sparkler of faceted glass. Wearing them in the street was asking for trouble. She turned them on her fingers. The evening held the knowledge of passing unnoticed in the world. Where was the gaze that would gather up her worthlessness and invest it with loving sense?

In the courtyard, a man was whistling. Phantom insinuations arrived through the wall: *But Assunta, my dear, we are all strapped to fortune's wheel. Why do you speak of betrayal?* On the day the world learned of Diana's death, someone had banged on Laura's door. Beyond the safety chain, an old woman scarcely taller than a child stood sobbing. Signora Florescu's Italian, stressed in all the wrong places, was a puzzle in which the dead woman's name recurred. She was crying for her: that much was plain. Laura put her arm around her neighbour—the bent neck was surprisingly thick. Placed in a chair and offered tea, the signora only cried harder. She picked up a cushion and blotted her face; afterwards, snot glistened on the mirrorwork. Laura put a saucepan of water on to boil. It took forever, and she wanted to weep. Signora Florescu had reverted to her own tongue, but Laura knew exactly what she was saying. Diana didn't come into it: she was only shorthand for the unbearable sadness of being. Laura could tell, because the same shapeless grief was working in her. 'Back teeth together!' she urged. She had intended a light note, audible only to herself, but it came out ringing. The water changed its tune, and Signora Florescu raised her white head—she really was powerfully ugly. A wrinkled child, she stuck out her tongue.

On Laura's birthday, the signora's TV kept up its whispered assault: *I may be your teacher, Massimo, but I am a woman first. And now another year has ended.* Laura countered it by cranking up the volume on Vivienne's boombox. A boy sang, *Hallelujah! Hallelujah!* His voice had always been unearthly; now he, too, had joined the dead. Laura Fraser sat alone, and turned her heavy rings, and wished what everyone wishes.

Ravi, 1990s

HIS FRIEND NIMAL COREA HAD been headhunted away from the university by an online agency that found accommodation for tourists in local homes. RealLanka was the creation of one of Nimal's former students: a singularly dull boy, a surgeon's son. His father had provided the seed funding and introduced the boy to backers who promised more. Nimal abandoned his master's degree, and moved to Colpetty to design and develop the agency's website on twice what the university had paid him. That still wasn't very much, but he was unable to help boasting that his stock options would make him rich when the company was floated. He posted a back issue of *Wired* to Ravi and swore that they would work together again on web design. 'Our portals will capture the most eyeballs,' he enthused.

There was another unsettling development. An Englishwoman had arrived to take up an executive position at the NGO, and one of those sudden, intense friendships had flared between Malini and the newcomer. Freda Hobson's father was English, and she had grown up in Surrey, but her mother's people were Jaffna Tamils.

'She's one of us,' said Malini. But she corrected herself at once: 'No, she's different.' Then she laughed.

She had her lovely wavy hair cut short. The size of her ears was revealed. Contemplating itself in the mirror, her smile was a little forced.

She had new clothes—jeans, a silky blouse—that had once belonged to Freda. There was also a skirt, blue with orange pockets and an orange band around the hem. It was perfectly decent and it suited Malini. But Ravi didn't like seeing her in it. Acknowledging this was unreasonable, he disliked the skirt even more.

Whenever Freda was mentioned, Ravi pictured a white woman with red elbows. Then they met, at last. The eyes were even darker than the skin, but their brown was haunted by purple. A hand covered in rings squeezed: 'Ravi! How super! I've been simply longing to meet you,' said Freda Hobson. And, 'Malini, darling, we've had masses of support for your idea for the refuge. Repeat after me: I am a genius and a goddess.' Her beauty was as extravagant as her way of speaking, and Ravi mistrusted both. He had recognised her at once: here was another rearranger.

Ravi's research into fractals was progressing slowly—he couldn't see the point. Nimal was confident that the following year, or the one after that, Ravi and he would be able to set up their web development company; their user interfaces would be unbeatable, stylish yet *powerfully simple*. But Professor Frog-Face wanted Ravi to apply for a scholarship, so that he could do a doctorate abroad; he kept Ravi standing in his office while he described his future. Ravi understood that if he spent his life at his desk and bullied his colleagues for thirty years, he stood a very good chance of turning into Frog-Face.

The professor liked to select protégés among his students: young men who were bright but not overly so. He treated them with light scorn, and expected obedience—they were his sons, in other words. He had directed each step of Ravi's career, even intervening to ensure that the university's website was entrusted to Ravi and Nimal. It was not that Frog-Face cared about websites, for he held all applied science in contempt, but he was delivering a snub. Who could stand the head of Computer Science? The man was in the habit of folding and unfolding his hands! A note was carried to the vice-chancellor's office reminding him that a website involved the prestige of the university, and that Mathematics took precedence over modish, upstart disciplines. The vice-chancellor had married Frog-Face's daughter—he was in a weak position.

Now here was Frog-Face offering Ravi Canada or Japan. But even if he did succeed in winning a scholarship, Ravi knew that Malini wouldn't want to go. When he said as much, speaking of his wife's responsibilities at the NGO, 'Leave her,' advised Frog-Face. He meant temporarily, because he believed in the sanctity of marriage just as firmly as he believed that if you didn't manage a woman, she managed you. Ravi remembered that when he had broken the news that he was a father, Frog-Face had replied, 'So now you are a slave.'

When Ravi thought of leaving his son, it was like trying to measure infinity: it couldn't be done. But before the year was out, without a word to Malini, he applied for and received a passport. He would have sworn that he had acted on impulse. How, then, to explain that he had been saving up for the fee for months?

Ravi kept the passport hidden in a pile of old exam papers in his desk. It was a talisman, comforting to have at hand. On the day it arrived, he had arranged to meet Malini after work. He came out of the Maths building and spotted her nearby. One of the stray dogs that lived on the campus was eating what appeared to be a roti. Malini, who was probably responsible for the food, was watching with her back to a painted wall. Once she had seemed the answer to every important question. But in that skirt, she looked like a target, standing there against the wall.

Laura, 1990s

LAURA HAD BECOME FRIENDS WITH one of her students, with whom she practised her Italian. They were at a restaurant for lunch when a man crossing the piazza stopped at their table. Silvia lifted her face to be kissed, pressed the man to join them, presented him to Laura: Marco, an old friend.

These days he ran a gallery in Rome. Laura saw him assess and dismiss her as a feminine object. But he had the Italian willingness to like and be likeable, and he turned to her with real interest on learning that she was Australian. His gallery specialised in tribal art, and he had travelled to Australia, 'a magnificent country, stupendous'. He spoke to Silvia in quick Italian. As he did, his hand rose like an independent appliance and adjusted her blue shawl.

He addressed Laura again. He had been blown away by the Northern Territory. 'The colours of the desert there. Wow!'

Long ago, Laura had noticed that Europeans who lived in the more desirable quarters of Paris, Rome, etc. were always going on about the desert. She thought, Now he'll say something about Aborigines. Or stars.

'The stars were amazing. So many!'

But he was not harmful, merely predictable. Laura remembered his hand, plump-wristed and busy, fussing at Silvia, and imagined it between her legs.

Marco began to talk about a crisis at the gallery. On their islands north of the mainland, the Tiwi people of Australia carved poles called *tutini*. He turned to Laura. 'You know these?' The carved wooden poles served two quite distinct purposes, Marco explained. Some, used by the Tiwi in their burial ceremonies, were placed beside graves. They weathered quickly, rotted. Others—no less beautiful, carved with no less care, *identical*, said Marco, spreading his thick brown hands for emphasis—were made to be sold in commercial galleries. He had been fortunate enough—*privilegiato*, was what he said—to acquire and sell a few *tutini* to collectors.

Now the art critic employed by a famous newspaper had published a feature in which she claimed that the *tutini* sold in galleries lacked the aura that attaches to the authentic. She had seen ceremonial poles in situ on Melville Island: decrepit, sublime. They were not to be compared with the pristine carvings created for Western consumption.

Soon after her article appeared, a client had returned his *tutini* to the gallery and demanded a refund. Marco feared that others would do the same. He would have liked to take legal action, but the critic had relatives in high places.

Food was being brought to the table. Marco excused himself—*la mamma* was waiting for him, he couldn't stay. A diversion arrived, a moon-faced beggar woman accompanied by a greybeard in a knitted jacket. It was Sunday, the day of beggars. The woman gave Silvia a handwritten sheet—a story, a history—repeating, *Per amor di Cristo*. Silvia ran her eyes over it but kept glancing at Laura, at

Marco. There was now quite a little crowd around the table, the beggars, the waiter, Marco, who had risen to his feet.

Laura handed one of her business cards to Marco, as the beggars closed in to impede Silvia's view. 'I'd love to hear more about your adventures in Australia.' Her jacket was unbuttoned, and she arranged herself in such a way as to afford him a prospect, from his not very great height, of the impressive expanse of her bust.

Per amor di Cristo, intoned the old man.

Silvia returned the beggar woman's letter. She lifted one shoulder, a movement that conveyed neither indifference nor acquiescence but helpless acceptance: '*Ma?*' What was she to do? The question, like her lips, remained open. Her eyes were the huge green ones Greece had bequeathed to Naples. They held the resignation of a people who, living in the shadow of Vesuvius, had long been exposed to unhappy conclusions.

Marco was the first person Laura knew to own a mobile phone. In her apartment that evening, he placed it within reach when he undressed. He played with it and Laura in turn, listening to messages. At one point, lifting his head from her breast, he cried, '*Che idiota!*'

'Who?'

'This crazy woman, this critic, this . . . this . . .' By the light of the bedside lamp, he had the pouchy, self-absorbed face of an old woman; *la mamma* would be waiting in the mirror as he aged. Another collector had contacted the gallery, insisting that his *tutini* be replaced at once with 'the real thing'. 'I want to say, go there then and live on those islands. Become a Tiwi. Because if there is a problem of authenticity, as this imbecile says, it is not in the pole but in your possession of it.'

He cupped Laura's instep. She had pretty feet, he declared, stroking her straight toes.

'I'm a product of the sensibly shod classes. And Sydney kids go barefoot a lot.'

But he meant something different. 'So many Australian girls, their feet are too big. They make me cold.'

She let it pass. She had no real interest in Marco, only in what he went on to provide.

Theo came in the spring. He had lingered in the south of France and the north of Italy, he had been moving towards her for days. Framed in the window of the train, he projected the curious impression that there was more of him and that it was less defined. Laura saw the swag of flesh at his chin. His face had slumped; there were little hammocks under his eyes. She saw that his beauty had gone from the world. She went swiftly along the platform and into his embrace.

He brought her a star made of ruby-red glass, each of its five points finished with silver. The hinged central compartment swung open so that a tea light could be placed inside. That evening, they looked at it shining in the window. Theo said, '*A tiny object in the night*.'

There was another present, too, an antique kilim. His mother had bought it in Kabul on her honeymoon. Laura saw a severe geometry of faded browns and greens dominated by a dull dark red.

That day was overcast, like the next. On the third, the sun, flattening itself between buildings like an assassin, found its way into Laura's room. At once the muted colours on the rug glowed with life. Thereafter she would find herself looking forward to that hour of the afternoon, waiting for the transformation. It would arrive like a loved face, remembered, anticipated, yet never exactly as she had thought.

There was always rubbish for sale in the streets, someone sitting beside oddments of nylon lace or rickrack braid, broken-down shoes, chipped enamelware. It was one of the ways Naples affected her, said Laura, this wringing of worth from things that would be discarded in wealthier places. Scenes she had once associated with far, tropical countries flashed up throughout the south of Italy: concrete-slab tenements festooned with exposed wiring, women fetching water from a public standpipe, children whose games centred on a plastic bottle—a worldwide web of making do.

Theo wasn't listening. From a tablecloth spread with a trashy assortment, he had snatched up a print. '*Exactly* what I need.' A Mediterranean beauty in a peasant blouse displayed her décolletage in a cracked frame.

His emails often came with an attachment showing a large, bad painting: galloping white horses, a violently autumnal forest, a paved beach where naked lovers sheltered under the wings of a giant swan. He said, 'But I have the feeling my collection of mass-market masterpieces is coming to an end. This one could even be the last—who can say?'

The streets laid down by the Romans were unflinching: narrow, sunless, slabs of black volcanic stone underfoot. A piazza or cross-road brought a shock of light. Theo was dawdling, pausing to photograph a carved door, flirting with a barista. A small glass case mounted on a wall sheltered a shrine to Maradona, worshipped throughout the city; here Laura turned to wait. Theo made his way towards her, now shadowed, now lit, through the blindingly obvious: the origins of chiaroscuro, the cosmic on/off of brilliance and dark.

A nineteenth-century arcade named for a king was colossal and derelict, historical as royalty. They revolved alone under its great glass dome. An ice-cream vendor hovered by an entrance, and now and then there came the grey-suited flit of businessmen short-cutting between two streets. These peripheral presences heightened the otherworldly quality of the pillared galleries, decided Theo. 'Like a figure that never shows its face on the edge of a dream.'

Laura felt a draught move through this remark. It was the kind of conversation they were having in Naples: glassy, high-storeyed, empty. They had talked about friends, of course, gossip moving smoothly in as intimacy ebbed. Laura learned that the Beloved actor, charged with the Saturday videos in Theo's absence, was depressed about his career: he wished for greatness but had found only success. The guerrilla gardener was threatening to write a memoir. He had never gone hungry, never been beaten, raped or addicted, his childhood had vanished in untroubled happiness—the book would be a sensation. And Dr Gebhardt? She had passed from his life, said Theo. At a conference in Chicago, the dean had collapsed from nervous exhaustion brought on by his dealings with Dr Gebhardt. His transatlantic colleagues had never forgotten the dean's magisterial treatise on Henry James. It argued that the best, the heroic work had been done long before James turned his back on his native land. The slippery narrators, the humiliations inflicted through the placement of cake forks, the bravura way with semi-colons: everything had been perfected in a tale written when the Master was twelve. Europe had merely overextended and ruined a blazing American talent. That every review dismissed the book as drivel was only another reason to look with gratitude on its author. A chair of creative writing was found. It was in a former steel town in the Midwest, but the offer was so lucrative and undemanding that Dr Gebhardt hadn't hesitated. Already her influence could be discerned in the stark Derridean fables accompanied by grainy images of footwear that were starting to appear in the *New Yorker*. In any case, added Theo, his thesis was almost done: all he lacked was a conclusion.

In all this easy nonsense something iron was present. It supported the airy edifice of Laura-and-Theo. She took his arm as they left the arcade, but the ice-cream cart intervened. A wish for closeness melted in indecision over pistachio or hazelnut, in Theo's remark that all the things Neapolitans loved—gelati, fireworks, music—were fleeting.

They fell back on tourism: food, shopping, sights. The overbearing façade of Mussolini's post office was scribbled with neo-fascist slogans, its marble pillars were as black as shirts. But day-to-day postal transactions were carried out in a hole-and-corner way in a kind of basement around the corner; and in the large, defunct telegraph hall above, one corner of a poster that had something to say about communication and speed had come unstuck. At the table below it, an African was sleeping, *dead to the world* with his round head pillowed on his arms.

Theo wanted to buy a postcard. After a long search, a rack was found. All the legendary images—the bay, the volcano, the opera house—were out of focus. Naples could madden by refusing to perform itself. It was such a slovenly, neglectful place. The cat hit by a scooter remained in the street to flatten slowly, the best room in the museum was closed without explanation, the seventeenth-century courtyard had been turned over to cars. Laura said, 'I'd like to stay here forever.' One possible response to that was, You can't—

how would I manage without you? Theo went on forking flesh from a shell. They were having lunch in a restaurant that catered to the staff at a nearby hospital. Two doctors in their white coats had just come in; the woman's face, a long oval with blank, tilted eyes, was a Modigliani. Theo's postcard, a blurry view of the Duomo, lay by his plate. It was addressed to Lewis Bryden. 'I know it's squalid,' said Laura. 'And to be honest, I can't bear it a lot of the time.'

'It's squalid because it's still alive,' Theo said. 'Only the dead are perfect.' On their way home, he returned to the theme. Paris, Florence, Rome were superb mausoleums. 'Europe's buried there. This is a deathbed.' He took Laura's hand, gripped. 'Every time I walk down a street here I feel I might burst into tears.'

By night he drank Lacryma Christi, grown on the slopes of Vesuvius. Yet Laura sensed him making an effort. Once he rose and poured the second half of a bottle into the sink.

She had just returned from giving an English lesson one afternoon when the phone rang. It was Marco—passing through, and hoping she was free *to discuss Australia.* That was their code, developed over two or three rendezvous. Laura said repressively that she had a friend staying. That evening, Theo was deep into his story of the pear tree when Laura realised that for the past ten minutes she had been thinking only of *discussing Australia* with Marco. Here was Theo Newman on tap, and she would rather that made-to-order little sleazebag. She got up. 'Sleep well. See you in the morning.'

So she was relieved when Theo ordered coffee in a bar or bravely requested mineral water with a meal. But the feeling persisted of something controlled in order to please. Once we didn't have to be careful with each other, Laura thought.

•

Theo invited her out to dinner; he was leaving the next day. When they returned to the flat, he poured himself a glass of wine. It sat untouched in front of him, a small red idol. Then he asked Laura to marry him. 'You know what I can't give. You know what I am. But I'd do my level best to see that no harm would come to you.'

My level best. It might have come from a Victorian poem: Theo Newman was promising to play the game. The grey eyes, still remarkable, were absurdly affecting. But the Boys' Own touch complicated. It worked at Laura's Australian suspicion of being manipulated by English public schoolboys for their private ends.

I found the dolphin in Tahiti, announced a disembodied voice close at hand. *Everything has been accounted for, whatever Pasquale might say*. Theo rubbed his forehead and said that Laura would be free to see other men, to do as she pleased. 'The thing is, I'd like to have a child. That's something we might manage very well together, don't you think?'

The evening had been cold, April filching from December. Walking home, Laura had worn gloves. They lay on the table—they had kept the shape of her hands. She picked one up and rolled it into a ball. At last, 'I'm sorry, Theo,' she said.

Later, she left her bed and went into the living room, holding her blue robe closed at the neck. Theo lay on his back on the pull-out sofa. A great sonorous rippling issued from him, now and then syncopated by a snort. He had neglected to blow out the tea light; the upper part of the star still gleamed. Those three red points made a boat-shape that floated in the darkness. Laura had told Theo—she had told herself—that she didn't like the idea of introducing a child into the arrangement he proposed. Now she thought, Why didn't you come up with this a year ago? At this moment, they might have been looking into the face of their child. There came the impulse to shake Theo into consciousness, to declare that she had changed her mind.

As if the thought had communicated itself to him, he ceased to snore. He flung one arm above his head and moved his fingers. Laura wondered if she ought to do something about the candle. The snoring started up less rhythmically, a hacking sound. She listened, closing her eyes. When she opened them, the reddish glow looked weaker. It would soon wear itself out, she thought.

A few days passed. She was prowling about the flat again. The telephone had woken her shortly after midnight. When she answered, the caller hung up.

The late-night calls had begun not long after Laura had arrived in Naples. They came two or three times a year, just as they had once done in Sydney. It was the thought of the caller's patience through all her phoneless years in London that chilled. The silence in the seconds that the connection lasted was enormous but contained a sound so faint it might have been the echo of a whisper. It suggested unfathomable distance, the stir of briny black depths, the sigh of stars. Yet it was profoundly unnatural: a wind from beyond the world. Laura's sleepy thoughts orbited with satellites. They pulsed with the fibre optical. They retrieved the black curve of a receiver against a fair head.

Night wakefulness is distinctive, sublime and blurred, consciousness peering through a caul. Laura switched on lamps and moved about the room, touching things, dreamily handling them. A tremulous whisper asked, *Surely, Mariana, you have considered bringing in an exorcist?* Theo's sweetish odour lingered in cushions.

Since he left, a headache had followed Laura, the kind like a bird that settles and soars. To keep her phone bill down, she tried not to check her emails more than twice a day; now she simply had to look. But there were no messages for her.

Ravi, 1990s

MALINI HAD BEEN PROMOTED AT the NGO and was working four days a week. That meant training, seminars, meetings which dragged on late. She pointed out that rather than the endless bus ride to and from work every day, it was easier for her to spend the occasional night in Cinnamon Gardens, at Freda's flat.

Around this time, Deepti Pieris resigned from the NGO. Freda Hobson had never warmed to her. When a literacy project Deepti was working on ran into difficulties, Freda suggested that she might be happier elsewhere. The breakdown of the project was dispiriting but hardly critical; looking into Freda Hobson's purple eyes, Deepti saw the unfolding of a plot. On the day she left, she engineered a row in which she accused Malini of conspiring against her with *that Tamil bitch*. Reporting this, Malini was delighted. 'It just proves what she's like.'

She had insisted that they go to a Chinese restaurant for dinner. Ravi ate tempered noodles and glutinous scarlet flesh. Malini was saying that Deepti couldn't see a glass door 'or the chrome on a car or even the bowl of a spoon' without pausing to admire her reflection. This was prompted by the huge mirror that covered the far wall of the restaurant. Waiters crossed and recrossed in front of it, and the big, animated room, which was lit by blueish-white electricity, went back and back forever—Ravi pressed his temples because they ached. Malini was drawing parallel lines on the table with her finger. Frowning at them, she said, 'In spite of everything, I feel sorry for Deepti. I can't help thinking we should have found a way to keep her. In the end, she couldn't look at anyone, not even the teaboy.'

The golden points of light had returned to her face that evening. They brought her sharply into view. Ravi realised that he never looked closely at anything. Knowing in advance what he was going to see, he paid it only scant attention; the world and his wife passed in a blur. But she was a woman concocted from spells.

Hiran now attended a kindergarten; soon he would be starting school. But he still came and went freely from the richly strange land of the very young. A murmured commentary hinted at its marvels and laws. 'The postman must come with baby birds. Seven, eight, nine, twenty, a hundred. His hand has a headache. Wish you happy year. All the motorbikes went to live in America. If you don't eat all your rice, you will get ill and die. Is she coming or not? The sun doesn't want the whole today. It can't be helped. There was enough bus.'

Hiran spent a night with his mother at Freda's flat. Questioning his son in private, Ravi learned that Freda had the biggest TV in the world. Malini and Hiran had shared Freda's bed, and Freda had slept in a different room. On Saturday morning they had all gone to a swimming pool before eating chocolate ice cream.

This furtive interrogation of his son sickened Ravi but was necessary. He was determined to keep his manner playful, his tone light. But Hiran answered in a forced way, feigning laughter and raising his voice, imitating his father's false ease. Recognising his own artifice in that truthful little mirror, Ravi was shocked.

The swirl of frustration, rage and misery he felt was so alien that months passed before he could give it a name. Malini was taking off her blouse, and he noticed that she was wearing a stylish pink and white striped bra that fastened at the front. At once he saw the Englishwoman's ringed hands easing it into place.

He lay on his wife, gripping her arms, and asked, 'Does Freda like girls?'

Her eyes widened. But all she said was, 'Maybe.' She even placed a heel on his buttocks in encouragement. Her nipples hardened as he watched.

Malini's voice came out of an open-fronted shop that sold cigarettes and soft drinks, and floated into the night. A man sat behind the counter on a stool, illuminated like a peepshow, picking his teeth beside a radio on a shelf. Ravi, loitering on a pavement pungent with grilled meat from the Muslim eatery across the way, listened to his wife appeal for help for women and children made homeless by the war. Her voice grew spiky as she denounced the Tigers' brutalisation of child recruits taken at gunpoint from their homes, and the murder of dissenting cadres. Then, without a pause, she listed the reasons why it was imperative to investigate the aerial bombing of Tamil civilians.

A rat ran lightly along the trapeze of a telephone cable. Ravi heard the bemusement in the interviewer's voice: 'So who are you saying is responsible for this situation? The government or the terrorists?'

Ravi went on his way without waiting to hear her answer. In an auditorium made airless by lawyers and intellectuals, he had recently listened to speeches about the routine use of torture by the security forces. When it was Malini's turn to speak, 'I am against terror,' she began. 'The terror of the terrorist and the terror of the state.' She recounted testimonies confided to her by village women with such calm power that Ravi saw a man sitting further along the row wipe his eyes. Freda Hobson sat beside Ravi and applauded with her rings raised in front of her face. One of them was a large blue sapphire; it dropped you to your knees, like her gaze. She was wearing a red-on-blue sari with a red blouse. Malini was in a blue blouse, and her sari was blue-on-red. She ducked away from the microphone, beaming and awkward, and joggled the stand. A schoolgirl was keeping a capital-letter promise: I RESOLVE NOT TO LIVE MY LIFE IN VAIN.

When he was still living at home, Ravi had once seen a shirtless boy dance on the beach under a string of coloured bulbs, watched by a group of spellbound foreign men. In Malini's escalating activism, he recognised the same shimmer of risky willingness. It was addressed to Freda, he was certain, and his heart twisted. Their saris called to and answered each other. *Maybe. Maybe.* He thought, When did she last say anything important to me?

He found himself prey to a lust he had last known in his teens: a vast, hormonal greed. His solution was technological. By now he had the use of a dial-up connection to himself at work. In a chat room, he observed for a while how matters played. Then he wrote: *hi, topaz here, 18, i like girls like me, do u want to talk?*

Responses appeared at once. Ravi waited. One of those who replied posted a second message and a third. Soon Aimee and he were in touch every day in their private message window. Aimee was compliant, acquiescing in Ravi's scenarios. These flowed with ease from his keyboard: all he had to do was transcribe what was going on in the video of his wife and Freda that looped endlessly through his brain.

Aimee offered elaborations. They were endearing and misspelled. Gradually Ravi tutored her in the sophistication of inference. He might describe nothing more than standing behind her while he fitted a front-fastening bra over her breasts (*c-cups just like yours*, she had informed him early on), the quasi-clinical portrait repeated, without variation, in a series of messages, until she climaxed or claimed to. About his own finales, there was nothing virtual. He had wired himself into his fantasy: at once witness, participant and impresario. He felt his body's drift, its effortless assumption and discarding of forms, even as his flesh turned adamant as stone.

Laura, 1990s

SHE WAS SHARING A FLAT in Kentish Town and freelancing for the *Wayfarer*. Whenever she had an assignment, there was always material that didn't fit the angle Meera wanted. So Laura would work it up into different stories that she sold elsewhere. She sold photographs, too, and reviewed hotels for a ritzy accommodation guide—that meant free ritzy hotels. When people asked where she lived, she would say London. But she might have replied, just as truthfully, that she lived in hotel rooms and gate lounges, in taxis and planes, on Eurostar and Heathrow Express, on moving walkways and escalators, in shuttles and courtesy buses. She was inert, strapped into place, yet hurtling and fast-forwarded. She could lay claim to two passports and three email addresses, she was between destinations, she was virtual, she was online, she was on the phone. She was a voice on a machine, she was neither here nor there. She swallowed small, extremely green pills against jetlag. Sometimes she thought, Why not just live at Heathrow? A family of robed Africans seemed to be doing just that. Why not sleep stretched out across plastic chairs, eat fast food, while away the time between flights by filling in questionnaires about her airport experience? The editor of a newspaper's travel supplement advised her, 'You're only as good as your content—you'll keep moving if you're smart.' Laura Fraser was a late-twentieth-century global person. Geography was beside the point.

St Petersburg, Jaipur, Ljubljana. Hill trekking in Thailand, a weekend in an abbey on the Isle of Wight. New York, where Laura realised that her first assessment of the city, shaped by those repetitive modernist grids, had been quite wrong. In Manhattan the contemporary wasn't architectural but invisible, hidden in towers full of screens, buried in coaxial cables, carried in bytes.

Hong Kong was a giant cash register where spending was soundtracked by the ringtones of mobile phones. Shanghai, pinned between capitalism and control, was all suspension: elevated expressways that ribboned past the middle levels of impossibly high-rise blocks, a glamour bar that floated in neon night. In Dublin there was Guinness and rain, Laura ate oysters in a pub where a man played a penny whistle and people with red hair spoke to her in soft, light voices—her mind was a caricaturist, fastening on to whatever was distinctive. She wrote well and efficiently, to length and to deadline, of flea markets, amusement parks, rituals, touts. Laura Fraser *checked out hipster bars*, woke to *mist-shrouded hills*, she *explored the Beijing art scene*. She wrote, *This is where worlds collide.*

A folder on her laptop held material she couldn't sell. On an icy Chinese evening her taxi took a wrong turn. A naphtha lamp flared. She saw bedding, cooking pots, the faces of labourers whose lives unfolded under the freeway they were constructing.

In Singapore, an open-sided truck transporting guest workers to or from a building site kept pace with Laura's cab. One of the dark-skinned men was asleep on a pile of bricks. The others stood braced against the sides, reaching behind for something solid to hold.

Hip-hop was blasting from a Bangkok arcade. Near the entrance, a beggar and her child had claimed a square of cracked pavement. In a faded red *intel inside* T-shirt, the little girl sat facing her mother with her legs stretched out. Laura had a note in her hand, ready to drop into the empty instant-noodle container. But as she drew close, the child spoke, her mother smiled and bent forward, the child laughed. Laura passed on, unwilling to break into that private moment, into the locked circuit of gazes and delight. But afterwards she wasn't sure whether her reluctance sprang from discretion or a nugget of ungiving in her heart. Later still, she was looking from her hotel window at vertical concrete curtained with light when it occurred to her that perhaps she hadn't offered money because happiness is not a beggarly attribute. Perhaps her failure wasn't one of charity but of imagination. Lives predicated on misery are not reduced to it, are humanly shot through with pleasure, with joy. But otherness is readily opaque, and she had been unable to see into it.

In Munich, a gargantuan helping of a moussaka no Greek would have recognised was placed before her, covered in chips. Laura deployed a cautious fork. A man was moving about the restaurant, peddling long-stemmed roses individually wrapped in cellophane; the mechanical gesture with which he held out a bloom acknowledged that he had no expectation of a sale. He had a neat moustache, light brown skin, grey hair streaked with black cut close to his head. An Iraqi, a Turk? He was, or appeared to be, about Donald Fraser's age—but the gulf between the two men was as wide as the world. The people eating barely looked at him, signalling their disinclination with a small flip of the hand. In his white shirt and blue suit, the man threaded his way through conversations, the smells of food, the racket of spoons. Waiters looked through him. Laura saw that he was expert at sidestepping them. Also that he was the oldest person in the room.

A German dining with his wife and sons was also watching the flower seller. His face was a blank pink page, but Laura knew what he was doing because she was doing it herself. They were trying to place themselves in the moment when the man stood at the door, in the wind that was slicing through autumn, preparing to sell what nobody wanted. Was that enough? wondered Laura. Were acts of imagination what people in her position would plead? The metaphor didn't escape her—its implication that justice would yet be done, her species' great, vague, consolatory fiction.

Incidents, scenes, reflections such as these were the et cetera of travel: intractable matter, material that couldn't be moulded into the shapely narratives Laura produced.

RAVI, 2000

MALINI DECIDED TO SPEND THE weekend with her parents. She would leave work at midday, collect Hiran from school and take a bus into the green monotony of the interior, returning on Sunday night. She liked to arrive unannounced at her parents'—that way her father had no time to hide the empty bottles.

The Mendises now occupied a large, quiet room tucked away down a passage at the rear of the rooming house. On Saturday afternoon, Ravi was correcting students' work when his pen ran dry. Looking for a new one, he found a bracelet of blue plastic beads inside a box of odds and ends. How was that possible? They had searched their old room so thoroughly for the trinket. He dusted the bracelet off and placed it prominently on the table, smiling as he anticipated his wife's delight.

That night, Ravi was woken by a distant shout. This would turn out to be the nightwatchman—he executed his duties by muffling his head in a towel and stretching out at the bottom of the stairs. When the police questioned him later, he would say that he had woken at a blow to his ribs; someone had stumbled over him.

He heard a car accelerate and realised at the same moment that the street door was open.

Ravi rose and opened the door of his room, his thoughts still molten. Seeing no one in the passage, he almost went back to bed. But something like instinct directed him along the corridor, towards the lobby; he was still sleepily knotting his sarong around his waist when he arrived. In the greyish dark, he could make out the chairs grouped around the television like guests who had fallen asleep at a party. But there was an unfamiliar bulk on top of the set. The watchman, arriving at the head of the stairs, switched on the light. Ravi blinked, and still couldn't decipher the object in front of him: a thing half known but unspeakably strange. Then he understood that he was looking at a female torso that had been sawn off halfway down the thighs and above the breasts. The cavity at the top had been enlarged and the amputated limbs crammed inside. The whole arrangement resembled a vase from which outlandish flowers of feet and hands emerged on fleshy stalks.

He must have moved closer, because just before he fainted he saw his name: RAVI, in white letters scratched on a shin.

RAVI, 2000

HE SLEPT AND SLEPT. THE shock, said Freda Hobson, the shots her doctor gave him and the pills he had prescribed. Ravi heard her out and yawned.

On the day of the funeral, he could barely keep awake. Finally released by the police, the bodies lay at Malini's parents' house. Mourners came from all over the island. They stood in line for an hour to file past the big coffin and the small one, both closed. Hiran had been found in the street, not far from the rooming house. In the uproar caused by the discovery in the lobby, the small body had gone unnoticed at first. Then a young constable, vomiting out of sight of his colleagues, wondered why the dog lying in the crevice between two buildings hadn't stirred.

A crone shrouded in silk rose up and embraced Ravi. Her arms were clammy and hard, and her breath was unfresh. It was like being clasped by something that had risen from a grave. 'That girl,' said Mrs Basnayake. Her spectacles appeared to be leaking. 'That wonderful girl.'

There was a commotion in the middle of the room. Ravi's father-in-law, drunk of course, had collapsed at the foot of his daughter's bier.

On the afternoon of the abductions, witnesses had seen Malini talking to a young man in wraparound sunglasses. Hiran was with her, in his favourite red T-shirt with the yellow smiley face. The stranger was leaning against an ice-blue Mercedes parked around the corner from the bus station. He held a ballpoint pen, which he clicked absently as they talked. The conversation seemed unhurried, relaxed.

When the man opened the rear door of the car, Hiran climbed in. His red Mickey Mouse pack, a birthday present from Freda, was strapped to his back. Malini followed her son, and the stranger went around to the driver's seat. The windows of the car were tinted. But there were those who claimed to have seen another man, waiting in the back.

The Mercedes was a novel touch. As a rule, a white van was preferred.

A pale-eyed man in plain clothes was always present when the police interviewed Ravi. He remained in the background but was memorable for the polished grey stones in his face. He spoke only once. That was at the end of the second interview, when he came up very close to Ravi and said, 'Don't you think there are questions it's better not to ask?' His tone was pleasant and conversational. He said, 'You're lucky. You know they're dead.'

Freda Hobson had scooped Ravi up and installed him in her flat. She lived in a district of expensive apartments, and large new houses that filled up their grounds as if they had been dropped into place by a crane. At first Ravi was in no condition to refuse Freda, and later he was glad. The flat was a blank place. He had never been there with anyone he loved.

What he remembered of those first weeks was brightness and space. Here and there, objects stood out as clearly as if outlined in black. Light moved through him unimpeded: there was a window at either end of the room in which he slept. Or so he thought—later he would be amazed to find that there was only a single long window above the bed.

Grief moved by stealth. In the act of putting on a shirt, he might think, 'The last time I wore this, they were still alive.' A banyan tree was always close at hand, now expanding, now shrinking. Its branches formed a black square. It encompassed all that was unimaginable: the future, for one thing, or the last minutes of his son's life.

A week earlier they had been alive. Ten days. Twelve. The last time he had cleaned his nails, the last time he had sneezed. *Run, run, run and bring me . . .* The roots of the banyan were lifting inside Ravi, and dry contractions seized his stomach. He couldn't remember the magical object that would restore his wife and child.

It was Malini's fault that their son was dead. He could have killed her at times.

Carmel Mendis, weeping into a neighbour's black Bakelite phone, nevertheless reproached her son for staying alone with an unmarried woman. What would people say?

Ravi repeated Freda's argument: he was safest there. The apartment block, white and streamlined as a plane, had a monitored alarm system and was patrolled day and night by a guard. The compound wall was three metres high and bristled along its length with upside-down nails. When Freda pointed out these defences, Ravi had thought how easily circuits are disabled and men frightened or bribed. But he said nothing. Precautions soothed her and left him unconcerned. Freda mistook his silence for dullness and listed the security arrangements again.

Ravi relayed them to his mother, and added that he had his own room. 'My own bathroom, also.' As he spoke, it struck him as extremely strange that two people should have *a bathroom each*.

He was providing all this information in an undertone. Freda had gone into her bedroom and shut the door when his mother called. This had the effect of making Ravi vividly conscious that she was there, on the other side of the wall.

Curiosity, a resilient emotion, rose up in Carmel. 'Son, what is it like there?' Her mind, running through scenes from *Dallas*, reached for something fabulous and unattainable, but stuck on an older ideal: Valenciennes lace. She also asked, 'Can't you get a chaperone, child?' The peculiar word, fished up from the sunless depths of his mother's girlhood, went through Ravi like pain.

Nimal Corea turned up with a laptop, a bottle of Johnnie Walker, and ganja already rolled into a joint. He wanted to show Ravi the website he had set up as a memorial to Malini and Hiran. There was an email address to which people could write if they had information about the murders. It was understood that faith in the police investigation was limited, at best.

Ravi refused to look at the photograph of his son. In fact he didn't want to look at the site at all but didn't know how to say so without giving offence. Nimal scrolled down, and Malini looked out from the screen in a mercilessly exact rendition of her gaze.

Nimal was wearing a ring set with a garnet on the little finger of his damaged hand. He had grown heavier, and called with corpulent oaths for justice and revenge. He spilled the contents of a manila envelope on the table, and Ravi shuffled printouts of emails. There were messages of sympathy and heartfelt, righteous denunciations, but no one had anything useful to say. Nimal looked on, jiggling his knee. But now and then he would lower his head and turn his ring with a sheepish air.

Ravi, who had never tasted alcohol, never used ganja, didn't hesitate to sample these gifts. It was like attending the funeral of his wife and son: not a thing he had expected he would do but suddenly unavoidable. A glassy remoteness encased him whenever anyone spoke of what had happened. It was not that he was unmoved by Nimal's efforts, but everything—the condolences from strangers, the modular leather furniture, his friend's declarations—had the overlarge quality of a film. He had noticed, and it was consistent with the fantastic unfolding of events, that one of the emails offering sympathy came from Deepti Pieris, Malini's old adversary at the NGO.

When the whisky was two-thirds gone, Nimal broke down. He wanted to offer Ravi a place to stay, he said, but his lodgings consisted of a room above the RealLanka office. With the collapse of dot-coms across the world, the public float of the company had been postponed, and Nimal's salary was devoured by the cost of living in central Colombo. And, 'Work, work, work, all the time,' he wept. There was no *time*, he said, over and over again, as snot and tears mingled on his plump, childlike face. 'Everything is faster, we must work faster, eat faster, shit faster.'

Ravi paid no attention. He had just caught sight of his hand—a surprise! What was it doing there at the end of his arm?

Time passed, and although he continued to swallow pills, Ravi stopped sleeping—so he would have claimed. But there were mornings when he could remember having spent hours on a beach looking out at black waves.

One day he asked Freda, 'Who would want to harm me? Why do I have to stay here?' She had just come home; her keys were still in her hand. She drew in her chin and looked hard at him, but it was plain that his bafflement was sincere.

Later on, when she was in her room, Ravi stood close to the door. Freda was talking on her mobile: 'I mean, yesterday I really thought there were signs of improvement. And then today, I actually had to spell out that he's at risk because it would be assumed Malini's passed on information they'd rather he didn't have. And he still didn't get it. He said, "But I've never done anything." So I said, "Exactly. And they don't want you to start."'

Then Ravi heard, 'I'm sure you're right, I'm sure it's the medication. He's just not making connections.' And, 'Yes. Super-sad.'

When Freda was at work, Ravi went into her room. It was his mother's bedroom, secretive and calm. But Carmel's room was crowded with heavy, dark furniture: a modest landscape packed with gloomy lakes and cliffs. Here, there were small, entrancing things: necklaces, painted boxes, photographs, the bright spines of books beside the bed. Ravi realised that when his mother had asked him what Freda's flat was like, what he should have said was that everything in it was new. He had just understood the meaning of money: it was freedom from ugly, inherited tables, from lumpy pillows and chairs that sagged.

Rings sparkled on a tray. Like all his countrymen, Ravi was a connoisseur of gems. He saw the diamond Freda called The Millstone and left lying around the flat, and the magnificent sapphire—he spied her Jaffna Tamil mother in its blue depths. There was a turquoise lozenge bound with silver, and an opal for bad luck. And there was sheer rubbish, a big red rose moulded from plastic, a glass band in which purples and lilacs merged.

He handled the jewels. They were cold as corpses.

From their first meeting, Freda had reminded him of someone. This impression, a bird he had to identify from its shadow, hovered fuzzy and persistent in Ravi's brain. He studied a group of framed photographs on a chest. A fair-haired man was genial in one of them; in another, his padded arms clasped Freda against a backdrop of snow. Ravi went out to the living room and examined the larger photo of him there. He filled the frame, a squared-off man. Ravi thought of good English butter. He thought of all the red roast beef the man contained.

The balcony where Ravi stood smoking looked into a broad-leafed tree. On the far side of the street, just where a bat had hanged itself in the power lines, a car pulled up and a girl got out. She wore jeans and a UCLA T-shirt, but her hair, lustrous with oil, flowed to her hips. When Hiran was very young, he had delighted in undoing his mother's plait and staggering around her with her hair in his fist, imprisoning her with its locks. Peering through leaves, Ravi watched the girl, who was now addressing an intercom. The gate before her began to swing open. There might still be time to leap from the balcony, seize her, shear the hair from her head.

•

Freda plugged in her PowerBook and answered emails. She was a news junkie, she informed Ravi with pride. 'Get this!' she would say. There might follow the *Washington Post*'s opinion of a summit about Palestine, or the *Guardian*'s retrospective take on the Y2K bug. A dead man hovered at her shoulder: Ravi saw his father, chin propped on hand beside his shortwave radio, lost in *Letter from America* or smiling at *Just a Minute* on the World Service.

When Freda invited Ravi to use her laptop, he declined. What he didn't say was that things had their own size and were not equal—even the primitive technology represented by Father Ignatius's old map had known that. But the internet, abolishing distance, undermined relativity; it offered sapphires and plastic with an even hand. When arguing with Malini, it had been usual for Ravi to say things like, 'These people who were raped or tortured or killed have no connection to you. Why are you concerned with them?' Why hadn't she replied, 'What connects you to the level of coffee in a Cambridge pot?'

The living room contained a phone and an answering machine, but it was often Freda's mobile that rang. Ravi watched her thumbs move over it, agile and dark. He noticed that she didn't like to be parted from the sleek little phone, carrying it with her from room to room and never leaving the flat without checking that it was in her bag. He thought of the oval St Christopher medallion that accompanied his mother everywhere, safety-pinned to nightie or bra.

Freda played her messages. *Hello, this is Luis. Just me, darling. Hi, it's Djamilla/Nick/Fran.* She would tell Ravi, 'Imogen and I were in college together. She's in Ho Chi Minh City now.' Or: 'Joel's such a sweetie. Nothing like one's idea of a New Yorker, actually.' The fair man had acquired a name, *Martin*, a job description, *head of client relations in an Anglo-American mining consortium*, and a vocation, *helping Africans see why they needed Anglo-American mines.*

A postcard came of the Valley of the Kings. Freda propped it on a shelf, beside a card from Seville. One of the magazines by the couch contained a map of the world on which swooping lines traced an airline's routes. Global, connected: that was how Ravi pictured Freda Hobson's life.

She was at work when the doorbell rang. Ravi knew he was going to be killed. Without hesitation, he slithered under his bed.

That evening, Freda asked why he hadn't opened the door to her cleaner. 'Were you out?' *Out* was discouraged if not exactly forbidden. Ravi usually bought cigarettes from the guard but had been known to walk to the shop on the main road. It was one of the tensions that thickened around his smoking. He hadn't realised that Freda employed a cleaner; had not, in fact, given any thought whatsoever to the cleaning of the flat, such labour having always been accomplished by this or that woman in his orbit. He might have pointed out that Freda had neglected to warn him the cleaner was due, but found he had forgotten the words. He couldn't remember how to say 'I didn't know'. Silently, he watched a scribble of irritation pass over her face.

Wherever Freda Hobson went, she made herself indispensable to a woman she had selected. Men admired her, at first. Very young, she had abstracted the pattern of her parents' marriage—*the blade and the block*—and rolled it into a tube through which to view the world. She had collected twenty or thirty close female friends, whose birthdays were noted in a book. Freda neither quarrelled nor abandoned, but with each new friend something would happen to make her feel tremendously let down. She asked herself again what a stranger could have said to Malini to lure her into his car. Her friend was prone to girlishness in the presence of fluently spoken men, a weakness explained, Freda supposed, by an early attachment to the unspeakable *père*. But how to account for Ravi? There was the obvious explanation, but Freda, having been careful to fall in love with a plain man, was unmoved by the other kind. Goldfish, too, are decorative. This business with the cleaner was the limit! The cleaner was erratic, and might not turn up for weeks; the day guard, a relative, offered far-fetched excuses that Freda neither rejected nor believed. As for Ravi, he hadn't so much as washed a plate until she made it clear that he was to do so, and then he hadn't known how to stack the machine. Freda had decorated the flat with pictures and carvings from home; she liked to keep a few of the beautiful, familiar things close. But a velvet rectangle stamped with the head of Nefertiti had blighted a wall, bestowed on Freda, like the cleaner, by her landlord. She had shut it away at once in a cupboard. Looking in from the threshold of Ravi's room one day—it was observation rather than intrusion, since the boundary was respected—she saw that he had propped the velvety abomination beside his bed. What was really unfathomable, however, was his inability to act in his own interest. What he had seen had left him blank-eyed, but he refused counselling. He had the soul of a—but Freda was unable to think of anything at once passive, exasperating and in need of rescue. Some kind of endangered slug that secreted a mild irritant, perhaps?

After the incident with the cleaner, Ravi turned jumpy. Night noises unsettled him, but silence swelled. He had believed that he was indifferent to dying; that he might even welcome the ending of his life. Others had feared the same. He guessed that he had been watched at first, never left alone. The faces of strangers, dark ones and pale, had hung over him in the room with a window at either end. But when the cleaner rang the doorbell, it was protest that sent Ravi to hold his breath in the dust under his bed. Stubborn life had asserted itself. He remembered a childhood experiment, a flower placed in coloured water that travelled up to stain white petals. He felt the red force that insisted in his veins.

The immediate media coverage of the killings had been extensive and sympathetic. There were brave editors, and those who remembered Malini's father from the old days. The child was photogenic, and where human feeling might have slumped, it was propped up by the piquancy of the way the woman's corpse had been displayed. But there were no developments, and the murder of obscure civilians was not exactly rare. As drama, the story was ill equipped to withstand the latest turn taken by the war. Talk of a ceasefire and international mediation had naturally led to an increase in slaughter. The Tigers were enjoying a string of military successes. Coverage of Malini and Hiran's case, like hope of a swift resolution to the conflict, flickered and went out.

Laura, 1999–2000

SHE PERSUADED MEERA BRYDEN TO commission a feature on Naples, pitching it as a neglected place. Thousands passed through on their way to Pompeii or the Amalfi Coast, but the city itself had slipped from the tourist beat. It was deemed too dangerous to visit or too dirty; pundits warned perennially of its collapse. Laura used words like *reveal*, *disclose*, *uncover.* Meera agreed at once, as Laura had known she would. Wanderlust, on which the *Wayfarer* fed, was only lust, after all, lustily excited by penetration and veils.

The old crowd around Theo was dispersing, allegiances shifting or falling away, careers and children claiming their due. The woman who had written about surfing had moved to Manchester and was marketing herself as a brand strategist, the letterpress printer had died. Bea had been promoted to working sixty-hour weeks. The guerrilla gardener had inherited a title and gone to live in a castle in Spain.

Theo had invented a new project. Laura had sparked it by telling him about the man who for decades had gone about Sydney chalking the word 'Eternity' on its pavements. Now, once a week, Theo went out after dark to blazon the latest entry in his Chalk Anthology in the streets. Laura came out of a Tube station one afternoon and saw *he whistles his Jews into line*. She walked about Swiss Cottage, spotting fragments of Celan's 'Death Fugue' on walls, pavements, kerbs—but she couldn't find them all.

He chose his poems at random from those he knew by heart, said Theo, the anthology didn't mean anything. He was trying to interest Lewis Bryden in it; they could go out together to chalk up the poems at night. The whole thing struck Laura as very *artskool*: hip, portentous, annoying. In the restaurant where she was having dinner with Bea, 'He's at least ten years too old to be carrying on like that,' she decided. Bea agreed; these two now permitted themselves that kind of acid judgment on Theo. Then Bea Morley set down her fork. It was one of those days when her soft yellow moustache was in evidence. She touched it, crying, 'But how awful if he was sensible like us!'

Laura had come to dread what she had once so looked forward to, evenings alone with Theo. When she arrived, it was usual to find him slow and slurred. His stories looped, drifted, tripped over themselves, grew labyrinthine. There was an evening when he endlessly circled a momentous yet enigmatic memory of setting off alone on a journey. A whistle had sounded, and his mother, dressed in a short blue jacket with silver buttons, turned rigidly away. Laura's thoughts wandered. When the fuddled account had trailed off, she asked whether Theo had finished his thesis. Suddenly lucid, focused, he snapped, 'When did you start to pry?'

There was no longer even the fiction that Theo didn't drink when he was alone; that was another thing that was now permitted. He told Laura that there were occasions when he was drunk for three or four days at a stretch. '*Pleasantly* drunk. You have no idea.

The far side of great drunkenness is just amazingly *nice*.' But Bea said that on a weekend when Theo had gone with her to Berkshire, she had heard him in the bath. He was moaning softly, 'Poor Theo. Poor Theo.' He came out at last, with pink cheeks and an empty bottle of gin.

The problem was no longer drunkenness—now it was being sober. When Bea invited a few friends to tea for Laura's birthday, Theo didn't show. Bea said grimly, 'His short-term memory's shot.' They waited and waited. There was no answer on Theo's phone. At last, someone switched off the lights, and Bea came out of the dark carrying a cake stuck with candles; the pennant flames flew sideways. Laura picked up a knife.

One evening in Hampstead, Theo fell asleep halfway through a sentence. The night was cold; Laura didn't like to leave him downstairs. She pushed and coaxed him up to his room at the top of the house—a journey both hazardous and dreary—where she covered him with a quilt and left him snoring. On the landing, she paused to recover and looked around. Mass-market prints covered the walls. There was the busty peasant from Naples, there was a half-naked female rising from a jungle pool, there was a Chinese girl with an angular blue face. But as Laura made her way down, the display was dominated by kitsch, reiterated weeping. The tearful, cherubic boys she had noticed on her first visit had proliferated. They had crept into the hall, they were creeping up the stairs.

In the days that followed, the memory of that late-night journey to and from Theo's room continued to nag. All the doors Laura passed had been shut against her. But there was something else—something that eluded and disturbed. *What is wrong with this picture?* But she couldn't work it out.

The puzzle slid away behind the mood that had prompted her question about Theo's thesis. Laura was in the grip of nostalgia. It had begun in Naples; when she went back there for the *Wayfarer*, she had dreamed of Sydney every night. The drift of these dreams was forgotten when she woke. But a filtered residue remained, to do with sandstone walls, beach towels drying over balconies, the small, mean kind of cockroach, bus drivers in shorts.

Laura put it down to the weather in Naples, a sultry dampness that recalled childhood and triggered her joyful Australian anticipation of rain. Arcs of purple bougainvillea, episcopal and disorderly, bore their share of responsibility, abetted by the port, the ferries, the ships that came and went.

But the reruns of home went on long after Naples and no longer confined themselves to dreams. With London concrete underfoot, the sole of Laura's shoe remembered the knobbly sensation of treading on a gumnut. Waking, she was hoisted into consciousness by the cutlery clang of a gangway hitting the deck of a ferry. The sung litany of currawongs arrived to obscure piped pop songs in a mall. Strap-hanging in the Tube, Laura swayed: she was standing on the deck of a boat, adjusting her stance to the wash from the Heads.

A jacaranda-haunting went on for weeks. Aerial views, sunsets, the twist in *The Sixth Sense*: Laura had missed them. Her mind's eye had drifted to jacarandas—the wild romance of the trees! They went unnoticed from one spring to the next, and then they were *all-at-once*: not a blossoming but an apparition. They purpled valleys, filled the funnel-shaped space between roofs, transfigured suburban hills. In rainlight, their lilac was also blue. It was the colour of nostalgia itself: elusive yet unmistakable, recollection and promise. Nostalgia floated jacarandas over London traffic, above the aisles in Sainsbury's. In Kentish Town, three floors above the high street, Laura's carpet was a pool of fallen blooms.

Time passed, and the jacarandas were replaced by a white-noise whisper. While Laura waited in a check-in queue or for the start of the inflight movie, when she plugged in her international adaptor or converted her receipts into sterling, when she used Google for the first time or sent a fax for the last, while she backed up her files, while she waited, with a flute of champagne, for all the computers in the world to crash, she heard: *Australian summer. Australian summer.* The dead grass browned the paddocks. It pricked like the beginning of tears.

Nostalgia has its correctives. Laura reminded herself that if you chose differently they said you were up yourself. She remembered that you could spend two days on a train and step out into sameness. There were the fruit bats draped like licorice chewing gum over the power lines that had killed them. And who was she kidding about summer in Sydney? When it wasn't pouring, it stifled with a thick yellow curtain. She called up several items along these lines, including a Fraser cousin who boasted of castrating sheep with his teeth.

The whisper turned insistent, grew intermittent, reverted to its old theme: *What are you doing here?* Laura bought pressure socks to guard against deep-vein thrombosis, she was upgraded on a flight to LA, an optometrist informed her that she neglected to blink. She went to the Screen on the Green with Theo, she had lunch with Meera, there was a weekend in Berkshire with Bea. Everything went on sort of as usual. The phone rang at night, and there was no one there.

Ravi, 2000

RAVI RETURNED TO WORK, TRAVELLING for an hour and a half each way by bus. Everyone—colleagues, students, the woman who served him in the canteen—treated him gently. Even the dogs lying about the campus seemed to turn a sympathetic gaze on him as he passed. Frog-Face avoided him and crouched at his desk—he looked as if someone had forgotten to inflate him. The professor kept an old manual Smith-Corona in his office, and could be observed squaring up to the machine as if to an opponent. The keys made a noise like quarrelling birds.

When the black square of the banyan threatened, Ravi would begin counting. *Zero, one, two, three, four* . . . Long ago, he had known a student who could recite pi to two hundred places. He considered emulating her or counting in primes. But with complexity came hesitation: the chink in the wall through which anything might slip. What was straightforward required no thought and provided the sturdiest defence. *Eight hundred and four, eight hundred and five, eight hundred and six* . . .

•

He dropped a glass bowl. It came apart in five toothed pieces. Horrified—he imagined that everything in Freda's flat cost the earth—Ravi gathered up the segments and dropped them in the bin. 'Not like that!' cried Freda. 'That glass could cut someone. Dispose of it thoughtfully!'

There was the rule that he had to go out onto the balcony to smoke. When he came back inside, Freda's silence was a shirt that scratched. Once she tilted her chin and asked, 'Is it super-sensible to expose yourself out there?' Her hands, beautiful even when she had forgotten her rings, were so satiny they looked polished. They moved, pushing something unwanted away.

Like Malini, Freda Hobson was a slim woman. But her gestures, like her voice, were large. It seemed to Ravi that she occupied a great deal of space. He spent evenings in his room, avoiding her. Luckily, Dutch friends of hers owned a house in the Galle fort; she often spent weekends with them. Was it possible that she was avoiding Ravi? The small, enforced intimacies of shared space were oppressive. About to leave for her daily swim, Freda was fumbling in her basket when a pair of skimpy blue knickers fell out at Ravi's feet. And although he was usually careful to emerge fully dressed from his room in the morning, he had once come out wearing only a sarong, having heard the front door slam. But Freda was still there. Ravi retreated to his room immediately, his cheekbones prickling. She appeared not to mind seeing him half naked. But she had minded about the knickers, Ravi could tell.

The idea of moving back into his old room grew compelling. Freda's apartment now had the look of a trap—a clean, scientific trap, where experiments that involved cruelty and mice were conducted. Ravi returned to the lane that led to the rooming house. He saw himself walking steadily up the stairs, crossing the landing. But, 'Could put a bomb,' said the manager sadly, and handed over a familiar suitcase. Why had Ravi imagined that his room would be waiting, just as he had last seen it with its rumpled bed? All day, he had pictured and feared the blue skirt with orange pockets draped over a hanger. Now the thought of it shut up in a suitcase was more than he could bear.

He had said nothing about his plan to move out, knowing that Freda would oppose it. At first, remembering her flow of favours and gifts to Malini, Ravi had decided that Freda relished the power that comes with a leash woven of debts. Later, when he felt sure that she disliked him, he saw her as a princess who kept her pea close. *He knew this because he felt the same way.* Freda Hobson was behind everything that had destroyed his life; he wallowed in the punishment of her proximity. Was there no limit to the harm that could come from two women talking with their heads close together? Ravi should have acted decisively, impressed the need for caution on Malini, he should have insisted and banned. What the situation had called for was a husband who thundered *I forbid*, someone moustachioed and unyielding. Not a fool who silently listened to plans for publishing the account of a boy whose eyes had been put out with rusty bicycle spokes.

Freda came out of her room wearing tracksuit trousers and a loose T-shirt. She had a headache, she said. The skin over her fine, high-bridged nose looked thin; the purple eyes had darkened in their sockets. Ravi saw the face that she would wear in her grave.

Now and then, at night or very early, he would hear her talking to herself. Remembering his son's long, murmured monologues, Ravi wanted to inflict bloody, physical damage on Freda. This was always followed by a wash of guilt. It was simple kindness that had prompted her to take him in and offer him her help. You're lucky to know her, he told himself. He was very super-lucky! He even knew that the two people he loved best in the world were dead.

•

Freda pressed her Discman on Ravi. His attachment to this gadget was ferocious and swift. As night deepened, he would lie on his bed listening to Freda's music. She had a fondness for homemade themed compilations. His favourite was *Colours*: 'Little Green', 'Baby's in Black', 'Purple Haze' and so on. He played the CD over and over, turning up the volume. The last time he had listened to music in this intimate, flooding way was on those long-ago Saturdays with Dabrera. Ravi remembered—but it was more accurate to say that his body remembered—his occupation by music, a sensation that began as invasion and ended as release. Songs ran loose in the gulfs and caverns of his being. He listened again to 'Red Right Hand'.

One evening, Freda's PowerBook caught his eye. His aversion to the internet, so definite just a few months earlier, suddenly seemed hazy and foolish. He missed internet magic, he longed to be *carried away*. What were the hundred best songs of all time, what was the Brent–Salamin algorithm? Ravi could Ask Jeeves. A streetcam would show him Montevideo, he could look at close-ups of Miss World. He could join the Michael Jackson fanclub, check the weather in Muscat, find a soulmate in Maine.

With a little shock, Ravi remembered Aimee. He had known every crevice of her, but now she was transparent and silvery. But that was an anachronism: memory, always old-fashioned, had called up an analogue ghost. Aimee was an up-to-date phantom, stored in code on a cyber-clipboard, readily retrievable. Ravi wouldn't be the one to do it, however. He stroked the laptop. An Apple—his mouth filled with anticipatory saliva. The white plastic lid lifted. But the PowerBook was password protected.

Ravi had only to tell Freda what he wanted; she was in the next room. But it would be conceding a little victory to admit that he had changed his mind.

•

A ringbound folder held printouts of reports from several NGOs, the relevant passages highlighted in sickly green. Four students shot at close range. Six farmers hacked to death. Eleven bodies in a trench. It went on and on. The catalogue had a cheerful, rollicking quality. *Eight maids a-milking*, sang Ravi silently, *seven swans a-swimming*. He hadn't thought of that song in years; now it bounced about his skull. He wondered if the folder had been left on the table for him to read. Freda Hobson clung to a belief in accurate accountancy. Her terminology, like Malini's, was juridical, circling around the fetishes of witnesses, evidence, proof.

Carmel Mendis rang. A letter had come from Roshi de Mel's father, Aloysius. An acquaintance in Vancouver, a man who had been a colonel in the Sri Lankan army, had told Aloysius that the police had orders *from high up* to do nothing about Malini and Hiran's case. The old tortoise gave it as his own opinion that Ravi should *let bygones be bygones*. Ravi lost his temper. Did Aloysius de Mel imagine that murder was a move in a squabble, something the magnanimous overlooked?

Freda said, 'We absolutely need that letter. Don't you see? It's vital, actually. Tell your mother to send it to you at once.'

Tell not *ask*. But Aloysius had instructed Carmel to destroy the letter—he didn't want any trouble, he had a sister in Sri Lanka—and she had torn it into tiny blue flakes.

Not for the first time, detectives asked Ravi if his wife had made enemies. It was not unknown, they suggested, for those who worked on behalf of women to attract a man intent on revenge. Officers had arrived at the NGO with no warning and a court order, and taken away files and the computer Malini had used. Ravi remembered stories that had hung over their bed in light, smothering folds: sons set on fire, daughters raped with broken bottles, brothers who had gone to a police station and never returned. What did he think? enquired Freda with light scorn. That the NGO would just have handed over material that put lives at risk? She had sent a letter to every English-language newspaper asking why, if the murders were the result of a purely private vendetta, no arrests had been made. She stood silhouetted against the window, her profile dark, faultless, frightening. Ravi realised, She is the queen of spades.

Freda closed her hand softly around a moth, carried it to the balcony, released it. If he had been forced to describe his life, Ravi would have groped for a word that meant something like 'dismantled'. When she came back into the room, dusting her hands, Freda spoke of trauma. Ravi learned that, being traumatised, he couldn't *get on with* his life. She suggested, yet again, that he 'talk to someone'. There were people who could help, trained professionals. 'When you're ready, of course. You must take all the time you need. But they do say talking is the most wonderful release.'

Even as Freda urged, her eyes were Hiran's, imploring forgiveness for this or that small crime. At intervals, advice about seeking help burst from her as if independently of her will. The first time, Ravi had thought, Who helped *them*? He would never realise that he had said this aloud. Now, looking at Freda's face, the close-grained skin, he remembered the pimples that had blighted his adolescence. Everyone had advised, Don't squeeze! Whenever Ravi had yielded to temptation, the little rush of pus and blood produced self-disgust. But it also brought relief.

Around this time, Ravi stopped washing. At first, he had relished the novelty of hot water on tap; had stood for ten minutes twice a day under the regulated cloudburst of the shower. Then he stopped. It wasn't a decision, merely a ceasing. He brushed his teeth, disliking staleness in his mouth, and soaped his hands when they felt sticky or were visibly grimed. Not wishing to draw undue attention to himself, he shaved every few days. But he no longer washed his body or his hair.

He bought a tin of baby powder with which he sprinkled his armpits and groin. His scalp itched for a while, but quite soon the discomfort went away. He continued to enjoy the fresh scent of his clothes, laundered in the washing machine. When it had completed its cycle, the machine played a tune. The flat offered various fleeting, electronic sounds, suggestive of a different kind of life. There was the ringtone of Freda's mobile, a DVD protested its ejection, emails announced their arrival. The microwave went *ping*.

LAURA, 2000

IN A HOTEL ROOM IN Prague, Laura answered the phone. Meera Bryden said, 'Laura, darling.'

The man who had travelled to Prague with Laura—a photographer she had met at the *Wayfarer* Christmas party—reached for the remote.

'Darling, the saddest, saddest thing,' said Meera's voice in the shocking silence. 'Theo's dead.'

He had fallen asleep drunk, choked on his own vomit, died. Lewis Bryden, having let himself into Theo's house two days after he failed to turn up to a dinner party, found him in the kitchen on a puffy leatherette couch.

Over the days that followed, Laura suffered the usual emotions, violent and banal. What was unexpected were the tiger stripes of jealousy. At the funeral, she could barely look at Lewis. That Theo should have entrusted him with a key! The man was a fool. How dare he appear haggard when Laura's mirror had returned a face that was tightly composed? She noticed with satisfaction that he was showing signs of baldness. And his head continued to give the impression that it would come away readily from his shoulders. Laura saw herself wielding the axe.

Gaby Shapton had her brother's solid black brows and none of his beauty. There were children about her, one an angel, all self-conscious with a sense of occasion. She bent over a dark head, retying a bow.

Laura went up to her, blurted, 'I'm so sorry.'

Theo's sister was a short, soft woman with an unfocused gaze. It gave her a wide, inhuman look. Her clothes hung from her in folds like a hide. She gripped Laura's fingers and said, 'Oh, so am I.'

The memory of the night when she had seen Theo up to bed wouldn't leave Laura. She stood once more on the landing, glancing first up, then down the stairs. She remembered the awful pictures. She saw the doors shut against her like graves.

She realised, *There was no window on the top landing.*

She was back in Prague; alone this time. She emailed Bea: Had Theo ever talked to her about reading for hours under a window on the top landing when he was a child? No, replied Bea, but he had often spoken of the pear tree outside his bedroom window and how much he had missed it when it had to be cut down.

Laura thought about all these things. She saw red apples in a market and thought about the apple tree in Theo's garden—its girth and reach. When she returned to London, she looked up Gaby Shapton's address. She wrote a letter, shoved it under a folder, read it a few days later, threw it away, wrote another.

Gaby's reply arrived before the end of the week.

The stories Theo used to tell you were our mother's. My guess is she never spoke about her family when she first came to live in England. What was the use of remembering what had gone forever? At school she was a dirty Hun who couldn't speak English. The past must have seemed as if it belonged to someone else, an adored youngest child in Berlin.

I think it was only when she had children of her own that Mutti allowed herself to remember. She was always telling us about Berlin, stories used to pour from her. It seemed perfectly usual to me, I thought everyone's mothers talked like that. She had the most amazing memory, heaps better than I can do when my kids pester me to tell them about when I was a little girl. It was like Mutti was looking into a book, describing the pictures there. She remembered everything, toys, curtains, puddings, the rain dashing against the small window with the round top, the doctor whose breath smelled of soup, the mignonette in my grandfather's buttonhole, the workbasket mandarin with the nodding head. She used to talk and talk, and it was so vivid, it was like seeing everything yourself. It's not really surprising Theo believed he had. Reading about the mandarin made me cry. I'd completely forgotten it till your letter.

Mutti loved Theo best. You're supposed to love all your kids equally, but everyone knows that's not how it works. I was a tomboy and a daddy's girl. But Mutti and Theo spent hours together, Mutti talking about Berlin, Theo taking it all in. When I think about it now, what strikes me is how happy Mutti looked when she was telling us her stories. Although 'telling us' isn't quite right. We were beside the point, in a way. I think she was happy because word by word she was collecting up everything she'd lost, recovering the past for herself.

After the divorce, when Dad moved to LA, I used to go out there for the summer. Theo always refused to come. I remember taunting him about it, this must have been when he was about eight, calling him a cowardy-custard who was too scared to go on a plane. I went on and on, and at last he said, 'I might not be able to come back.' There was such anguish in it, it stopped me in my tracks. One way or another, the favourite pays.

After Meera's phone call, Laura had left the room in Prague, left the man in it without a word, left the hotel. It was a glorious afternoon, blue-skied and cold. She walked across a square that went on and on, she walked along the river, first on one bank, then the other, she crossed and recrossed a famous bridge. A queue of patient, scarved tourists waited for Kafka's castle, another for an organ concert. Laura passed a street portraitist, and people eating pickled vegetables behind glass. There was a terrible sentence in her mind: *Now he no longer lacks a conclusion.* Nobody spoke to her, although she wore thin clothes and no coat and walked crying and clutching her hair. A green saint sat on a green horse. She passed marble men.

The frosty weather was back, or had never gone away, when Laura returned to Prague to research her story the following month. It was so cold that as she passed shuttered shops one evening, looking for somewhere to eat, her eyes began to water. A woman stopped her under a streetlamp; a soft North American voice enquired if she was okay. A few blocks on, there was another woman, a girl really, with thick yellow plaits and a knitted hat. She let go of her boyfriend's arm and put out a hand to detain Laura, offering impenetrable syllables of consolation or help; reassured by a smile, she continued on her way. Laura walked on, dabbing at her eyes with a glove. Then she found that she was crying in earnest. On waking, her mind still reached for Theo. But already there were whole hours in a day when she didn't think of him. And he had been dead less than a month. Forgetting was the real meaning of death. The same thing had happened with Hester. But Laura hadn't minded so much, then. Her great-aunt had been old. She had always belonged to *the past*. Caught up in finals, caught up in the future, Laura had let the old woman go, as a tourist looks for the last time on a landscape that has contained happiness: reluctantly, even sorrowfully, while picking up a bag with a sense of onward motion. Life asserted itself as one small betrayal of the dead after another. It began beside the bier, with an adjustment to a ribbon. Laura vowed, I won't forget, Theo, I won't forget. Tears continued to well. Behind her eyes, a picture arose; it was the meal she craved, something starchy that steamed.

Ravi, 2000

A LETTER ARRIVED, ADDRESSED TO Ravi. It contained a sheet of paper on which the security code for the building was printed above a stylised drawing of a vase of flowers.

Freda was still holding her small silver phone. She had alerted the police and arranged for the security code to be changed. She had the rather baffled air she wore when the planet didn't fall into step, but repeated the first thing she had said: 'It's only a frightener. Otherwise there'd be no warning.'

Ravi thought of the man in sunglasses casually clicking his pen. He thought of Hiran in the Mercedes, looking out at billboards and bikes. The house of fear rose and rose with no need of a blueprint: an airy edifice to which it would always be possible to add yet another wing. He realised that he was looking at a picture of the rest of his life.

He would leave at once, he said.

'And go where? Home to your mother? A rooming house

like the one you were in? They'll be expecting you to go to those places.'

The topmost branches of the tree beside the balcony cast uncertain shadows on the living-room wall. Ravi couldn't stop looking at them: the soft shapes, the way the light probed.

Freda took him to a flat in Havelock Town. It was rented by a friend of hers, a Frenchman. Ravi saw an eagle, beaky and hunched. That bird's face was one of those that had floated over him in those first sleep-shrouded days; he remembered the shy, wild smile. The fridge contained only a bottle of vodka, two limes and a mineral-water spray. 'There is nothing better for the complexion,' said the Frenchman, squirting water into Ravi's face. The flat was dim, and the airconditioning fit for icebergs; small ones had sprung up in corners. They turned out to be glass ashtrays, many of them full of butts.

Every night, fully clothed and shivering under his coverlet, Ravi heard footsteps and whispers in the garden. There was no tree at the window here, only a winding, thick-limbed creeper. Its black roots, rummaging in the earth, intruded on the dead. Hiran's voice found its way out and followed his father. It warned of *a devil with long ears*. But the devil who came had worn wraparound glasses—no one had mentioned his ears.

Ravi returned to work. A week later, a drawing was delivered to the Frenchman's flat.

'You can't go on working. They'll just follow you home. You have to get right away.'

At one in the morning, Freda had driven him, via insanely circuitous routes and two checkpoints, to a five-star hotel.

Ravi went on protesting in an undertone while the desk clerk accepted her Visa. She said, 'It's not a problem, actually.' And finally hissed, 'I can afford it, you know.'

The clerk slid a keycard over the counter. He avoided looking at Freda, but understanding quivered in the glance, immediately screened with lashes, that he offered Ravi.

Freda's logic was severe. Even if Ravi could find new employment, he would be traced. He needed an income. Therefore he had to leave the country.

She said, 'What about studying abroad? I remember Malini saying you were thinking about it.' So they had talked about him! Ravi's scalp crawled—he could imagine what his wife had said. He wanted to lie down and go to sleep and never wake up. He also wanted to hit Freda Hobson, or at least shut her in a drawer where he need never see her again. He began to tell her about scholarships and application procedures and the unlikelihood of succeeding. Freda addressed a fool: 'Obviously, we can't risk waiting till next year.'

Of late, she had often worn that pinched, thin-skinned look. Now her eyes snapped, there was a new light in her face. She can't wait to be rid of me, Ravi thought.

Three evenings later she was back in his room, with a beer she had bought at the bar. She told him what he already knew: Sri Lankans who applied for residency abroad could wait years for a refusal. Freda had talked to a few foreigners, friends who could be trusted and were knowledgeable, and everyone had advised her that Ravi should try for a tourist visa. It was quicker than applying for residency and likelier to succeed.

Once at his destination, he could apply for asylum, went on Freda. 'Can you get a letter from your university saying you've got a job to come back to? You won't get any kind of visa without one.'

Ravi saw that she had anticipated everything, including any objections he might raise. She was saying, 'I'll need your bank details so I can transfer money into your account. You'll need proof you can support yourself when you get to the other end.' She would *take care of* his ticket as well, she added, raising her chin. She had the potency of a figurine placed out of a child's reach: tempting, expensive, not to be touched.

The hotel room contained only a single chair, and Freda had ignored it. There are people who fit themselves into rooms, and those around whom space is arranged. Ravi had seen policemen, journalists, his grief-maddened, terrifying father-in-law take on the imprint of Freda's will; rooms were the least of it. With her spine against the headboard, she sat with one denim leg stretched on his bed. There was a large, faceted stone on her hand. It had been bought on a visit to Galle when Ravi was still living with Freda; she had thrust it at him as soon as she returned to the flat. 'Isn't it super-gorgeous? A green amethyst. I had to have it. It's the colour of the bay where I was swimming this morning.' What a ridiculous reason to buy a ring! The woman could afford real stones: rubies, emeralds. An amethyst meant one thing only: quartz.

Freda's springy hair had grown; Ravi watched her lift it away from her neck. He remembered two saris that had called to each other, dark hair clipped above two pairs of ears. Friendship was conducive to imitation and doubling. He was traversed by a vision—brief, unwelcome, shockingly explicit—of Freda naked and inviting on the ivory spread.

She was saying, 'Actually, we might run into a problem. As soon as any embassy runs a check on you, they'll find out about the murders. No one's going to believe you're just taking a holiday after that. You won't get even a tourist visa if an embassy thinks you're likely to be applying for asylum when you get there.' The back of her hand trailed across her mouth, wiping away beer. That she drank alcohol was one of the things about her that fascinated and repelled Ravi. Glancing around the room as if enthralled by its bland orthodoxy, she said, 'But we'll just have to chance it, I suppose.' Then she went away.

Five minutes passed. She scratched at his door. 'Ravi, it's me.' She came in and sat down on the chair and ran a contemptuous eye over the curtains. 'There *is* another way you could get a tourist visa, actually. I just can't make up my mind if I should even mention it.' She moved her hands—there was white fire and blue. Ravi found himself the object of her knock-you-flat look. 'There's an Australian. At the high commission.' Freda sounded uncertain, explaining what would be required of Ravi, but he was the one who lowered his gaze.

When she had finished, he was silent for some minutes. Then he asked how Freda knew about this man.

'J-P.' That was the Frenchman. 'He got a Tamil boy out that way last year. We'd have to arrange everything through J-P, actually—the Australian guy'll pull out if he gets so much as a hint that anyone else knows. And it might come to nothing. He's super-cautious. Only one or two a year.'

If the Australian accepted, went on Freda, he took care of various tricky formalities: the police check, for one. 'It's a vile way to do things, of course. But he does help men who are in danger.'

When she said, 'Before he decides, he'll want a photo of you,' she looked away at last. Plucking an imaginary thread from her jeans, she murmured, 'Of course we could just keep trying Canada or Ireland or wherever in the hope that someone'll give you a tourist visa. I completely see why that might be what you'd prefer.'

Ravi said, 'No. I'll do it. If this man is willing.'

'It would be marvellous if you could go to London, of course. But Australia's rather good, as it happens. I know the perfect person in Sydney.' Her composure was back; her voice was as polished as her hands. Ravi saw that he was to be disposed of thoughtfully and with minimal inconvenience to Freda; Australia was perfect, actually. Freda Hobson, who knew people in Sydney, in New York, in Ho Chi Minh City, was running the world again.

The Frenchman had what Freda called *a genius idea*. She was unpacking a small, wheeled suitcase as she spoke. It contained a daypack, thick-soled runners, German sandals, a camera, clothes. There were also sunglasses and a First Boston baseball cap. While he waited for his visa, Ravi was to adopt the guise of a migrant on a visit home. As soon as he had changed into his new jeans and a T-shirt with a Nike swoosh, Freda drove him to a different hotel.

Ravi, 2000

AT NIGHT, STRINGS OF LIGHTS twisted through the trees in the hotel garden; Ravi knew that a man stood pressed behind each trunk. Fear came to find him like steps approaching the bend in a corridor. He rose from a table, leaving a meal half eaten, a head waiter hurrying forward. He was certain there were watchers: on a bench in a marble lobby, in a deckchair on the far side of a lawn.

One of the dreamlike aspects of this time would become apparent only long after it was over. Then it was the weddings that fanned out to command the retrospective screen. Ravi would turn a corner or step out of a lift and find himself caught up among confident, bare-armed bridesmaids. On dates deemed auspicious, the wedding parties followed each other in swift succession. Restrained in formal clothes from the cruder expressions of hostility, men hit each other on the back. Mothers searched their handbags for something vital, a lipstick or a warning. Lobbies filled up with boys in miniature bow ties; rose, lilac, tender blue flower girls gathered in bouquets. Ravi looked on from terrace or restaurant. Tourists lay like offerings beside the pool.

•

The black square rose and widened without warning. Then the convulsions clutched. Ravi would begin counting: *One, two, three* . . . The struggle against memory exacted its revenge. Having placed food in his mouth, Ravi might realise that he didn't know what to do next. He would sit on and on at the table with his mouth full. Removed from time, he watched it pass. Sometimes leaving a room posed a riddle. How did anyone contrive to move through a door or escape from a chair?

He turned his head and saw Malini. She was descending a polished staircase. By the time Ravi reached her, she was a fat woman in checked trousers. For the first time, he registered: *They are gone.* Who can say where the dead live? Certainly not here. Time was a magician, it always had something improbable up its sleeve and the show lasted an eternity. But two had been dropped from its routine forever.

Ravi took a three-wheeler to a craft shop, where he bought Freda a handloom tablecloth. It was handsomely striped in cinnamon and red. Paying for it, he was struck by the notion that even the banknotes she had given him were cleaner and crisper than any he had previously handled. They seemed valueless, notes from a children's game. He gave them away in handfuls, until the afternoon when he saw a man come out of the relaxation centre in his hotel. An ayurvedic masseur followed. 'Sir! Sir!' When the man turned, the masseur joined his palms and brought them to his chest, murmuring, 'Sir, tip, sir?'

The man spared him a look as blank as it was blue. 'A *tip*?' There was a pause, exquisitely prolonged to allow hope its full deployment. Then, 'No tip. I've only got plastic.' He patted the place where tradition locates the heart.

Thereafter Ravi tipped sparingly—he was less conspicuous that way. Mirrors showed him a soft-fleshed stranger with a familiar face. His appetite had revived; in fact he was ravenous. He ate doughnuts for the first time and gorged himself on protein, returning to buffets for second and even third helpings of prawns, beef, chicken cooked in cream.

At some point, he started to breathe well, his ribs opening sideways and folding without haste. No one spied on him over a newspaper or waited in the shadow of a colonial clock. Even the country's leaders, cut off at the neck and preserved behind glass, looked no worse than smug. Evil was a real thing. Ravi had seen it—it had looked like a vase. What flourished here was as harmless and false as the piano player's smile. A bride floated past in her sari, upside down in the gleaming floorboards. The sky darkened, as if something enormous had spread its wings. But only tourists came running in from the rain.

Every few days, Freda would pick Ravi up in the evening. Flicking her eyes at her rear-view mirror, doubling back on their tracks, now and then pulling over to the side of the road, she would drive him to his next destination. Journeys that might have been accomplished in fifteen minutes stretched to fill an hour. This expansion of time, too, was dreamlike, with a dream's spellbound stagnation. As they approached whichever hotel she had chosen, Freda would call ahead; if a room wasn't available, she would drive to the next place she had in mind. She was forbearing and humorous on these occasions, as if playing her part in an entertainment organised by children. Ravi decided that she relished the intrigue. He wasn't wholly immune to it himself.

Ravi Mendis, Tourist played only to select audiences. Registering required ID, so the desk clerks always knew that Ravi was a local. But he had refused television interviews, and most picture editors had succumbed to a dramatic image that showed a man slumped forward with his hands over his face. No one appeared to connect that ill-fated figure with the one advancing across a lobby in Reeboks and American jeans. In any case, when Freda produced one of her three credit cards at reception, every clerk drew the same conclusion as the man at the first hotel.

At checkpoints across the city, Freda's passport was glanced at, Ravi's ID card inspected. She would lean across. 'My friend's with me. We're on our way to my flat.' They would be waved on with obscenities only one of them understood.

Anyone with official connections, or the money to make them, could gain access to the registration data collected by hotels. But what happened was that Carmel Mendis rang Freda. An elderly neighbour of hers had fallen into conversation with a stranger at the train station. They had chatted of this and that, and at one point the stranger mentioned that years ago, at university, he had known a Ravi Mendis who came from here. He wondered aloud what had become of him. The old man replied that he lived near Ravi Mendis's mother but hadn't seen her son in a long time. A few days later, turning the conversation over in his mind, he grew uneasy and went in search of Carmel.

'Did he describe the man at the station?' asked Freda. But the neighbour was absent-minded or frightened or both. When Carmel called on him, primed with questions dictated by Freda, he claimed not to remember anything more. His wife assured Carmel that it was *all a dream*, saying that her husband hadn't travelled by train in years.

The dreams that came to Ravi during this time were often of his father. Once they were in a car together. They had overshot their destination, even though his father drove, as he had done everything, without haste. They had to go back, Ravi insisted. The rooms in his parents' house were involved, as well as a roadside stall where small precious figurines made of green glass were sold, and these were sites it was important to recover. Like all the dreams about his father, it was deeply satisfying. Ravi emerged from it soothed and refreshed.

But sometimes there was the policeman with pale eyes. In these dreams, which were brief and had the force of nightmares, Ravi might be in a garden with the man or seated near him on a bus. Everything was calm and ordinary and frightening. There was a dream in which Ravi noticed that although his companion's shoes had been polished to a high gloss, he wore no socks. That was particularly horrible.

A letter was delivered to Carmel. She forwarded it to Freda, who passed it on. The typed note inside stated that a man of around thirty, *smartly presented*, had been asking about Ravi on the university campus. He had let it be known that the police had a fresh lead regarding the murders and were keen to talk to Ravi. The note was unsigned, but the typewriter pointed to Frog-Face.

Freda rang the officer in charge of the investigation. She had heard a rumour, she said, that new information regarding the murder of one of her colleagues had come to light. The detective assured her that she had been misled. He was polite and regretful, and enquired casually after Ravi. She had no idea what had become of him after he had left her flat, said Freda. She was unable to resist adding, 'Isn't looking after him what you're paid to do?'

She was jubilant. 'You see? They're looking for you in all the wrong places.' But then she decided that it would be more prudent if Ravi didn't spend all his time in Colombo. So he began to join tours that took him away for a night or two. He saw famous places:

an elephant sanctuary, fabulous ruins, the precipice at World's End. He told everyone who asked that he worked in customer relations in Phoenix, where he had lived for the past nine years. He took photo after photo; a metronomic clicking marked his way. *Taking, taking, always taking*. He told Malini, 'Do you know what I've just realised? A camera hides a face, does away with the need for conversation, gives you something to do with your hands. Maybe tourists always have something to fear.' He used up the first roll of film, threw it away, didn't bother to buy another. The Frenchman's Minolta Memory Maker clung to Ravi's neck and nuzzled his breastbone: a hard little child.

On a tea estate, a girl removed her hat and shook out hair like a sheet of copper foil. She asked, 'So have you seen many changes?' The upcountry morning had been misty; a cardigan dangled from her waist. Its neat emerald pattern replicated the rows of tea on the flank of the hill. Her voice grew serious. 'You must have been so homesick. This has got to be the most beautiful place on earth.'

Early on in his travels, Ravi had grasped that the most effective way to avoid questions was to ask them. Most people offered conversation only as a preamble to talking about themselves. The girl replied, 'Oh, everywhere. I've been here twelve days. I've seen everything.' Her skin was so white it was green.

Sightseeing took place in a time out of time: greased, touching nothing as it passed. Scenes, succeeding each other swiftly, bore Ravi away on their surface like a corpse. His schedule was full, but nothing was required of him. *That was the point of a holiday.* Coaches carried him past dagobas, sandbagged gun emplacements, stilt fishermen, soldiers alone and in knots. In the old days, Ravi would have avoided the eyes of soldiers. Now, safe behind tinted glass, he looked into their faces. Many seemed nervous and most were young.

There was an endless flow of pedestrians beside the road, women carrying bags or a baby, boys with their hands swinging free. Ravi thought, That's how poor people get around. As a student, he had thought nothing of walking for an hour or two to see a film or a girl. Now the patience of these slow journeys, their human pace, seemed remarkable. He realised, Tourists see invisible things.

Sometimes their point of view eluded him. By now, he was often the first in the group to raise his camera: to a roadside shrine or a sunset, to a buffalo ploughing a paddy, ribs curved like a boat. But why were the others laughing at a billboard advertising Perlwite soap? What was fascinating about two village women grinding chillies on a stone? The dust of familiarity still lay in patches on the scenes through which he moved.

He attended a programme of Kandyan dance held in the ballroom of a famous hotel. Applauding with his hands raised, he smiled at the woman in the adjoining seat. She drew her shawl closer against the air-conditioning and murmured, 'I don't know why I agreed to this. These tourist shows always seem so contrived, don't you find?' Her husband, a bear in linen trousers, leaned across. 'Astrid and I are into authentic local culture. Any idea where we'd go for that?' After reflection, Ravi gave them the RealLanka URL.

In a white-faced mansion, now a hotel set in landscaped jungle, the bathroom was as dim and marbled as a tomb. Ravi ran a tap into a veined bath. He even opened one of the scented lotions provided and poured a little into his palm. But when night fell, he remained unwashed. A reddish rash went on spreading in the creases behind his knees.

•

They were on the Kandy road in heavy traffic, the minibus labouring up a series of hairpin bends. Somewhere along this stretch of highway, dozens of students suspected of involvement in the first insurgency had been brought at night, stood at the side of the precipitous road and shot. During the endless evenings imposed by curfews, every aspect of this tale had been polished to a high sheen. Ravi had been very young at the time, but the story had persisted, passed around in conversation like an object in a game that went on for years. It was said that instead of disappearing into the ravine, some of the corpses caught on bushes and rotted. The stench was reported to be foul.

These things—the bodies crumpling backwards in the dark, the reek—entered the child Ravi's repertoire of horror, where they occupied a vivid niche. His thoughts would glide almost pleasurably towards the scene. He re-enacted it with his sister's dolls, kidnapping all three, lining them up on the edge of the veranda, hitting them with a stick so that they tumbled into the dirt, repeating the routine until Priya saw what was going on.

When Ravi peered through the window of the bus, pillowy clouds had smothered the sun. The old story still trembled and glowed in his thoughts, now twinkling surface, now mysterious depth. He saw a few stalls selling plantains and pineapples, and a tiered arrangement of cooking pots. A sleek mongrel stood on three legs, clawing his belly. The minibus inched forward, and the far side of the valley, dingily lush, was revealed.

Where exactly had the killings taken place? It was hardly the kind of incident that would attract a memorial plaque. The story floated unanchored; the scene sank back into landscape. It occurred to Ravi that the tale might have been no more than one of those blood-soaked rumours people love to invent. He aimed his camera at the murky panorama anyway. Settling back in his seat, he smiled at the Finn next to him. 'View,' he explained. The Finn nodded. But he obviously thought that Ravi had wasted a shot.

With his hands held stiffly at his sides, a small boy ran across a roadside yard. Seeing the minibus, he stopped and waved. Several people waved back. But every bolt in Ravi's body had come undone.

Malini had become a frequent visitor. If Ravi went up close or gazed too directly, she changed shape. They had long, silent conversations. In a restaurant, she said, 'Are you mad? You know you don't like squid.' Startled, he looked across at her. She was a bald American, eating ice cream with a long-handled spoon.

In a gem-mining town, Ravi came out of a shop where blue moonstones had trickled through his fingers. Malini was waiting: she launched into a rambling account of a strange incident that had taken place when she was a girl. On a visit to Colombo with her parents, they had gone to the cinema. Just before the feature came on, Malini went to the toilet. A woman followed her in; she was one of the ushers. She told Malini that ten minutes into the film, the doors would be barred, and the audience whisked away to a secret destination. There, everyone would be fed and watered and held captive in pleasant, solitary surroundings until they died. Pets were allowed but not radios. Malini smiled—it was a joke! 'I'm not playing the fool,' said the usher. 'Don't forget that the man who sold you your tickets was missing an eye. He was the only one who escaped last time. He hid behind the curtain.' Frightened now, Malini asked why the outrage was necessary. It was scientific, she was told, the experiment would be filmed and studied. In order to advance the store of human knowledge, it was vital to ascertain what happened when people were supplied with every comfort but never allowed to hear another voice. But the usher, a lovely person, was on Malini's side. She stood by the door to the foyer, holding it open with one arm, and urged the girl to run. Malini felt the sun on her face. She was advancing in slow motion. The usher had climbed onto her back and was clinging there like a monkey.

Ravi found the whole story frankly incredible. It almost turned into one of their rows. But policemen began ordering people off the street and herding them behind sandbags. Outriders approached on motorbikes; a cabinet minister was visiting the town. His car flashed past, flanked and followed by more armed escorts. 'I must say it's heartening,' murmured Malini, 'that our leaders know how greatly they're loved.'

Twice a week, Ravi had an appointment in Colombo. After nightfall, he would take a taxi to an outlying area of the city—he was following instructions issued by the Australian diplomat and passed on by the Frenchman. A concrete stair waited in an empty apartment block at the far end of a cul-de-sac. In a flat on the top floor a tap was always dripping; Ravi heard but never saw it. He always climbed each thrice-grooved step slowly, but was terrified only once. That was the first time, when the door to the flat opened and Ravi saw the devil. The devil was a tall, two-legged figure with Hiran's Mickey Mouse pack for a head.

The Australian seldom spoke and never took off the mask. It continued to frighten Ravi. Fear worked to his advantage: sensing it, the man grew aroused. Everything happened quite quickly after that. The ceiling fan was set to high, but Ravi's skin was always clammy. Once or twice, when Freda was driving him along a dark road to a new hotel, she said vaguely that she hoped everything was going all right. At no point was the mask ever mentioned—the horror of it. The face Ravi pictured underneath belonged to a fox; that was because red hair curled on the back of the man's hands. The little knotted whip was a further revelation. When it began to claw, there were so many reasons why Ravi was glad—he was alive, for a start. He was also waiting for someone in authority to say, 'Now you have earned the right to go into that room over there. Your wife and son will be so happy to see you.'

The apartment block had only recently been completed. Shades had yet to be fitted to the lights in the lobby, and the smell of paint loitered in the stairwell. The smell was quite strong but Ravi only noticed it on the way up. It seemed to mount with the stair.

When he had climbed to the top twenty-four times, his passport was returned. It contained a visa for Australia, valid for a stay of three months. Freda bought his ticket the next day.

Laura, 2000

WATCHING FOOTAGE OF THE SYDNEY Olympics, Laura saw Australians gathered around a giant public screen spontaneously boo their prime minister as his rat-smile menaced a victorious swimmer.

She went to her laptop and googled *london sydney one way*.

Ravi, 2000

CARMEL MENDIS HAD WORKED HER bunions into high-heeled shoes. Powdered and lipsticked like a wedding guest, she stood with her knees apart and slightly bent. Her shimmering pink dress was creased across the hips. She had grown stouter, which gave the impression that she had sunk into her shoulders. As soon as Ravi saw her there, waiting on the platform, he knew he could never go away.

Priya had married and now lived near the Dabreras' old place. Her husband was a well-to-do man, a widower of almost sixty with two grown sons. He was also an inch shorter than his wife. When she thought of working at the hotel, and how it had seemed as if that life would go on forever, Priya counted her blessings. She was expecting a child, she was mistress of a house with four bedrooms, her stepsons were placid men with nondescript wives. But sometimes she couldn't suppress a pang for the stilettos she would never wear again.

Ravi's gaze kept returning to his sister's stomach. In the last month of Malini's pregnancy, he had been in the habit of whispering to her navel, 'Hurry up! Amazing things are going on out here.'

•

A string-hopper feast was waiting at Priya's house, where the cushions had been set on their points in Ravi's honour. Over the meal, Carmel lamented the absence of her youngest child. For the past two years, Varunika had been working as a paediatric nurse in a German hospital in Tanzania. Ravi was shown photographs: Varunika in uniform with a small African child attached to each hand, or wearing jeans in a group on a lawn bordered with flowering shrubs. How neat and self-possessed she looked. Ravi remembered her way of holding herself aloof from his titanic quarrels with Priya when they were all children. But there had never been anything controlled about her smile.

He remarked that she looked happy. Carmel tightened her lips and tucked the photos away. Her son seemed to have forgotten—they all seemed to have forgotten—that the following day was Varunika's birthday. Recalling the protracted labour that had preceded the birth, Carmel thought, This time twenty-seven years ago I was in agony! The baby had turned and slipped and wedged its head sideways across the passage above her groin. But her children didn't care about any of that. And now the bird-boned infant they had wrenched from her was walking about in Africa, and sending home money and presents. 'Africa used to be where poor people live, isn't it?' wondered Carmel aloud. 'My God, what if she goes and marries one?' she cried.

Ravi could tell that Priya was ashamed of her husband, who picked his teeth without covering his mouth. Lal Fonseka never ran out of platitudes, which he produced with the weighty deliberation of one proffering pearls. Ravi learned that the Tigers were *in for one helluva shock* if they thought the government was going to give in to them; and that *things were bound to get worse before they got better*. Then Lal scratched his scalp and examined his nails. Not for the first time, Ravi reflected on what he owed this amiable dimwit.

Leaving his mother and Priya would have been impossible if not for Lal.

Priya was thinking that it was just like Ravi and Varunika to come and go as they pleased, leaving her responsible for their mother—did Ravi even know that Carmel had recently been diagnosed with high blood pressure? Then the reason he was going away came to Priya with force, and she spread her hand over her stomach and went into the kitchen to visit the welter of her emotions on the cook.

Ravi went for a last walk along the beach that evening. On the way home, he encountered the familiar odour of frying fish. He felt . . . not joyful, for that was a house locked and barred against him, but in possession of himself and at one with his surroundings—a brief, bright plenitude of being. His childhood, a lost country, had offered friendliness, frog song, the grit of pipeclay on his fingers from freshly whitened tennis shoes.

A creeper—was it antigonum?—was offering up big green hearts and tiny pink ones to the barbed-wire fence. Ravi recalled the frustration of living here, how it had seemed as if nothing would ever change. But the possibility of happiness had beckoned and sustained him then. Now all that was *the past*.

He had reached the place where the banyan tree continued its assault on the asphalt. The vegetable violence of the tree was both more horrible than Ravi remembered and disturbed him less. Standing in its shade, Malini had once licked ice cream from her wrist. She had been talking about her schoolgirl fascination with detective novels. Over the course of a year, she had read all her father's Agatha Christies and Ngaio Marshes, secreting herself away with their mouldering pages. She was severe in her condemnation of any failure to comply with the conventions, requiring genuine and sufficient clues, subtlety in the matter of red herrings and a plausible solution. Once, unable to bear the suspense, she had turned to the end to learn the name of the murderer. She still felt bad about it, she confessed. At the recollection, a flash opened behind Ravi's eyes: it was iridescent, persuasive, mad. It insisted that if only Malini had told that story to her abductor, Hiran and she would have been spared. To die was to be transformed into an object—but even as the thought came to Ravi, it was overtaken by the memory of his son's corpse. Damaged and icy, it had remained a person: agonising because, laid out in a mortuary, it still seemed to hold wishes, sorrow, fear. Conversely, what Ravi had seen on the TV set in the rooming house was neither person nor thing. It was a no-thing. Why hadn't Malini told the man in the sunglasses about flicking ahead to find out whodunit? That small transgression was so irreducibly human. Surely even he would have understood that?

Ravi had intended to observe everything carefully on his way home, according these familiar sights the gravity of *the last time*. But enmeshed in his thoughts, he allowed his feet to carry him forward mechanically and noticed almost nothing that he passed.

Priya had said that she would be arriving early the next day to prepare milk rice for breakfast. But when she came, she disappeared into their mother's bedroom and came out a few minutes later wearing a faded cloth tied above her breasts. To Ravi she said, '*Aiyya*, come.'

The well in the courtyard still supplied the kitchen with water. Priya lowered the bucket and drew it up carefully, refusing her brother's help. Then she upended it over his head.

Ravi was wearing a T-shirt over his sarong. Priya said, 'Why don't you take your T-shirt off?' Busying himself with the bucket, Ravi turned deaf. As he let out the rope, he launched into one of their mother's old songs: '*John, John, the grey goose is gone, And the fox is on the town-o.*' The marks of the whip were still fresh on his back. The fox's den had a bathroom where everything Ravi could possibly need was waiting when the fox had finished playing with him. There was always a clean towel and antiseptic and lotions that soothed. One had a name like a beautiful, mysterious heroine: Aloe Vera. The first time, cautiously twisting to look over his shoulder, Ravi had inspected his back in the mirror. Then he had addressed his frightened face: 'They're only a fox's tracks.'

Brother and sister sang, '*He didn't mind the quack, quack, quack, And the legs all dangling down-o.*' Priya broke off to exclaim, 'What a thing to sing to children!' Her eyes were complacent; with pregnancy, she had drawn close to Carmel, whose advice on grave maternal subjects Priya systematically sought and rejected, saying, 'Nowadays, it's all different.'

Ravi and she took turns at throwing water on each other. Priya produced a fresh cake of soap, a new bottle of shampoo. While they anointed themselves with these luxuries, Priya told her brother that Aloysius de Mel, now a widower, had returned at Christmas, along with his oldest daughter and a Canadian son-in-law. 'But when you meet him, he's Chinese.' All the de Mels had been back at one time or another, she said, except Roshi. 'That one has a child and no husband. Uncle let the cat out of the bag. No wonder she's ashamed to show her face.'

As Priya spoke, she was remembering Roshi's big, greedy teeth shining with spit. How pleasingly life distributed its punishments sometimes! A little grunt of approval escaped her. It encompassed her bare arms, which had rounded beautifully in pregnancy, and the diamond speck on her finger. There would be another ring for her, a ruby, if the child was a boy.

She told Ravi something the de Mel girl had said. When the family emigrated, Aloysius had carried with him a plastic bag containing a handful of his native soil. In Vancouver there was trouble at Customs, and the bag was confiscated. It had become one of the ridiculous stories that the de Mels specialised in turning out, recounted with rowdy glee. But as they dried themselves, Priya and Ravi confessed to amazement: what a gesture, foolish and splendid, for the old tortoise!

While breakfast was being prepared, Ravi ran a caressing hand over the sideboard on the back veranda. All the drawers were now stuck. But when he squatted before a door and tugged, it opened. Something yellow lay inside the cupboard: Hiran's toy viewfinder, mislaid on a visit to his grandmother's house.

Freda drove him to the airport. The last thing she said was, 'She was so brave.'

At the barrier that separated them, Ravi didn't look back. On receiving his boarding pass, he had entered a new country. Its citizens were all around him, the young with their surfboards and backpacks, the rich with their matching luggage, the swarming poor, who as usual outnumbered every other group, as ubiquitous as their duct-taped cardboard boxes, mysterious bundles and suitcases peeling at the corners.

Ravi's hard grey case had accompanied his parents on their honeymoon; his mother had insisted on giving it to him. When he asked if she was sure she didn't need it, Carmel had said, 'Where will I go now, child? Only into hospital.' Ravi didn't want the old suitcase. It was heavy and impractical with silver locks that snapped.

When he opened it, he found a pocket formed by ruched blue satin and a card from his mother emblazoned with *Bon Voyage* in raised, flowing script. The card had yellowed along the fold, as if it had lain too long in sunlight, but it was imported and must have once been expensive. Above his mother's message to him were printed verses:

Kiss the Blarney Stone for me
And if you get the chance,
Give my dearest love—Oui, oui!
To the President of France.

Bring me back a Pyramid
Or else a Spanish comb.
And don't forget that I'm all set
To welcome you back home.

Freda's last present to Ravi was a dossier. She had kept multiple copies of everything: newspaper reports, signed statements, notes of telephone conversations, the terrible little sketches, the anonymous letter from Frog-Face. There was also a long, formal statement from Freda testifying to Malini's activism and everything that had happened since the murders. At her insistence, Ravi had lodged a complaint with the Human Rights Commission. His pen had wavered above the simplest questions on the form: was he Rev, Mr or Mrs? Freda instructed, 'Put "Criminal Investigation Department, Sri Lanka Police Force" where it asks who you're complaining about.' Ravi wrote down everything she said. There was a copy of the form in the folder Freda handed him, and an acknowledgment of receipt.

While waiting for his flight to be called, Ravi went to the lavatory. There he took Freda's phone from his pack. On arriving at the airport, he had made a great show of patting his pockets before announcing that he couldn't find his passport. When Freda and he had searched the floor of the car and the seats, she suggested, in desperation, that it might have ended up in the boot and went to check. At once, Ravi removed the mobile from her bag. Then he called out that he had discovered his passport safe at the bottom of his pack after all. In the toilet, he dropped her phone into the bowl, flushed, and left the cubicle, picturing her distress when she discovered her loss.

A stylised electronic map appeared from time to time on the screen at the front of the cabin. In Thailand, a green word shone beside a green dot: *Kanchanaburi*. Ravi was awake, then asleep, then awake, and a green chant came out of the past to find him. *Kang kang buuru! Chin chin noru! Run, run, run . . .*

Somewhere between Singapore and Sydney, he woke and sat up straight. The cabin was in darkness. Ravi looked out of the window: the plane was suspended in an enormous night. He had just seen that *everything Malini did was for her father.* Freda Hobson had never come into it, after all. It was like passing a house after dark at the moment when the door opens and carves out a corridor of light. The beam showed two coffins and a drunkard. Malini was lounging across the aisle, and Ravi turned to her in fury: 'Do you think he was worth it?' But her seat was occupied by a stranger, a man masked as if for execution and strapped into place.

To work and suffer is to be at home.
All else is scenery . . .

ADRIENNE RICH,
'The Tourist and the Town'

LAURA, 2000

SHE HAD TIMED HER RETURN with care. With the seatbelt sign lit up, she craned to see the loose purple canopies among the right-angled turquoise of backyard pools.

In the taxi, Laura couldn't keep from remarking on the trees. 'Can't say I look forward to the jacarandas, love,' returned the driver. 'That's when me melanomas start to itch.'

Six months later, what still struck Laura were the hats, the babies in sunglasses, the Factor 30 sunscreen, the little kids at the beach in neck-to-knee cossies. The familiar summer scents of frangipani and barbecued lamb persisted. Pineapples, ripening in bowls, still overwhelmed at dusk. But parks no longer held the remembered reek of coconut tanning lotion. The planet's ills came home in six words: Australians were afraid of the sun.

Laura spent her first month in Sydney at her father's house. Her anaesthetising stepmother had warned that workmen were attacking the dining room, that Donald Fraser, although retired, had never been busier with consultancies, that her mother, on an extended visit from Melbourne, was occupying Laura's old bedroom, that there would be no one home at Christmas, which they were all spending with her sister in Portsea, that she couldn't answer for the Rottweiler around strangers, and that Laura was welcome, of course.

Ravi, 2000–2001

THE FIRST TIME RAVI STOOD on a headland above the Pacific, a jogger cried, 'Geddout the fucken way, mate!' The command reached Ravi obscured by wind, the pounding of feet, the slap of waves. It had contained the word 'mate' but had sounded hostile. While he was trying to work this out, he was elbowed in the chest by a man speeding past on the narrow track. The word *Aspire*, embroidered in gold, bounced on green satin buttocks. An old woman going the other way said, 'That was a very rude man.' She walked on, swinging her arms.

Freda's Sydney contact, an immigration lawyer called Angie Segal, had sent a friend to meet Ravi at the airport. Helen Guest spoke slowly and distinctly as she drove him to her flat. 'Angie's been held up in Port Hedland for three days. Do you understand?' She held up three fingers. 'She's processing asylum-seekers at the detention centre there. In Western Australia. She can't afford to turn it down, it's really well paid.'

Helen's face, like her hair, was long and pale. Standing in her kitchen, she asked if Ravi was a vegetarian. Then she said, 'That's a relief. I hate picky eaters.'

She served him a bowl of spicy, delicious soup. When it was empty, she filled it again. There was bread on the table, butter, red apples on a white plate. Helen addressed Ravi as they ate, feeding him stray facts in clear-cut sentences. 'We're in Clovelly. It's east of the city. From the front door, it's a ten-minute walk to the beach. On Wednesday morning, I'll drop you off at Angie's office in the city. We were at school together. I've left a key beside your bed.'

When Helen had cleared the bowls away, she sat at the table drawing him a map. Her hair lay against her brown shirt in flat, shining bands. She asked if he was a Tamil. She also said, 'Angie's taking you on pro bono. Do you know what that means?' Ravi realised that she was kind, and that his need to get away from her was acute. Otherwise she might go on telling him things for the rest of the day.

Her map took him over tarmacked hills. Gardens held shoe flowers and oleander and flowering creepers known to him from home. There were pink blossoms and creamy ones underfoot—Helen had scattered the same scented flowers on her table. Touching one lightly, she said that she hoped they made Ravi feel at home. 'They must grow in Sri Lanka?' Ravi nodded: 'Temple flowers.' 'In Australia,' said Helen, 'they're called frangipani.'

Everything bore the glaze of strangeness, the fast, baleful traffic, the pavements where the only rubbish was fallen blooms. What he saw on that first Australian afternoon had a bright outline setting it apart from everything that followed. Thirsty boats stood in the streets, each covered with a blue wave that had crisped and been reborn as tarpaulin. A wall bore the large painted hieroglyph <<+#>> , an algebra too far advanced to understand.

But the energetic smell of the sea was familiar. On the clifftop path, the wind stirred coldly in the roots of Ravi's hair. It went away, returned and ran over his eyeballs. There was sunshine, and Ravi was wearing a long-sleeved shirt, but he wouldn't have said he was warm—logic had come loose, as in dreams. There was the dreaminess, too, of finding himself beside the Pacific. He tried to recall what he knew of it, other than its immensity. Names lifted from a blue page to float in his mind like wreckage: the Mariana Trench, the Bering Strait.

Presently, he came to a cemetery set, in shallow terraces, on the side of a hill. Ravi went in and, forsaking the path, climbed the grassy tracks between the graves. At the summit, it was one long seaward rush of marble and flowering weeds. What Ravi knew of cemeteries was a composure that might on occasion pass for majesty. The dead lay flat under its weight. Here whited sepulchres set the light bouncing. An air of recklessness prevailed: at any moment these stolid monuments might rise and hurl themselves over the cliff, choosing obliteration over endurance and sham. The Pacific yawned—there was all the time in the world. It shuddered in its blue skin.

Ravi wandered around, noting the variousness of the memorials, the mausoleums and headstones with their stark or elaborate inscriptions, the mottled or snowy marble, the shining granite, the angels, crosses, photographs, railings, the coloured china bouquets. Each element had been chosen, he supposed, to accord with the preferences and personalities of those they enshrined. But what was overwhelming wasn't individual at all but the common outrage of death.

Angie Segal had round black eyes like a bird, and a bird's darting quickness. She looked through Freda's dossier, asked questions, keyed Ravi's answers into a laptop. He would come to associate the sound of the keyboard with her voice, that quick clicking chatter.

She crossed to a filing cabinet, from which she drew a form. There was a landline on the desk and a mobile beside it. One or the other rang frequently. Angie, too, seemed to vibrate and trill. She asked, 'Did you have trouble getting your travel documents?' She looked up from her screen because Ravi didn't answer at once. He was remembering the smell of paint on a concrete stair.

The morning passed. Angie fed them both sweets from a tin. She would read back what Ravi had said, then press him for more. 'Your application will stand or fall on credibility. That's where details count.' Ravi stared across the street at an identically grey building with slits for eyes. There was so much he could say: an exercise book opened at a capital-letter promise, we fed our son *anamalu* plantains, she had a blue skirt with orange pockets—Ravi's brain held nothing but details of the wrong kind, details that proved nothing. Angie Segal shook her head over Frog-Face's letter. 'It's useless without a signature. You could have typed it yourself.'

When they took a break, she walked Ravi down the street to a bank. He examined this new currency with interest, the colourful plastic notes, the heavy coins. When he came out, Angie was waiting with two rolls from which there protruded lettuce and flaps of ham. She produced her mobile, called a number, nibbled her knuckles. Sitting across her desk from Ravi, she had said, 'Most asylum-seekers from Sri Lanka are young Tamil men. The department understands that. I'm not saying they're sympathetic, I'm saying their imagination's limited. A Sinhalese like you, it's not an everyday scenario.' Then she offered Ravi another mint.

Now he heard, 'Hazel, hi, it's Angie. Yeah, he's here. Oh, I forgot—hang on.' She lowered the phone and asked, 'Are you okay with dogs?' Then she said, 'No worries, he's good.' She bit herself some more.

•

The following day, Angie collected Ravi and his suitcase, and drove them across the city. Her car held a great mess of juice bottles, wrappers, parking tickets, ballpoints, grease-stained paper bags. 'Air-con's bust,' said Angie. 'Sorry 'bout that.' When they stopped at a light, she fumbled for a newspaper and fanned herself. 'Now it'll stay muggy for months.' These remarks were mysterious to Ravi, whose notion of weather was inseparable from this dense and vaporous warmth.

A taxi cut in front of the car. Angie said, 'Don't you love a dickhead?' Ravi didn't immediately realise that these events were cause and effect. He had been marvelling afresh at how little the Australian traffic wove about. Like Helen, Angie drove in a straight line and was at once irritated when someone swerved.

Halted by the traffic, she said, 'Would you believe there's a Sri Lankan guy at Port Hedland with the same name as you? His wife's a Tamil. They've been in detention a while.' Then she said that Hazel Costigan, to whose house she was driving Ravi, had worked at the DHS. 'She used to be in Admin with Mum. Before the cuts.' All this, too, was obscure, but after Helen, Ravi was grateful for talk that didn't automatically instruct.

Angie had given Ravi a street directory when they set out and told him to navigate. 'I'm Castle Hill born and raised. Wouldn't have a clue south of Parramatta Road.' Signs often prevented them from turning right at intersections. Angie sighed and tossed chocolate-coated peanuts into her mouth. Ravi consulted the map for alternatives, and quite soon they had arrived at the address in Hurlstone Park. At the sound of the gate, a dog began to bark.

This dog, Fair Play, a beagle–whippet cross passed off by the pet shop as a spaniel, had once belonged to Robbo, Hazel's second.

The puppy was named by his girlfriend, Sooz, for a horse on which Robbo won *a shitload of money* and for the first year of her life was greatly indulged, dressed in fairy wings at Christmas, encouraged to occupy couches and growl as she pleased. Then Bettany was born, and Fair Play was banished to the shed. Naturally she chewed woodwork, ruined petunias, charged the usurper. Sooz was all for taking her out Dural way and letting her go, but Hazel intervened.

Fair Play rushed Ravi, barking extravagantly while sizing him up. All that first day, she growled each time he ventured into the yard. That was where she lived, for it was the kind of house where there were always visitors and grandchildren, some with allergies, all of whom Fair Play resented. For Bettany she reserved an implacable hatred, surging forward in ominous silence whenever the lumpish child appeared—which luckily was seldom, for Robbo and his family had moved to the Sunshine Coast, where the birth of a sister had presented Bettany with a fresh set of complexes.

Hazel Costigan lived in a small house on a big block, the opposite of how they now came. The sleep-out in the yard had seen a parade of occupants, and Fair Play had ruled them all. On Ravi's first night, she scratched at his door. She kept this up until he opened it, whereupon she sprang onto his bed and curled up. In summer, she preferred to spend the night outdoors, where small lives offered themselves up for extinction. But this was a test.

Fair Play was a beauty: satiny black coat, narrow waist, a hunter's muscled thighs. All day she danced through the pumpkin vine, chasing skinks. She wore her long ears turned inside out when hunting, so that two pink roses adorned her head. In this guise she had the look of a cheetah or a bat. There was always something to investigate or kill, leaf shadows thrown by the overgrown shrubs, doves in the sweet long grass. Sometimes Fair Play's mind turned to geology: she kept a small collection of stones down the side of the shed. Sometimes Kev, Hazel's fourth, dropped in with Lefty, his big blond labrador. Fair Play, who detested all other dogs, loved Lefty. Devotion required her to tug with all her strength at his cheek. There was also standing under Lefty's belly, reaching out her muzzle and sinking her teeth into his neck. Lefty, a romantic, was tolerant of these coquettish manoeuvres and only occasionally sat on her head.

When they remembered, the boys urged Hazel to open up the back: bifolds, a deck. The view, they said, nodding from the kitchen door at sunsets lolling above the river. But Hazel liked the dim kitchen where her mother had cooked, and the sunroom with its row of windows like a train. When they were first married, Len had put in new kitchen cabinets and an indoor toilet. As the boys grew, a second shower had gone into the laundry, which Hazel still called the washhouse, and that was quite enough of renos for her, thanks.

There had always been someone living in the sleep-out: Hazel's uncle Vic, who had never been the same after the Japs, then Len's dad, later one or another of the boys. It was Damo, Hazel's youngest, left alone at home with her, who had suggested foreigners. He was different, Damo, he went out into the world and brought back urgent ideas that he handed his mother like thorny bouquets. There were migrants who needed a place while they found their feet, said Damo, there were overseas students being ripped off in unheated rooms.

After Hazel had been made redundant, the boys said, Mum, you have to charge more than utilities. It was none of their business, replied Hazel, and pushed her grey fringe from her red face. She had her redundancy package. And, lately, her chairs.

Throughout her grown life, Hazel had renewed old chairs, collecting them from the side of the road and heaving them into the back of her station wagon. She stripped, sanded, cut foam to size, tacked piping into place. Her father had been an upholsterer, and Hazel couldn't remember a time when she hadn't known about grip clamps and webbing. All the chairs in the house were her remodellings. Fair Play had a throne, out of the wind on the back patio, a cosy Victorian affair with maroon velvet cushions and flokati-covered wings.

Hazel passed on her creations to neighbours who needed seating for a veranda. She gave them to the boys when they had places of their own. They were not always welcome gifts. 'What's wrong with a nice neutral?' asked Sooz, striking to the heart of things, for Hazel salvaged her materials and favoured boldness. All the old bedspreads and tablecloths and curtains in the street found their way to her. 'And it's such a wog suburb,' said Sooz. This was provoked by an armchair upholstered in an embossed lime and turquoise fabric that had once covered the Katzoulises' bed. The back of the chair was a Sacred Heart tapestry: Mrs D'Agostino specialised in them. 'Do you realise Indians bought that place two doors down?' warned Sooz. Sure enough, next thing there were three kitchen chairs flaunting scenes from Bollywood, and Hazel cutting up a vinyl shopping bag for a fourth.

Then Damo had a barbecue at his house. The new art teacher at the school where he taught English came. Confronted with a pair of Hazel's chairs, she grew agitated. Her husband owned a shop that sold recycled furniture. One thing led to another. Not only was Hazel doing commissions now, she couldn't keep up with the demand. Kev had been to Surry Hills to recce the shop. He emailed photos to Robbo. One of them showed a price tag. As Sooz concluded, 'There's always people with more money than sense.'

The sleep-out held a wardrobe, a microwave, a bar fridge, a TV on a stand. The bed was already made up under a yellow chenille spread. The mustard wall-to-wall had been put in for Col, her eldest, when his father died, said Hazel. 'Carpet can be crucial at a time like that.' The sleep-out also contained two of her chairs, one easy, one upright, but she didn't draw attention to them, of course.

'Anything you need, give us a hoy.' She had already shown Ravi the dunny, down near the fence, its louvres obscured by passionfruit vine, and the laundry off the patio where he could shower and wash his clothes. As soon as he was alone, Ravi remembered that he didn't have a towel. But he had made up his mind not to ask for anything again.

The first thing he did was unhook a picture from the wall and slide it face down under the bed.

Angie Segal said that it would take Immigration a year, and very likely longer, to rule on Ravi's application for asylum. The waves of refugees coming in from Afghanistan meant the system was more than usually slow. Meanwhile, Ravi was on a bridging visa—or would be, once three months and his tourist visa expired. Because he had entered Australia legally, his new visa would allow him to work. But when Angie spoke of organisations that helped people in his position find employment and what she called *support*, Ravi's stomach clenched. He didn't want to be *put in touch* with people like him.

Angie asked fiercely, 'Are you okay for money?' and 'What's Hazel charging you?' She pressed a mini Mars Bar on Ravi along with a mobile phone. There was a year's credit on it, she said, because she had to be able to contact him. Fresh from Freda, Ravi feared finding himself in a new labyrinth of obligations. Angie Segal and Freda Hobson had shared a flat in London for two years. 'Isn't she completely amazing?' Angie said.

Gathered around yum cha in Campsie for Col's birthday, the boys analysed and assessed.

Russ, Hazel's third, said, 'Any of youse see that thing about queue-jumpers on Channel 7?' Then, 'Yeah, I know Howard's a slimy turd. I'm just saying, if this Lankan bloke's a refugee, why isn't he locked up?'

Kev said, 'Those Reeboks he's got didn't come cheap.'

Damo said, 'His *face*.'

LAURA, 2000–2001

RAMSAY PUBLICATIONS WAS ADVERTISING FOR a commissioning editor for its European guidebooks. Why not? thought Laura. She had to do something for a living.

The great thing about putting together a CV for a guidebook publisher was that there was no need to obscure the gaps. On the contrary, the missing years were converted into an asset: travel, experience!

At her interview, she told the story of *It's Australian. But good.* Somewhat to her consternation, she was hired.

Aspects of it were magical: the regular infusions of money into her bank account, the rostered days off, the prospect of paid leave. But there was getting to a laminated desk on time and remaining there for hours, there was overcooled or stuffy space where only Windows opened, there were key performance indicators and the corporate *we*.

At general meetings, new employees were introduced to the rest of the staff. Invited to *tell us your reasons for choosing Ramsay*, Laura mustered a *love of travel* that drew decorous applause. Then the other new hire, a cartographer called Paul Hinkel, flung his arms wide. 'You guys!' he cried. 'You're the reason I want to work here. You're such a great team!'

Cheers. Fists punched air. Laura waited for someone to shout, 'Let's all have a Coke!'

The world of work. She heard doors sliding shut.

Ramsay's head office occupied a former knitwear factory in Chippendale. Laura caught a bus or walked to work through fume-rich air. She had moved to affordable Erskineville, where she shared a warehouse apartment that belonged to a journalist called Danni Holt. Warehouse living suggested capaciousness, but so many flats had been squished into the building that Danni's rooms were poky, her ceilings oppressed. Five years earlier, when she bought it, the apartment had possessed the virtue of being new. Now the collapsing baseboard, the creeping stains testified to the effects of climate and greed.

Condensation, on its way to becoming mould, had settled between the heavy panes of the door to the balcony. There was a view of a car park, more apartments, antennas like Chinese script. Quite often, the sky was replaced by a low-flying plane on its way to the airport. Danni said, 'You get used to the noise.' Laura hoped not—it would mean she had died.

In her sunless flat in Kentish Town, she had harboured a fantasy of greenness and growth. Now she had tomato seedlings in mind, and a trough planted with spring onions. Meanwhile, the balcony boasted a bloomless gardenia in a pot.

There were nights when she left the apartment and went out walking. The west was gentrifying: there were For Sale signs in every street. Laura paused before a shuttered house In Need Of

Complete Renovation. One photo showed a backyard deep in weeds, another a mirrored mantel above a bed. Poverty slept on a bare mattress draped with an orange, satin-bordered blanket. *BYO Imagination!* invited the sign. Laura conjured wintry midnight journeys to a tacked-on lavatory, she pictured the kitchen where the airbrush hadn't dared.

Where spooky blue TV light had once indicated a fellow insomniac, her sleepless neighbours now sat before bright screens. Laura mentioned this evolution to Robyn Orr, with whom she had become friendly at work. 'Late-night searches for twentieth-century exes.'

Robyn headed up Marketing. 'They'll be downloading porn,' she said.

Ravi, 2001

FREDA HAD SAID, 'ONCE YOU'VE got a bank account, send me the details and I'll transfer more.' But instead of opening an account, Ravi had merely converted her rupees to dollars. He hid the cash in his wardrobe and resented each withdrawal. The sum that Freda had calculated would cover four weeks lasted twenty-one.

The phone Angie Segal had given him rang. She said, 'I've got an email for you from Freda. Actually, I've got three. I've been in Bris-Vegas visiting the rellies. Should I print out your messages and post them? Or have you got an email address I can forward them to?'

'No.' Ravi added, 'Thank you.'

'Fair enough,' said Angie, after a while.

He lived on cheap, delicious food, baked beans, pot noodles, sugary tea, spaghetti onto which he poured tomato sauce, toast made from plastic packs of bread that didn't dry out or grow mould. For feast days, a hamburger or chicken nuggets or pasta with tinned tuna. The smell of the fish brought Fair Play. Her eyes were as large and lustrous as those of cartoon aliens. Ravi poured the juice into her dish.

Hazel gave him pumpkin scones and a jar of her marmalade. It was a street where vegetables and gossip and plants were exchanged. Hazel passed on a foil dish of curried beans. 'Dr Mishra, God love her. I didn't like to mention the ulcer.'

Whenever Hazel grilled sausages and chops on the barbecue, there were extra. She said, 'You're doing me a kindness,' and 'I'm used to a crowd.' The thin sausages tasted of soap. Ravi loved them, as he loved all Australian food.

In flower-sprinkled grass, Fair Play was liberating a moth from the wheel of existence. Plumbago draped the fence; the blue of the flowers turned unearthly at dusk. In the middle of the yard rose what Ravi had taken for the skeleton of a giant shade umbrella. Hazel showed him how to peg his washing to its ribs. It was called a Hills hoist: 'A great Australian invention.' For a long time, Ravi went on thinking of it as something broken.

The dunny door was made of clear glass. That was Damo's idea, said Hazel, he had taken down the old door saying, Why waste the sunset? She offered to rig up a curtain for Ravi. 'But you'll be quite on your own down there.'

From his perch, Ravi looked out at prosperous clouds. When he rose, the wet gash of the river came into view. Leaving the dunny one evening, he forgot to switch off the light. Anyone else would have thought that the lighted lavatory had the look of a phone box. When Ravi remembered and turned, he saw a glass-lidded coffin from a tale.

Damo had made it his business to ask a question or two of Angie Segal. Then he had googled *sri lanka politics*. When he had finished reading, what he needed to do at once was to *give Ravi something*. He drove to his mother's. To Ravi he said casually,

'Got this fleece that's too small. Could come in handy when the weather turns.'

He told Hazel that Ravi had refused counselling. 'Angie told him she could put him in touch with people from his own community but he doesn't want that either.' He fetched two stubbies, which Hazel and he drank peering through the sunroom windows at the sleep-out. Hazel said nothing of a discovery she had made. The lock on the sleep-out door didn't always catch. When Ravi was out one windy morning, the door had begun to bang. Hazel, giving in to temptation, had seen at once what was missing. The small mystery gnawed. Had Ravi sold the print? But it was more or less worthless. Thrown it away? Kev had bought it long ago in his creative phase. Hazel wanted to tell Damo that the picture was gone but it would mean revealing that she had snooped. Her youngest had strong, formidable beliefs. He seldom left her house without having first forced an act of submission from Fair Play—this or that small frustration of the dog's will. It wasn't cruelty and passed as discipline. Now and then, his mother spared a thought for the teenagers Damo taught.

Ravi spent fine days out walking. It exhausted him and passed the time. In his pack was bread spread with peanut butter and a soft-drink bottle filled with water. The cushioned sneakers of Ravi-Mendis-from-Phoenix carried him along the river in both directions, across suburbs, to shopping centres. What he liked best were parks and streets of houses. The mouth-watering smells of food he couldn't afford mocked him in the malls.

Long afterwards, when Ravi thought back to those endless summer days, what he remembered was loneliness. No one spoke to him. No one knew where he was. He missed Malini. She refused to be coaxed out, claiming that the light hurt her eyes. Ravi blundered into a tiny park that had been arranged as a giant's sitting room: the vast couch had an antimacassar of coloured tiles, and a flight of concrete steps for a seat. He thought how Hiran would love it. A banyan tree appeared at once—Ravi saw the great black square of its head. It blotted out a mirrored fireplace in which a kiosk took the place of a grate.

A plane roared so low overhead that it must have been navigating by a street directory. There was a row of birthday-cake houses, green, pink, yellow, with marzipan trims. Fences and railway arches were sprayed with the symbols Ravi had seen on his first day: <<+#>>. And the flowers—he hadn't known a city could contain so many flowers. There were mandalas of fallen blossom studded here and there with a squashed cockroach; he stared at them as if they held messages. His mind grew white-hot—it was the mind of an animal in a searchlight.

Angie Segal had held up a hand, folding down fingers as she cited the recognised motives for persecution: race, religion, nationality, membership of a particular social group, political opinion. 'In your case it'd be the last one. Political persecution.'

He had never been politically active, said Ravi.

'But your wife was. And whoever killed her made sure you feared for your life.'

No one expects you to do anything. In the fierce summer streets the light was incontinent, and Malini's voice was a scythe. Ravi would have to stop walking and rest on a wall or a bench. Sometimes he sat on and on—who was he waiting for? He looked up and saw Freda in her baggy T-shirt with rings on every finger. She was coming to save him. They would drive down empty streets to an air-conditioned room. 'Can I help you?' asked Freda. She had disguised herself as a square, exhausted woman pushing a stroller hung with shopping. She said, 'My husband doesn't like people sitting on our wall.'

Walking is a porous activity: the outside seeps in. By the end of that summer, Australia had entered Ravi. Now it would keep him company no matter where in the world he went.

All the houses in Hazel's street were built of dull red brick. A lane ran behind the yards on one side. Ravi had explored it, and seen extensions and a swimming pool and ramparts of hydrangeas. There were expressions of individual style—the Katzoulises had replaced their timber veranda posts with handsome fluted columns and paved their drive with big orange tiles—but the core of all the houses was the same. Over a barbecued T-bone, Hazel filled Ravi in on the neighbours. Dr Mishra was a dentist and her husband was an engineer. Mr Katzoulis worked at the airport. The D'Agostinos ran a deli, and their daughter, who lived three doors up, was a teacher. A Russian at the far end of the street drove a bus. Ravi saw people leave for work dressed in uniforms at the same time as their neighbours were setting out in shorts or suits. At home, where the humble lived in small, flimsy houses, the wealthy in large, solid ones, such miscegenation was inconceivable. Hazel mended chairs, which made her a kind of carpenter in Ravi's eyes. But her house had ceilings more beautiful than he could have imagined, fit for a palace with their plaster fruit and birds.

Malini went on refusing to show herself but sent Hiran to appear in a dream. The child was only a tot. He clapped his hands or sat up on his mat and smiled. Ravi cut him a slice of birthday-cake house. They took bites from it in turn. Hiran spoke up, telling his father that it was vital not to look in the mirror over the mantel. The queen of spades lived there. She could reach out and pull you in.

At night the flowers returned as scent. Woken by his bladder, Ravi would step outside and be met by a great whorl of perfumed air, gardenia, frangipani, the jasmine that starred the length of the lane.

The shower recess in the laundry had a screen of ridged amber glass. One morning Ravi was certain that someone had entered the laundry as he showered, and was waiting. Thereafter, even though it was draughty, he left the sliding door open when he had a shower.

There was a dream in which Priya drew back a curtain, and Ravi saw worms consuming his son's face.

The first time he went to Circular Quay, he walked all the way. It took so long that he had eaten all his sandwiches by the time he arrived and was hungry again—it had also started to pour. After that, Ravi always caught an upstairs train to the harbour. In fine weather, he would make his way over a headland to a quiet bay. One of the wharves there offered a good place to sit, in the angle of a building. Hours passed. Skeletons of light twitched in the water. Ravi would smoke a cigarette—he had discovered the Bangladeshi shop where cigarettes were sold singly. Meat was cheap in Australia, and cigarettes were expensive. Like the cold sunlight on his first day in Sydney, it was an other-way-around thing about life here.

Sometimes a fine morning had turned to rain by the time his train arrived at the harbour. Then he didn't leave the station but went across to platform 2. That was *the marvellous platform*. The view, framed by the bridge and the opera house, had been known to Ravi as long as he could remember. Someone had paid for it, scribbled on the back and posted it to his parents. What was amazing was that the original was given away to commuters. Oh, open-handed Australia, lavish as light! Silver trains came and went unnoticed at Ravi's back.

Another place he liked on rainy days or when heat struck was the Hungry Jack's at Central Station. For the price of a small French fries, he could sit on and on at one of the tables on the concourse, and only the eyes of pigeons reproached. Children and suitcases were led to trains leaving for the country. There was always an old lady peering up at the number of the platform with her top lip raised at one corner. There was always a free newspaper to read.

Next to Hungry Jack's was a pub with doors to the concourse. Ravi could see the waistcoated barman and the chained lamps that shone all day. It seemed a tremendously luxurious place, with its patterned ceiling and curved, gleaming bar. Unlike Hungry Jack's, it was patronised exclusively by Australians. What Ravi meant by that was white people. He would have liked to go inside, just once. At the same time, there was something about the men perched in formal jackets over golden drinks that was obscurely sad. Ravi worked out what it was, eventually. Hungry Jack's drew schoolboys, violent-eyed girls, women with firm-fleshed babies. There might be someone eating chips who was openly or secretly broken. But everyone in the bar, whatever their age, looked old.

Ravi's thoughts often strayed to the cemetery above the Pacific. Seen on that first strange Australian day, it had entered his imagination and was lodged there, as plain and bright and talismanic as a scene from the deep past. He considered asking Hazel how he might find it again, but realised, after a while, that he was keeping the cemetery for *a special occasion*. He had no idea what he meant by that.

Although his pace was steady and slow, walking tired Ravi. What he had known all his life was sea level. The ache in his shins informed him that he didn't have the habit of hills. Sydney tricked with deceptive gradients even in streets that started off flat. The lie of the land was still unfamiliar, so the way a street plunged to reveal the river or the suburb cladding a distant valley always took Ravi by surprise. It was called a view but had the force of a reward. And the sunsets—he was no stranger to their conflagrations, but walking uphill into the blaze sent a shiver along his nerves.

Ravi walked and walked, but he couldn't outwalk Australia: only the scenery altered. There were days when he felt trapped in red-roofed valleys. A small plane flew through the depths of the river; Ravi looked up and watched it moving far above the roofs. Clouds parted, and a great rib of light reached into a valley like an illustration from a Bible story. *Hills are God's gift to our imagination*, said Brother Ignatius. *Who can say what lies on the other side of a hill?*

LAURA, 2001

EVERY DAY, THE NEW, THE unexpected, the arbitrary arrived in Laura's inbox, in her in-tray, in person. Accustomed to working alone and without interruption, she was ill prepared for office life. It was like being dropped into a country where she didn't understand the language: the disorientation, the constant switching of focus, the way the trivial and the momentous presented on the same plane. Cubism must have looked like this in 1911, thought Laura, a lunacy that admitted no hierarchy of interpretation, no fixed point from which meaning might flow.

A typical day began with an email from Gina Piggott. Gina ran Ramsay's London branch and liked to copy her messages to the head of Publishing. The latest listed thirty-one errors in the new guide to Brittany. *This kind of carelessness is so damaging to our credibility*.

The mistakes, typical of first editions, didn't amount to much. But Gina wanted editorial on the European guides transferred to London. London office space like London labour like London on-costs like London everything was pricier than in Sydney. Gina knew all this. Everyone did. But Ramsay UK was solely a marketing office, and editorial was the core of publishing. Gina longed to speak of *my editorial team* and she had the mulishness of the successful empire-builder. It was apparent to Laura that Gina would prevail—the rest of them would simply get tired of arguing with her.

In Sydney, Gina Piggott's staff were known as *the little victims*.

Her emails, always aggrieved or accusatory, arrived overnight. They were never a good way to start the day.

An email flagged with an urgent red ! proclaimed that someone in Sales couldn't find his coffee mug.

An email requested a meeting about freelance editorial rates.

On the other end of Laura's phone, Jenny Williams I, who ran Production, said, 'Got a moment?'

In her office, Jenny silently held up an advance copy of a guidebook. Silently, she turned it around so that Laura could read the spine: *Swizerland*. Ramsay printed offshore, usually in Singapore or Hong Kong; it was cheaper than printing locally, and more efficient for shipping books to warehouses around the world. Recently, however, Jenny had been using a firm in Indonesia, where printing was cheaper still.

'The usual illiterate in Design. And no one at the plant who reads English,' said Jenny. 'Twenty thousand copies,' she said.

•

There was a meeting to discuss proposed changes to map keys. It was confined to commissioning editors and senior cartographers. But a memo from Paul Hinkel, suggesting an alternative set of symbols for hotels, restaurants and places of interest, was circulated. It was well written, closely argued. People were impressed.

Afterwards, Laura saw Paul in discussion with his line manager, arms folded across his chest. As she passed, his eyes ran over but didn't acknowledge her: she might have been a blank space on a map. His small, red mouth went on pulsing—Laura could see why he would appeal to a certain kind of woman. He looked capable and generic, like a man in a training video demonstrating CPR.

An email requested a meeting about price points.

An email reminded that the brief for the *Ireland* update was due the next day.

A letter offered the exclusive opportunity to publish the writer's tales about his travels around Europe in a campervan. *Family and friends have found my stories hilarious!*

In the kitchen, Laura stood chatting with Helmut Becker from Design. 'I am an artist,' declared Helmut as Laura's herbal teabag brewed. 'Art is elusive. It is inspiration. They cannot just say, do this, Helmut, do that, we need six covers, *schnell, schnell*, like bastard Nazis in a movie. There is a creative ambience—you know? When things are flowing, I could start work at dawn, I could stay at my desk all night,' announced Helmut magnificently. He had never been seen in the office after half-past six or before ten. Laura liked him a lot.

An email from Rights proposed a seminar on intellectual property law.

An email from Nadine Flanagan, the webmaster, requested copy for an e-feature on Russian churches.

An email from Sari Gardiner, one of the researchers on the *Greek Islands* update, complained that her deadline wasn't realistic. It was Sari's first assignment. She had yet to realise that guidebook deadlines were never realistic. Information dated quicker than it could be gathered—that was the built-in use-by date that made publishers of guidebooks rich. How it went with new researchers was already sadly plain to Laura. They clamoured to be hired, brimful of energy and enthusiasm, thinking *Free travel! Cool!* A few days into a gruesome schedule of fact-gathering, it began to dawn on them that this was nothing like a gap year. And that *interacting with other cultures*, always cited in their letters of application as motivating their desire to write guidebooks, would be confined to wheedling information from expatriates and bureaucrats, who lied reflexively—the first group to aggrandise their experience, the second to cover their tracks.

An email from HR outlined changes to Ramsay's corporate membership deal at the local gym.

•

An email requested a meeting about blurbs.

Laura had lunch with Robyn Orr at their usual Korean restaurant. Over a soundscape of Carla Bruni, Robyn said, 'So I'm in Cliff's office, running through this deal I've negotiated with the airport bookshops, and suddenly he goes, "What do you make of this?" It's this letter—*typed*, can you believe it, pages and pages—from this guy in India who used to distribute us. London's dropped him and he's writing to complain, saying he was the first to distribute us in India, he's served us faithfully since like the Dark Ages, yadda yadda. So I remind Cliff that this guy was always months late paying us, Gina was totally pissed off about it at our last conference. I mean, we all know what Gina's like, but this guy's the limit, I'd've dropped him too, in her place. Anyway, after a bit Cliff goes, "We could choose to be kind." And then he just vagues out, clicks his pen, you know the way he does when he's miles away?'

Laura looked sympathetic. But Cliff Ferrier's Hawaiian shirts and Mambo Ts, so unsuited to a CEO, had already recommended him to her.

On the other hand, she was not Robyn: twenty-eight, narrow rectangular glasses with red frames, going places.

A tiny woman bore down on them with a large dish of kimchi pancakes.

'Those Sixties guys!' said Robyn Orr.

A voice-message from her dentist's receptionist reminded Laura that she had an appointment the next day.

•

Twenty-three emails replying to the email about gym membership had been copied to her.

An email from Clive Mason, a longstanding Ramsay researcher, complained that the money he'd been offered to update the *Vienna* guide wasn't realistic. He provided a detailed breakdown of costs, exchange rates and so on. The new researchers complained about time, the veterans about money. It had been explained to Laura that after five years a researcher either went feral and disappeared in a series of savage and minatory emails, or became an old hand. Old hands combined the unshakeable certainty that they were being ripped off by Ramsay with a pathological inability to contemplate alternative employment.

An email from reception announced a garage sale the following Saturday.

An email requested a meeting about performance reviews.

Laura endured her weekly meeting with Quentin Husker, the head of Publishing. Quentin's soul was corporate. But his flesh was weak. It had succumbed to chicken parmigiana in the pub at lunchtime. Now it wished to succumb to Jenny Williams II, the publishing assistant, in her flat in Darlinghurst. She had already briefed him by email, and the rendezvous was scheduled for the end of the working day.

Laura finished running through her titles. She had confessed that one of them was over budget and two others were running late. The silence went on, for Quentin was still admiring Jenny, in her boots and nipple ring, illuminated by black candles. A tomato fleck lingered on his shirt, which he always wore open at the neck to signify openness. Arabella, his sister, had once been married to Alan Ramsay. In office lore, the wedding coincided with the hiring of Quentin, the birth of the Ramsay heir with his first promotion, the divorce with his second. At the pub on a Friday evening, deep into sauvignon blanc and the train-wreck of another week, Jenny Williams I liked to return to the topic. 'I swear to God Arabella had it written into the settlement. *Facework every two years and Quentin stays.*'

At last Laura ventured to ask for guidance, speaking of deadlines and escalating costs. Recalled from his erotic duties, 'Your call,' said Quentin. The management handbooks that guided him all advised delegation. And cunning. 'To be honest, I'm not feeling the best.'

Laura offered an ambiguous noise.

'Yeah, thanks.' Quentin glanced ostentatiously at his watch. It was not quite three. 'You're right, I might just have to call it a day. We have so much to learn from the wisdom of our bodies.' His eyes, a damp brown, were guileless and alarming.

The latest draft of the revised Ramsay style manual (one hundred and eighty-three pages) waited on Laura's desk. Her comments were required by the end of the week.

A second email from reception apologised: *Duh!! I meant to flag my garage sale email as Spam! Sorry!!!*

•

There was a meeting to discuss font sizes. Dropping down a point would make it possible to include more information without affecting the length of a book, and therefore its portability and price. Against these advantages, there was the matter of legibility. Someone under thirty looked at the sample page and asked incredulously, 'Is it really too small to read?' Laura stared at the blurry print.

A Post-it stuck to her screen reminded her that she owed petty cash $9.15.

A letter from a woman in Aberdeen threatened legal action because her B&B was described in the *Scotland* guide as 'pleasingly ramshackle'.

Laura studied the first of three costings on which she had to sign off by the end of the day.

Occupational Health & Safety emailed about a fire drill.

Eleven emails, all copied to Laura, went on arguing the new gym-membership deal back and forth.

An email came in from Alan Ramsay, founder and sole director of Ramsay Publishing, to his staff worldwide. More than twelve months had passed since Alan had handed over the day-to-day running of the business to Cliff Ferrier, his former general manager. Now, as Alan wandered the globe with his new young wife, a Croatian underwear model, noblesse obliged him to gladden tinier lives. Their brains dulled by conditioned air, their eyes reddened by screens, his employees would learn that the skiing at Aspen had exceeded all expectations or that the truffle restaurant in Haute Provence totally deserved its third Michelin star. *Hi all, We're in Milan and Qantas has managed to lose our luggage again. Jelena had to go shopping all yesterday and was so exhausted, we had to cancel our private viewing of* The Last Supper. *But New York was great. Bill Clinton is terrifically friendly. He sat next to Jelena and*—But Laura had deleted the message.

Ravi, 2001

PRIYA HAD POSTED HIM A photo of her daughter, quite unconsciously selecting an image that displayed her plump, pretty arms to greater advantage than the baby. Now she was pregnant again. Whenever Ravi checked his email in an internet cafe, there would be a message from Priya. Her emails rambled at length, full of carelessly spelled complaints and news about friends Ravi barely knew. So many people had left that Priya had correspondents across the globe. A girl she had gone to school with lived in Perth, her husband's niece was studying in Canberra, Carmel's cousin had been in Sydney for years. Priya provided addresses; Ravi should visit these people, she urged.

Varunika, too, was emailing him. Not regularly, like Priya, but surprising him from time to time. She had been home on a visit but was back in Tanzania. Her first email was only a subject line—*Thought you might like these*—with two photos of their mother attached. When there was a message from her, Ravi's thoughts would drift to it all day, although Varunika's emails were brief and usually unremarkable. But once: *I'm filled with hope in this place*, she wrote.

Nimal, too, kept in touch. He no longer worked for RealLanka; the company had folded. Hugely successful at first, it had fallen to a creeping malaise. Clients began to complain that the experiences for which they had paid handsomely and in hard currency lacked authenticity. Those who chose to stay with urban families were affronted when their hosts addressed them in English or invited them to watch reruns of American soaps. A Norwegian wrote that the household into which he had been thrust was *grossly materialistic*. He had been assured that these people were Buddhists, yet five curries had waited on the table, including beef. A New Zealander demanded a refund: her hosts' eleven-year-old daughter had confided that when she grew up, she wanted to be just like Britney Spears.

RealLanka broadened its strategy. It billeted its clients with villagers who spoke nothing but a pure and incomprehensible vernacular. Tourists laboured in paddy fields, ate malodorous rice and fiery sambols with their fingers, slept on beaten earth in mud huts where mosquitoes sang. In towns, they were received by slum dwellers, queued to squat in communal and stinking lavatories, went down with dengue fever. An Italian ethnographer was so enamoured of these trials that she returned with a group of graduate students. One sliced his foot open on a rusty blade, contracted septicaemia, died. Seizing the day, RealLanka organised a traditional funeral ceremony to which tickets were sold at US$30 a head.

Yet discontent continued to fester. There were the usual complaints about smoking—but that was a trifle. The ease and rapidity of electronic communication ensured that the suspicion of fraudulence couldn't be contained. However vigilantly RealLanka eradicated all taint of pamper from its programmes, the rumour gained strength. Emails circulated. It was inconceivable that people really lived in such conditions, all the time, 24/7. It was all spectacle and show. The student's death was a gimmick, the funeral rigged, with actors hired to impersonate monks. There was an experience beyond RealLanka's offerings, something neither cosseted nor exposed, something exotic yet persuasive, for which its clients yearned. Vaguely defined, it was keenly missed. There was wild interactive chat about malpractice. Bookings fell away.

Nimal wrote that he no longer cared for a career in IT. As for picking up his abandoned thesis, he couldn't imagine returning to academic life. Fortunately, he had come into a small inheritance. He returned to the south, where he had been raised, and went into partnership with his brother. They set up an internet cafe near a beach where tourism flourished. Now Nimal asked for nothing more than to smoke ganja and marry a foreigner who would take him abroad. The Russians were pitiless but Germans abounded. Even their elderly were technologically proficient. He had nurtured great hopes of a retired principal from Bonn. But she got an email telling her that her cat had disappeared, and Nimal's campaign was cut short.

Every week, without fail, Ravi received an aerogramme from his mother. The thin blue sheet was covered with anxiety and advice. But once Carmel had momentous news: Freda had visited her. Freda had worn a denim skirt and was accompanied by her fiancé, *a very nice fair boy*. They were touring the island for the last time because Freda was going back to England. The fair boy ate two wafer biscuits, but Freda left her tea untouched. There had been no ginger beer in the house, and this failure of hospitality haunted Carmel; also, she had come to the door in slippers. Her visitors brought flowers, velvety white orchids from a shop. The fair boy admired a photo of Priya's baby. Freda said that she hoped Ravi was well and to please give him her love. Carmel's disapproval showed in the detail of the tea not drunk, as well as this: *They're planning to marry in a registry office.*

Ravi responded, as he did to all his mother's letters, with informative evasions. *I am well. It is cool but sunny. There is no news about my application. My room is very comfortable. Yesterday I visited the harbour.* He had perfected the style on school compositions: My Holidays, My Family. A teacher learned much and nothing that mattered. When his father died, Ravi had written: *My Christmas was quiet because my cousins didn't come from Galle. I had two pieces of chicken and they will keep my box of hankies for another occasion.*

Scrolling down through an email one day, he found a second message from Priya. It was more or less identical to the one above but included the information that the baby's nose was flattish—Priya pinched up the bridge every day. She must have decided that babies were a tactless subject, and copied her email in order to censor it. But then she had forgotten to delete the original. It brought her sharply into focus, the care with which she typically blundered.

Varunika wrote: *Do you remember when you fell from the mango tree and broke your wrist? It was just after Priya cut her chin open when she fell off someone's bike. I was so frightened, thinking it was my turn next and wondering what was going to happen. All these years I've had this idea, at the back of my mind, that a horrible accident was waiting for me. Last week, a dentist replaced that tooth I chipped when I fell down those steps at school. I looked in his mirror and realised I've been expecting a disaster that happened when I was nine.*

Night after night, Hiran cried, 'Daddy! Daddy! Daddy!' Rain was pounding the sleep-out roof when Ravi woke from the latest dream. The thought of what was under the bed grew unbearable. He pulled it out, put it into a plastic bag and wrapped the package in newspaper. It was only a short dash to the shed and worth the soaking.

Rain obliged Fair Play to suspend her midnight sorties in favour of Ravi's pillow. Reared on raw drumsticks, apples and grass, she gave off a reek as strong as freshly turned earth and as sweet. Her eyes were open as Ravi settled in beside her, but she didn't stir. Humans were a noisy species, given to the production of clamour—like Sit! like No! like this keening—none of it any concern of hers.

RAVI, 2001

AT BANKSIA GARDENS AGED CARE Facility, with his hair in a hygiene cap, Ravi scrubbed surfaces, put crockery away, stacked a dishwasher, matched meals to trays. Red was diabetics, blue meant pureed, grey was everyone else. Working as a kitchen hand required just enough concentration to keep him from thinking. Old Mrs Katzoulis, across the road from Hazel, had arranged it all. Her great-granddaughter, playing in the street with older children, had fallen, grazed her knee, howled. Mrs Katzoulis reached the gate just as Ravi, who happened to be passing, crouched before the child and set her upright. At once the little girl shouted, 'I hate that man.' She said 'hate' because fear was an emotion she couldn't yet name. Mrs Katzoulis could tell because she knew what it was to be frightened of dark skin. That was why she made Ravi sit on her best chair—not one of Hazel's—and placed cakes that oozed honey before him. Of the two hundred and nine English words she knew, many pertained to rheumatoid arthritis. But when her granddaughter, the manager at Banksia Gardens, collected her children that evening, Mrs Katzoulis told her that Ravi was looking for work.

One of his tasks was to write up the daily menu on the whiteboard in the dining room. The fare struck Ravi as sumptuous. A choice of dishes was always offered: between, say, Sausages & Mash and Shepherd's Pie at lunch, Chicken Vol-Au-Vents and Welsh Rarebit for dinner. There were sandwiches for residents who preferred a light meal, as well as soups, salads, desserts. Friday brought fish; Sunday was a roast.

Mandy, the busty RN, joined Ravi in the brick-paved courtyard where he liked to take his tea break on sunny days. 'God, the smell in this place! Mince and disinfectant. Gets me every time I walk in.' She eyed Ravi over her cup. 'Must be awful for someone with your ethnicity. How do you stand it?'

Ravi smiled cautiously.

'But what I mean to say is, you're better off here than back there, aren't you?' Then she laughed, which was alarming. 'See that over there? That container-type thing with the broom in it? My first day here, right, I read the label on it and I'm thinking, "That's not a very good name for a paint colour, I wouldn't want my walls painted Gravy." And it's like a full two minutes before it clicks that it's not an empty paint tin, it's what it says. The gravy comes in twenty-litre cans here. That's what they're serving up on the meatloaf. Isn't that gross?'

From Mandy, Ravi learned that what he called a shoe flower was known to Australians as a hibiscus. Tiny birds with bright blue breasts were investigating the blossoms on a tree. Things were as calm as an egg out in the courtyard. Old women and George, the only male resident, came out to stand in the sun, frozen to their walkers and slowly thawing. Ravi contemplated the mysteries of this new climate. Cold air came in a great flood from the west. But he was warmer, that winter, than he would be in those that followed, though that had nothing to do with the way the courtyard trapped the sun. People who have spent their lives in tropical places carry the memory of warmth in their bodies. It sustains them for a while, despite their cheap nylon jackets, because *they are unable to believe in winter*. Later a fatal stretch of the imagination takes in the cold. Uselessly, they discover fleece, padded parkas, scarves.

A landline had been installed in the sleep-out as soon as Ravi could afford it. Then he had bought a laptop and a modem; three months interest-free, but he was still paying them off at Bing Lee.

He went straight to the website that Nimal and he had designed; it had scarcely altered, only the list of academic staff having changed. Ravi was unprepared for the effect of the site, the intensity with which it conjured the sensation of concrete against his bones, the particular itch of mosquito bites, the maddening power cuts. More dangerously, it brought back Malini. He saw her hands, the short fingers flashing over a keyboard. There was the lively weave of her hair.

The contrast between his old site and the rest of the web could hardly have been greater. So much had changed, was brighter, speedier, there were images everywhere. It was the reign of Google. Ravi discovered weblogs. He discovered RSS feeds. Everything, it seemed, was for sale online. A link in a page of text was no longer signalled by a clumsy underscore but by a change in the colour of the font. The web had grown from usefulness into beauty. It was as complex and various as a world. What was in Ravi's mind was the waterfront at Circular Quay, its kaleidoscopic gathering of shipping, idlers, commerce, performers, its dazzling mutations and flow. The web was like that, a city of strangers and connections: people with different needs were drawn to it from far and wide. It thrilled with potential, magic, risk. Ravi's mouse clicked and clicked as if keeping time—but that was an illusion. Time spent online disappeared with the smooth efficiency of Ctrl-A + Delete. There was so much on the web that beguiled and blinked.

That was the winter when Hazel Costigan first felt old. It was nothing specific: a recognition rather than a particular limit or a new kind of ache. In dreams she was always a bride with long yellow hair. But when she opened her teledex, she saw a line drawn through yet another name. Towards dawn, when Hazel rose to make a cup of tea, she would find herself looking for Ravi's light. Like unhappy countries, the sleep-out was a place from which people couldn't wait to get away. Built of boards, it was draughty in winter, hellish in the heat. There were the drawbacks of the external shower, the outside dunny. When Ravi found work, Hazel had expected that he, too, would leave. She sipped her tea, standing at the sunroom window, going over the rollcall of the sleep-out's inhabitants. The teledex, the sleep-out: it was becoming a tic, this preoccupation with vanished names. Ravi had sought her out one evening after dinner, remaining on the step in his diffident way. Hazel thought, Here we go. Fair Play interposed herself between them, standing over Ravi's shoes with her back arched to remind him of his inferior status. He interrupted himself to pick her up, and compounded atrocities by tugging her ears. He was insisting that he pay more rent. 'It's not right to take mean advantage of you.' *Mean advantage* was one of Carmel's phrases; Ravi was pleased to have found a use for it. Hazel almost laughed, but saw that he was in earnest. They settled on a sum. He paid fortnightly in cash. She passed it on to a charity that worked with asylum-seekers.

•

On the web, JenniCam was still going, although access to the site was no longer free. But the coffee pot site at Cambridge was defunct. The last greyscale picture of the empty pot looked so shabby and defenceless that Ravi moved away at once. However, a few days later, he returned to the site and bookmarked it.

A large envelope came in the mail. It contained a padded one with English stamps, addressed to Ravi care of Angie Segal; he recognised Freda Hobson's hand. Inside the second envelope, a small white cardboard box held a squishy rectangle wrapped in silver paper. Ravi didn't have to open it to know what it contained. *Remember me by the river, remember me on the lake . . .* She had remembered him on her wedding day and sent him a piece of her cake.

Ravi, 2001

THE THOUGHT OF HIM, ALONE in Australia, ate away at Damo. He wondered if Ravi might like to do a bit of sightseeing?

They would set off early on Sunday in Damo's car. Ravi inspected Australia through glass: a Pink Panther waving outside a discount-furniture showroom, a horse standing under a blanket, biscuity cliffs. One showery morning, Damo announced, 'Today we're going over the bridge.' They approached the landmark through a sci-fi landscape of expressways and glass towers: it was futuristic, Damo said. Then he said, 'Why does the future look like Melbourne?' He referred to the Harbour Bridge as 'the coathanger'. That made sense to Ravi: you could hang your dreams on it. Damo's voice had turned disparaging and proud. It was the tricky Australian voice. It was Hazel saying, *It's a great Australian invention*. Ravi remembered that *Can I help you?* meant *Go away!* He remembered that *mate* could hold a threat.

At Palm Beach, where Damo and Ravi took off their socks and shoes, the sand was damp and pink. A fresh shower sent them to a restaurant where Damo ordered tea. It was too early for lunch, and the only other customers were a group of girls at a table on the edge of the veranda. The rain, slanting in, brought them to their feet. 'I'm getting *wet*!' they told each other, amazed that anything in the world might do them harm. Their limbs and hair were solid and golden, and they wore, in spite of the weather, tiny dresses that seemed to float. While they clutched their purses, two waiters gathered up their cups and resettled them at a different table, whereupon the rain ceased. Damo and Ravi went on to Pittwater. The sun came out, went in, came out, while they took a ferry between green islands. Weekenders, returning to the city, carried musical instruments, pillows, babies. One man had a turquoise macaw in a cage. The girls appeared on a white wharf, their bright hair dense as clouds. One moved away from her companions, and the wind grabbed her skirt. She tried to hold it fast between her knees.

It was warm in Damo's car, Ravi and he talked or followed their own thoughts, there was usually music, Damo would plan their next outing. What he loved best was bushwalking—the native forests were Damo's sacred sites. He belonged to a continent where nature so far outstripped anything humans had produced that those in need of something to worship turned to it as a matter of course. The cult produced pilgrims, schisms, prophets, doctrine, blasphemers who dedicated their lives to desecration. Out of a sense of fairness, Damo showed Ravi the Hawkesbury, the south coast, a derelict township where gold had been mined. But they always returned to the national parks, to the signposted tan-bark trails. The bush closed in about them. Damo spoke of acacias, rockwarblers, seasonal blossoms, not as one imparting instruction but because he was moved by these things. Quandong, elaeocarpus, ironbark, howea: the names of the trees were a poem. But the forests were cold and blue. The beaches, couched between headlands and devoid of coconut palms, didn't correspond at all to Ravi's notion of a coast. It was in the forests, however, that he felt the planet's scale.

He got through bushwalking by looking forward to lunch. Like all the Costigans, Damo thought of food as fuel. He would lead Ravi to an authorised picnic spot, and unzip his pack for thick white bread, hardboiled eggs and slabs of yellow cheese, along with bananas and chocolate. Where there were public barbecues, he produced chops, T-bones, sausages, a container of ketchup. While they ate, the talk often turned to Sri Lanka. Damo asked impersonal questions about cricketers or tea—politics appeared only in ruins that bore witness to the ambitions of kings. Gratefully recalling the guided tours he had taken, Ravi told Damo a great many things, quite a few of them inaccurate, about temple architecture and the habits of leopards.

One day, they were eating bacon sandwiches beside a lake when a car pulled up. A woman arranged plastic containers on a picnic table, children released from confinement screamed their joy, a man used a breadknife to scrape grease from a grill.

Damo wondered if the newcomers were Sri Lankan. 'Can you tell?'

The mother was calling to her son, warning him in Sinhalese against eating so many potato chips that he would have no room for lunch. 'Indians,' said Ravi. The brilliant pink folds of a sari smothered by a belted cardigan struck him as the saddest thing he had seen in Sydney. The boy, now galloping sideways, was the same size as Hiran.

The Sunday outings were irregular. Damo might be busy with a school camp, a friend's wedding, a lingering flu. Sometimes it rained all weekend. There was also a man, very young and rattled about love, who was jealous. Damo had invited him to meet Ravi, to accompany them on their sightseeing, but the man, preferring his intrigues orchestrated by invention, had refused. Ravi missed and didn't miss the Sunday tourism. The memory of fish and chips, consumed on yellow rocks in La Perouse, made his mouth water. But what he would have really liked was to return to the cemetery above the Pacific. He had never proposed it, believing that destinations weren't for him to choose. On the first excursion, he had offered money for petrol, too much and awkwardly, that Damo waved away. He said, 'You can cook me a curry sometime,' alarming Ravi, who had no idea how to set about such an undertaking. It loomed in his mind, a pledge as perilous as the eucalypts he had been told were prone to crush the unwary. The fish and chips had been paid for by a walk that went on forever among scrubby coastal bush. It rose just above Ravi's head, so there was nothing to see. Damo spoke stirringly of a fungus that wasn't in season. In the 1930s, the area had been a vast makeshift slum of the unemployed who had drifted from the city. No trace remained of the settlement, which had been elaborate, with leaders and rules. Of all this, Ravi would retain the word 'Depression'.

In a cafe in Katoomba, on a leaden mountain afternoon, they ate scones and purple jam. They were making their way back to the car when Damo, glancing into a shop that sold mid-century artefacts, spotted a red ceramic horse. Ravi turned over a tray of oddments while he waited. A box held snapshots, dozens of them, of Chinese couples posed beside shrubs or fountains, always with a background of skyscrapers. The women had beehive hair and tight, shiny dresses. Ravi remembered the flyaway dress on the wharf. Everyone in the photos, too, was young and looked happy, although the colours had faded a little. Damo came out of the shop without the horse. All the way home, the men and women in the snapshots asked Ravi why the people who loved them had permitted their photos to cross an ocean and end up in a box.

•

Passing the newsagent's one day, he puzzled over a headline: *Tampa*.

At work, people were talking about it: Afghani refugees were involved, and a Norwegian ship. The government was standing firm. In the courtyard, Mandy said, 'I'm not racist but I'm against queue-jumpers. Fair go for everyone.' She settled her uniform, plucking at it under her bust, and explained, in a kindly tone, 'That's the Australian way?'

When she had gone back inside, Ravi's gaze met that of the Ethiopian nurse's aide. Abebe Issayas preferred to work nights; the two men's shifts didn't often coincide. But there was a feeling of sympathy between them. Bespectacled and neat, Abebe looked like the accountant he had been in another life. One day, his face would fit him again; he was studying part time to get his Australian qualifications. He said, 'When politicians say, "We mustn't be sentimental", you know something bad is coming.' His speech was deliberate and faintly inflected with American. A long time ago, he had spent a high school year in St Paul.

The new resident, Beryl Doone, trundled her walker into the courtyard. At the sight of the two men, she screamed, 'Get away from me, you black shits.' Unlike, say, little Glory Warren, who was prone to fits of rage in which she hit people, Beryl didn't have dementia—she was merely insane. She filled the doorway, shouting, 'Don't you put your black hands on me! I'm warning you!'

'Bit of shush, love,' flung Mandy, through flyscreen. She had her pets and didn't care for the independent voice no matter what it cried.

Beryl stood and trembled. Her complexion, like her blouse, was mauve. In a ruminative, mauve undertone, she repeated, 'Black bastards. Black bastards.' This was aimed equally at the trees, which made everything untidy with their leaves. She rolled her wheels back and forth over those she could reach.

Sandra, who managed activities, appeared at Beryl's elbow. 'Singalongs, darling. Everyone's waiting for you.' And threw over her shoulder, as Beryl wheeled tentatively about, '*Sorry*, guys.'

A while later, Beryl could be heard warbling of a track winding back to an old-fashioned shack. Her voice was low, velvety, true. The dining room adjoined the piano room. Setting the melamine-topped tables for afternoon tea, Ravi had damp eyes. The old people's singing never failed to affect him. Abebe came in, holding Glory's hand. Glory wished not to sing along, but to sit and fold a napkin that resembled the only doll she had ever owned. Next door they were on to 'Waltzing Matilda'. 'Under the shade of a coolibah tree,' harmonised Ravi. Mandy, on her way through behind her trolley, pounced. 'How come you know that?'

'I learned it at school.'

'But it's an Australian song,' objected Mandy. Then, as her trolley encountered an old woman stalled in the doorway, 'Keep moving, love! Whatever you do, don't stop!'

When Ravi was waiting for the bus that evening, his phone rang. Angie Segal said, 'I guess you've heard Labor's backing Howard on the *Tampa*. Bastards.' Then she said, 'Hang on.'

He could hear her mobile's ringtone in the background. He pictured her at her desk, he saw the bones close under the skin in her sharp little face.

When Angie returned, she said, 'I've been fielding calls from clients all day. Everyone's afraid this is going to mean bad news for them.' She told Ravi that he was not to panic. 'The pollies are just behaving like the bastards they are. It's electioneering. It doesn't have a bearing on your case.' She repeated the injunction about not panicking. Her need to hear it was plain.

Ravi's usual shift was an early one, finishing at three, but that day he had started at nine. The bus taking him home snuffled slowly through the traffic, pausing here and there to ingest more victims, and songs looped through Ravi's mind. When he was a child, the pattern of things had brought neighbours to the Mendises' house on Saturday evenings. Ravi's father played his guitar and everyone sang. The night and the songs grew older together. At Banksia Gardens, too, they liked 'Don't Fence Me In' and 'Galway Bay', songs of yearning and flight. How easily music travelled the world! Malini had sung Beatles songs to Hiran and 'The Carnival Is Over'. Hearing her warn that the joys of love were *fleeing, far beyond and far and wide*, Ravi had said that she had the words wrong. But try as he might, he couldn't supply a plausible alternative. That annoyed Malini, which was understandable. Snug in a rush hour that lasted three, Ravi might have begun counting but hummed noiselessly instead.

LAURA, 2001

SHE WAS WALKING TO WORK through weirdly hushed streets. No one was revving an engine or screeching away from a light. The newspaper uppermost in the stack in the takeaway place where Laura went in to buy a latte displayed a photograph that already looked iconic. She changed her order to a double espresso. The previous night, she had been getting ready for bed when the phone rang. Danni said, 'Switch on the telly.' Laura spent most of the night in front of the set.

The plane came in, big-bodied and low, at the end of the street, the noise of its engines magnified by the unnatural calm. It was an everyday sight that had been altered forever. People looked up, then away, and tightened their hold on something: a steering wheel, a cup.

The boy was on the other side of the road and some way ahead of Laura. It was rare to see a kid that age walking alone to school these days. They were packed into people-movers by Yummy Mummies, or flocked, wheeled goslings, about a Boho Daddy's bike. But the reason Laura noticed the child was something alert in the way he held himself. She thought, He's not looking forward to school. There returned mornings when she had longed to stay at home, and had discovered that her stomach ached or her throat, and tears had gushed. And Hester, kindly and implacable above an apple and a cut lunch, would enquire most tenderly before concluding, 'But if there is no reason . . .'

How could six-year-old Laura have found the words for her apprehension of a vast and pitiless trap? How awful school was, when you thought about it, each programmed year opening its jaws upon the other, and fastening about the growing girl. How reasonable of children to weep and wish to flee.

At the intersection, Laura glanced to her right, which was the way the boy with the red backpack had gone. But he had vanished, presumably into a side street and school.

LAURA, 2001

DANNI WAS HAVING *a few people around for Chrissie drinks*. Over the sparkling and dips, wounds inflicted by the federal election were still being probed: 'I mean, can you *believe* it? Who are all these people who gave them a third term?' Laura escaped to the balcony. A girl with dappled hair and the native uniform of sprayed-on denim, halter top and four-inch heels said, 'Hi, I'm Alice.'

They were obliged to stand close to each other—there wasn't a whole heap of room on the balcony. The green globes of a staked tomato shone in the fading light. A second tub held veined silver-beet. Wild festoons of green that might have been a zucchini had spread from a trough to begin their overwhelming of the galvanised balustrade.

'I'd love to grow veggies,' confided Alice Merton. 'Only Woolies is easier.' Then her perfect golden nose crinkled. 'What's that pong?'

It was the top note still emanating from the chicken poo recently applied by Laura. Enlightened, Alice exclaimed, 'Did you do all this? I thought it was Danni!'

Alice's lover squeezed onto the balcony to see what was going on. He was Danni's editor, a big, pretty man. Afraid of losing Alice Merton, he seized her at once by the wrist. But the girl's attention was on Laura. 'Are you like totally committed to living here?'

The house at McMahons Point had blistered green shutters. Breaking from window boxes, plumbago intensified its blue against streaky ochre walls. Half the small garden was taken up with a lemon tree and a density of summer vegetables. On the other side of the path, a grape arbour was surmounted by an orange plush dog.

The man who opened the door had a face known to Laura, not as it appeared now, but when its perfection wasn't only of the bone. Time hollowed: she was standing uniformed and slouched before painted Carlo Ferri, and Miss Garnault was explaining that the gallery had acquired the portrait ten years earlier, when it had won the Archibald—controversially, of course—for Hugo Drummond.

These days, dead Drummond's lover had a third leg that ended in a chrome claw.

Carlo refused to have the operation that would give him a new hip, according to Alice Merton. Nor would he leave the house where Drummond had lived and died. She would move in herself, said Alice, for her parents were just down the road and she had known Carlo all her life, but—

But his brown hand slid into Laura's.

At the foot of the stairs, he raised his stick. 'Up and up.'

The second flight of stairs was little more than a ladder. She opened the door at the top and went out onto the roof.

The bridge, the boats, the boisterous light, the whole glam, prancing, knockout show.

Laura spared it barely a nod. She was taking in oleander, pomegranate, gardenias, everything terracotta-potted. Olive, rosemary, mock orange: the Mezzogiorno! Frangipani fallen pinkly upside down. She noted a tap and a retractable hose, a whippy bougainvillea. The logistical riddle was plain, the need for nutrients, mulch, water at one end of a stair, at the other a deficiency of cartilage about a joint. At the thought of the old man making his way up to the roof, Laura could almost hear the grind of bone on bone.

A room clad in trellis and leaves wasn't locked. A cupboard beneath the sink revealed practicalities, like secateurs. And a window the view, of course. Here, with the harbour rolling over at his feet, Hugo Drummond had produced the tortured monochromes of his late period, burning layers of colour onto canvas with a blowtorch.

She tramped back down. The old house shuddered along its spine.

In the kitchen, Carlo Ferri waited behind an interrogative espresso.

'I think the murrayas could do with a tip-prune,' said Laura. 'And a dose of Seasol all round couldn't hurt.'

His eye was appreciative. 'Nice big girl. Run up and down stairs with dung.'

Each contemplated this vision.

Friends said, 'It's the wrong side of the harbour! You can't possibly!'

But Laura could.

Laura, 2002

ROBYN WAS SAYING, '. . . CALLED MAO? It used to be a shoe-repair place?'

Laura shook her head.

'Oh yeah, I know where that is,' Crystal Bowles said. 'They've got that funky Cultural Revolution decor. What's the food like?'

From her desk in the e-zone, Crystal had spied Robyn Orr heading for the kitchen and had followed. Robyn was cool. And a manager. There had been a time when Crystal's sister, Jade, had worked with Robyn. So when Crystal applied for the editorial traineeship in web publishing, Robyn had been really helpful.

'Who'd even think about calling a restaurant Hitler? Or Stalin? So how come Mao gets to be funky?' Robyn applied herself viciously to a coffee plunger. 'Because the millions he murdered were only slopes, that's why.'

Crystal explained patiently, 'The name's just a joke. Like the Mickey Mao T-shirt I got when Jade and I went to Hong Kong.' Because it never hurt to remind Robyn of the Jade connection. 'It's an ironic thing.'

'That's such crap, Crystal. How come the Holocaust isn't'—Robyn's fingers inserted scare quotes—'ironic? Because, *a*, bad stuff that happens to white people isn't funny, and *b*, after blackfellas, Chinese are who Australians hate most.'

'But there's Chinese people working at Mao. I've seen them through the window.' Crystal thought, Aborigines! They're *soooo* touchy about ethnicity. She felt quite compassionate as she pointed out, 'Nowadays Mao is like a brand name?' Whereupon, having deposited her soggy Celestial Harmony teabag in the sink, directly beneath the sign that said DON'T BE EVIL. PUT YOUR GUNK IN THE BIN!!!, she sashayed away.

Slumped against the counter, Robyn said, 'I had such a crap weekend, you wouldn't believe. Ferdy and I came yea close to calling it a day.' Her teaspoon was beating against the rim of her mug. 'The whole band thing's never going to happen. Not in any financial way. Meanwhile, Ferdy's happy spending his life stacking shelves at Woolies. I mean, I love the guy, but he just, I don't know, it's like he's got no *drive*.'

Ferdinand Hello played bass in a band that refused to give interviews and performed wearing cartoon masks. His name was self-awarded. In Cambodia, a long time ago, he had had a different one, but all the people who remembered it were dead.

'I'm good at marketing, I could help him with his resumé,' said Robyn. Then, 'Shit! I was supposed to be in a meeting five minutes ago.'

She went away thinking, I shouldn't have lost it with Crystal. Even if she's full of crap. Like the global management meeting to which Robyn was making her way. She'd seen the agenda. Post-9/11, Americans weren't travelling. The profits from the US office were down. You didn't need to be a genius to figure out where that scenario was going.

But moral indignation was so not managerial, Robyn knew.

•

Laura took the ferry to the city, then a bus to the office. The train was fast, cheap, efficient. But who wouldn't choose the ferry?

In the evening, she would realise that she couldn't wait to get home. So the train would rush her across the bridge. She just about ran upstairs.

When she left Erskineville, Laura had donated the little she owned in the way of furniture and so on to Alice Merton's student household. Robyn had driven her and a couple of suitcases over the bridge in her Charade. In McMahons Point, Laura's room was the back one on the first floor; she stored her clothes there. It had a door to the bathroom, and a rubber tree in a glazed Chinese pot. And an embroidered white cover on a nun-like bed.

But Laura preferred Drummond's daybed in his studio on the roof. She kept an electric jug beside the sink, along with a bowl, two mugs, a corkscrew, equipment for coffee. Forks etc. She was welcome to cook downstairs: 'You not be shy,' Carlo Ferri had said. But Laura preferred to tuck in to takeaway laksa or sushi or beer-battered fish on high: at a small slatted table beneath the frangipani when the weather was fine, by the window in the studio when it wasn't.

Oh, Sydney, with your giant moon!

And prawns.

There was a quilt for cool nights. And Theo's red rug on the paint-splattered floor.

Ferries passed, lit up like cakes. The bridge went on holding the two halves of the city apart. On Saturday evening, everywhere was oysters and mozzies on sandstone terraces. Screams of gaudy terror noosed the minarets at Luna Park.

•

Laura rose in opal dawns to hose, and manoeuvre shade cloth. On weekends, she deadheaded and pruned, topped up potting mix, measured fish emulsion into a watering can, hefted bales of pea straw, swept.

She photographed the plants from different angles, uploaded the images, carried her laptop along with seven gardenias and their shining leaves to Carlo.

On the ground floor, walls had been knocked through. Here Carlo cooked, watched TV, smoked. He greeted Laura with tiny cups on the brown and red oilcloth. An archway separated the kitchen from the living area. Under the bay window, a sofa served as his bed. There were actually records, and a player with an arm you moved out. A song as thick and syrupy as the coffee mingled with the smell of garlic, liniment and Camels. A lamp raised by a naked black female always shone, for at all times the shutters were closed.

The courtyard at the back was for the compost bin and a fruiting fig. There was a bench that got the morning sun and a bed of herbs. Here, as among the vegetables that flourished at the front, Carlo refused help and was to be observed kneeling on a mat before a perennial basil as if to pray.

Once a day, on his own two legs, he made the grim journey up and down the first flight of stairs. 'The old guy, he not finish yet.' No matter what the weather was doing, morning found him creeping up and down green gullies and streets that followed the unreasonable contours of the bay.

'You think I marvellous for my age?' When Laura assented, he pounced. 'I marvellous at all age. Always!'

Tracy Lacey was so happy for her friend. Although personally she'd always thought a harbour view was just that little bit obvious. For her bohemian soul, there was nowhere but a heritage terrace in Paddo. It was the simple things that mattered, as Tracy had always said. And that was where she and Gary had been fundamentally unsuited, that way he always judged and grasped. Still, water under the bed now, darl, Tracy was totally Zen that he'd repartnered with Bruce, no hard feelings—they just fell away when you had a good divorce lawyer. But the Melbourne scene was so up itself—people there carried on like it was Manhattan or something. Dream on! The vibe here was totally different, so laidback, and Sydneysiders were really open to innovation. 'You know I'm in charge of new media, darl?'

Laura congratulated. Then spoiled the effect by asking dreamily how long new media stayed new. 'When does it become old media?'

Honestly, anyone less loyal would have just ignored Laura Fraser's email. But there was something of a buzz around Hugo Drummond. At the gallery, they had been all ears when Tracy happened to mention where her friend was living. Torquil from Modern Australian had invited Tracy to lunch and told her that Carlo Ferri ignored all his letters. Drummond's dealer got the same cold shoulder; there had been one falling-out too many in the Eighties, when no one was buying Drummond and he blamed everyone else for it. Torquil had known him: 'a terrifying old bastard'. Then he had died, and Carlo seemed to be under the impression that the art world was to blame for that, too. Torquil would love a retrospective to coincide with Drummond's centenary, but who could say what Carlo Ferri had done with the late work? He was Neapolitan and excitable. Torquil, staring into his third pinot grigio, saw canvases slashed in unfathomable Latin frenzies, tossed out with empty flagons, carved up to fire pizza ovens. Long ago, when Drummond was still accepting commissions, a society hostess whose portrait he was painting had invited the pair to dinner in Double Bay. Carlo took offence at something her husband said about Italian opera. He refused the oysters and said he had to have spaghetti. When it came, he ate it with his fingers. The guests included a bishop, and a Dane who was very possibly titled. 'Drummond told that story for years.'

Tracy moistened her lips with peppermint tea and explained to Laura that she was part time at the gallery. Because Destiny was only three, although you'd never know it, everyone from the swimming coach to the piano teacher said she was so advanced for her age. That was when Tracy had known she'd made the right decision about her future, meeting Stew the very same week she moved back to Sydney. You had to believe in karma, *n'est-ce pas*, darl? Had she mentioned that Stew was a Buddhist? But not in that fundamentalist vegetarian way.

It was Saturday morning, and the two women were sitting under the frangipani on the roof. Laura was wondering, How could I have gone without this all those years? Just as, in London, Sydney had always come to her as a Sunday in summer, now when Laura thought of London everything seemed to have happened on a winter afternoon. She had been young, undoing her soiled apron after the lunch shift in a pub; the windows were steamy because she had just mopped the floor. Bea came into a dark room carrying flames that streamed sideways, a door opened to admit Theo and the scent of rain. The cold came off a marble pillar, and Laura, wearing a knitted scarf, hurried across a vast courtyard after her breath. A bundle of rags extended a mitten that she filled with cold coins. She saw the red sun.

She offered almond fingers.

'No sugar or carbs for me, darl. I'd bloat straight up to a size eight.' Tracy Lacey spoke mechanically because she was thinking she would rather die than endure the cultural wasteland of the North Shore. But she was like that, she required constant intellectual stimulation. It came with being vibrant and thin. Fat people's thoughts moved sluggishly, it was to do with their high GI intake coating their brains with cholesterol. You only had to look at Laura Fraser, sitting there chewing poison, her eyes empty and content. She was actually going to eat another biscuit—amazing! And the hair! A friend less sensitive than Tracy would have handed over Fabrice's card and urged—he was so worth it. You could tell straight off he was French. The way he had known, just by looking, that Tracy had arrived at that point on her journey when she needed streaks.

Through half-closed eyes, Laura was watching the tingle of light on the water. And fearing that she might be slipping, slipping into the Great Australian Smugness produced by the blandishments of climate and scenery, not to mention the world-class varietals you could pick up in any bottle shop these days. With the special fervency of the unbeliever, she prayed, Keep me from *It's great for a while but*. She would email Bea that afternoon, vowed Laura, she would arrange to meet up in Hanoi or Split. The thought of travel summoned a Sicilian day when she had taken a long, dull bus trip to a grey town where it was raining. Laura had asked directions, persevered, peering out from the hood of her jacket to struggle with the conditional tense and the Sunday stupor of the streets. Opinion as to whether the famous site could be visited on a weekend wavered. A signpost led uphill, into a suburb of guard dogs and villas. Here more roads branched away, and there were no directions. The local bus, on which Laura had counted, didn't run on Sunday. The rain stopped, September asserted itself, she grew hot. When she came, at last, to the ruins, the caretaker waved away her money. It was National Monument Day, there was no charge. And yet no one else had come for the silence, the damp Greek stones, the paths devastated by grass. When Laura eventually made her way back to the town, the cafes that hadn't begun serving lunch when she passed them the first time were now closing. It was raining again. She had to run for the bus. Already she knew that it had been a day that redeemed the boredom and indulgence of tourism. What she had in mind was the hour spent alone with a horizon of poplars and a National Monument. But with time, every aspect of the day had come to seem integral and precious: hunger, the frowning baroque square, the uncertainty attending her ascent through the suburb, the bus filling up with students and immigrants returning to the city now that leisure was done.

The time! Where were the keys to the Range Rover? Destiny's class in Free Expressive Movement had less than ten minutes to run. And in just half an hour, there was Italian For Under-Fives over in Leichhardt. 'Mind you, it's all dialect where we have the farmhouse. Stew wouldn't buy anywhere that wasn't authentic. But Destiny's teacher says she's so gifted, she'll pick up Tuscan in a flash.' All the while peering and wondering as they descended. For there was not so much as a drawing by Drummond on view. A Whiteley on the landing, Molvigs along the stair, a row of Carl Plate collages to follow. And Tracy driven at last to enquire, for all the doors were shut.

No, there were no Drummonds in the house, said Laura. A Giacometti lithograph hung in the downstairs toilet off the laundry, but without Carlo, she didn't feel she could take Tracy through. Every Saturday, Carlo Ferri's cousin Rosalba carried him off to her house in Haberfield. He would return the next morning, bearing damp parcels from the fish markets at Pyrmont and the cousin's own ravioli.

Not long after moving in, Laura had encountered this Rosalba in the hallway. She was Europeanly groomed, her hair a bronze stiffness, her feet defying the dread humidity in closed and shining shoes. They were broad across the toe yet stylishly heeled and indefinably expensive—and how they clashed with the pastel summer suit! Laura deduced: Peasant thrift offsetting the price tag with serviceable black. This spurt of snobbery was born of the antagonism, inaudible to an onlooker, deafening to the protagonists, that rustled at once between the women.

Faced with this large new person, Rosalba said merely, 'So you are here.' Her voice was husky, with the downward inflection that Italians so often carried over to English. It made everything she said sound ironic.

RAVI, 2002

HE COULDN'T GET OVER THE things people threw away in Australia. Bedsteads, TVs, tennis balls, mattresses, couches, T-shirts, computers, toys: in Sri Lanka, there were many who would take these pavements for a showroom. Sneakers swung from the power lines. Coins glinted at Ravi's feet. He always took the tennis balls home to Fair Play—ripping open a furry green sphere in a private place brought gratifying memories of entrails. Ravi pocketed the money, of course.

The profligacy of the streets explained why it was a long time before the grassy strip outside Hazel's house caught Ravi's eye. At the foot of a majestic municipal fig, the vestiges of children's games were frequently to be seen—at least, that was how Ravi interpreted these exhibits. There might be a scattering of paper stars, coloured with crayon and clumsily scissored. Or gumnuts or plastic figurines or a configuration of white pebbles. Once a small grey rubber elephant lay half buried on its side.

At first, Ravi merely registered the changing display. Later it began to preoccupy him. What did it mean? Who were the children behind it? The Mishra girls were too old, the Katzoulis children too young. Hazel's house stood near the middle of the street. Children lived further along, in both directions, but Ravi had never seen them playing near her gate. It was true, however, that a troop led by a girl with bold black eyes went shouting and running by from time to time.

Ravi began to watch out for this brigade. He saw it charge past, chanting, te-le-*phone*, te-le-*phone*. The black-eyed girl was called Layla. She was a tyrant. Ravi heard her command, 'Give me your Fighting Energy card or I'll bash you.' She threw stones at a cat in a tree. He was returning from work one afternoon when he saw her astride a wall. Her face, screwed tight, showed concentration and mirth. As Ravi drew level, she farted. Admiring and fearful, her subjects snickered on the porch.

A mirror with a plastic loop at the top, the kind designed to dangle in a birdcage, had been driven into the tree with a pin. It flashed in the sun, three feet above the ground, at child height. On the grass below it lay the knave of hearts. This assemblage disturbed Ravi in a way he couldn't name. On warm evenings, people would sit out on their verandas and conversations netted the street. Ravi, standing with a cigarette at the gate, was offered coffee. Lit by calm candles, the children gathered on a carport deck and sang, 'Red, Red Wine' in their birdlike voices. The mystery continued to nag.

He answered his landline one evening and said, 'Priya!' But it was Varunika, who never rang him, laughing in Africa at his mistake. The line was clear, but as sometimes happens, they kept cutting across each other's remarks. Each would apologise, wait politely for the other to speak, and they would end up saying something at the same time.

Into one of their silences, Varunika came out with, '*Aiyya*, do you think I would like Sydney?'

So that was why she had called.

When Ravi asked if she didn't like where she was, she replied that it was fine. But recently she had been thinking about other possibilities. *Dreaming*, was what she said. 'In the end, I'll probably stay here. I'm used to it.' Her tone was casual, but Ravi sensed unhappiness. When Priya called him at New Year, she had suddenly asked, 'Do you think *nunggi* is one of those?' Ravi knew what was meant but feigned mystification. He was punishing Priya for voicing an idea that had crossed his own mind. Priya had evoked a recent photograph of their sister. 'Did you see how short she's cut her hair?'

When Varunika rang, Ravi was sitting in front of his laptop. Listening to her voice, he found the email with the photo and opened the attachment that brought up her face. She was smooth-skinned and delicate-featured, her mother's pretty child—but it was true that the haircut was brutal. Ravi told her what he had heard at Banksia Gardens, that nurses were in short supply in Australia.

A few days later, his mobile rang. It was Angie Segal. She had spoken to Ravi's case officer—'a bit of a dick but not actually a bastard'—because his application for asylum had now been before Immigration for fourteen months. 'He was pretty evasive but in the end he hinted that some applications might have gone astray last year. *Gone astray!*' Angie said, 'No, not lost, I promise. Just mouldering at the bottom of an in-tray while someone's brain went AWOL.' She also said, 'I tried to make him promise he'd fast-track your case. But there's a limit to how far these guys can be pushed.'

Her voice had faded. Ravi heard a tearing sound and pictured Angie ripping open a packet of sweets. He asked, 'Has the other Ravi Mendis heard?' This met with silence, so Ravi specified, 'The man in Port Hedland?'

Angie said, rather indistinctly, 'Their appeal was rejected.'

'But his wife's a Tamil,' implored Ravi.

Before ringing off, Varunika had said rather coolly that she would *look into* Australia; Ravi was left feeling that he had failed her in some way. Why hadn't he said that his life would be transformed if she joined him? He was unable to stop thinking about her in Sydney. He was unable to stop thinking about his namesake, seeing him circling the world, now and then arriving somewhere where he and his Tamil wife were always unwanted. Ravi wished he had asked Angie how old the man was, what kind of work he did, how long he had been married.

Into his dreams that night came a long-ago scene of a girl stumbling along in front of soldiers. When he woke, what was in his mind was not an image but, as sometimes happens, a sentence: *There's no limit to how far people like that can be pushed.*

LAURA, 2002

NINETEEN JOBS WENT AT RAMSAY'S Sydney office. The announcement followed a fortnight of speculation and closed doors. The HR people were always going into or coming out of meetings with their faces arranged to convey importance and concern.

Laura thought, This is it. She rotated her shoulders: Unemployed at last!

At first, there had been the satisfaction of acquiring a trade. She learned how a book was put together and how to decipher a sales report. There was budgeting and blurb-writing, and what to look for when checking artwork. She was shown how to calculate a researcher's fee and how to plan a first edition. There was the satisfaction of staying late to lend a hand with proofs so that a colleague might meet a deadline, although it was not required or even expected of her. There were the delights of a specialist vocabulary. Ozalids—fabulous word!

There was the wonderful moment when an advance copy arrived: an object in the world, satisfyingly material, labour rendered tangible and solid. People would smile as it passed from hand to hand.

These pleasures, of solidarity in work, of making and learning, had carried Laura through meetings, through the seminar on Mission and Vision, through the annual cricket match, through mandatory enthusiasm, through more meetings, through the slump of Wednesday afternoons, through her first year.

Once mastered, however, skills returned as routine. There was a special monotony to the production of guides. Out of date before they were published, always in need of renewal, they were the perfect commodity. When Laura had been at Ramsay for a month, the bestselling guide to France had gone to the printer. Now, consulting her schedule of titles, she saw that it was time to start commissioning the next edition. The horror this aroused in her seemed disproportionate. In an effort to shake it off, she mentioned it to an editor called Tony Highmore, with whom she happened to fall in on her way to Central Station that evening. 'Oh yes,' he said, and adjusted his pack so that it sat squarely against his spine. 'They come around. When people ask how long I've been here, I don't say ten years. I say three editions of *India*.'

All the way home, Laura had wondered, How do people put up with it?

So she anticipated the email summoning her to the meeting that would inform her of her fate with something approaching relief. But it wasn't unalloyed. She was getting on for thirty-eight. Fear wriggled in and out of her ribs. Meera Bryden had said, 'We'll always want you back.' But Meera had left the *Wayfarer*, following the birth of a baby with cerebral palsy, and no longer answered emails. Laura didn't know the man who had replaced her. There were other travel magazines, of course. But: the train to the airport, the safety announcements, the keycard that controlled the lights, the invoices that were ignored. And *the hunched craftsman in the narrow alley*. And *there are myriad Mumbais, clashing and intertwined.*

Lack of a tolerable alternative: that was why people put up with it. As to how: by paying attention, Laura saw that ambition was useful. Ditto intrigue, adultery, gossip, myth.

Overcome by the need to say *something true*, she went into Robyn Orr's office. There was a whiteboard on Robyn's wall. Every manager had one, to encourage creativity. Robyn's said: *Brad Pitt called AGAIN*. Laura recognised Ferdy's hand.

An award-winning poster urged *Do Your Country A Favour—Leave!* Laura sat down under it and said, 'Ramsay's in the business of manufacturing guidebooks, right? Things that can be sold. The success or failure of what goes on here can be expressed as sums.'

'Sure,' said Robyn. 'Listen, I'm leading this think-tank with the marketers tomorrow. I was going to kick off by asking, What is the core of Ramsay? But then I thought "essence" would be better than "core". It's cooler, isn't it?'

Distracted by what she had come to say, Laura replied, 'It sounds like aftershave. "Essence of Ramsay. For Today's Traveller".'

'Ha ha,' said Robyn. Her clever face had shut down.

Laura saw the wisdom of stopping right there. But she had been thinking about all this for a while. It was clear in her mind and bore her along on its flood. 'Have you noticed, the only word you never hear around this place is "tourism"? Because tourism's about dollars, no argument. But "travel" lets you pretend. Travel has an aura. It allows us to believe that publishing guidebooks is, you know, a good thing. We can tell ourselves that what we do contributes to global harmony, international understanding, you know the stuff I mean. It's understood without being spelled out.'

She paused for breath. Robyn blinked.

Ramsay was a successful community, went on Laura, and what successful communities had in common was a self-flattering mythology that encouraged loyalty and dedication. 'That's why a downturn in sales gets everyone jittery. Not just because jobs will go. It's more insidious. Suddenly the profit aspect's upfront. For a little while, there's no pretence.'

Robyn was thinking, Editors!

Laura said rather desperately, 'What I'm getting at is, there's this warm fuzzy feeling people have about travel that inspires them to put in extra hours, meet deadlines, take pride in their work, all that self-motivated stuff. It makes them easier to manage. Ramsay reaps the benefit.'

'People like working here because it's a good place to work,' said Robyn. 'We have flexi-time and paid parental leave, we pay above-award wages, that kind of thing.'

'Okay. Sure. But isn't the dedication also down to people feeling they're working for a larger cause? That travel is, you know, a good thing?'

'Well, it *is*, isn't it?'

Laura thought, It's another thing that most people in the world can't afford. And yet none of this was exactly what she had wanted to say. A picture appeared in her mind: outside a bar in Manhattan, snow was falling like tattered lace. Then she was walking down a street in Singapore where washing hung in grubby tenement windows; a white dress swayed on a hanger, sheer across the midriff, lacy above and below. Try as she might, Laura was unable to connect those scenes with her daily work—perhaps that was all she meant. But *something true* hadn't turned out, after all, to be the same thing as the truth.

She stood up. 'Sorry. I shouldn't have bothered you. It's all this uncertainty about who'll be here this time next week. A weird vibe.'

'Oh, *right*.' Robyn Orr was a kind person. She said at once, 'Look, I don't know anything for sure. But my guess is you're safe.

It's the people who've been here ages who'll go. Their wages have crept up over the years, for a start.'

Laura went away in shame: for Robyn's failure to understand, for her own readiness to retreat from treacherous ground. If the dynamic that governed her relations with her colleagues had a name, it would be something like *comprehensive fraudulence*, she thought.

It was, indeed, longstanding staff who went. Clifford Ferrier, addressing the assembly, expressed regret—his thick blue eyes bulged with it. But it was a question of ensuring the survival of Ramsay post-9/11. That was decisive. What was human unhappiness when weighed in the life-or-death balance of a brand?

Cliff went on to announce an indefinite freeze on new hires. Replacement hires would be evaluated case by case and limited to short-term contracts. Finally, 'I'm pleased to tell you that the global management team's agreed to take a ten per cent cut in wages.'

The silence that greeted this was dense with astonishment. Then someone—it spiralled from the vicinity of Paul Hinkel—began to applaud.

Every employee who completed a year at Ramsay was presented with a trophy at a general meeting. Humiliation, necessary to any tribal induction, was represented by the awfulness of the prize, sourced from Vinnies or a two-dollar shop. The bestowal of a kitsch little object embarrassed and confirmed, signalling belonging and the renunciation of any higher ideal. A chunky, gilt-rimmed ceramic ashtray had been awarded to Laura. She kept it in a drawer, into which she glanced now and then to puzzle over what she had freely accepted. The hollow for ash, a fleshy pink, was ambiguously moulded. It suggested a heart or perhaps a vulva—in any case, a receptacle deemed suitable for the grinding out of fire. But the award ceremony had not been without solace. It had presented Paul Hinkel with a little nodding dog. Seeing him now, glitter-eyed and compliant, Laura thought, Bow-wow.

Robyn said, over coffee, 'Look, I'm not complaining. The wage cut was the right thing to do. But it's different for Cliff. He doesn't have a mortgage.'

Alan Ramsay emailed staff@ramsay.com to assure everyone that the decision had been a difficult one, taken reluctantly. He apologised for the lateness of his support: the eco-resort in Brazil had no internet access. Jelena and he had intended to go on to Kenya, but it didn't feel like the right time for elephant polo. Instead, the Ramsays were retreating to their apartment in Paris *to reflect and take stock*.

At a meeting of the commissioning editors who had been spared, Quentin Husker said, 'Team, I suggest we keep our thinking flexible on this one. Try looking at it this way: isn't redundancy another name for opportunity? A fresh start. The push-off into the unknown. I'm really pretty excited for those guys.'

The silence that greeted this was devoid of astonishment.

Jenny Williams II, taking minutes, thought, Ooh! When Husky talks like that!

Laura came across Paul Hinkel and another cartographer in the kitchen. With his arms folded across his chest, Paul was speaking of dead wood. It was a metaphor that Quentin, too, had employed—this despite habitually referring to his own corporate longevity as *runs on the board*.

The afternoon brought an email from HR. There had been a micro-restructure in Mapping following two redundancies and a resignation. The department required a new senior *to implement leadership initiatives at this time of change*, and HR was pleased to announce that Paul Hinkel would be *stepping up to the role*.

These were grand days for HR, the chief purpose of bureaucratic process being to stave off the tedium of bureaucracy. The department was living through its Renaissance, an era unsurpassed in meetings and confidentiality, grave with strategies and recommendations, incandescent with grief counselling and exit interviews.

The dead wood had gone; the green bay tree of Ramsay could flourish. A corporate guru, hired to *turn the mood of the office around*, spoke for an hour and $800 on 'Mind Maps: Their Role in Creativity'.

Tony Highmore was one who fell to the pruning saw. In time, it was learned that he had moved to Melbourne and was working for Lonely Planet. Thereafter he was spoken of sorrowfully and always in the past tense.

Ravi, 2002

THE SUNDAY EXCURSIONS WITH DAMO had fallen away; among other reasons, because Damo was preoccupied with a new man. The old one continued to crash about, called five or six times a day, kept vigil outside Damo's house, sobbed. He had always known he would lose Damo, had imagined the unfolding of events from every angle, and the foreknowledge had been useless, had failed to ward off or even mitigate the calamity. Damo and Tyler were sorry for him, in a theoretical fashion, but the length of time they had known each other could still be numbered in days. They were unable to muster real interest in anyone else.

Seated on a stackable orange chair under a Hand Hygiene poster at Banksia Gardens, Abebe Issayas was reading a newspaper. An ad placed by a new budget airline took up the back page. It was offering mystery tours: a forty-dollar, one-day return flight to a mystery destination in Australia. Beryl Doone stood beside Abebe, on guard. Her pills had changed, and her eyes. Now she knew what it was to hate in a cold, marvelling way.

That Saturday, Ravi caught the first train into the city. He was at the airline office before six, but a queue had already formed. Nevertheless, he got a place on a flight to Canberra. He was back in the queue the following week, and every Saturday thereafter for the three months that the promotion lasted. Sometimes he missed out, but the mystery flights carried him far and near. In Melbourne there was a toothed wind and swaying trams, and why was everyone dressed for a funeral? Ravi was still in the centre of the city when night came, at five. In their dark clothes, all the people disappeared into it and left their faces floating down lanes.

Everywhere he went, Ravi met friendliness. Angie Segal, groping for consolation, had said, 'I know the uncertainty's very hard on you. But at least you're not in a detention centre. What's going on in those places, it's not much better than torture.' In Adelaide, the southern light, ricocheting off sandstone, knew no mercy; Ravi shielded his eyes with his hand. A day's drive away, detained behind razor wire, the children of refugees were sewing up their lips. But what Ravi took home was the knowledge of how kind Australians could be.

There was a long, dreamy flight to and from Perth, when invisible zones stretched and collapsed the day. On the way over, Ravi had a window seat. There was a peculiar moment when, looking out, he realised that he knew the landscape below. Time pocketed, he sat at a wooden desk into which he had carved his initials, Brother Ignatius was describing a treeless expanse. Not sure that he could manage his face, Ravi kept it turned to the glass.

He worked as much as he could, willingly replacing workers who called in ill. For leisure, there was the internet. Ravi visited chat rooms, read the diaries of strangers, grazed on images. He googled the names of old friends, and found a caterer in Orange County, an accountant in Penang. Roshi de Mel's older sister, the one with the Chinese husband, had written a book about spices. But Roshi herself, like Ravi's friend Mohan Dabrera, had left no digital trace.

Ravi scanned sites devoted to the habits of beagles and those that described the customs of whippets. There was an insistence on the sweetness of both breeds—Ravi concluded that Fair Play was unique. He came across a webpage that a young boy in Alice Springs had dedicated to his dog, a beagle called Boogie, run over the previous year. There were photos of Boogie, her birth and death dates, a list of her favourite toys and the tricks she could do. The boy's family and friends had left tributes. The nature of these messages suggested that they dated from the days and weeks when the loss was still fresh. Its mournful purpose served, the site had been neglected; Ravi noticed that no message had been posted to mark the first anniversary of the dog's death. He guessed the arrival of a new pet, a fresh cycle in the boy's life. He bookmarked the site.

Over time, he came to build a collection of abandoned websites. If an official site fell into obsolescence, it was remodelled or removed from the commissioning organisation's server. But sites set up for private purposes merely languished when the need they fulfilled had passed. These derelict places drew Ravi. Some, like the Trojan Room coffee-pot site, had once been famous. But most of the sites he bookmarked were as obscure as Boogie's memorial. There were caches and site archives, there were abandoned blogs and personal webpages, there were sites dedicated to family trees that hadn't been updated in years. Behind the beguiling, hypermodern façade of the web was a landscape littered with ruins. It resisted tourism. Ravi would stumble on its untouted landmarks, their melancholy charms attended by the shock of the accidental and the unforeseen. It was like wandering through a brand-new, labyrinthine mansion in which a door opened to reveal a grave.

In the wake of Varunika's phone call, Ravi gave way to a fantasy in which she came to live in Sydney. Dreamily, he plotted expeditions with her: to the harbour, to shopping centres, to visit Hazel. Varunika drew up a chair, and they ate a meal she had cooked. A monologue ran incessantly under Ravi's thoughts, advising his sister on the weather, on bargains and bus routes, on the idiosyncrasies of their co-workers at Banksia Gardens. An ingrained association showed him women as sources of food and receptacles of instruction. He would have denied the pattern, but it had survived his marriage, its relationship with reality at once ambiguous and firm.

On real estate sites, he visited first flats and then—why not?—houses Varunika and he might rent together. Details of properties that had been let or sold sometimes hung about on a real estate site for months. Ravi bookmarked these ghost listings. His childish daydream of entering the houses of strangers was realised. He walked unseen through home gyms, eat-in kitchens, lower-level laundries. Sometimes a child ran ahead of him, always out of sight. A voice floated back, announcing that the dog had drowned in the pool. It asked, Why are all the children in the photos so fat? Ravi followed the voice to *an entertaining backyard* and *a full-brick family.* There was also *a duel residence—perfect for the in-laws.* The TVs in the photos were bigger than desks. But that was a false comparison: there were no desks. All the concrete paths led to Hills hoists. All the vanities gleamed. Frightening photos, taken at purplish dusk, showed new, empty houses whose windows shone yellow—for whom?

A kitchen in Enfield belonged to *Retiree moving out*: a lace tablecloth drooped over one patterned with fruit. Set around it were three wooden chairs. The fourth stood with its back to a wall, its place at the table taken by a chair with a tubular frame and padded arms. An African violet bloomed in purple plastic by the window; beyond it, shrubs pressed green faces to the glass. A striplight struck glints from teacups suspended like carcasses from hooks.

Carmel Mendis's letters to her son were vigorous and combative, detailing the foolishness of Priya's notions on how to rear children. But occasionally they mentioned breathlessness or a blocked sink. Squabbles had sparked between mother and daughter as long as Ravi could remember, but now he feared a conflagration. What would become of his mother if the one child left should grow estranged? Who would summon the doctor, who would deal with the drain? Residents newly arrived at Banksia Gardens sulked or cried until, exhausted, they grew resigned. Their pets had been put down—a brother would mention it in passing on the phone. The old women were offered safety, a choice of crumble or tart, sometimes kindness, and there wasn't one who wouldn't have left if she could.

The tubular chair in Enfield, its seat raised with extra cushions, lingered in Ravi's dreams. Banksia Gardens had instructed him: the hollow steel frame made the chair light to manoeuvre, but what mattered was that it had arms. All the upright chairs at Banksia Gardens were provided with them. Arms were what you needed when your knees let you down. They got you to your feet when the garden had run wild and what you were left with could be contained in a pot.

In February, Ravi had called his mother for her birthday. The receiver passed in turn to Priya, to her husband, Lal. Everyone asked the same questions about the weather and the time, and rejoiced at the ceasefire with the Tigers. It wasn't that Ravi wanted the war to go on. But he couldn't shake off a sense of things slipping from his grasp. The blue house was not an earthly edifice but the space where his life had taken shape; abandoned by her children, his mother drifted through rooms as formless and echoing as the past. She stumbled, smashed her hip, died alone in a version of Banksia Gardens. The last face she saw was Mandy's. Forsaking email, Ravi wrote a letter, a sign of gravity. It urged conciliation and prudence, and mystified Carmel. She accused Priya of complaining to Ravi behind her back. For the first time in months, the two women had a row.

Laura, 2002

SHE WONDERED WHERE CARLO WASHED. Certainly not in the bathroom on the first floor, where the only damp towels or stray hairs belonged to her.

The flush sounded in the downstairs lavatory. Perhaps he made do with the basin there. Or the kitchen sink. Or the laundry trough.

He was unfailingly spruce: cheeks smooth, nails trim. Clothes mattered. For going out, there was a pale straw hat, and a blue shirt playing a cadenza against his tan. His shoes gleamed and fastened with laces. Even at home, and with the air-conditioner purring, there were thin socks and leather mules.

The upshot was just a little bit woggy. But what was moving was the endeavour. Once, it hadn't been necessary. Photographs provided evidence on the mantelpiece, the cabinets. A child collared for first communion, a man wearing only cotton trousers and the golden pollen of youth: they had been effortlessly ravishing.

His orange-blossom cologne was over-sprinkled. Passing down the hall shortly after he had gone out, Laura was in a patisserie in Agrigento and they were carrying in a silver tray of cakes.

These things marked Carlo's zone: fragrance, excess.

He invited her to lunch one Sunday. They ate late, well after two, spaghetti with mussels, a firm fish baked with tomato, zucchini and peppers, a salad of bitter pink leaves. Laura noticed that her glass was cloudy. She noticed that a speck had dried on his spoon. The kitchen was a little grubby, there was a dark line where the draining board met the bench, the tea towel slung over Carlo's shoulder was stained. None of this really merited attention, but a Fraser had no truck with dirt.

Carlo's vanity precluded spectacles. He would poke about the kitchen, trying to locate a grater or a sponge. Events unfolded slowly in his vicinity. That stretching of time, too, was characteristic.

There was the bright room on the roof and the shadowy one below. Things happened differently in each, each had its own weather and codes, its specific aetiology. Linking the two was the picture-hung stair.

After they had eaten, Carlo lay on the sofa, head propped on a cushion, and smoked. Laura stretched Gladwrap over leftovers and scrubbed pans.

Then came coffee, and *cassatine* from Haberfield in a white cardboard box. Carlo offered liqueurs from the sticky bottles on the varnished sideboard. That was where he kept his shirts, he said. Laura accepted a Camel. 'Ave Maria,' cried Mario Lanza, and the needle jumped. A very long time ago, the walls had been painted wine red. Somewhat less long ago, in an age when the sun had been permitted to sprawl about the room, they had faded to an uneven rose. There were darker rectangles where pictures had once crowded, there were peacock feathers in a green-glazed jar. The lamp raised by the naked female stood on a table covered with lace. All trace of Hugo Drummond had vanished with the paintings: absorbed into an oleographed Infant, into damask upholstery draped with protective polycotton, into four upright chairs lined up like victims in a row. Carlo's cigarette glowed in a Cinzano ashtray. Laura remembered rooms glimpsed off alleyways in Naples. She searched the shadows around her, half expecting a framed dollar bill on the wall.

The flowers were fresh but suitably vulgar. Their scent fanned from three cut-glass vases, big velvet-stamened lilies from a greengrocer's bucket, all pinkly suggestive and past their prime.

On top of the TV, a plaster statuette stood on a runner. Carlo followed Laura's gaze. 'You know this one?' She learned that in 1958, Pius XII had chosen Clare of Assisi as the patron saint of TV because she had seen heavenly visions projected on the wall of her convent cell. Her statue on the set was said to guarantee good reception. 'My mother, she no have telly. She buy Santa Chiara for keep on table. Every day pray God to send her TV.'

It became a Sunday ritual. They would eat the meal he had prepared, there were sauces made from his tomatoes and herbs, there was always something that tasted of the sea. They ate greedily: he pushed his tongue into shells, she wiped her plate with bread. The wine, made by a friend from Carlo's grapes, was pale, slightly *frizzante* and came in an unmarked litre bottle. They nibbled on small, heavy cakes, Carlo lay on the sofa in one of his beautiful shirts and smoked. They sipped coffee. There was sugar, in lumps, in a tin. The afternoon, darkening, was thick with tobacco, with garlic and swooning flowers.

They painted out towards the edge of the canvas, filling in the past for each other.

He had been born in a village in the foothills of Vesuvius. When he was still very young, there was an accident—Carlo was vague about it, and much else—and his father died. His mother went to live with relatives in Naples, among the tenements of the Spanish Quarters, taking the three children with her. She gave birth to a female infant, who obligingly died.

The oldest son was killed at fifteen during the *quattro giornate* that liberated the city from the Germans.

Some years later, Carlo was unloading artichokes in a market at daybreak when a party of revellers swept into the square. They were led by a woman with hair like a flame. She was a *principessa* from Palermo. At her strawberry-pink villa on Ischia, Carlo was appreciated by her husband as well.

The garden was magnificent, with a stone terrace and a century-old avenue of palms. The prince was a botaniser, interested in everything that grew. Carlo learned to use a budding-knife. He learned about drainage, soot water, the testing of seeds for vitality, how to puddle roots. Planting was best carried out when it was wet, said the prince. In streaming rain, Carlo planted yuccas, mauve eucalypts, a ficus from Ceylon. The prince, under a yellow and blue umbrella, brimmed with directions and pride.

They were marvellous years, magical. 'Everyone come.' There was always champagne on the terrace; in the green Japanese salon, someone was always losing a fortune at cards. There were foreigners and artists, there was an indigent colonel and a diplomat who had fallen from grace. An Argentinian industrialist was a permanent fixture along with a dwarf from Macau. Film stars came, and the intelligentsia. 'This man Wystan, *Inglese*—you know this one?'

Hugo Drummond came. He caused a sensation by asking for beer.

Eight months later, he returned.

He went away for good on an afternoon of rain, and Carlo went with him. The *principessa* threatened and raged. She offered a ring with a square-cut jewel the size of a stamp. The prince said nothing, but walked in the avenue without his umbrella, under the dripping palms.

They travelled. They lived, for years, on a farm near Calès in south-western France. The *mas* was partly ruined and the colour of dried leaves. They raised ducks, knowing nothing about poultry, and lost money they didn't have. Once they were saved by a letter from Drummond's mother with banknotes in the folds.

Drummond gave English lessons in the nearest town. Carlo worked on a neighbouring farm. They didn't like the French: '*Tutti fascisti*.' There was a painting by Drummond, *Les bourgeois de Calès*. 'You know this one?' There was no more to be said.

Carlo's mother died, her prayers for a television still unanswered. It was a mild, death-laden autumn. Drummond's father went a month later. He had not been heard to mention his son in years.

In the depths of November, yet another letter came from Sydney. This time it was Cousin Maeve Ebury's turn. Her solicitor wrote that she had left her money and furniture to a Jain temple, and the freehold in her house to *her beloved godson, Hugo Drummond*. A copy of the will was enclosed.

Drummond hadn't seen Cousin Maeve since he was eleven, when she had reprimanded him for swiping at a fly.

All winter they debated whether or not to sell her house and remain in Europe. Carlo said, 'You know what we decide.' Then he corrected himself. 'Hugo decide.'

He pronounced it halfway between Italian and English: *Yougo*.

Now and then, letting herself quietly into the house or descending the stair, Laura would hear him addressing a ghost. *Yougo. Yougo*. The first time she had thought, with a clutch of dismay, that he was speaking to her.

Ravi, 2003

RAVI TORE A STRIP FROM the flatbread and used it to scoop up his stew. Abebe Issayas was demonstrating the technique to Jian and Irene and their husbands. Ravi knew the two Chinese women, both aides, from Banksia Gardens. The picnic was taking place around a woven mat in a park. Hana, Abebe's sister, was present, along with her daughter, Tarik. There was another Ethiopian family as well, and a girl called Jodie who worked with Hana. Jian chewed and said, 'Yum.' It sounded like a question. Irene and the Chinese husbands smiled when asked if the food was to their liking. They ate hardboiled eggs, and tore small corners from their bread. The children, who were plentiful, were eating corn chips. Actually, in the way of children meeting for the first time, they were establishing hierarchies. Now and then, one would turn with real interest to a bucket of KFC. Two were Australian, with round mouths and round eyes. They owed their presence there to Jian, who was doing a neighbour a kindness, but Ravi assumed a connection with Jodie. He would never see through the children's freckled exteriors to Jian.

The flatbread was spongy and faintly sour, and reminded Ravi of a hopper. The lamb stew had a slippery texture, but its fieriness satisfied a need. Once a week, the Bangladeshi shop supplied him with curried goat in a foil container, and small green chillies in a ziplock bag. Eaten with cheese slices and bread, the chillies brought on mouth ulcers—but Ravi couldn't do without them. Hana broke off a conversation with Jodie to pick up an enamel bowl. 'This is *azifa*. It's lentils cooked with mustard seeds. I made it specially.' Sitting up on her knees, she offered a large spoon. The children, facing each other on the limp grass, were intent on a game or a struggle to the death. The Chinese continued to smile.

Hana turned to Ravi. 'How are you?' Like her brother, she was broad-backed and held herself very straight. Ravi and Hana had met when she turned up at Banksia Gardens one morning. She had been to a hospital for tests, there was good news, she had wanted to tell her brother in person and straight away. Beryl Doone was lying pure and triumphant in her own warm shit: when contaminating black hands approached, she was warding them off with howls. Glory Warren had tripped and cut her lip—Abebe could not be spared. Ravi made a cup of tea from his own store and carried it to Hana, waiting in the dining room. She looked up from a stack of André Rieu DVDs and announced, 'I'm very hasty.' Ravi remembered something Malini used to say: that people confess only to failings of which they're proud. He became one of Hana's impulses. Abebe would call him on a Sunday, inviting him to a street festival or a day at the beach. In the background, Hana was audible: 'Tell him two o'clock. No, better say quarter past.' What Australia took away, it tried to make up for with food fairs, free guided walks, concerts in parks. Hana said, 'It's a wonderful country.' She was at least ten years younger than her brother, could not have been more than thirty, but now began talking about Paris with the words *when I was young*.

Hana told so many stories about Paris that Ravi assumed she had lived there for years. When he asked one day, she said, 'Thirteen months.' Her daughter, aged seven, had shown Ravi a photograph of her father. Ravi was looking from the child's eyes, which were shaped like leaves, to identical paper ones, when Hana turned from the kitchen bench with a pan of coffee. 'Tarik, how many times must I tell you not to bother our guests?' The child had a flair for irritating her mother. It might have been clumsiness or an instinct for revenge. 'Tarik, how many sleeps to your birthday?' asked Abebe. But he counted for nothing. Hana was the shadow her daughter had to escape, the sun to which the child was pulled. She wanted to watch TV but wasn't allowed to while Ravi was present. This drove her to say, 'Do you know I'm French?' What she meant was that her father had been a native of Lille. One day Hana would tell Ravi why she had chosen the name Tarik. 'It means history. And a marvel.' But when she spoke to the child, it was like someone going through a house snapping off the lights.

At the picnic, the Paris story was about the time when Hana, disoriented from a long journey underground, emerged into daylight and walked the wrong way across a square. When she realised she needed directions, she approached a passer-by. But her mother-in-law had said that in Hana's mouth, the language of Racine sounded like someone scraping out a saucepan. Remembering this, Hana grew nervous about grammar and pronunciation, and asked the stranger the time instead. 'You know what he told me? "Do you think I'm an information desk?"' All Hana's stories were like that, testimony to French barbarism. Her husband's director at the hospital had sacked her au pair after a week because the girl, a Canadian, had drunk milk instead of wine with her food.

Adseda, the other Ethiopian woman, said that she had once visited an uncle in Italy. It was plain that she had no wish to go there again. Ravi, who was sitting next to Irene's husband, asked where he had lived in China. 'Shanghai,' said Rong. That wasn't true. Ningbo was one of the oldest cities in the country. In the war, the Japanese had bombed it with fleas that carried bubonic plague. But in Australia no one had heard of it. It was easier to say Shanghai, which was separated from Ningbo by only a few hundred kilometres. Then people could say, Oh, I'd love to go there! and Rong could look thrilled. It was defeat of a kind, but there are only so many fronts on which you can fight. A month after arriving in Sydney, Rong thought he had got to the end of the witticisms provoked by his name. Six years on, he knew that he never would. At the factory, some of his workmates called him Ron; they meant it as a kindness, to spare him embarrassment. Irene urged, encouraged by example. But Rong wouldn't change his name.

Dessert was a pavlova made by Jian. It drew the children in. A tiny paper flag flew above the strawberries and kiwifruit because Abebe, Hana and Tarik had been granted Australian citizenship. A toast was drunk in Fanta and Coke. Awarded a blunt knife tied with green and yellow ribbons, Tarik contrived to sink her fingers as well as the blade into the cream. At once her gaze flew to her mother. She turned away and licked her fingers quickly. Although not pretty, the child was enchanting. Her expression, like her mother's, could change quickly. Part mineral, part jewel, she was solid yet caught the light.

The pavlova had produced a brief, deep silence among the children. Now, with serious faces, they sang 'Advance Australia Fair'. After the first verse, two of the Chinese boys branched into

'God Save the Queen'. Their father remarked that there was no end to the rubbish they picked up at school. Across the park, a man shouted, 'Turn it off!' The children went on chanting this, stamping their feet in rhythm, long after the pavlova was a ruin. Jodie and Hana had got on to the topic of the supermarket where they worked. Jodie horrified and amused everyone with her account of shoppers who handed her half-eaten bananas or chocolate bars to scan. She was a ham-faced girl with a mouth that invited kisses. Hana observed that what she hated most was cashing up at the end of a shift. 'Counting all those dirty five-cent pieces.' At the start of the meal, she had used a strip of bread to pick up some stew and placed it in Jodie's mouth. This was a *goorsha*, an act of friendship, she explained.

The talk of work seeped into the mood of the afternoon. People started to grumble about managers, conditions, the idiocies of co-workers; Monday threatened like a chill. A musical horn cruised out of a side street, and a van came to a stop on the other side of the park. 'Ice cream!' whined a child, hopping up and down on the spot. 'Daddy, kenivenicecream?'

Hana said, 'You know what my daughter used to believe?' At which Tarik shrieked, 'Mummy, no! Shut up!'

'I told her that when Mr Whippy was playing that tune, it meant he had no more ice cream left.'

Everyone laughed. Tarik screamed, 'I hate you, Mummy!'

On the train home from Belmore, Ravi's mind slipped between two pictures. Hana's long fingers moved among greasy coins; Tarik, turning her back on the company like an animal, cleaned herself with her tongue. At some point, Ravi realised that what had really drawn him was Hana's hand at her friend's plump lips. The gesture was both electrifying in its intimacy and contaminated by association with the coins.

For a long time, nothing had been left on the grass near Hazel's gate. But now there was a model aeroplane in the power lines overhead. Ravi drew closer and saw that the plane had feathers. It was a gull, its white wings fused to the wires.

The sleep-out door clicked shut behind him, and the phone began to ring.

Afterwards, Ravi sent an email to Angie Segal. She wouldn't read it until the following day, but to transform what had happened into sentences was to enter into the long adjustment to truth. He walked about the room. It had begun to rain, or he would have walked out into the dark. Hazel was away, visiting Robbo and Sooz. Ravi thought of Damo, who had tried to make him feel at home. He thought of Abebe Issayas, the steadfast apex of a triangle, the separate shimmering points of Hana and her child. But he had only just left the Issayases—anyway it was Sunday evening, when people withdrew from the world. Ravi had seen the lighted windows and the empty streets. The sleep-out, six metres long and four wide, was more space than he had ever had to himself. Within it, he was alone. He looked at Fair Play, sitting in the middle of his bed. She looked back, her beautiful eyes unblinking. She cared nothing for him, but he had forgotten to feed her. It was a measure of the arrogance of his species that when she threw up her muzzle and began to bay, he took it for solidarity and grief.

Ravi returned to his laptop. He had switched off his modem from a sense that he ought to keep his landline free, but saw his foolishness now. The critical phone call had already come through. He had already spoken to Priya, to Varunika, to Lal Fonseka. It was Varunika, home for a fortnight's holiday, who had risen late, found the house silent and gone into her mother's bedroom.

While Ravi was at the picnic, they had been trying to call him. Priya had said, 'She didn't suffer,' and started to cry. Her husband, taking the receiver, imparted facts. Less than a month had passed since Carmel's heart had been monitored. Lal Fonseka said this, and everything else, twice. The situation was made for him, a showcase for masculine calm, rich in sonorous phrases. It was clear to Ravi that for weeks his brother-in-law would go about saying *full check-up, all clear, cardiac arrest.* But it was Varunika he hated. By the time they had spoken, there had been nothing left to say. Her voice had thickened, then quavered—but she had been there, the discovery had fallen to her. It was a pattern Ravi recognised: the fortunate youngest, shielded and spoiled. Old injustices clawed at him, paramount among them this: *Varunika had got away with refusing to eat tripe.*

When he sat in front of his laptop, Fair Play came and laid her head on his knee. Still he ignored her. This was powerful, unprecedented, baffling. Fair Play contemplated an age-old female dilemma: was the masterful man to be punished or followed to the ends of the earth? Ravi had remembered Nimal and decided to email him. But he went instead to the site dedicated to Malini and Hiran. Their faces, backlit and smiling, were shockingly specific. Years had passed since he had seen them. He was braced for the familiar spasm in his entrails, but it was his hands that danced. Malini's name and year of birth constituted one of his online passwords, Hiran's another; now his mother would make a third. It was a modern memorial, coded as bullet points or asterisks. The dead appeared and vanished, ghosts in the machine.

When his hands grew quiet at last, Ravi scrolled down the screen. Dozens—hundreds—of messages had been left on the site. Nimal had alerted him long ago to the phenomenon, had urged him to read the tributes. Ravi began to do so, when an electronic melody started to play. Rather than reading in a concentrated fashion, he was merely allowing his eyes to glide over words, and the music seemed only to accompany this activity; then he realised that it came from his mobile. To her partner's annoyance, Angie Segal had checked her work emails on Sunday night.

LAURA, 2003

THERE WAS A RECORD PLAYING, one of the treacly arias in which Carlo wallowed. Rain fell, heavy and warm. Sweaty with summer, languid with prawns and limoncello, Laura heard syllables felted by the roar of the downpipe, by a tenor's protestations. She stirred herself to shout, 'What?'

The depths of the sofa bellowed, 'Beautiful titties!'

Inside the racket, everything was as hushed as the moment before music, hushed as the Lower North Shore on Sunday.

Laura considered, Ha-ha-ha!

Or: Gross! Get away from me, old person!

Cliff Ferrier reminded, *We could choose to be kind.*

How truly disgusting limoncello was—a drink for old men and tourists.

Or did she mean old men and lovers?

Whatever the case, the limoncello was definitely siding with Cliff Ferrier.

So Laura undid a button.

When she rose, something furtive skipped across Carlo's face. But she stayed where she was, only stripping clothes from herself like petals. Knickers presented their usual awkwardness. When she had dealt with it, she posed and stroked. Beautiful titties! Laura closed her eyes and hummed along. She felt corny, self-conscious, astonishingly powerful. Sexy in a sub-porn, exciting kind of way. But as the tenor persisted, her thoughts strayed. She remembered a day in London when she had gone to a cafe to meet Bea. Laura arrived a little late, but there was no sign of Bea—only, sitting alone, a man with a large head of thin, fair hair. He looked up and raised a hand: it was Bea, of course. Recalling this, Laura combed her hair with her fingers. She peeped: on the sofa, a veined hand was at work. The aria ended, another began. He shivered, at last.

The performance inserted itself into Sunday, one with the raised lamp, the small, sticky cakes, one more aspect of the rose-red room. The afternoon would flounder, she or he would select their record from the stack, it would start.

Laura always left straight afterwards. They never touched each other, they never referred to what went on. But after some weeks, a letter came from her bank. The rent she transferred to Carlo's account had been returned.

It became her habit, on a Sunday, to wear nothing under her clothes. Or, as the season cooled, only a confection of silk and lace, swiftly discarded.

She worked late. Everyone did, titles had been put on hold, schedules stretched, and still Ramsay was understaffed. Laura's mind buzzed long after she came home.

Sleep was elusive. She was reeling it in. Then it gave a wriggle and was gone. She never went walking at night around here. The pavements were deserted, the walls high, there were surveillance cameras and intercoms. In Drummond's lair on the roof, she switched on her laptop. There was an email from Theo's sister—Gaby had attached photos of a child on his eighth birthday, a black-browed angel. He collected snowdomes. Laura had sent him a fabulous one, emerald and orange fish hanging about the opera house, while iridescent flakes fell slowly over the bridge. The studio offered only brutal fluorescence, so Laura kept matches and candles to hand. Her face, candle-lit, was a visitation at the window. On both sides of the harbour, towers were fallen constellations. The tea light shone in Theo's red star.

Laura googled names. Sometimes an image turned up. A girl she had known at school, now a dispute resolution counsellor, had disguised herself as her mother. The apple cheeks of a once longed-for boy had assumed the lacklustre mask of middle age. Steve Kirkpatrick had vanished, leaving not even a death notice. There was a review of Charlie McKenzie's latest show: the gallery was middling, Laura noted cattily, and the praise distinctly faint.

She remembered that only four or five years earlier, 'the information superhighway' had been a fashionable term. *Information* encouraged thoughts of newsrooms and statisticians, of gravity and weight. But Laura's experience of the internet was of invisibility, exoticism, discontinuity: a lightness. She moved from site to site in an exhilarating patternless dance. One step led to another, performance and choreography the same. It was true that she usually set out soberly—tonight she had begun with an analysis of neocon strategy offered by the *New York Times*. So how come forty-three minutes later she was reading a blog about street fashion? Along the way, there had been a review of a Mexican film, an Oberlin sophomore's blog about her yoga class, an advertisement for weight loss, an interview with Louise Bourgeois, a site where one click fed starving children while another conserved 11.4 acres of rainforest, a vituperative forum about global warming and a Japanese designer's take on the uses of bamboo. Information abounded, but what triumphed was partial and individual. Glimpsed lives were addictive: Laura cruised the confessions of strangers, their aversions and apartments, the recipes they recommended, their responses to the news.

She googled colleagues. There was a photo of Robyn Orr accepting an award on behalf of the budget travel agency where she had once worked. Quentin Husker had left no digital footprint, but Marion, his wife, dispensed interior design in Woollahra. *Floor-to-ceiling shelves of books are considered sophisticated, but the same effect can be achieved with wallpaper*. Marion's personal style was influenced by India, where she loved to holiday with her family. What others called the Raj had provided her breakthrough concept: 'The Greater Shopping'. Global fusion was timeless and now! Laura saw paisley throws, rosewood consoles, an antique Buddha coupled with a pith helmet on a brass tray.

The only living Paul Hinkel she could find taught economics at a college in Baltimore. But an online genealogy unearthed a dead one in The Hague. That'd be right, thought Laura, for whom tulips had a regimental air. First up to the dyke with his loud, heroic thoughts, the fool.

The lyrics of songs were an education. Ancient riddles dissolved. So it was not, after all, *She keeps a mohair champion in a pretty cabinet*. Not *Cheap wine and a teenage goat*, not *I'm a pool hall ace with every breath you take*. But oh, how Laura yearned for Bryan Ferry to go on singing, *Analogue. Analogue*. She had thought it wonderfully modern, a love song to technology.

Google was ravenous: Laura fed it hour after hour. Her laptop kept up the noisy breathing of a drugged child.

There came an afternoon when, at the end of yet another day of cant and emails, Laura was fed up. It was not quite four. But she left work and walked all the way up to Circular Quay, looking into windows, scraping off the office like something stuck to her shoe. She went into a shop and bought a single, expensive chocolate. She bought red gerberas from a stall. Wind sliced her cheekbones on the deck of the ferry, but inside was stagnant with office-workers. As her destination loomed, Laura saw that a group of Asian men were setting up lines and rods on the wharf. One settled himself beside a tartan thermos, another snapped open a plastic box. The passengers in their severe city clothes began to disembark. No one looked at the fishermen, and they appeared not to notice the stream of commuters. Laura had the impression of living through something remembered or imagined: a scene in a film, tense with meaning and possibility, or an incident in a dream. A straggler from the fishing party came hurrying down to the water, wearing tracksuit pants and sneakers, swinging an old TAA bag—the crowd parted before him as for a messenger. He was younger than the other fishermen; Laura tried to smile at him, but he wouldn't meet her eye. A large yellow car, unnaturally luminous in the gathering dusk, was parked at the bottom of the street, a battered old Kingswood with one dull pink door. Around here, if you had the misfortune to have to park in the street, you made up for it with a RAV4 or a Subaru. Where had the fishermen come from? Laura wondered, and drawing closer, read their licence plate: *Peril*. It made her smile all the way up the hill.

From her roof, the wharf was invisible. But when Laura woke that night, she thought she could see the spangle of the fishermen's lights. There was the smell of food, she thought, a wafting of spices. She was sure she could hear the men, their talk as alien and appealing as birdsong. Far away, but clearly, Theo was laughing. The harbour was an alchemist: a radio blared, a baby cried, and Theo's wild hoot erupted. In spring, when the ascending whistle of koels rang through Sydney, Laura could have sworn he was laughing at her. The light in his star fell across arms pimpled with goosebumps. The past had come strolling over her grave.

Close at hand, the darkness shrilled and frightened. Laura located her phone. Its face shone, it was a live thing in her hand. The number had been withheld. There would be only the familiar, faintly echoing silence if she answered. She switched off the phone. Once, startled from sleep, she had shouted, 'Cameron, what do you want to *say*?' Her caller broke the connection.

Laura made herself a mug of lemongrass and ginger tea. Despite the florist's wire, her gerberas were heavy-headed—she had known they would droop. But after work she often craved flowers, or a yellow pear in a twist of violet paper, something pretty to salvage from the day. She wondered again how her brother had got hold of her phone number. When giving it to their father, she had asked him not to pass it on. But Donald Fraser was of the generation that relies on address books. His was easily found beside the cordless phone in the hall. Cameron was devious by nature and training. Laura pictured him pocketing the book, turning to L behind a locked lavatory door. She had seen her brother only twice since returning to Sydney—he was a stranger, in fact, as opaque to her as the young fisherman hurrying down to the wharf.

When she tilted her mug, a scene from the afternoon rose from the dregs. She was walking away from Ramsay, and there were three apprentices, two young men and a girl in buff overalls, on the far side of the street. A child walked with them—or so it had seemed. But now Laura wasn't sure; he had walked a few steps behind. She had seen him before, she recognised the red pack and the shock of black hair. A voice accused silently: *You should have gone over and spoken to him*. The presence of the girl had misdirected. It had caused Laura to believe, somewhere deep in the brain where such links persist, that the child was with the trio. Actually, she had barely noticed any of them—they were heading in a direction she was intent on leaving. The frustrations of the day, the memory of Quentin Husker prefacing yet another idiocy with 'Let's just run this up the flagpole', had crowded the scene from her mind. Now it came to her as a bungled occasion, attended by urgency and regret.

Ravi, 2003

ON THE DAY OF HIS mother's funeral, Ravi called Banksia Gardens and said he was ill. He took an upstairs train and then another to Bondi Junction, where he caught a bus. It was a roundabout route, but he was in no hurry. There was a moment when the second train, burrowing up from the city, shot out into light: something that had been constricted fanned open. Ravi noticed this, noticed spaciousness presented like a blue volume—an idiotic gesture.

Along the cliff path, the light was an anaesthetic. Ravi walked south past sea baths and secluded coves. Beach towels had been hung out to dry over balconies. An old Chinese man walking the other way was shaking his wrists.

A tree bristled with grey cones and white birds; Ravi could name them and the tree. Hana knew things like that, and pointed them out to Tarik. Ravi, eavesdropping in the passenger seat as Abebe drove, learned *hoon*, *nature strip*, *servo*. 'How do you know these things?' he had asked one day. Hana looked surprised. There were library books, she listened to people talking at work, there were nature documentaries. She kept a list of Australian plants and made Tarik look up their pictures on the computer. But it was Tarik who informed her mother that it was not a swimsuit but a cossie. 'Or you can also say swimmers.' Hana was delighted: she wanted an Australian child. In Addis Ababa she had worked as a secretary in a firm that imported medical equipment. That was how she met her husband. A shell had killed him as he tended the dying on the fourth day of the last war with Eritrea. The family had applied for residency in Australia, where Abebe was already living. The papers had come through, the date had been decided, there was no need for the Frenchman to go to the front. But he had the foreigner's hazy vision of Africa. 'To give his life for those people!' Hana's tone was the barbed wire on which an old quarrel was stuck. As for herself, she couldn't wait to get out. When she was fifteen, Marxists had hanged her father. Once, and never again, she referred to *my mother*. Abebe, turning the steering wheel, had nothing to say.

In Ravi's first week at Banksia Gardens, 'What brings you here all the way from Sri Lanka?' Mandy had asked. 'Politics?' After a moment, Ravi assented. Politics would cover it. It covered most things. At work, he never spoke of the past. Or rather, he talked about curried seer fish, monsoons, the blue house by the sea. Most of his fellow workers were immigrants. Reminiscing of home, everyone stuck to food, plants, childhood, the weather. Ravi assumed that somewhere else, if only on the treadmill of the mind, the reasons that had brought them to Australia were rehearsed. Or perhaps that was how memory triumphed, in the end, over regimes: by according politics less significance than a flower.

There were more cockatoos ahead, strident in a park. One, further off, was shifting about on a shrub. Fixing on the acid-yellow fan of its crest, Ravi willed the bird to fly. *Before I count to ten*. At twenty he looked over his shoulder. The cockatoo lifted a leg and scratched its head. On the balcony of Freda Hobson's flat, too, Ravi had searched for signs: that his dead were at peace, or at least within earshot. *If the crow calls thrice. If the leaf falls.* The Pacific slopped over rocks—it was beautiful and careless. But the city of the dead was in sight at last. All morning Ravi had feared that the cemetery would be ordinary. Then it was before him, and it was not.

Under the blind gaze of an angel, Ravi took out an aerogramme. It had arrived the previous day. For the last time, he messed up opening the flimsy blue sheet, leaving the lower section to flap over the middle of the letter. His mother had written of a downpour, a grandchild's fever, the present that Varunika had brought her. Three days later, her heart had stopped. Ravi read the letter again. Again there was nothing, between *Darling Son* and *Your loving Mummy*, but rain, medicinal tea, a watch set with stones. When he could have closed his eyes and recited each sentence, he looked at his wrist. She was under the earth now. The sea coughed and coughed, but what Ravi heard were the first slow steps of rain through a mulberry. It was answered by the slap of rubber slippers passing in and out of rooms: his mother was sheeting the mirrors against lightning. Until now, all that had belonged to a time that was distant but ongoing, still susceptible to surprise and flux.

The Irish girl found him sitting beside a tomb with his knees drawn up in a sliver of shade. Keira had thought that she had the marble books and jittery sea-light to herself, but the first thing she offered the man was her smile. It was one of her grandmother's precepts: *Christ comes as a stranger*. The old woman was the reason she was visiting the cemetery, Keira told Ravi. 'Her brother's buried here. He left Ireland when he was seventeen and they never saw each other again. Isn't that sad, now?'

The cone of pink paper she was carrying was full of red flowers. *J'aime Paris* announced her T-shirt in dancing script. Ravi couldn't always follow what she said. At first, not realising that she was speaking English, he heard only the dappled noise of a breaker or a bird. In the shadow of a cotton brim, her face, too, had its mysteries. A sentence detached itself: 'Isn't it special here?' The graves, pointing to the drop, proposed no limit to loneliness or risk.

When she set off again, Ravi went with her—it seemed expected. Keira said, 'We're looking for the name Sims.' Soon enough, it was there. From the glazed photograph on his headstone the dead man peered out boldly. Ravi saw eyes that were an argument for placing corpses under granite and concreting around the base. The girl shook crisp brown roses from the jar under the photo and filled it with water from her bottle. Her sunglasses slipped when her hands were full; she pushed them up with a knuckle. While she arranged the flowers she had brought, Ravi looked away. Keira went on talking. Sims had a Protestant wife—she was somewhere nearby, packed into an urn. Ravi learned that the rift caused by the marriage had seen out two generations.

When Keira stepped back from the grave, she did something Ravi had never seen before: holding up a phone, she took a photo.

He had read about camera phones on the net. 'Duty-free,' explained Keira. Ravi asked, 'Will you take my picture?'

A pattern slotted into place for the girl; she almost heard it click. Between Dublin and Sydney, she had stopped only in hot places. In each of them, black-haired men had requested a photo. She regarded Ravi, in her viewfinder, with disappointment; also with the first faint prickle of something else.

Unable to sleep the previous night, Ravi had switched on his laptop. He searched his emails for the first message Varunika had sent and chose one of her photos of their mother. After some fiddling, it reappeared as his screensaver. Then he set four candles around the computer and began his vigil. The rosary clicks of his mouse ensured that Carmel went on looking out at him, the machine, too, prevented from slipping into sleep.

In the morning, confronted with a mirror, Ravi saw an effigy. Thinking, This is what grief looks like, he had wanted a photo of it. One of the things he couldn't forgive Freda Hobson was her doctor. If you have spent a season in hell, you should have something to show for it. Ravi's souvenirs were the memory of a syringe, a recollection of pills. This time he wanted a keepsake. But he had returned the Memory Maker before leaving for Australia. He stared straight at the Irish girl's phone. An image Keira had known all her life came into her mind: a sorrowing face imprinted on a veil.

Her cousin's flat was a few streets inland. As they walked, Ravi learned that Keira was on her way to Cairns. A friend was waiting there, and a job serving beer to backpackers. 'What do you think, Ravi? Will I like Queensland? The pay's rubbish, but I can't wait to see the reef.'

In the hallway, released from hat and sunglasses, her face was ordinary and more satisfying. Around her throat was a band woven from tiny red and blue beads. Among the tombs, she had written down Ravi's email address and suggested tea. What she produced, however, were slices of lemon in a pitcher of cool water. Her eyes were the faraway blue of hills.

The cousin's living room was as dim as a grotto. From a sideboard shaped like a coffin, the dead man smirked in the gloom. Long ago, lumpy forms had sunk to their graves here and grown encrusted with cushions. Weedy leaves trailed from a shelf, and there were clumps of round and branching coral. Ravi saw more photographs: a white dog and a black cat. Keira confirmed that the animals, too, were dead. Her cousin worked in the city and wouldn't be home for hours. Every morning, she renewed her instruction about shutters: light ruined the upholstery. Keira wet her finger in the moisture on the pitcher and dabbed at her temples. She remarked that the view, in any case, lay to the east.

A door at the end of a passage opened on to a backpack propped against a filing cabinet. 'If you squeeze yourself in there, next to the desk, and stand on tiptoe, you'll see a piece of ocean'—but Ravi was looking at her. Under her T-shirt, her body was white as a candle. The room, like the sofa, was grey and comfortless but wholly adequate to their needs.

He returned by the route he had come, along the cliff path. Dogs and the people they walked were everywhere, and joggers in tight, expensive gear. Workers, released for the evening, were hurrying to the beach. Children screamed in the luscious bays. Ravi passed families around picnics and a group doing tai chi. He marvelled at the ease with which Sydney shrugged off drudgery, slinging a towel over its shoulder, heading for the waves.

A woman scolded her phone in a foreign language, and Ravi thought of the Irish girl. When her fingers found the embossing on his back, they had paused. Ravi could have said, A fox passed that way—it's nothing. But he remained silent, watching the wide eyes fill with tears. At the last minute, he had substituted a .net for a .com in the address he gave her. 'Greensleeves' started up like a dirge in the distance, and behind the greedy thought of a choc-top came an aerogramme from the previous year. Halfway through, his mother had written, *There was an old song I used to sing, 'I would give all for a moment or two, Under the bridges of Paris with you.' Do you remember that?* Ravi had ignored this when he replied. Now he saw that the reference made no sense but answered a need—it was like his decision to abandon the photo he had requested. His image would travel with the Irish girl until she deleted it. As with any graveside ceremony, what the photo would mark wouldn't be a connection but a defeat. In the end, that was what everything recorded. Papering over absence, his mother's letters had proclaimed it. He would google the song as soon as he got home, but what it had come to tell him had always been clear. His mother had missed him to the end of her days. Each punctual aerogramme had played the same tune.

He was almost at Bondi before he noticed that the long day was weakening. There were more people on the path than on the beach below. Ravi remained where he was, grasping a protective rail. *If I see the first star. If the last surfer leaves the water.* Then Malini was at his shoulder. He couldn't see her, but she was pointing out what he had missed. Along the horizon, a ribbon of darkness had broadened. Night was rising over the earth.

LAURA, 2003

CARLO RARELY SPOKE ABOUT NAPLES. But he once described his mother and other women going from house to house in the Spanish Quarters to recite the rosary.

There was a Sunday when Laura was holding forth about the suburbs of Naples, the hideous towers crammed together, firetraps no doubt, the work of the Mafia's property development arm. She had visited one of those blocks, she told Carlo, invited to lunch by one of her students. The scrape of the neighbour's cutlery was plainly audible, and the names of the saints he invoked before eating. Laura described a concrete lobby with graffiti and syringes, and the three extra locks fitted to her student's door.

Carlo exploded. 'In Quartieri Spagnoli plenty beautiful. My mother, all her life she no have water from tap. No have toilet inside. When she old woman, seventy-one years, still go in courtyard in night, in winter, for take a piss.'

It became a quarrel. They spoke viciously and coldly. His sister lived in a suburban tower, he said. 'Have warm, have toilet, when come rain, no leak roof. But no beautiful. Beautiful good for rich people take photo. Like you. No good for live.'

That was unfair, said Laura, she had never said slums were picturesque. There was no reason why affordable housing couldn't be—she sought a phrase that might crush him—'aesthetically pleasing. And by the way, I'm far from rich.'

'You not rich? *You not rich?*'

They were glaring at each other.

With an effort, he heaved himself up on the sofa. This evidence of feebleness repelled her.

'You look.' He had kicked off a slipper and was dragging at a sock. 'See, look!' he shouted in a spray of spittle. The sun-starved growths had the look of creatures blind from birth and preserved in formaldehyde. The third crossed over the second; here and there a misshapen stub protruded.

'My sister same. My cousin same. All same. For go school, must have shoes. Is rule.' He wiped his chin. 'We wear same shoes three years, four.'

Rosalba's shoes, black and sleek as pups on the Persian runner, came vividly to Laura—they went with everything, she recalled. She had put it down to thrift when she knew nothing about cost.

What happened next was born of impulse but had the formality of protocol. Laura plucked a peacock feather from the mantelpiece and brought it down in a great slow arc across Carlo's toes. She drew the gorgeous green and blue object this way and that, caressing his terrible flesh. She stroked lightly around the heel, the ticklish length of the sole.

From that day on, Carlo spoke more freely of Naples. He picked up the tin in which the sugar was stored. It was pale green and square with a pattern of orange roses. A painted spray of emerald leaves, crudely veined in white, had been grafted onto the rose printed on the lid. Carlo's mother had given him the tin, he told Laura. She couldn't afford the tin of biscuits for which he longed. But a neighbour sold her an empty tin, and she begged a little paint at one of the workshops where wooden Nativities were crafted. Using a twig as a brush, she created an object unlike any other for her son on his name day. There was a tremor in Carlo's hand as he told this story. The sweet white cubes rattled in the tin.

Laura had ascribed his reticence about childhood to self-protection. The deep past was dangerous, she knew. She had imagined Carlo thinking of his life as beginning with Drummond. In the same way, she figured the years before she had gone abroad as a prelude. Real life began with a decision: a lover commanded, an inheritance arrived to squander or save. Before that were only things that had been done to you. It was a dream of self-fashioning, deeply Australian. But now she saw that she had been wrong about the Spanish Quarters. Carlo had known himself loved in that dank room. The barricades around it didn't serve to seal off the past—they kept intruders away.

Laura had been wrong about Drummond, too. She had thought his ghost banished from the rose-red domain. But it had merely taken up residence in Carlo. Now and then, it peered out. It was responsible for *take a piss*. 'Give me strength,' Carlo/Drummond might say. Or when someone pinched the orange scarecrow dog: 'Bloody yobbos.'

On an evening in summer, Laura had taken part in a rally against the imminent invasion of Iraq. All day she had pictured people eating, kissing, scratching themselves, impatient because a bus was running late. Very soon, they would be dead. But on the way home, her thoughts were of Ferdinand Hello, who had walked beside her on the march. 'Hello' was the first word spoken to him in Australia. As for 'Ferdinand', who could say from what dream or farce it came? Aged four, the child who would become Ferdy had seen his mother, condemned for wearing glasses, beaten with a spade until she died. A depressive decade later, his father had plunged from a bridge in Melbourne.

Carlo was pottering about his tomatoes. At the sight of Laura's face, sorrowful and righteous, he said absently, 'What's up, chook?'

Ravi, 2003

ANGIE SEGAL BIT OFF THE head of a chocolate teddy bear, and Ravi noticed the new golden circle on her finger. He repeated the first thing he had said on learning that his application for asylum had been rejected: 'I should have gone back then.' *Then* would have taken him to his mother's funeral. Ravi would have led the straggling procession from the church; he saw himself bending over the lip of a grave.

'Two years, and a rejection without an interview.' Angie was running through the letter from Immigration as she spoke. 'I'm so sorry, Ravi. It's outrageous.'

Ravi had been judged lacking in the *well-founded fear* based on *a real chance of persecution* that was required in those who sought asylum. The Immigration Department could find no substantial evidence for the applicant's claim that the murder of his wife and son were the work of the state. It could have been a purely criminal matter, which meant Ravi had nothing to fear in Sri Lanka. Definitions were offered in lieu of sympathy: 'A fear is well founded where there is a real substantial basis for it, but not if it is merely assumed. A real chance is one that is not remote or insubstantial or a far-fetched possibility.'

Angie put down the letter and took off her glasses. The glasses, too, were new. 'It's outrageous,' she said again. 'There's no lack of independent documentation, from Amnesty for a start, about what happens to people like your wife who speak up about human rights abuses in Sri Lanka. The department's just chosen to disregard it. But look, Ravi, it's a setback but it isn't the end. It just means we'll go to review.'

Her mobile rang. She held it at arm's length, frowning. 'I have to take this.' But with the phone at her ear, she continued to address Ravi. 'The tribunal costs fourteen hundred bucks, but only if you're unsuccessful. You've as good a chance as any.' She pushed a saucer of bears across her desk.

Ravi was now in the habit of visiting Malini and Hiran's webpage as soon as he woke up. At first, he had taught himself to look at the photos. Then he had started reading. Most of the messages dated from the period immediately following the murders, but fresh tributes continued to appear.

The first time he read it, Ravi hadn't paid particular attention to a recent message. So many had said more or less the same thing. *A brave woman and a lovely person. Sadly missed. Deepti P.* But that night, unable to sleep, he remembered an old disagreement. Deepti Pieris was the woman who had left the NGO after quarrelling with Malini and Freda. What had impelled her, after all this time, to send a message of condolence? Then a damaged hand wearing a red ring flashed over a mess of printouts. One of those first messages Nimal showed him had come from the Pieris woman. Ravi was sure of it. He lay rigid in his bed.

He relayed all this to Angie as soon as she was off the phone. He spoke fast and got things out of order, and was obliged to lay out his suspicions again.

Angie Segal was accustomed to gifted fantasists. Asylum-seekers made what they could of loneliness, sorrow, uncertainty, fear. She said, 'People feel bad when someone they know dies. Even if they didn't like the person. Maybe especially then.'

'But two messages!' It was the repetition that felt wrong, an excess cloaking a pit of falsity. 'A long time apart,' Ravi insisted.

'It's usual to go on thinking about terrible things.' Angie's voice was gentle. She means me, thought Ravi, and was filled with rage. Angie Segal was a woman who found consolation in sugar! What she had seen was a drawing of a stylised vase. But Ravi had seen the thing it mocked.

He made an effort to speak calmly. The Immigration Department was right, he said. It was obvious, he should have seen it at the time. The vase of flesh was spiteful and personal. 'My wife's murder was organised by someone she knew—someone she'd told about a prediction in her horoscope. It said there would be flowers in her destiny.' Ravi knew it in his marrow, as he knew that the woman on the other side of the desk pitied and didn't believe him. She was addressing him in phrases that soothed and concealed a verdict: *remote*, *insubstantial*, *a far-fetched possibility*.

Since their mother's death, Varunika had taken to calling Ravi every week. The last time, she had asked, 'Do you remember when we saw those bodies near Galle?' She had never forgotten it, she said, the formal repetition of driveways and corpses. 'It was like an arrangement in a shop window. Or pieces of a puzzle.'

But neither of them had seen any such thing, protested Ravi. A file of prisoners was all they had passed. Their cousins, frightening their guests with atrocities, had confused her.

'I know what I saw! Maybe you didn't see anything, on your side of the car.' The child Varunika ran through time, and his sister's voice shrilled: 'Don't try and say what you don't know!'

That was what Ravi would have liked to shout at Angie Segal. Who was saying that people didn't have each other killed over arguments at work. 'Though God knows the temptation's there.' She had brought up the memorial site on her laptop and was scanning it as she spoke.

Ravi began again. 'This woman's brother-in-law . . .'

Angie heard him out. Then she angled her laptop towards him. 'You said Deepti Pieris's name was on that first email. This latest message is from Deepti P—is Deepti a really unusual name?' When Ravi admitted that it wasn't, she said, 'So how can you be sure it's the same person?'

Angie's mobile rang. She picked up the phone and said, 'Sorry, Ravi, I'll be back in two secs.' In the toilet, she listened to her mother talking. Angie's eyes were closed, but imprinted on the inside of her lids was the face of the child she had seen on her computer screen. On her honeymoon, Angie Segal had lost a baby to a miscarriage. She bit her thumb. She didn't know how Ravi Mendis managed to go on living.

'I can go back home now,' said Ravi firmly, as soon as Angie returned to her desk. The plan had taken shape over the last few days: *the good place* was now a narrow one. It was a clean, firm bed into which he could fall after an exhausting journey. At first, Ravi had seen himself rising refreshed from sleep to seek out the Pieris woman. He had walked up to her desk carrying a jar of battery acid concealed in a plastic bag. Or a can of petrol and a box of matches—he couldn't decide which. But Nimal, asked to find out whatever he could about Deepti Pieris's whereabouts, had replied that morning: the Pierises had sold everything months ago and emigrated to the States. Nevertheless, a crucial shift in Ravi's thinking had occurred: now *going back* was robed as a wish rather than a rejection. Deepti Pieris might have slipped free, but the inviting bed remained: Ravi longed to lie down. He would be able to stay still and watch light move around the room. If he turned his head on the pillow, he could see three graves—they were immaculately kept, he could tend them from where he lay.

He told Angie the news about the Pierises, ending with, 'So there's no danger for me now.'

Angie snapped a teddy bear in two. She said, 'Are you sure of that? I don't see how you can be.'

A girl Ravi had known a long time ago had grown up in the north of Sri Lanka. Her father, a magistrate, had been shot in front of his children by a man he had invited to tea. Since then, at the sound of fireworks, his daughter didn't look to the sky but for cover; in any room, the seat she chose faced the door. History was a lesson for the unblinking, it delivered its messages in the flesh. There were bodies tied to lampposts, eyeballs laid out on satin, skulls that smashed with a noise like coconuts: but who had done these things? The need for certainty produced a romance that came between damp-spotted paper covers and was known as a whodunit. The guilty party was assigned a face and called, say, Deepti Pieris—everything was revealed if you flicked ahead to the end. A voice cried, 'Don't look!', but the prisoner was always pushed on by the soldier. How could Ravi be sure of anything? Not knowing whose face the mask concealed: *that was the meaning of fear.* The roots of the banyan tree lifted, its dark arms spread. Fear found Ravi swaying on a bus, entering a supermarket, taking a shower. It was ungovernable but was it well founded?

Angie said, 'Let's take your case to review, okay?'

The next time Damo dropped in, Hazel showed him what she had found. 'It was in the shed, shoved behind that old kero heater.'

The ball of green gardening twine had rolled away from her hand. Mildly blasphemous, she had bent to retrieve it and spotted the plastic bag.

'Three years running, Kev's best subject was art,' remembered Hazel. On the dresser in the sunroom were five photos, hated by the boys, that showed each one as a baby. What their mother saw, however, was not a row of placid or spirited infants but five emblematic scenes. Kev, chubby in a paddling pool, conjured a teenager looking at a painting of sunflowers. He had saved up for the print, made a frame for it in woodwork, suspended it from a nail over his bed. His face at fourteen was freckled and reverent. It had unsettled Hazel, who desired something solid for her sons, like plumbing. But the backward gaze sanctified. Something precious to that vanished boy had been consigned to cobwebby darkness—it might have been lost forever. Hazel, who had never gone in for religion, not even when the Beatles discovered India, found a word she needed: desecration. 'Why couldn't Ravi just take it down if he didn't like it? Why stick it in the shed?'

Damo said nothing. But he could recognise a taboo. He had been eight when his father died in an accident, and he still made looping journeys to avoid that section of Parramatta Road—there were days when even the sight of a motorbike augured ill luck. His hand moved over the print of tawny flowers in a vase.

The five photos on Hazel's dresser were souvenirs of a country, outdistanced by her children, where her presence was all they knew of bliss. In her relations with the occupants of the sleep-out, a point always arrived when Hazel resented them for not being her sons. She was unaware of this, of course, and a more immediate grudge was usually at hand; the latest was written in water. In December, fires had encircled the city. The weather was changing: every week on the news, a graph dropped with the level of the dams.

Hazel's doctor, thundering about cholesterol, had condemned her to vegetable soups. She rinsed zucchini, broccoli, celery in bowls she upended over gardenias to save water. Over the whirr of the Bamix, she listened to the pipes gurgling in the washhouse as Ravi showered. At Christmas he had stood with Hazel at the bottom of the garden looking at the smoke. He could hardly have missed what was going on with the weather. *But he still took eight-minute showers.* Hazel had never felt the cold, never feared winter, never known the dread of stepping from steam into a cube of chilled air. A radiator in the laundry might have accomplished wonders, but her imagination had never strayed to that outpost. Every day she made up her mind to say something to Ravi. Then he would appear, and Hazel would see eyes that had peered into hell.

A scheme that had been gathering at the back of Damo's thoughts assumed its final form. Standing outside Hazel's house, he took out his phone. Nine red camellias, waxy as candles, made a square on the nature strip. Damo saw and didn't see them.

Laura, 2003

AT THE PARTY AFTER THE global marketing conference, there was a joint going around on the terrace of the beachfront hotel. Laura wandered out from the bar and into a discussion about decades: did the Eighties end in '87, when the stock market crashed, or two years later with the collapse of East Germany? Wall Street or the Wall? Opinion leaned this way, then that. It was agreed that in any case the Nineties had hung on until 9/11. Across the moonless beach, the Pacific growled and showed its teeth. Stoned Cliff Ferrier remarked in his sleepy voice that the Sixties had held out until the fall of Saigon in '75.

'No way, man, it all went up at Altamont.'

'That's where you're wrong, my girl. Vietnam *was* the Sixties.'

Heidi Koss, the head of Ramsay's American branch, had lost one in five staff to the cuts. She wasn't giving in on another thing. It was, furthermore, a deeply held conviction of the Brooklyn and London offices that they were misunderstood, neglected and victimised by Sydney. In much the same spirit, legionnaires along Hadrian's Wall had grumbled of Rome's ignorance of fog.

Cliff Ferrier's bulbous gaze hadn't budged. 'God, you're sexy, Heidi,' he said. 'You're the sexiest female at Ramsay. Possibly on the planet.'

You could have heard a pin.

Until Laura Fraser shrieked, 'That's the exact same thing you said to me last Friday, Cliff!' A part of her mind was wondering, Where did a phrase like *the exact same thing* come from? While she continued, in the same borrowed screech, 'You're making me jealous, you know.'

So everyone else could join in the joke. Even, grudgingly, Heidi. Because—Laura Fraser!

Laura's fingers closed around Cliff's arm while she cackled, 'They're playing our song!'

Docile now, Cliff allowed her to lead him onto the dance floor. There he said, quietly reaching under the techno thump, 'Jeez, I'm a pretty bloody hopeless case.' And followed with, 'I always go and forget that girl's a lezzo.'

When Laura protested, he ground out a laugh. And collapsed on her breast.

Robyn Orr, in a red silk camisole, was watching the dancers. Robyn was flying, she was walking on water. The conference had run like honey, weeks of meticulous planning culminating in two days of potential fuck-ups that didn't occur. Robyn's presentations were crisp and forceful, none of the sessions ran over time, some *really interesting stuff* came out of the workshops, even the caterers got it right, even the vegans were contented. Best of all was the vibe. Robyn had worried that the sales figures would be a downer, especially for the Americans, who had arrived tense with the need to defend. Instead, the statistics served to energise everyone, creating the determination that *together, they were gonna turn this thing around*. You could feel the buzz.

Minutes earlier, Robyn had been dancing with Sayyid Jamir from the London office. She lusted after Sayyid a bit. She was pretty sure he lusted after her. 'You look wicked,' he murmured into her ear. Not that it would go anywhere, they were both way too smart. So she didn't dance with him a third time.

All at once there was Laura: pushing Cliff before her, hissing an appeal. As soon as she took her hands off him, he ambled away.

'Cliff making an arse of himself? It's okay, I'll keep an eye on him,' said Robyn. She was just a little bit pissed, she decided, but her mind was as cold and clear as vodka. She disappeared after Cliff. There was nothing she couldn't sort today.

The DJ launched into a mash-up of 'What's Love Got to Do With It?' Laura returned to the terrace. There was no one else there. She strolled to where the shadows lay deepest, tilting her throat so the easterly could fan it. She had forgotten her watch, and was wondering how soon she could go home and how much she was going to have to fork out for a cab.

A voice said, 'That was smart work with Cliff.'

Laura could smell the beer on him. 'All that stuff about decades,' she said. 'Do you think people are fascinated by eras and endings because it's a way of preparing for death?' She had knocked back her share of Stollies with Robyn at the start of the evening and found herself speaking to Paul Hinkel as if he were quite another kind of person.

'What I think is Cliff's a dickhead.' His voice was serious and low. 'Anyone can see you're far and away the sexiest woman here.' He put one hand under her breast and began to kiss her.

When a group of smokers came out onto the terrace, he moved away. With his palms flat on the balustrade, he addressed the quaking black expanse. 'Got your phone on you?'

She had left it in her coat. So she repeated his number after him. Something as frenzied as surf kept crashing through and causing her to fluff it. But in the end she had it by heart.

'Okay, so here's what we'll do. You're going to get your things and say goodnight to a few people in there. Then you're going to get a room from reception. When you've gone up, call my mobile and tell me where to find you.'

She did each of these things, one after the other, just as she would have carried out any instruction he issued: calmly drained the hemlock, smashed a skull.

That Sunday, she was so tender with Carlo. All through lunch, she chatted and gulped wine. Poor old man, she thought, poor old guy. She smiled and smiled.

The first notes of the aria found her as fluid as a woman in a dream. She realised, with a pang that would have been guilt if happiness had left space for another emotion, that her performance in the red room had grown perfunctory of late. But today she had rubbed her limbs with a scented lotion. With grand, gentle objectives in mind she cupped and arranged herself, she trailed her fingers through her hair. She offered the grace of her glorious flesh to an animated husk, thinking, Poor old man. At his spasm, she smiled.

Laura, 2003

ALMOST AT ONCE A PATTERN was set. They met at lunchtime on Tuesdays and Thursdays. On Wednesday he was at a gym with a climbing wall, Friday meant deadlines. There was a reason Monday was out of the question, but Laura could never remember it. Her usual thing on Thursday had been lunch with Robyn, but that was easily changed.

She would walk to the motel. He drove, so that they weren't seen to leave or return together. The car park at the rear of the office had no more than a dozen spaces, occupied on the principle of early birds and worms. Most people stuck to public transport: Ramsay was so handy to Central. Paul Hinkel preferred to drive. It was *good discipline*, he said, it got him out of bed and at his desk *bright and early*. That was the way he spoke, camouflaging needs that were urgent or particular to him with banality. One of those needs was Laura Fraser. Gripping handfuls of her, he might gasp, 'You're . . . *great*.' She thrashed about under his ministrations. He promised nothing on which he could not deliver, he was focused and skilled—one could say professional.

Sometimes, hurrying towards the motel, Laura heard an old whisper: *What are you doing here?* But there was the human wish for an end to loneliness. There was the human need to believe that existence was larger than the plain fact, demonstrated every Sunday, of flesh alone, desiring and laborious on a couch. Sometimes, at the end of an endless avenue, she saw a little dog dance. But the sun intervened and dazzled. It wore Paul Hinkel's face: ecstatic, overwhelming, gilded with lust.

On learning that Paul was enrolled part time in an MBA, Laura remarked that in her opinion the administration of business could be summed up in a single axiom: 'Profit first.' He answered mildly that someone had to *keep track of the numbers*. He was not the kind of man who took offence easily, nor the kind who laughed.

Time ticked through their encounters. They had to *keep an eye on it*, he said. Unravelling, Laura remained bound by schedules, heard the fidget clock.

Afterwards, he showered while she lay in their bed. She should have dressed and left, but then they might have arrived at the office together. It was understood that she could spend longer away from her desk—as if what she did there counted for less, thought Laura resentfully. But it was also true that she could stay at work later. He had a young child and childcare arrangements.

All this—the resentment, the reasoning—flowed in an underground way that bubbled only intermittently to the surface of Laura's mind. It remained invisible to Paul Hinkel. His shower, her delayed departure belonged to a programme he took for granted. Besides, she colluded in it. She wished to impress her nakedness on him, so that what he carried away into the afternoon would be the painterly image of rumpled polycotton and luxuriant female flesh.

But she dragged on her clothes pronto as the door closed, and walked fast.

She was only yards away from the office one Thursday when he loomed before her. He had that fair skin that reddens at once. He nodded behind his wraparounds and strode ahead. By a sun-blighted shrub near the entrance stood a man with smoke coming out of his face. Laura recognised the new web guy, Ravi. Paul paused to say something to him. Twenty minutes earlier Paul Hinkel had left the motel with freshly soaped armpits. Passing him now, Laura caught the delicious tang of his sweat.

A visitor, turning up at Ramsay for a lunchtime meeting, had stolen his parking spot. Paul had been obliged to drive about before he found one three blocks away—with an hour's limit on it at that. All afternoon he had to go up and down with coins. At one point, he had to leave a meeting called by his line manager and sprint. This trauma leaked from him the following week while he was still resting inside Laura. He couldn't afford too many repeats, he declared. What he had in mind wasn't clear, a tightening of managerial features, parking fees, his exertions, all of these. She rubbed herself against his thigh, prey to a terrible premonition that he was about to veto Thursdays or else Tuesdays. But he merely squelched free.

Afford. He had said, Afford. She was facing up to his tightness with money. The first time in the motel, stripping clothing from each other, she had gasped, 'Condom.' He had none. They managed, of course, just as they had done the previous time, after the party. As he fitted himself to her, he murmured, 'I can hardly get about with condoms.' It crossed Laura's mind that he might have stopped at the 7-Eleven on his way. But it was no time for talk.

Thereafter she came supplied. She paid for the room, since she always arrived first. Soon the receptionist, a plump teenage Goth, would have the key waiting, wouldn't even glance at Laura's signature on the slip. Often she didn't trouble to break off her mobile phone conversation, merely ran the Visa through the machine while pinning the phone to her shoulder with a metallic ear.

In case he should find his parking space nabbed, Paul now allotted no more than an hour to Laura. There was a constriction in her throat as the minutes fled. He plunged about her, and she thought, Tick-tock. Her picture of his life was an Excel spreadsheet. She tried to imagine joy, fatherhood, craving, hope as so many challenges in time management. She might have confided at least a version of this, but they were running out of time.

But there were such glories, such redemptions! There was a weekend that dragged on forever, followed by an interminable Monday. On Tuesday she was at the motel early, but his knock came almost at once. He dropped to his knees and hooked her knickers aside. This unscheduled haste so astonished him that he was moved, in time, to a redundant confession: 'I couldn't wait.'

A dreamy benevolence continued to emanate from Laura. It extended to Ramsay, which had brought her Paul Hinkel. Office life, yoking unlikely temperaments and unequal talents, taught, or at least exacted, tolerance. When Quentin Husker spoke of *strategising our focus on delivering unique content* and was so struck with his poetry that he repeated it, Laura felt only a mild desire to vomit. Then HR produced an eighteen-page document that every employee was required to keep up to date titled *My Aims & Development*. If its authors had noticed the acronym, they had judged it unimportant. It provoked only amusement in Laura; once it might have brought despair.

Even having to work late to make up her hours was soothing. Here and there, fluorescence showed as bright as the onset of migraine, but the calm of the office at evening was largely undisturbed. Laura signed off on a costing with her favourite kind of pen, a four-colour Bic. It was an object that had come into the world in her lifetime. She always kept a spare in her desk. It aroused a strong, primitive emotion in her: not quite a *lucky pen* thing, but not far off it either. The Bic wasn't standard issue from stationery and was touched with magic, one having appeared on Laura's desk on her second day at Ramsay. She had asked around, but no one claimed it. Office life abounded in these small mysteries. Post-its went missing. Staplers appeared. The flash new photocopier always jammed, while the ancient one reliably produced single-sided A4 copies (b&w only) in batches not exceeding thirty. Urgent emails failed to arrive, spam turned up twice. Documents vanished from hard drives. Screens brightened, then dimmed. The workplace was organic. It had its own vital signs. It was shifty, endowed with speed and cunning. It breathed.

The curtains in the motel, always shut, were printed with waratahs. That October Laura raided florists, swooped on markets, surrounded herself with sculpted red blooms. Would Paul Hinkel understand the coded declaration on her desk? Everything charmed and delighted her. Her laugh rolled from meeting rooms, was heard on the stairs. An advance copy of a guidebook arrived from the printer, and Helmut Becker propped it beside Laura's computer wedged open with a piece of fruit. She returned from the motel and discovered the assemblage with its handwritten caption: *Last Mango in Paris*. She sought out Helmut and hugged him. She laughed and laughed.

RAVI, 2003

A LONG TIME AGO, SOMEONE relieved by Banksia Gardens of the burden of a parent had expressed thankfulness with flowers in a shallow china bowl. They had remained in the entrance hall, the petals stiffening and darkening, finally assuming the appearance of wood. One day, Glory Warren slid white pebbles, stolen on an outing, between the rigid stems. This aroused the competitiveness that beats savagely in aged breasts. Pine cones came to augment the arrangement, a tartan ribbon was fastened anonymously around the bowl. The result, the first thing a visitor saw, was judged *really creative* and certainly good enough for the indigent old.

At Ramsay, artfully disarranged blooms, renewed twice a week, greeted in reception. Ravi was able to ignore them—lounging in a brushed-metal bucket rather than jammed into a vase, the flowers didn't disturb him. He had been a designer in the e-zone for a month, and still his thoughts skittered between his old workplace and the new. Thus tourists, trying to decipher strangeness, compare home and here. Here, everyone sat before big, bright screens. Everyone was connected. Souvenirs proclaimed a casual familiarity with the planet:

a mouse mat from the Guggenheim, a Javanese shadow puppet, an Eiffel Tower snowdome. Postcards were Blu-Tacked to monitors, screensavers showed fiords or a noodle seller's stall. *Keep moving, love!* remembered Ravi. *Whatever you do, don't stop!*

Mortgages and tertiary education debts were spoken of in Ravi's hearing, but what he noticed was the magic of money. Disposable income was as silent as snow and as transformative. It softened monotony, blurring its workaday bones with MP3 players, camera phones, negative ionisers, takeaway coffees in environmentally responsible mugs.

When Ravi looked back at Banksia Gardens, he saw lives marked by before and after. Youth, health or the simplicity of belonging were landscapes that had been lost. Much had been patched up but nothing could be mended. On inspection, the crack always showed. His new workplace, on the other hand, was forward-oriented: the Mission Statement required it. Ramsay was firm flesh, blonde streaks, the smiles that only fluoride and first-world dentistry can achieve. Diversity, diligently practised, was an HR crusade, but everyone looked alike to Ravi. On the train, in the streets, there were so many different kinds of faces—it was one of the wonders of Sydney. But at Ramsay, China, Ireland, Hungary, Lebanon had brought forth identically clear eyes and gleaming hair. Ravi saw energy and confidence and post-industrial track lighting. There was nowhere to hide. People spoke kindly, and he had difficulty following them. What did *Give it a burl* mean? The girl who sat across from him swivelled her chair to ask, 'Are you a Tamil?' and 'So when exactly did you leave the detention centre?' Her hair and her eyes were bright brown shot with gold. Ravi willed himself not to stare. Even her name was beautiful: Crystal Bowles.

•

Tyler had protested, 'A Sri Lankan site in the Nineties? No way would he have the skills.'

'A trainee,' said Damo. 'He'd save you money.'

That was cunning. It was Sunday night, the first time they'd seen each other that weekend because Tyler had been working on budgets. He hesitated: the kind of small, fatal mistake to which Tyler was prone.

'His case has gone to review.' Damo improvised: 'A job at Ramsay could work in his favour, swing the decision.'

Tyler rallied. 'There's travel experience. That's crucial at Ramsay. A designer has to know where the user's coming from.'

'Ravi's travelled around Sri Lanka.'

'He's local. It's different for foreigners.'

'Exactly. He'd provide a fresh point of view.'

Tyler changed direction, another error. 'There's a freeze on new hires.'

'Only permanent ones.' The relationship was still in that phase when Damo and Tyler actually listened to each other's complaints about work. 'You could offer him a contract,' said Damo. He also pointed out that from one postal delivery to the next, Ravi could find himself with twenty-eight days notice to leave the country. 'Which is the likely scenario. So it's not like he's going to be on your payroll for too long.'

Later he said, 'A refugee, Tyler. You could change his life.' And, 'It would be a visionary thing to do.'

It was *visionary* that affected Tyler, loosed the tinsel-twirl of possibility in his mind.

Back in the day, newly recruited to head up IT at Ramsay, Tyler had worn cargo pants and held grown managers spellbound. He had bounced a little on his exercise ball, incandescent with can-do. He sprinkled words like magic dust: electronic editions, fully searchable knowledge bases, intranets, interactivity. Drifting through the minds of his listeners, these terms left little impression but glittered with efficiency and profit. They sparkled with the promise that all who heeded them would be carried along into the digital age. Even the newcomer's name suggested a spell: Tyler Dean, an incantation that worked backwards and forwards. It sounded American: youthful, state-of-the-art, *now*. No one wanted to be left behind in the old century, as has-been as analogue. Success was a god with a single profile, and it wasn't directed at the past.

Back in the day was before dot-coms mutated into dot-bombs, it was before 9/11. It was before the global sales dive, before a ruinous Ramsay e-venture into smart cards for travellers. Tyler still had his soul patch and his place on the management team, but the glamour had gone. Thoughts strayed when he addressed meetings. IT was back where it had once been, a service division to the rest of the company. Tyler would have liked to *move on*. He had been four years at Ramsay and should have left after three. He had heard vaguely, as he had heard of Machiavelli, that a career had once been considered a matter of long-term development. Tyler conceived of his as a series of short-term stays. He saw himself flowing freely from one organisation to another, changing tactics and style as required—only losers got stuck. But the headhunters who didn't answer his emails knew that the market was oversupplied with start-up whiz-kids who'd left it too late to cash in their stock options.

At twenty-eight, Tyler Dean was *history*.

But in the modern workplace, flexibility was a watchword. Solidarity with refugees was cool. Taking Ravi on, equipping him with marketable skills: it would be a first at Ramsay. A strategic staircase was taking shape. It was smarts plus heart. It ticked boxes. Tyler was updating his CV, cascading his vision through the ranks.

He said, 'Let me think about it.'

Damo kissed him.

The Wayback Machine preserved webpages over time, offering a record of the digital past. A few days after his conversation with Damo, Tyler used it to reach the archived site of a university in Sri Lanka. Just as he'd expected: frames, static content, low interactivity. Where was the call to action? To think there had been a time when the whole web was like this! Tyler took note of the clashing typefaces, the untidy navigation, the amount of white space on the pages. He thought, Dead links!

It was hilarious, really. At the same time . . . it was sort of great. It was just a few years old and it was pioneering. These guys had been cowboys, making up the web as they went along. Gotta love that, thought Tyler Dean.

In his gap year, Tyler had travelled to Zimbabwe. In the company of a cousin, he visited his family's old farm. There was an avenue, a mile long, of flame trees and jacarandas. Tyler had always believed that he had forgotten everything about the first three years of his life. Then he saw the trees.

When they set off again after lunch, the cousin stopped in a town to pick up some fertiliser. A dusty eucalypt was all elbows on the far side of the street. On the farm, the trees were in flower. Tyler's life stretched before him like the view from his cousin's veranda in the morning. It was only the way back that was barred, electric with wrongdoing, patrolled by dogs with angry faces. His cousin drove with a handgun in her glovebox. If he had been alone in the car, Tyler might have cried.

He got out and wandered along the street, looking for something to photograph. He came to a recreation centre, identified by a sign above the door, and went in. The hall housed a concrete stage and a table-tennis table. Tyler, navigating around the Sri Lankan website, found himself remembering that hall. He saw the breeze-block walls and the dust on the table. The net sagged, and so did the light. It revealed the figure who had come to greet him: Dean Tyler, a double, a visitant, a there-but-for-the-grace. On Tyler's screen an open stairway climbed into a colourwashed building, and that shade of yellow, too, was something he had seen. Tyler was arrogant or kind or blundering enough to imagine that he knew what Ravi had been up against, designing that site. He went into his email and began composing a message to HR.

Crystal Bowles glided into Tyler's office. When he took out his earbuds, she said, 'Guess what I just found out about Ravi?'

'Hi, Crystal.'

'He's never been in a detention centre!'

'Yeah, cool.'

'You said he was a refugee. *He* says he's a refugee. So how come he wasn't locked up?'

'Have you asked him?'

'Didn't you see that email HR sent round before he started? About appropriate conduct with a refugee?' Conscious of virtue, Crystal said, 'I've been approaching Ravi sensitively and respecting his right not to talk about what he's been through.'

'Boat people get locked up.' Tyler had Damo's explanation by heart. 'Plane people like Ravi come in on a visa, so they live in the community while their applications are being processed. It's part of the government's strategy to distinguish between the two groups. To boost their line that boat people can be treated like shit.'

During the weeks of the restructure, Tyler had scarcely slept. In management meetings, the phrases that rang around the table were *re-engineering* and *scaling back*. Tyler saw cells in a spreadsheet vanish with a mouse-click: the process was painless, efficient, clean. Then Clifford Ferrier had to say, 'What this means is people are going to lose their jobs.' The other faces in the room instructed Tyler in what he felt: a pure, consuming hatred for Cliff.

Tyler slashed jobs, suffered, learned whose skin he would always put first. He called together those who were going from IT. 'You're a great bunch of people. You've been responsible for the most creative, inspirational, even provocative work to come out of Ramsay.' When he began to cry, some of his victims wept with him. They had been spared war, starvation, plague, but knowledge of those ancestral catastrophes was coded into their DNA; what was novel and terrible was mundane disaster. Each felt personally to blame. They should have gained new, indispensable skills or at least *moved on* sooner—after all, wasn't it their *love of travel* that had brought them to Ramsay? Dave Horden, the webmaster, spoke up on behalf of everyone: 'Dude, thanks for sharing our pain.'

Tyler consoled himself with the thought that he had hung on to a couple of *really great people*. Also Crystal. She had finished her training shortly before the restructure, she cost less than anyone else in the e-zone, she was smart, it had made sense to keep her. Nadine Flanagan, who had replaced Dave, preferred email to talking, so Tyler had become the screen on which Crystal projected her effects. These days he thought of her as a punishment. She was saying, 'So Ravi's definitely a refugee? Even though he wasn't locked up?'

'Would it've been better if he'd been locked up?'

'I'm just saying,' said Crystal Bowles.

Laura, 2003

THE KOREANS WERE PLAYING CARLA Bruni again. Robyn said, 'I'm seriously going to bring them a new CD next time.' She shook out her napkin and inspected Laura. 'You're looking indecently good. Love that shirt.'

It was a delectable grape-green with concave buttons of opalescent shell. Laura was buying a lot of clothes, spending Saturdays checking out the little designer places in Surry Hills, the gear in Oxford Street. She had lost weight. Her hair was different, too. It was a matter of camouflage, concluded Robyn, noting the uniform darkness of Laura's head. There wasn't a female on the North Shore under the age of eighty with grey hair, and like any good tourist, Laura Fraser was blending in.

Robyn said, 'Looks like this lunchtime exercise plan's suiting you. Where do you walk? Should I come with you, maybe?'

There was friendship's ever-present invitation to confide. And beyond that, Laura's wish to proclaim the miracle, to shout the holy syllables of Paul Hinkel's name.

Fortunately, seafood hotpots intervened. 'Maybe when I get back from Vietnam,' went on Robyn. 'You know what it's like when you've got holidays coming up. I've got back-to-back meetings between now and then.'

'How long are you going for?'

'A week.' Robyn repeated, 'You know what it's like.'

Laura did: you dreamed of working at Ramsay because you loved travel. You had one of those passports with the extra pages, your gap year had turned into three. Asked where you would like to go next, you answered, Away. It was the reason they hired you. Thereafter, what you knew of travel was your daily commute.

'How's it all going with Ferdy?' asked Laura. Because Robyn, once unfailingly upbeat, had seemed dispirited of late.

'Yeah, good.' Robyn's chopsticks grasped a cube of white flesh. Lifting it required an effort, like the discretion she was tired of practising. She longed to tell someone what had happened after the conference party, but Laura was rising from the table. She fled from the restaurant, her face a consternation. Robyn twisted to look out of the window, but there was only the lunch-hour street.

A waitress was asking if everything was okay.

Laura, returning, apologised. She sat, rather heavily, and said, 'This kid, I've seen him before. Wandering about on his own but he's not that old. It's weird.'

'School holidays,' said Robyn. 'Lots of short people with time on their hands. You sure he was alone?'

Laura could only resume her hotpot. Eventually remembering, 'Were you saying something before?'

She'd forgotten, said Robyn, it couldn't have been important.

•

Laura volunteered to email the senior cartographers about *a few editorial issues*. She did so, then sent a PS to Paul for him alone.

When they next met, he told her that he didn't trust in-house email. 'The techies monitor it.'

'Really?'

'It happens everywhere. In case some creep's downloading kiddie porn on a company computer.' There had been a guy he'd worked with in the public service. The cops were called in.

She hadn't known that Paul was ex-public service. What she knew of him was as intimate and as superficial as skin. Of facts, there were these: Paul Hinkel surfed whenever he could and was *into photography*. He loved Thai food but disliked fish. A long time ago, he had worn a surplice and sung in a cathedral. His daughter was called Anouk. His father's people had come to Sydney from Rotterdam. He suffered from hay fever, each sneeze an explosion. When Laura learned that he had spent almost two years in London, their histories drew together. He had worked as a barman in Shepherd's Bush; there had been a time when she had passed that pub almost every day. Entwined, they recalled Cool Britannia. (Oh, Britpop days of our youth! Truly, was there anyone in big spectacles more major than Jarvis Cocker circa 1995?) They were pretty sure they'd gone to the same Elastica concert at the Hammersmith Palais; he ta-tummed a riff from 'Stutter'. They might have travelled on the same train, stood within feet of each other. *London* became their repository of might-have-been. 'If I'd seen you then,' he would say and cover her mouth with his. The sentence remained unfinished, the consequence at once all-encompassing and vague.

At saner intervals, Laura could see that the only future his tenderness implied was retrospective. Yet on ferries, at the checkout, in her eyrie above the flexing harbour, geography dissolved—Laura was rushing upstairs to the room she shared with Paul Hinkel in

Ladbroke Grove. They went travelling together. In a bar in Berlin, they toasted each other in a mirror. They picked through jackets in a flea market in Bucharest. In a mall in Pasadena, they agreed that the Nineties were pastel-hued, smelled of Obsession and tasted of Starbucks. In the shadow of a domed palace in Jaipur, they bought a mirror-worked coverlet for their bed.

Thus Laura substituted fantasy for history—in fact, it wasn't just the past she remodelled but time itself. The scenarios she constructed belonged equally to once-upon-a-time and still-to-come, to *one day* and *back then*. The unwritten, endless letters she addressed to Paul Hinkel were more knowing. They revived what had taken place in the waratah-curtained room, and proposed inventive variations. Grammar, syntax, vocabulary remained steadfastly erotic, although straying on occasion into the more banal endearments. Beyond that, her sentences refused to progress.

If obliged to alter their arrangements, they would text each other. They shared a fondness for electronic gadgetry—he bought an iPod two days after she acquired hers. She enquired into his playlists so that she might download the same songs. He declared that the White Stripes were even more amazing than Coldplay. His iPod nuzzled her breasts, and 'Seven Nation Army' cascaded through her while he showered. He surprised her, too, with a taste for lush romanticism. At night, she would listen over and over to 'The Ship Song', to 'Ruby's Arms'. Her phone went everywhere with her, was switched on the instant the credits came up or the chairs scraped back, even though his texts were rare and of the *meeting delayed 30 mins* sort. He was the kind who reduced morality to caution, thought Laura. It was one of the sour, forensic insights that streaked across her mind, self-protective and useless. How perfectly texting was suited to adulterers, instant, private, as readily mastered as erased. This reflection was provoked by the sight of Quentin, who famously had once required a techie to point out the on button on his computer, in adroit manipulation of a Lilliputian keypad. Yet to associate anything that emanated from Quentin Husker with that communion in the waratah room was a form of sacrilege.

At work, a group email from Paul Hinkel contained an emoticon. Laura remembered that she had despised them—why? What a snob she was! Those little winks and smiles were charming. They enlivened her own messages now.

He mentioned that he had given Ravi Mendis, *a really nice guy*, a lift one evening. Laura was conscious of shame—although she felt enormous goodwill towards Ravi, she had never actually spoken to him. Now she made a point of saying, 'How's it going?' and beaming at him if their paths chanced to cross.

There was rugby talk around the water cooler. Why was Laura Fraser hanging about? Because the state team was called the Waratahs. Not that anyone had mentioned the Tahs. But the word shone unspoken in the air.

There came the thought: What will be left of this when it's over? She knew every inch of him but not his handwriting. She had no letters, no photographs, no gifts, not even any emails. There would be a handful of text messages, as anodyne as business, and a few schmaltzy tunes on her playlist. There would be the Visa statements that recorded her squandering on flowers and a motel. This was modern love: traceless, chilling. But *when it's over* was as empty of meaning as a faulty proposition in logic.

His phone rang as she was bending over him. He pulled away, located it, was stumbling, already flaccid, into the bathroom. He emerged and told her that he had to leave. His child, Anouk, was asthmatic and was having difficulty breathing. So Laura knew that, too. She knew that his thumbs were double-jointed and his parents divorced. It was like her late-night trawling of the internet: she learned a great many things that had no bearing on each other and were of unequal worth.

Sometimes Laura tried to account for it, this need, this infatuation, this . . . but she resisted the word 'love'. 'Lust' wasn't right either, although lust was inseparable from it. It was folly and it was clarity. One tiny part of her mind never lost sight of her original verdict on Paul Hinkel. But it was without importance.

At night, with the red star presiding over her vigils, Laura was inclined to ascribe Paul Hinkel to Theo Newman. Theo had offered a risk, she had refused it, he had died. So now it was necessary to persist: to accept adventure, to follow to the end of a path haunted by a corpse and the child he had proposed. The dead are called ghosts, but what name could she assign to the never-were? By day, however, what happened in the waratah room was sufficient unto itself, unghosted. It was something to look forward to, it excited—as work didn't—with hazards and thrills. And why look further than the animation of a biological clock? But that was simplistic. What Laura finally settled for was merely simple: *Parce que c'était lui, parce que c'était moi.* It was no reason, the only one.

On a Saturday morning in Blues Point Road, she came face to face with Alice Merton. Alice was attended by a large golden beast. She was walking her parents' retriever while they were on holiday—as it happened, she was on her way to visit Carlo and Laura, she explained. But Carlo wasn't there, Laura told her, Rosalba had carried him off as usual. She invited Alice to brunch in a cafe, instead. The retriever, who loved indiscriminately, laid his head against Laura's knees and pressed.

The sight of Alice was especially welcome that morning. Of late, Laura had tended to neglect her duties on the roof. Working back meant coming home too tired to think about gardening. On Saturday, she shopped for clothes, she dawdled and dreamed. There was often a film or a meal with Robyn and Ferdy. On Sunday, Laura rose late. Soon it would be time to go down to Carlo. Meanwhile, she made half-hearted passes with secateurs or hose.

Carlo took his time over eating. Laura would grow impatient. She was down there for one reason only, and *tortellini boscaiola* didn't come into it. She stuffed plates any old how into the dishwasher's orthodontic maw. In the rose-red room, she gulped coffee, positioned the needle with brutal precision. But on the couch, Carlo was still taking his time. Laura made an effort, stroking and arranging herself with extravagant, baroque gestures. If she closed her eyes, she could almost believe that the gaze she nourished was Paul Hinkel's. But the scent of the rotting lilies intruded. The aria ended and another began. Even the tenor strained, even the glide of the needle was effortful.

One day Carlo said, '*Non posso.*'

Laura was willing to help—it was her declaration of independence from Paul Hinkel. But he was at hand while she caressed Carlo, their invisible third. She felt his disgust and his excitement. When she gathered her clothes and left, it was Paul's face, its blurring at the moment of climax, that followed her.

The rain that drenched the city at night in winter, the summer downpours: of late, these had abated. Elsewhere, the continent might wither, its ancient skin split. But this was Sydney! It oozed damp, it was made of water! How could the dams be down by a third? Drought, a disease that had once remained politely out of sight, was spreading to the face and neck. Carlo said, 'You no forget mulch?' Pea straw lay thick among his vegetables. There was another bale of it in the shed at the back, delivered by the friend who made his wine. 'You take upstairs.' There was no need, called

Laura, rushing for the ferry, she had already mulched everything up there.

That was true. But she had put down the straw in autumn and failed to renew it in spring. On the Saturday that brought Alice Merton, Laura had spotted a lifeless gardenia on the roof. She waited until the sound of Rosalba's car faded, then uprooted the crisp brown shrub, emptied the planter of compacted potting mix, attacked the terracotta with a hammer. She broke up the soil and scattered it about. Snipped into sections, her floral victim vanished into the compost. A plastic bag concealed the pieces of clay. Minutes before spotting Alice, Laura had dropped it into a municipal bin.

While envisaging these actions, while carrying them out, she had known that Carlo would forgive her at once if she confessed. Like anything that mattered, gardening was inseparable from losses. And a single gardenia! A dozen remained. But Laura knew she could never tell Carlo. The shame that burned if she allowed it oxygen had little to do with shrivelled leaves. It was fuelled by the clinical determination, untainted by tenderness, that had come to govern her in the rose-red room. These days she undressed for Carlo as if lashing him. To admit to the lesser dereliction was, in some obscure yet unmistakable way, to own to the other.

As she bashed the earth-stained planter, one part of her mind writhed. Another shrugged: why waste time beating herself up about an old man and his affairs? But on meeting Alice, that clear young face, Laura was overwhelmed by what she had done. So it was crucial to ply the girl with food, to heap her with muffins and love.

Alice sipped guava juice, spoke of university, spoke of films. Light floated in her hair, and homemade muesli with quinoa was set before her by an appreciative waiter. She was writing a screenplay, Alice confided. What she actually longed to divulge was the brilliance of the man she would receive that afternoon. He lectured her in Communications, so the affair was conducted in secret. A woman hovered in the background, and a child from an old marriage, but Alice had seen her new love tremble when she undressed. Laura Fraser sliced open a Florentine egg, and Alice was compelled to speak of decisive choices. For what would have become of Carlo and Rosalba, she mused aloud, if they had married each other as planned?

It was news to Laura!

'They were, like, engaged. Then he met this princess. Just like in a book? It was the *coup de foudre*,' declared Alice, whose lover was French and made the most of it.

Carlo hadn't breathed a word, said Laura, somewhat miffed. All she knew was that Rosalba had married a stonemason who brought her to Australia, where he made a killing in wholesale fruit.

Oh, Carlo'd never said anything, it was Rosalba who'd come out with it, said Alice. 'When Mum did the extension on their house? Mum thinks Rosalba's really amazing. She left school at thirteen but she used to do the books for her husband. He was a creep, Mum says. Rosalba refused to go on wearing mourning for him. Some people still cross the street when they see her.'

The retriever, who had shown admirable patience, began to lick Laura's ankle. But she failed to understand and allowed the waiter to carry away her crusts.

Ravi, 2003

PAUL HINKEL HAD CRINKLY BROWN hair and crinkly brown eyes and he wasn't too tall—so many Australians loomed over Ravi like a tree. On a Sunday in spring, upstairs trains carried Ravi to a station where Paul was waiting. A short drive took them to the Hinkels' townhouse. As the car turned in to the driveway, the door opened. Paul's wife appeared at the top of the steps. She greeted Ravi with her head inclined and her palms joined.

Over lunch in the courtyard, the Hinkels told Ravi about their honeymoon in Sri Lanka. Lunch was marinated chicken breasts, Thai-style prawns, roast potatoes, an orange salad and a green one. The plates were large and white, the platters heaped. At the first mouthful, Paul said, 'Mmm-*mmm*!' and to Ravi, 'Martine's a brilliant cook.' It was a bright day, but the flats next door threw the courtyard into shadow. Against the only sunny wall rose a flat tree whose arms had been forced along wires; Ravi hadn't known that crucifixion could extend to the vegetable kingdom. Another peculiarity was the large garden bed with concrete sides raised six inches above the ground on which the table and chairs had been placed. It gave the impression that they were lunching on a grave. The design was loony, said Paul, they had intended to level the bed, break up the concrete and pave over the courtyard. But the baby had come early. This was by way of apology for the table, which shook despite wadded cardboard. Here and there, in the rectangle of grey earth on which it stood, a blade of grass struggled, or a weed.

A southerly arrived at the same time as whipped cream, and a chocolate and hazelnut cake. Glass doors led from the dark courtyard into a room that was dimmer still. In the galley kitchen at one end, Paul stacked the dishwasher. Martine went around switching on a heater and lamps. Then she sat on the couch with Ravi and turned the pages of a photograph album. The past reconfigured itself as scenery. Ravi saw a temple he knew, a stretch of little shops, the remains of a Dutch wall. A white-haired woman had strayed into a photo taken in the fish market: it was Mrs Anrado, Ravi realised with a little shock. He hadn't thought of his mother's old friend in years. Her guesthouse had flourished for a while, but she had borrowed heavily to establish it. When tourists fled, in the late Eighties, the bank was intransigent. Mrs Anrado lost her house with its bedrooms and hot water, and had to appeal to a brother. He allowed her to live in his kitchen and treated her like a servant—her teeth had fallen out, Ravi saw. He was conscious of comfort and warmth, and the clean smell of Martine's hair. She spoke softly, an innocent enthusiast, now and then touching her throat. Her oval nails were a pale, pretty pink. Paul moved about the kitchen, wiping surfaces with a sponge.

The doorbell commanded. 'That'll be Mum,' said Paul. When he came back, he was carrying a miniature replica of himself: 'This is Anouk.' Martine was already reaching for the child. The woman who had entered with Paul said, 'Hi, I'm Leonie,' and

'Oh, no need to get up,' and 'Can't stay long, I'm due at the gym.' She wore tracksuit pants, and a tight-fitting vest that showed her fibrous brown arms.

Martine returned the baby to Paul and passed into the kitchen. Standing at a bench, she began setting out white cups. Leonie's hair was as parched and yellow as grass in midsummer. She asked, 'Has Paul told you he's got ancestors on his father's side who were in Ceylon?' and 'Which detention centre were you in?' Her voice, too, was dry and blonde. Ravi thought of the cornflakes tipped into bowls at Banksia Gardens while Glory Warren cried, 'Snap! Crackle! Pop!' Something had changed in the room: the difference encompassed Leonie and the silky-haired child and the music of teaspoons, but had angles Ravi couldn't measure.

Leonie was saying that for two years she had visited a Tamil asylum-seeker at Villawood. 'Nasedan? No, Nadesan, that's it. Lovely guy. Everyone called him Neddy. Have you ever met him?' She also said, 'I'm a librarian. When Paul was a little boy, he used to tell everyone that his mum was a lesbian.' Her smile was sparkling and wide. It was difficult to believe that she had a son who was older than Ravi. Another thing Leonie mentioned was that before the divorce, she had owned an antique dresser carved from Ceylon ebony. Paul went to a shelf, and then to a different room, stepping over the gate at the foot of the stairs: he was looking for the photo that would prove it.

An electric jug began to rattle in the kitchen, letting off steam. The baby clambered off the couch and staggered about, then sat down all at once and opened her eyes wide at her cleverness. Ravi gathered her onto his lap. She had been premature, explained Leonie, and wasn't really slow for her age at all. Ravi would have liked to have gone on sitting there forever, the baby smiling and touching his face, while Leonie said, 'Sri Lankans are so gentle,' and the past, sectioned into 4x6 rectangles and protected with plastic, could be safely shut up in a book.

Fear was rising like water in Martine Hinkel as she tilted the jug over the pot. Teaspoons had provoked it. Long ago, people she loved had taught her that black skin harbours germs. No one, learning what Martine's life had been like, would have held her responsible for it. But the past was a trinket she kept locked, lied about, wore always around her neck. One of the things that lay twisted inside was love; she would never betray it to the light. The rest, Martine wanted to believe, had withered to dust. In Asia, in Africa, dark children had enchanted her. But that was before she had a child of her own. Just now, she had been arranging teacups on a tray when time had flashed forward. It was the following morning, or the one after that, and Anouk opened wide, as Mummy requested, to receive a morsel of soft egg. *Into that trusting mouth went the teaspoon that Ravi had touched.* Reason said, Dishwasher, Sterilisation, and, loudest of all, You are vile, you are mad. But Martine shivered in a shadow she couldn't outrun. The baby was patting Ravi's cheek, but that was of no importance—what menaced was the conjunction of mouth and spoon. Did the bibbed child in Martine's vision come from the future or the past? Her hand flew to her throat, checking that something was in place.

Leonie said, 'How's that tea coming along, love? I've got five minutes.'

Martine's fingers found what she needed at the back of a drawer. Coming forward with the tray, she looked for a way around Paul. The lines of a toaster, the heft of a jug: things like that mattered to her husband. They had sat on floor cushions until they could afford the couch he had chosen. There had been chopsticks or tinny two-dollar-shop knives until the desired canteen came up at a Peter's of Kensington sale. Distributing cups, positioning the sugar bowl,

Martine knew that Paul had spotted the anomaly. On a leather ottoman at Ravi's feet, she murmured, 'This is a souvenir from Alice Springs, I thought you might like to keep it after you've stirred your tea, a dingo's an Australian icon?' The baby said, *mmm-mmm-mmm*, leaning out from Ravi's lap. He exchanged her for a spoon.

Ravi, 2003

HE HAD NEVER MET ANYONE like Crystal Bowles. He had never seen anything like the streaky brown and gold of her hair. She wore it in pigtails or piled carelessly on her head. When they were both facing their screens, Ravi could study it or the solid column of her neck. He never saw her without thinking of his favourite supermarket dessert: caramel, cream and chocolate packed into plastic and individually served. She wore tiny skirts over jeans. On a cold morning, she arrived in a leopard-skin coat. It seemed the height of luxury to Ravi, who had no idea that the leopard had been made in China. Under this glamorous garment, a much-washed green T-shirt asked *Do I Look Like A People Person?* Ravi had heard Crystal say that she shopped for clothes at Vinnies. He couldn't understand why a girl like that would rummage through the cast-off garments of strangers. She often called in sick. Ravi felt sure that the germs trapped in the seams of her clothes were exacting their toll.

He was sent on a short training course in web design held in the city. Images faded or flared as a cursor moved over them: the first online tutorial was in creating rollovers. When they broke for coffee, a boy standing near Ravi remarked, 'Should be called a glideover. It's not like anything actually rolls.' Ravi thought of the older model of mouse with a hard rubber ball embedded in its base. He could remember the shape of it in his hand, and blowing on the ball to free it of dust. The boy wrinkled his nose. 'Oh, right. Interesting.' Ravi felt old.

Work was lessons, parables, mysteries. Nadine Flanagan, the webmaster, sent Ravi an email called *feedback. hi ravi, it would be great to hear your own ideas in meetings. we're proactive players in the e-zone!* Ravi looked up 'proactive' in his online dictionary. In the weekly think-tank sessions, he listened with interest to everything his colleagues said. If asked what he thought, he would agree with either Nadine or Will Abrahams, the unit's design guru. That had seemed natural, courteous, safe. Everyone had more experience and was senior to him. Ravi rarely left his desk, never made or received personal calls, completed his set tasks in the allotted time. He looked across at Crystal. She was asking her phone, 'So did Adam get kissed in the end?' There was a pleasant, rasping quality to her voice. She was wearing long grey socks, bronze stiletto sandals, a short blue dress. Light caught the clear plastic combs in her hair.

He took a cigarette from the pack in his drawer and made his way across the office. Someone or other was always coming or going at Ramsay, to and from the stationery cupboard or a meeting room, out to the car park, where they could smoke. People on the move often carried a phone, grabbing the opportunity to make a call. Down the stairs they went and up, in and out of the photocopying room or the kitchen. Sometimes his workplace looked to Ravi like one of those hand-held labyrinths contained in plastic in which a tiny silver ball can be set rolling. That was an idea of his own, but he could see that it wouldn't do.

A terrace of narrow houses backed onto the car park. They sheltered small businesses: a barber, a Chinese herbalist, an artists' co-op. At the bottom of the barber's yard, a crooked hibiscus rose above the fence. On the Ramsay side, the lower branches had been lopped off to ensure safe passage for the trucks making deliveries to the warehouse. Long strands of a creeper, too, hung over the palings. Against its green vigour, the hibiscus looked arthritic. But one morning each grey twig flaunted a swirl of red silk. Now the maimed glory of the hibiscus spoke to Ravi of *a different thing*. Eventually, he realised that it was twinned with the old sideboard in the blue house. Whenever he came out to have a cigarette, the first thing he looked for was the tree.

Every time he told Hana about something that had surprised him at Ramsay, she would say, 'Oh, Australians!' She told Ravi that when her brother first came to Sydney, he had worked as an assistant to a house painter. There was far more work than the two men could handle. 'The first thing Australians do when they buy a house is change it. Why don't they just buy a house they like?'

She would like to rent a house, said Hana, so that her daughter would have a garden to play in. But the exams that would authorise Abebe to practise accountancy were more than a year away. Until then, Hana hoped that the rent on their flat wouldn't rise. It gave on to the parking area at the front of the orange-brick block. The main room contained a sofa bed where Abebe slept, a TV, a computer, a table at which the family worked and ate. At one end of the room was a small kitchen; at the other, the door to the bedroom that Tarik and Hana shared. Ravi thought of the child riding her scooter up and down the concrete side passage. The rubbish bins were kept there. 'That's another thing about

Australians,' remarked Hana. 'They think everyone in Africa lives in a mud hut.'

This conversation was taking place, not without difficulty, in the middle of a carnival crowd. A street had been pedestrianised and lined with stalls for a Spring Festival. There was a Cook Islands Cultural Association, an Islamic Women's Aid Agency, a police recruiting booth. Rice-paper rolls tempted, along with Turkish pancakes, Malaysian noodles, Lebanese pastries, Indian sweets.

Near the first stalls, Abebe had led Tarik away. When Ravi next saw the child, by a stage where four West Africans were setting up their drums, she was nibbling a pink cloud. Then the crowd bellied and she vanished again. Ravi never questioned or teased Tarik, remembering how, as a child, he had resented the intrusiveness of adults. But now he bought a box of honeyed sweets that he pressed on Hana. That was his strategy, to arrive with chocolates or little cakes, a gift that didn't single out Tarik but had been chosen with her in mind.

Hana stopped to examine a display of shoes. She picked up a blue ballet slipper with a beige and blue bow and turned it over to look at the sole. She turned it over again and slipped it onto her hand. She held the shoe up, then put it down and turned away looking bored. They were almost at the end of the street, and Ravi calculated that he had seen no more than a dozen white faces. One of them belonged to the local MP, who was handing out unwanted flyers, baring his teeth. The banner over his head proclaimed that *Richard Madison Supports Diversity*. Hana said, 'He looks like he's hoping someone will give him a medal for it.' She paused before a dispiriting array of cheap homewares and cosmetics offered by Ethiopian Community Aid. Hana exchanged a few words with the women behind the table and came away with a scented candle. Tucking it into her bag, she told Ravi, 'At home, I'd never speak to people like that.'

Children were everywhere: sturdy babies in strollers, boys and girls wheedling treats from a parent or weaving independently through the crowd. Tarik appeared, leading Abebe. 'Mum, see what I got?' The child's face had been painted with pink and orange petals. She blew a soap bubble at her mother through a plastic loop. 'Very clever,' said Hana, not as if she meant it. Tarik began dancing up and down on the spot, making an irritating noise with her lips pressed tight. Abebe placed his hand on her shoulder and said, 'Shall we meet back at the car in half an hour?' He looked from Ravi to Hana. His expression was interrogative but not only that; it looked to Ravi as if Abebe had reached a conclusion. On their outings, he often found a reason to go off with Tarik, leaving Ravi and Hana together. Ravi had read this as a tactic for sparing mother and daughter from each other. Now he wasn't sure.

Hana drew the candle from her bag and held it out to Tarik. 'Yuk!' said Tarik. 'Yuk and double yuk to you,' replied Hana. 'A million billion trillion yuks to you!' 'Go and put your head in a bag!' Hana and her child had the same long cheeks and sharp nose. They were dressed alike, too, in windcheaters and jeans. Ravi was thinking that Hana always wore that type of thing, when he understood what he found disturbing about Crystal Bowles: her clothes didn't go together. They formed a sentence whose parts were individually alluring but made up a grammar that bewildered. In meetings, the way Crystal had written up a destination was often admired. She whipped up airy marvels from a stodge of facts: 'Be Amazed By History!' It was *really creative*. Studying one of her articles after he had returned to his desk, Ravi realised that it accorded equal weight to a civil war and an anecdote about an emperor's horse. He found it unsettling in the same way as stilettos worn with socks.

Hana had mentioned that as a child she had spent long months in bed. 'There was something wrong with my heart.' From time to time, it still beat irregularly. There were days when she wore a monitor; Ravi had seen the wire taped down near her collarbone. Hana's fingers often went to that spot. The gesture was an invalid's, plaintive and fussy. Once, as Ravi looked on, that beautiful, bony hand found its way to Tarik's arm. A faraway look came over Hana's face as she pinched up the flesh under her fingers. The child sat wide-eyed, faintly smirking, still.

On weekends, Sydney waited. A magical bus route wound east, attended by the shimmer of bays. Ravi saw an image from a book: sandstone shaped into arches and towers and piled on a hill. Set against clouds, the convent? school? hallucination? was charged with prophecy and haunting. Then the bus had left it behind and found its way to the sea. Sometimes it seemed to Ravi that the city and all its inhabitants sought only that untrammelled blue terminus—the Australian mind slid towards it on shining rails. Even in Oxford Street, where the traffic dragged itself forward in agony, or moaned and tended its wounds, the fumes were edged with brine. Encouraged, the cars crept on, hoping for a glimpse of waves before expiring. Ocean delirium was pervasive. Parched inland suburbs boasted Beach roads, Bay streets, Seaview crescents. Ravi remembered his first Australian day, the boats dying of thirst in the streets.

One Sunday evening, he found himself in a neighbourhood where people wore leather, tattoos, an arc of studs along the brow. A man with long silver hair glided past a wellness centre on a skateboard. Distracted by the spectacle of two women kissing, Ravi almost collided with a third. Robyn Orr said, 'Oh—*hi*, Ravi.' Her glasses were framed in the same bright red as the building from which she had emerged. She said, 'I live just around the corner, this place is really convenient.' A broad-shouldered form against the long perspective of the street, Robyn gave off a kind of brilliance: her glasses, the metallic clips in her hair. This glitter was also a projection of the power she wielded at Ramsay. She might have stepped from a spacecraft dispatched by a superior civilisation. At the thought, Ravi glanced at the red building behind her and saw that it was a Chinese restaurant. Robyn said, 'Actually, Mao's like a brand name now?'

These days, Ravi examined the west of Sydney with an eye tutored by the luxuriance of other quarters. He saw that the hills flattened out there and potholes appeared. Even the climate was distinctive: the west was breezeless and hot—the promise of the sea had been withdrawn. In compensation, showrooms grew larger. They lured with novel galaxies: Sleep World, Carpet World. The suburbs streamed towards the mountains bearing a cargo of saris, *pho*, Korean pickles, Iranian raisins, taxation advice in Mandarin, wines from Portugal, headscarved grandmothers, the purple flesh of ritually slaughtered goats. Thus the known world conspired to offer a reprieve from Australia. Ravi might have been back in Hungry Jack's at Central. In the west, too, people came from everywhere to consume, snatch a bargain, sink into dreams. They pushed strollers before them, trundling their vigorous, greedy, Australian children into the future.

Ravi consulted the Ramsay guide to Sydney. Surf, museums, sandstone passed in review. He flipped to the section called 'Secret Sydney'. It provided directions to a nudist beach, a street of polychrome-brick mansions, a gay cabaret, a cafe that never closed. When Nadine called for ideas at the next e-zone meeting, Ravi spoke up. He had noticed, he said, that the guide to Sydney made no reference to the city's west. Why not feature this neglected region on the web? It was—he brought out the Ramsay idiom with nonchalant pride—*off the beaten track*.

Crystal shot a look all round, then dropped her gaze over her coffee. Some of her smile had come off on her cup. Obliged to respond, Nadine said, 'Okay, so what would you list as attractions in the west?'

'Fat people,' intervened Crystal. 'And that hotel in Milperra where there was that bikie massacre.'

Suggestions poured forth. Art Greco houses. Lebanese gangs. A world-class Kmart. Heritage fibro. Not to mention brick venereal. When everyone had finished laughing, Nadine was still looking at Ravi. All he had in mind were the minglings and partings of a shoving, kaleidoscopic crowd. But it was as multiple and hard to take hold of as life itself. He fumbled about in the whirligig and came up with, 'A lot of different people live there.'

Nadine Flanagan's face grew whiter than a screen. Meetings were mountains; Nadine toiled upwards in boots that bit. But she strove always for fairness or at least logic. Ravi was a trainee, he needed training. It was her duty to explain that visitors to Sydney—like travellers anywhere—were in search of the iconic. She rattled off the trinity: Bondi, the opera house, the bridge. 'Typical places where people hang.'

Ravi was enlightened. 'Westfield Shopping Centre in Burwood.'

Nadine's armpits turned damp. She managed to say, 'Typical but not . . . ordinary.' Crystal arranged her face to fit the sentence in her mind: *She controlled herself, but laughter played about her lips*.

Ravi had the impression that anything might happen next; events at Ramsay often found him in mid-air. But Will Abrahams observed that Ravi had a point, the Sydney guide was hopelessly white bread. It was decided that Crystal would write up Cabramatta as a destination. In time, 'Saigon in Sydney' was published on the web. *Ho Chi Minh and Buddha, two pretty cool guys, meet 30 km west of the CBD* . . . Crystal swivelled her chair to inform Ravi that

Cabramatta station was known as Smack Express. 'When some Swede or Japanese goes and gets killed there, will that be typical? Or just ordinary?'

Ravi asked where Crystal lived. 'Bronte. If you're more than five minutes from the beach, you might as well live in Melbourne.' She stretched out her legs, flexed her straight toes. She was wearing a lace shift, a chunky cardigan and rubber slippers called Havaianas. Ravi and she admired her feet: two flawless little golden animals. Crystal said, 'It's a lifestyle thing.'

Laura, 2003

THE THREAT OF CHRISTMAS BROUGHT a summons from the anaesthetist. Not to the feast itself, for Portsea was a sacred ritual. But to drinks on New Year's Eve. Afterwards, Donald Fraser and his wife had competing invitations—from an embassy that was showing minor royals in captivity, and an orthopaedic surgeon with a yacht—so dinner was out of the question. But a family had to get together sometime.

This assertion made such a clang over the phone that it precluded further conversation.

Over the years in Bellevue Hill, the dining room had been made over as a gym, the terrace revisioned as casual dining, the outside ordered in, the inside shoved out, every vanity cantilevered, every counter Carrara-ed, the spare room conquered by landscapers, the jacaranda vanquished by architects, the kitchen revolutionised with an ensuite, the porch upcycled with underfloor heating, the living spaces compelled to flow, the study repurposed as a plunge pool, the basement revealed as a wine cellar, the Rottweiler converted to ashes, a car stacker installed in the garage, until finally, when the house was perfectly luxe, and painted throughout in Lubyanka with the wow factor supplied by feature walls in Goanna Moderne, it was fit only to set a record at auction, and the Frasers downsized to a penthouse at Darling Point.

Where Laura, proffering crimson mallets of protea as if they might tenderise the moment, *mwa, mwa*-ed at the appointed hour. She crossed the living room as commanded, a journey of several minutes, to admire The View. This was reduced by twenty-one floors of steel and reinforced concrete to a scale model of itself. Laura contemplated the iconic sights: a midden of white shells, a toytown arch spanning a blue puddle. The value these diminished splendours added was laid out for her delectation along with the *amuse-bouches*.

There was a tripod-mounted telescope on the terrace. With his eye to it, Donald Fraser stood and searched the horizon, as he did for hours every day, and was reluctantly persuaded to turn his gaze onto his daughter.

Who was different, the hair at least. Something flashed in her face, and Donald saw his wife—the real one, the dead one—signalling to him. She, too, had been in the habit of doing things to her hair. Donald's mind sought and closed around a word: backcombed. Laura advanced, and he realised that the suggestion of snout would always hover. He was resigned to it now—as to so much else—and succumbed to her embrace.

Cameron arrived in the company of a woman. He guided her with a hand on her neck, propelling her before him across the parquet steppe in the manner of a criminal manipulating a human shield. It was the third time Laura had seen her brother since returning to Sydney. Accompanied, on each occasion, by a different female, he had addressed each one as Car. All his Cars had long, graceful necks, presumably to facilitate his grip.

He mashed Laura's hand, calling her 'Sis'. It was the same breezy style he had adopted at their previous meetings. She remained unconvinced. Only a week ago, her phone had cried out at three in the morning.

Car said, 'It's Catriona, actually.'

Cameron, who had released her neck, seized it again. She was pushed forward into The View.

The breeze refreshed ruthlessly on the terrace, so after an appropriate interval, everyone was shooed inside and ordered to Sit. Laura couldn't prevent a glance at the distant console where the Rottie was cradled in a cloisonné jar.

The anaesthetist called her chairs by names, like children—there was even a Ghost. They all took after her, being firm, clean-lined, impervious. Car was parked on Tulip, Cameron directed to 'take Egg'. Donald Fraser subsided into Barcelona and closed his eyes. Ghost, the favourite, was spared material buttocks, and Laura positioned at one charcoal extremity of a leather couch so long that the anaesthetist, at the other, appeared perspectivally shrunken.

Cameron told entertaining stories about people he had ruined in the line of duty.

Car said, 'Actually, the ruling might just as easily have gone the other way.' It was plain that if she outlasted the year it would only be by hours. She rotated her long neck to smile at Laura and enquire what she did.

While they were talking, the anaesthetist rose to leave the room. This she eventually achieved.

As soon as she was gone, Cameron leaned forward. 'Sis!' He drew a BlackBerry from his person. With one thick finger poised above it, 'What's the best number for reaching you?' he asked.

When Laura had recovered, 'Don't you have it?' she countered. Cameron's brazenness had to be a form of insanity. Yet beneath its polished thatch, his monumental façade was as bland as a bank.

Words rushed from him, their father and Car of no account. It was the difference, calculated in millions, between *the family home* and *this place* that was preoccupying Cameron. Why shouldn't the money come to him—and Sis, of course? 'Now, while we can enjoy it.' He wished Laura to broach the subject with *the old man*. He would *brief her* as to wording.

Laura remained mute and unseeing. She was picturing Quentin Husker, in a room like this one (only smaller, of course), constructing, for the benefit of women, fables that starred him as victim, dragon and knight. For the first time it occurred to her that Cameron, too, might be merely average—no worse than a type.

Her brother's voice rose. 'You could get away with anything. You were always his favourite!' It was a cry in which disappointments echoed up from a valley forty years deep. Laura accepted a card and agreed to call him, knowing that she never would. His judgment had come unhinged. It stopped at surfaces: took punishment for justice, silence for complicity, a chequebook for tenderness, profit for inheritance, the curve of a neck for submission. Car proved his miscalculation, helping herself to independent Mumm.

Donald Fraser, trapped in Barcelona, was afraid. *His wife's eyes were smaller than her rings.* He had noticed this quite recently; it coincided, more or less, with the move. The light hoovering over the terrace removed everything that wasn't essential. Now the realisation wouldn't leave him, panting in his ear. A few days earlier, he had thought, I am dogged by misfortune. Ever since, the Rottweiler, too, had followed him. The dog's crime, as it grew old, had been to fart unreasonably. What could Donald do but scan the sky? Once it had been a source of help, or so he seemed to recall.

Ushering Laura to the security lift, the anaesthetist came in close. The lift began its weary ascent, and she confided, as if referring to a particularly pernicious kind of weapon, that Cameron 'had ideas'. Laura was the sensible one, she declared. Neither woman referred to the change in Donald, although it was as inescapable as The View. His wife had diagnosed a minor stroke, but Donald refused to submit to tests. It was unscientific, therefore dangerous, but the anaesthetist couldn't help associating the telescope with his new stubbornness. She remembered that she had always been against it, picturing it in advance, a large black insect cluttering the pure sweep of the terrace. A word that meant something like *witnesses* had been in her mind when she consulted the calendar and picked up the phone to call the giant humans who passed as her stepchildren. For the same reason, her mother had been summoned to stay not long before the Rottie embarked on his last journey to the vet. Afterwards, the anaesthetist could say, 'You saw for yourself what he was like, the poor old boy—it just wasn't practical to have him around the house any longer.' When you married a man who was nineteen years older, you married a risk. Silently, Donald Fraser's wife renewed her annual vow. She had formulated it when she was fifteen, and kept it against parental expectation, professorial sarcasm, the bullying of surgeons: *I won't be a nurse*.

Ravi, 2004

PRIYA AND HER HUSBAND WANTED to sell the house that Carmel had left to her three children. Ravi saw strange faces at the windows, rooms ripped open, the mulberry on its knees before an axe. A desk occupied the wall that belonged to his mother's dressing-table. *He saw the house painted a different colour.* Varunika, too, didn't wish to sell. The argument went on in emails and phone calls, now intensifying, now fading.

It echoed another conflict. In the last months of his mother's life, she had shared her house with a servant. When Carmel was a girl, this woman had cooked for her parents. One day she was there on Carmel's doorstep. She was seventy-eight and had nowhere else to go.

Several weeks after his mother died, it occurred to Ravi to ask what had become of this servant. She had gone away, replied Priya. Where? Priya didn't know. She had her own cook who came in every day. In any case, the old woman was useless, she could barely see to pick stones out of lentils. Ravi answered this email with accusations. Then he called Priya. What he really wanted to say was that they should send the old woman some money. But his sister would scoff; the words stuck in his throat. Meanwhile, Priya shouted that it was easy to stay away and find fault.

Now, with no message of her own to accompany it, she forwarded an email from their mother's cousin, who lived in Sydney. It was an invitation to lunch. Ravi had avoided getting in touch with the Patternots. He had feared interrogation and tedium. Desmond and Merle would want to discuss the events that had brought him to Sydney. Then they would call up an age when everything was better in Sri Lanka—it had ended when they left.

Their nostalgia was what attracted Ravi now. The Patternots would talk about Carmel. Although Malini and Hiran were never far, what had seemed unimaginable had come to pass: days went by and Ravi didn't think of his mother. But the Patternots would recall a party or a scandal, and he would retrieve her. He would see his mother as she had been before they knew each other: hesitant or idly flirting, but in any case ignorant of the spotlit role in his life that was to come.

When picturing the Patternots' house, Ravi had seen a hallway and a room opening off it to the right. In fact he stepped straight from the door into the living room. It was full of people because it was Merle's birthday. Desmond went among his guests saying, 'This is Carmel's son.' An old lady told Ravi that she would have known him anywhere: 'You have the van Geyzel face.' Desmond said, 'Carmel Sansoni who married Suresh Mendis.' The old lady looked dashed but said, 'Never mind, darling, I recognised you anyway.'

A large brass tray in the shape of Sri Lanka glittered on a wall. Ravi was conscious of something he hadn't missed until then: a friendliness that wasn't personal but originated in family. However mistaken the identification, among these people he would always be someone's son. More guests arrived. No one sought Ravi out, but someone always turned to him in conversation or refilled his plate. There was no talk of the old days—all the gossip was of Sri Lankans in Sydney. The three Australians present, two girlfriends and a son-in-law, smiled to show that they were keeping up or at least didn't mind.

The new podiatrist at the health centre had complimented Merle on her English. 'What do they think we speak?' Her nephew worked in a shop where a recent immigrant from Sri Lanka was also employed. It was assumed that the two men would be friends, having a country in common. But the newcomer was a Tamil who ate rice with his fingers. Tania, the Patternots' daughter, said sharply, 'What does it matter, Mum? We're all Australians now.' The Australians in the room received this in silence. Ravi realised that Tania had that the wrong way around. What she meant was that in Australia, they were all merely Sri Lankan—Burgher, Sinhalese, surgeon, sweeper, it was all the same. Immigration was the triumph of geography over history. *At home, I'd never speak to people like that.*

The old lady told a filthy joke about John Howard and a kebab. Everyone laughed, but afterwards Desmond said, 'They are keeping the economy on a firm rein, isn't it?' Ravi took this to mean that the Patternots voted for the government rather than Labor. For that generation of emigrants, the Left was the torch applied to the thatch. It was mob rule, clothing coupons, the erosion of standards, rationed and stinking country rice: the rising flood from which they had run.

Tania was moving about the gathering with pieces of love cake nestled in a crumpled handkerchief made of red and white glass. She told Ravi that she had just returned from her first trip to Sri Lanka with her family. A fantastic holiday, you could buy anything you needed, and the kids just loved the hotels. Tania had steeled herself for misery, but the ceasefire had brought hordes of tourists—there was no poverty these days. Mind you, the pollution was another story. Desmond said, 'They went to Kernigalle and saw our old house. It's owned by some Muslims now. They showed the children around, let them take photos and everything.' 'It's not Kernigalle, Dad,' said Tania, 'it's Kurunegala.' Ravi remembered that his parents, too, had used the old name and been corrected by their children. Not only had a way of life gone, even the memory of it was passing. Each year, there were fewer who made the old mistakes.

Tania's husband, Jared, said that they had used the Ramsay guidebook on their holiday. 'It was pretty good on background, but the prices were totally out of date.' He asked Ravi how he could become a guidebook writer. 'I've always loved travelling, I reckon that'd be a great job.' Behind his back, his wife's eyes were expressive.

A lift home had been arranged to spare Ravi two changes of Sunday trains. A tea-planter in his youth, Desmond had worked for the railways in Sydney; he was retired now, but could still recite a rosary of timetables and routes. Merle had a parcel of lampries ready in a plastic bag. 'I always make extra. And two per gentleman.' The old lady took Ravi's face in both her hands and said, 'Darling, you are the spitting image of your mummy. I was in class with *her* mummy. What do you think of that?' Then she urged him to marry a nice Australian girl.

A compromise was reached: tenants were found for Carmel's house. Ravi gave his consent on condition that the old sideboard remained in place. He had returned Angie Segal's phone and bought himself an up-to-date model. In the efficient shorthand of SMSes, he discovered new ways of complaining to Varunika of Priya's heartlessness and greed.

LAURA, 2004

ON A THURSDAY IN FEBRUARY, Paul Hinkel told Laura that he was leaving for Bali on the weekend. It was offered casually, but he took refuge in the shower at once.

When he came out, Laura was ready. 'I think it's time you paid for this place for a change.'

In emergencies, he adopted the humorous tone of an adult obliged to negotiate with a perverse, engaging child. 'But you've already settled up, haven't you?'

'You can *settle up* with me, then.' Seeing, as she spoke, two unequal columns of figures that ended in red, something final and blazing.

'I've got a mortgage. It means a budget.'

'You're about to go to Bali!'

He said, in the same equable tone, that the holiday was budgeted for. Besides, it was only for seven nights. Laura noted that: not seven days, not a week, not the language in which humans reckoned, but terminology lifted from the special offers of travel agencies. But it was the thought of those tropical nights that lacerated.

Distress showed in her face: it was the signal that he was safe. Between her breasts was a flat, furry mole the size of a ten-cent coin. It was one of the places where he liked to kiss her. Straightening, he added that the prices in Bali had never recovered from the bombing. 'You can pick up these amazing deals.'

That Sunday, Carlo lowered the needle while the pasta was coming to the boil. It was a song he loved, a thick old record Drummond had discovered in the *mas* when he turned the mattress on the first fine day of a long-vanished spring. *Nuits de Chine, nuits câlines, nuits d'amour* . . . In France they had been too poor for a record player, so they had waited until Sydney, until the Archibald, to hear the song. But it belonged to cold, thick-walled rooms in a house the colour of dried leaves. Hugo Drummond clasped Carlo by the waist, and he hazarded a tricky half-turn around an occasional table. That was love, realised Laura, pouring herself a third glass of wine, it was good for years, you risked your bones for it, risked even the ravioli. '*Nuits d'ivresse*,' sang Carlo, oblivious to the timer, '*de tendresse*.' Santa Chiara, expert in spectral visions, looked on.

Seven nights passed, and Paul Hinkel came back to Laura. His neck, always furry, was now sunburned as well. When they were lying beside each other at last, she asked the question that was asked at Ramsay when you returned from a holiday: How was the book? Out of date, he replied, turning his head on the pillow to answer, taking it earnestly. He was incapable of doing otherwise. The room had been paid for, the condoms supplied, as usual, by Laura. Accounts might be left in abeyance but someone had to keep track of the numbers.

Nevertheless, Bali marked a change. The part of Laura that had remained aloof, that had never ceased watching and weighing Paul

Hinkel, was gaining strength. He had a wife. He was tight-fisted. The only books he read had titles like *127 Paths to Organizational Success* and *The Six Key Strategies of Excellence in Management*.

Tragedy touched their workplace. A freelance cartographer died in a car accident. Laura had barely known the girl, but she had worked for Paul's unit. He texted Laura to cancel Tuesday because it coincided with the funeral. She saw people return shaken from this event. On Thursday, wishing to console, she asked about the ceremony. 'It was really good,' he answered. 'Lots of managers went.'

What had driven him to approach her on that hotel terrace? wondered Laura. She was pretty certain that she represented his first affair. Perhaps she was an item on a checklist: the wild oats of Europe, the career back home, marriage, mortgage, fatherhood, adultery, the mandatory stopping places on the Ordinary Aussie Grand Tour, with renos, divorce and a coronary to follow.

Thoughts of his wife, until now only a moral unease that occasionally showed its teeth, became regular callers. She had probably been present at office parties, at the only Ramsay cricket match Laura had attended—but Laura was unable to place her. One memory, however, was vivid: *la famille* Hinkel, mother, father, baby in a sling, at the anti-war rally the previous year. Laura had been walking with a group that included Robyn, Ferdy and Jenny Williams I. Someone said, 'There's Paul.' Laura caught sight of him, the baby on his chest. She was faintly startled by his presence, having assumed that 'corporate obedience' was an acceptable synonym for 'right wing'. 'Good on him,' said Jenny, her tone hinting that Paul Hinkel had surprised her, too. The crowd shifted and engulfed him. But a woman with red hair had walked at his side. A thin woman, Laura recalled grimly, and not very tall. 'Petite' was the word. Laura tortured herself with it. To Robyn she said, in an absent-minded way, 'What's Paul's wife called? I'm hopeless with names.' Robyn thought, wrinkling her nose. 'Natalie? Something that begins with N. Or maybe T.' Laura knew better, having looked up the phone book: Hinkel, P and M. 'I know: Diane,' said Robyn firmly.

Learning that Paul had lived in Thirroul as a child, Laura mentioned D.H. Lawrence. He remembered that film, said Paul, the one with Peter O'Toole, but he'd had no idea that Lawrence had visited Australia. On the other hand, he was able to tell Laura that Brett Whiteley had died in Thirroul. History, for Paul Hinkel, began more or less with his birth. The boy who had sung in a cathedral knew the Inquisition as a Monty Python skit; he would have been hard pressed to say whether Galileo came before or after Gallipoli. But like many of their colleagues, he possessed a keen knowledge of brands. All her life Laura, poor fool, had bought things if they pleased her or answered a need. At Ramsay, she learned that a kettle was coveted if it was an Alessi, a stereo was desired if it was a Bose. Mystified, she heard, 'Love ya Campers!' and 'You're wasting your money if it's not a GHD.' Paul Hinkel was fluent in this argot, spoke with offhand familiarity of Gaggias and Cons. How he would love, he confided, strapping on his watch, to own a Patek Philippe. 'A what?' asked Laura. An expression that might have been pity crossed his face. She had no way of knowing that it mirrored hers when he had mentioned Peter O'Toole.

For a period of about ten days, Ramsay turned feverish with rumour and speculation, the collective lunacy that breaks out in every community now and then. Some, Laura among them, remained untouched, learning of the epidemic only when it had passed. Eventually, it would be confirmed that it had originated with Sammy Maroun and Mike Rosen in Sales, a conversation that must have gone something like this:

'You know the way place names are becoming brand names? Like Telstra Stadium, Optus Oval?'

'Yeah?'

'So I'm thinking the logical next step is for countries to change their names to global brands. Like instead of Ecuador or whatever, you could be called maybe Nike. It would cost the corporate sponsor a serious stash. Obviously. But it would be the naming-rights deal of the century.'

'You know, you could be on to something there. It's not like there's a lot of leverage to be had from naming yourself after an imaginary line.'

'Right. Whereas if you call yourself Nike, all your citizens get great sportswear. And there'd be the dollars as well. Obviously. Dude, it's gotta happen. I'll make a note of it in my MAD folio.'

'You see a cross-business opportunity for us there?'

'Well, obviously we couldn't afford a country right away. Not to start with.'

'Obviously.'

'But we could maybe afford a city. A cheap one. Somewhere Indian?'

'No, they changed the names of all their places like a few years back, they won't want to go through all that again. Think what it'd cost them in mapping. No, I'd say China.'

'Way to go, dude! And everyone who lives in Ramsay, China, would get our books for free, right?'

'For sure. The Chinese are like the fastest-growing market in independent travel. They're gonna love the concept.'

In the pub on Friday, Jenny Williams I, mischievously po-faced, shared the idea with Peta Bayley in Finance, swearing her to secrecy first. As well as being of a literal turn of mind, Peta consumed a large quantity of alcohol between Friday evening and Monday morning, when she told Ameena Khan, at the adjoining desk, that Ramsay was contemplating setting up a branch in China.

'I really hope it gets off the ground. I'd love to live in China. Just, like, for a bit.'

'Yeah, me too. They have great shopping. The fakes are amazing.'

'I'm going to put it in my MAD folio. That I'd like to spend six months in the China office.'

'Yeah, me too.'

The story went underground, developed a tangled root system, spread. It surfaced in Editorial, with Rosie Gatt and Ben Thwaites.

'Heard the latest?'

'The China thing? It's outrageous.'

'And crazy! Outsourcing production to the Chinese! Like how's that going to work? Sure it's cheaper, but what about the whole language thing for a start?'

'Yeah, I know. Wonder which management genius came up with that one!'

'And when are they planning to tell us? It's our jobs on the line here.'

'Maybe Alan's going to announce it whenever he's next passing through on his way to nirvana. Like: "Great news, everyone! You don't have to come back in 2005."'

'I'm going to put it in my MAD folio. Like how does it square with that bit in our Mission about *Treating everyone with courtesy and consideration*?'

'That's our Vision, not our Mission. Anyway, Alan'll probably announce it courteously. And with consideration.'

Not long afterwards, Gemma d'Cruz from Design, out smoking in the car park with Jason Townsend from Tech, asked, 'Do you think it's definitely happening, this China deal?'

'Yep. Everyone's talking about it. Any idea who's bought us?'

'Just that it's a huge Chinese consortium.'

'Unreal! I guess Cliff'll break the news when he gets back.'

'So do you think the Chinese will keep us on? Or will they want to bring in Chinese people?'

'Wouldn't have a clue. But what I've heard is head office will be based there. Seems they've already got a business park set up, like there's this bit of Shanghai that's going to be called Ramsay? So unless you want to move to China . . .'

'But I'm in a new relationship! That is so unfair.'

'Ancient Chinese curse, Gem: may you live in flexible times.'

'And what about human rights in China? I'm going to put it in my MAD folio. How it goes against our philosophy.'

'One problemo, Gem: flexibility *is* our philosophy. It was one of the Seven Key Innovations we took away from the restructure.'

Thus it was that Alan Ramsay, midway through a Caribbean cruise, received an email from Gina Piggott, who demanded to know why, as the head of Ramsay's UK operations, she hadn't been *kept up to speed* with the company's expansion into China. At more or less the same time, Cliff Ferrier, back in Sydney from a Tasmanian bushwalk, found himself facing a delegation from HR demanding more or less the same thing. Heidi Koss, supine on a couch in Brooklyn, had already informed her analyst of the latest *harassment situation* emanating from head office. She couldn't see her way forward: the game plan was fundamentally flawed. For Americans to have to take directions from Australians was just plain wrong.

Twenty-four hours later, Laura Fraser, pillowed on Paul Hinkel's breast, said, 'Isn't it brilliant? Chinese whispers!'

He shifted, freeing himself of her. All *rumour-mongering* did was make work for management, he declared. Two journalists had already called Robyn Orr. It was particularly irresponsible of Jenny Williams I. 'For a senior manager not to think through the implications.'

'It was a joke! Cliff isn't fussed.'

'Cliff's a dickhead.'

This had the inadvertent effect of reminding them of the terrace above the Pacific where all this had begun, and so of their present purpose.

Afterwards, while she was getting dressed, it occurred to Laura that she might be Paul Hinkel's mid-life crisis. But he was only thirty-six! She thought, Maybe he's getting it out of the way early so he can concentrate on his career. This led her to wonder if what she satisfied was his traveller's itch for variety. Stuck in marriage, stuck at a desk, he had found a way to keep moving; their affair might be no more than proof of his commitment to the Ramsay code. I'll end up as a bullet point on his CV, Laura thought.

The previous year, when she had been more or less infatuated with Paul Hinkel, she would have been able, nevertheless, to do without him. Now that she judged and condemned, her craving was consuming and pure.

Ravi, 2004

ABEBE ISSAYAS SAID, 'MY SISTER had a son.' And, 'She is someone whose life has been, I would say, very difficult.' He gave the last syllable its full value: diffi-cult.

Aged seven months, the infant had died in his sleep. The tragedy dated from the Paris era. Hana's husband, Pierre, was working late; she was alone in the apartment with the baby. There was no sign that his death was anything other than the blackest misfortune, but the police questioned her for weeks. 'You cannot imagine how excited my sister was when they went to live in Paris. It was her dream. Her idea of the French was Pierre.'

That afternoon, a Sunday, Ravi had accompanied Abebe, Hana and Tarik to a university in Parramatta. Jodie, Hana's friend from the supermarket, had recently enrolled in a major in Tourism there. Further study, until then a misty blue realm of fantasy, had suddenly pressed against Hana's window, and she was as fidgety as a child cooped up. She remarked that Jodie was a nice girl, but no one could call her clever. 'Her till never balances.' Hana had read online about a course in Early Childhood Development, but was drawn also to counselling. The question was whether her high school diploma would hold good in Australia, or whether she would have to re-sit Year 12; Hana was investigating this. Meanwhile, she was under the governance of a vision, and it had ordained that she visit the campus 'to look around' without delay. In the back seat, she was by turn critical, amusing, enthusiastic, sharp. Away from her, Ravi would look forward to their next meeting. What he recalled then were her full lips, her wide, straight back, the way she so often made him laugh. She had her own distinctive sayings, like 'Go and put your head in a bag!' Sometimes, and Ravi could not have said why he found the change so funny, this became 'a brown paper bag'. Hana was a landscape smoothed by distance; up close, the weather struck.

An impasse that mother and child had arrived at weeks ago was being circled again on the way to Parramatta. Hana had kept her surname when she married; that was the Ethiopian custom. But Tarik had her father's name, Giroux. Now she wanted to replace Tarik with Sophie; it was her middle name, and the name of her best friend at school. Mother and child tugged the argument this way and that, like something shapeless and heavy. 'Why can't I be Sophie?' 'Your father chose Tarik. He wanted you to have an Ethiopian name. You should be proud of coming from the oldest independent country in Africa.' Along with Hana's disavowal of home went a store of patriotic facts—she had told Ravi, more than once, that the word 'coffee' came from Ethiopia. 'If we call you Sophie Giroux, people will think you're French. They'll think you eat bread full of holes.'

The campus was by the river, far from the centre of the suburb. Hana wondered aloud how students who had no car managed: the station was nowhere near. 'Bus,' said Abebe, indicating a stop. He proposed dropping Hana off, then driving Tarik back to a park they had passed. He looked at Ravi. 'You could come with us or stay with my sister.'

This pleased no one. Tarik drummed her heels against the seat: why couldn't she see 'Mum's university'? Hana said, 'Don't start,' and to her brother, 'This is Australia. My daughter's going to university, and the sooner everyone gets used to the idea, the better.' Abebe raised both hands briefly from the wheel: okay, okay. Ravi looked out of his window, embarrassed by the crudeness of Abebe's tactics, sorry, too, that Hana had misunderstood.

A few students were making phone calls or smoking outside the library, but the campus was largely deserted. Hana paused by a signpost. In a musing way, she read aloud, 'Auditorium'. In the same way, she kept stopping in front of buildings to read out their names. 'Whitlam Institute'. 'School of Law'.

Tarik had reverted to babyishness. She clutched her mother's hand and walked with her gaze on the ground. If Hana freed herself, the child would at once stick her thumb in her mouth. Her gestures were stagy, yet both men saw that her unhappiness was real. Soon, for Ravi, this became unbearable. Hana wheeled on him without warning. 'What's wrong with you? You have a face like a month of Sundays.' Ravi muttered of a headache. 'Give him the keys,' said Hana to Abebe. 'He can wait in the car.'

It was a relief to walk away. At the same time, Ravi felt like a book that has been shoved back into a shelf. To prove his independence, he went down to the path beside the river. The water, glimpsed through branches, was thickly green. He spotted Malini on the bank, ducking about between the mangroves—but she turned out to be only a trick of the light. There was no doubt, however, that Hiran was very near. He called, 'Daddy, Daddy, Daddy,' while running up and down a locked passage in a handsome sandstone building. It was a former school for female orphans established in the early years of the colony. Hiran's arms rose, but he couldn't reach the window. Ravi headed back to the car, walking fast.

On the way home, Tarik announced that her throat hurt. Hana shifted into the middle of the back seat, and Tarik huddled against her. Abebe asked if he should stop off for lemons. A little later, Hana asked, 'Do you have a sore throat as well as a headache, Ravi?' When he turned in his seat to deny it, she said, 'Are you sure? These things are very infectious.' Her tone was severe, but she was smiling. Ravi wondered which way she pictured the flow of contagion. Absurdly, he felt himself to blame.

Tarik said, 'Mum, you know Jacinta in my class? I really hate her hair.' The child often ignored Ravi, greeting him with her eyes dropped. Sometimes, when she was snuggled up against her mother or seemed absorbed in a game, Ravi would discover that Tarik was in fact observing him. In the same way, Fair Play curled on a chair, seemingly asleep, would keep covert watch. Their eyes had the same look: cold but lively. They were waiting to see what he would do. Ravi realised, with a jolt, that he might represent a threat to a small female. At other times, he was an opportunity. Child and dog would stare openly or even cavort, willing him to produce a sardine or a sweet.

Hana murmured, 'School of Law.' When Ravi looked round at her, she said, rather defiantly, 'You know about these things. Before today, I would have said "Law School".' Whitlam Institute, Campus Service Centre, Auditorium: they were not names on a board, Ravi saw, but steps carved into a golden mountain. At its peak, Hana, gowned and mortared, waved goodbye to the conveyor belt, the flat that smelled of exhaust, the bed she shared with her daughter. She upended a bag: an avalanche of dirty five-cent pieces fell on her French mother-in-law and killed her.

Ravi asked to be dropped off at the station, but Abebe replied that he would drive him home after leaving the others at their flat. 'That's a good idea,' said Hana. 'There's always a cold wind when you're waiting for a train.'

Outside Hazel's, the two men sat on in the car. Abebe had offered Ravi a cigarette, then told him about Hana. When the ambulance came, she had asked, 'Is my son completely dead?' It was one of the things about her that Ravi would never forget. Shivering, he found the button that raised his window. When he got out of the car, he trod on a paper plate of caramel popcorn. He scraped his sneaker back and forth on the grass. Abebe, who had turned the car around, saw him and laughed.

Ravi, 2004

A LONG, BITTER EMAIL CAME from Nimal. For months, he had laid siege to a divorcee from Nevada who was renting a house near Galle. She was forty, looked fifty and brought a touchingly clumsy enthusiasm to everything she did, whether performing fellatio or rolling a joint. With a flow of phone calls and emails supplemented by almost daily visits, Nimal beat off a trishaw driver and an upstart waiter; like most foreigners, the divorcee had no appreciation of the local social stair. At last, as his campaign reached its strategic climax, Nimal drew the garnet from his finger and placed it on hers. Two weeks later, he demanded its return. In the interim, the divorcee had steadfastly refused to entertain any suggestion of returning to her native land. She was never going back to those winters, she declared. Nimal pleaded for California and Hawaii, he googled the average hours of sunshine in Santa Fe. It was all useless: all through their idyll, when he had been dreaming of SUVs and steaks, her imagination had thrilled to rice paddies and crisp, fresh hoppers at breakfast.

Ravi saw Hana almost every weekend now. Their relations had taken on a tinge of self-consciousness; or perhaps it was only Ravi who had changed. Hana was buoyant with plans. Her brother would sit his final accountancy exams at the end of the year, and then it would be her turn to study. Hana had sent off certified copies of her high school diploma to a government office for assessment—she wondered if she would have to do a bridging course. 'There's no hope if you can't imagine your life changing,' she said. 'That's why places like Banksia Gardens feel sad.'

Tarik and her mother had a new game: When We Live In A House. They took turns: When we live in a house, we'll plant roses and figs. When we live in a house, we'll have two cats. Hana tired quickly of these mundane visions. 'When we live in a house, we'll keep a kangaroo.' Tarik would shriek with glee, but her amusement was shot with panic. If Hana continued in the same vein, the child would beg her to stop. The game was solemn to her, a ritual. What counted was this pledge: *When we live in a house, Tarik will have her own room.* And what would she have in her room? enquired Abebe. 'A TV!' shouted Tarik, bobbing up and down. That was intended to divert. Already the child knew that it was prudent to conceal what was precious. But her wish was strong and it wriggled free: she wanted 'a painted cupboard with lots of drawers'. Revealing this secret, she watched Ravi, the outsider, from the corner of her eye. In fact, what he had been shown was only a casing, the leaden casket around the jewel. Tarik cupped her hand around her mouth and whispered at length into her uncle's ear. 'I *see*,' said Abebe. His face, seen close up with its pores and hairs, stirred disgust in the child. But she knew that Abebe would never harm her. '*You* say,' she urged him, for with Abebe as its custodian, the treasure was safe. 'Are you sure?' She nodded. 'Okay. Well, it's like this: Tarik will have a drawer for her socks and another for her hairbands and another for her T-shirts. And she will open each drawer in turn and put both her hands inside and everything will have its own place.'

It was the kind of exchange to which Ravi could have listened for hours. He missed the plot of family, its nonsense, quarrels, intrigues. Abebe, Hana, Tarik: what drew him was a triad. In short succession, he had the same dream twice. He was in the grey room where he had gone with the Irish girl. He saw the rumpled couch, the sheet thrown back. But it was Hana's face on the white pillow. Her full lips closed around his fingers and sucked. There was a waking dream, too, in which he undressed her without haste.

He wanted to divulge their symmetry. In private, he recited, Malini, Pierre, Hiran, a baby who turned to ashes in Paris. He could have talked to her of death or love, inexhaustible topics. Then she was before him, and he said nothing important. A piece of paper in her possession gave Hana the right to live in Australia. Ravi didn't want her to think that he was interested in it. The old lady at the Patternots' raised her ruined face: 'Darling, when are you going to marry a nice Australian girl?'

His landline rang at eleven on a Saturday night. He thought, as anyone would, of home and bad news, and sprang to answer it. A woman said, 'Ravi? This is Martine.' The old film Ravi had been watching was louder than her voice. He said, 'Wait, please,' and found the remote. 'Paul's wife,' he heard.

She apologised for calling so late. Paul had gone out earlier that evening and hadn't returned. His mobile was switched off. 'I thought . . .' Then she said, 'He talks about you, I know he likes you. It was so nice that day you came.'

At which, Ravi recalled the spoon that Martine Hinkel had offered him. He had left it on his saucer and quite forgotten it until now. How rude she must think him! Her presence came vividly to him, her gentleness and the smell of her hair.

Fair Play, who had lifted her head at the disturbance, rose from Ravi's pillow and resettled herself. For some weeks now, she had been transferring her collection of stones, one by one, to the middle of the bed. Ravi was obliged to shift them when he wanted to go to sleep—it was no use returning them to the garden because Fair Play fetched them in again. When Ravi lay in bed, the stones prevented him from stretching his legs. Their presence was proof of great trust. Also a consolidation of territory. Curved like an apostrophe beside her treasure, Fair Play snored with content.

Ravi asked after the Hinkels' little girl. The conversation convulsed back and forth, until it succumbed to silence. The silence went on and on. There was something very restful about sitting in TV light, with the phone at his ear, while a beautiful woman who carried a candle and feared for her sanity crept mutely along a corridor on his screen. For a few minutes, Ravi allowed himself to be caught up in her black-and-white intrigue. Then a faint sound reached him down the phone, and he repeated that he was sure there was no cause for worry. As if that was the signal for which she had been waiting, Martine wished him goodnight. She hoped he would come again soon, she added. Ravi thought of a child whose face was the only bright thing in a room. He remembered the tortured tree.

LAURA, 2004

SHE WAS LOOKING AT THE name of her caller. It was a sign and a wonder: Paul Hinkel on a Saturday night!

He said, 'Are you at home? I'm outside.'

It so happened that Tracy Lacey had invited Laura to dinner that night but had cancelled at five: Stew was running a temperature, the poor darl, the motivational guru circuit was so draining, he just gave of himself constantly, she knew Laura would understand. Laura Fraser, pounding down the stairs, having decided to stay in because there was nothing she wanted to see at the cinema, offered brief, wild thanks to whichever god was lurking in the vicinity.

On the step, in the hall, Paul Hinkel repeated, 'I can't live without you.'

But she was leading him up the stairs.

On the landing, she remembered the spinsterish width of her bed. She turned: 'Not there. Here.' He swerved, clutching her hand. She understood that he would have followed had she said 'Mars' or 'the moon'. Triumphant, half mad with victory and wanting, she reeled into the big front bedroom, hauling her prize. Hugo

Drummond eyed them with distaste. He reared above the mantel—one half of his face was green.

His paintings were stacked everywhere, covered all the walls.

They were cleared without ceremony from the bed.

Time passed.

Laura went downstairs. Returning with a jug of iced water, she almost tripped over a canvas. That might have been after or before she raised the blind and the sash.

Paul Hinkel crouched above her, saying that he had gone out to get milk and had just kept driving. His voice went on and on, a gibbering so fast that at one point a rivulet of spit ran out with the words. He had emptied himself into her twice and still wasn't drained. She heard him declare that he was *tired of the lies*. Laura had a glimpse of their life together: a soundtrack swelled between the bouts of canned laughter. There was no mirror in the room, but she had the impression of receding depths. She turned her head and encountered the famous whirlpool of Drummond's gaze.

They slept. She woke to Paul's hand grazing between her legs.

It was cold on the roof, and they were only half dressed. But Laura had felt compelled to display them both to the harbour. So animals are paraded before a sacrifice. Or had she pictured Paul inside her, up there, as the first birds sang in the dark? She had thought about that often enough, waking alone to the dawn havoc. Marching ahead of him now, she said something about the brassy birds of home. Did he miss the blackbirds of London? It was nonsense—in Kentish Town, she had woken to the sigh of air brakes. But with her first step on the roof, Laura had surrendered to a mechanism that ran on preset laws.

Paul Hinkel was navigating past dangers. A chair threatened, bougainvillea clawed. The moon dribbled just enough to obscure what was withered and rampant alike. Leaves, towers, eyes, all that was individual showed solid in its grudging light.

They stood hip to warm hip. A clockwork tour guide went on saying things like, Look—the bridge! Or: Over there—see? Luna Park! She drew assiduous attention only to whatever was obvious. Goat Island! she cried, as if it might hear and be moved to come to her aid. Birchgrove! And, finally, in despair: 'Hugo Drummond's studio—would you like to go in? The palette scrapings are authentic!'

Then she had exhausted her repertoire, and it was no longer the monumental that couldn't be avoided but silence.

You could have heard a pin.

The sky paled.

Where was the tour guide when you needed her?

So it was left to Laura to tell Paul Hinkel what he had really crossed the dividing water to say: 'It's no good, is it?'

He protested. Rather, he piped. For a moment, his voice changed pitch with relief. That was merely a confirmation, however. Here was the giveaway: his breath smelled fresh. When he had stood on her step, when he had squatted above her to proclaim *starting over*, a foul current had carried his words. Laura had assumed a sanitary oversight: naughty Paul Hinkel forgets to brush, burns bridges! Now, on the roof, she remembered having read, in a novel or two, of that smell. What it betrayed was terror. Paul Hinkel had faced love, as another man might confront a firing squad, with fear on his breath. How amazing, thought Laura Fraser, that life should bear out a phenomenon she had believed the invention of novelists. *I can't live without you* and *I'm tired of the lies* and every other heartfelt platitude Paul offered had actually been addressed to his wife—thank goodness his breath had known it. *We have so much to learn from the wisdom of our bodies*. Sadly, Laura acknowledged that Quentin Husker and Paul Hinkel had always been cut from the same template. If she hadn't felt so cold, she might have smiled.

In no time at all, he was dressed and down the stairs. The sun was still working up the nerve to peer over the horizon when he drove away. When adventure palls, little dog scampers home to dry rations and forgiveness. But first, turning to her on the doorstep, he spoke with odourless breath. 'You're right—it's best this way. A clean break. It's cleaner.'

Noon was gathering itself to strike. Carlo was back from Haberfield. Laura could hear him in the kitchen; something fishy was going on down there. Oh, she could murder a great big serve of tortellini followed by a selection of yummy little pastries! These days, after they had eaten, the old man arranged himself on the sofa. There he looked to her meekly for a verdict. Laura might reach for their record or not. One Sunday she had tormented him by slowly shuffling the stack of vinyl as if searching for something infinitely rare; later she picked up her clothes and left the room while a crescendo was still building in its rosy crevices. Lingering in the hallway, she grinned to hear him curse. *How dare he expect*. Let him taste what she did twice a week in a motel, naked, waiting, certain it was all over. But today she would be merciful, she decided, she might even fondle him. After all, she had cause to be grateful to Carlo. He had shown her the scraps on which life could be sustained. Carbs for fuel, sugar for solace, an occasional perv at a spectacle that aroused.

In the front room upstairs, Laura smoothed the powder-blue satin coverlet. Piling it with canvases, she looked at each one first. How much time had passed since Carlo had done the same? When had she last seen him heaving himself upstairs? The room into which she burst towing Paul Hinkel had held an accumulation of silence. It was already thickening afresh over their disruptive moans. When the door closed behind her, neglect would resume its occupation. The front room faced north but struck chill. Like all altars, it required proof of devotion from the faithful. All it asked was a pilgrimage of pain up a stair.

It had begun to rain. Not the tremendous Sydney bucketing of yore but a stringy sort of music. At the window, Laura listened to water running off the roof. Now and then, it shuddered down the pipe and came out as a splat. On a different day, it would have sent her up to the roof to watch rain running over the harbour. But as long as the sash remained lifted, the blind raised, jug and glasses uncollected, traces of a pattern called Laura Fraser and Paul Hinkel twinkled through the dusty coat of indifference that time slapped over everything in the end.

Then it couldn't be postponed any longer. *Back teeth together!* With the window fastened, she bowed her head before Drummond. You fool, he told her, the difference is Carlo was loved.

Weeks passed before Laura saw that the rooftop above the harbour mirrored the hotel terrace above the ocean. Symmetry was the imperative that had made her drag Paul up there. A good editor, she hadn't forgotten to provide the bracket that marked the close of a parenthesis. Now the main story could start over. Hinkel, P and M would march on.

Ravi, 2004

IT WAS ONE OF THOSE days when the shade made Ravi shiver. He took his cigarette across the car park to the patch of sun beside the fence. Further along, where winter had stripped them of obscuring greenery, white symbols showed on the palings: <<+#>>.

A woman was making her way between the cars. Laura Fraser often put Ravi in mind of upholstery: an armchair advanced across the concrete, bearing a mug.

She announced that it was a beautiful day. Then she asked if Ravi had done anything interesting on the weekend. Presently, she indicated a blue Mazda. 'I think that's Paul's car. There's a kiddie seat inside. You know Paul Hinkel, don't you? Everyone knows Paul.'

In cold weather, Ravi's lips were always dry. He licked them as she continued, 'You'd have to be a dickhead to bring a car in here, wouldn't you say? With Central so close. He must be a dickhead.' She grinned broadly, while her brown eyes glared. How small they were and how savage! Ravi watched their depths turn to rust. 'I must say I pity his poor wife,' she went on. 'Who'd want to be Mrs Hinkel?'

All the time, Ravi had the unnerving impression that Laura Fraser, while looking at him intently, was not talking to him at all but to an invisible figure at his shoulder. He placed his back to the fence and was moved to say, 'Mrs Hinkel is a very nice lady. Very kind.'

She drank her coffee after that.

More or less daily, she began turning up in the car park with her mug. The hand that held it wore a big red worthless ring. Ravi grew used to her. One morning he drew her attention to the white hieroglyph. 'Oh, it's been there ages,' she replied. It was the name of a band. 'You say it like this.' Her tongue clicked twice. 'Ben Thwaites—do you know him? That really tall editor? He's their drummer, and there's three other people in it, including the guy Robyn Orr used to go out with.'

But why didn't the band have a proper name?

'It's their philosophy. They're against commercialism, that sort of thing.' She looked into Ravi's face and laughed. 'They're better than you might think. Funny. In a good way. I could burn you a CD.'

Laura Fraser's hair was heavy around her face. Sometimes her hand closed around a clump of it. Now that Ravi had seen her amused, he realised that he had thought of her as unhappy. The burden of her hair suggested it. Sometimes, like sorrow, it was heaped on her head. He got into the habit of looking for her, as he looked for the hibiscus, when he went out for a smoke. But he never forgot that she had frightened him, that first day.

Varunika called to say that she had decided to go home when her contract expired the following year. 'I keep thinking about our house.' It would be easy for her to get work at the local hospital.

She added, 'Of course, *akka* won't give me any peace as long as I don't have a husband. Did I tell you they sent a photo of Lal's cousin? So ugly he must have broken their camera.'

Ravi asked if she wanted to get married.

'What do you think?'

Priya, apprised of Varunika's plan, hastened to inform Ravi that she didn't believe a word of it. 'She's changed her mind before. Wait and see, she'll renew her contract at the last minute.' Then she began to grumble about the tenants in Carmel's house. Priya believed that they brought about problems in order to hold back the rent. This conviction enabled her to convert their grievances into swindles. Their latest ruse was bandicoots in the roof. Ravi heard the relish in his sister's voice: the tenants, their slovenliness and cunning, were Priya's live teledrama. The plot gratified, being both ingenious and reassuring. Each fresh development confirmed what Priya already knew. Now a grandmother had taken up residence behind a partition on the back veranda, and the *biling* tree had promptly died. That sorcery was involved was plain.

If Varunika returned, the blue house would come, by imperceptible degrees, to be looked on as hers. Ravi opened the sleep-out door and stood there surveying Hazel's yard. It was one of those golden winter afternoons slashed by a southerly; the canna lilies were in rags. The sunshine, having lured with a thousand brilliant promises, delivered the unwary to the wind. Whatever knocked on the door at home, the weather at least didn't smile and knife. Recently, on just such a day, Ravi had realised that Hiran was somewhere outside in the wind with no one to take care of him. It was not a dream or a delusion but a matter-of-fact acknowledgment. More than anything in the world, he wanted to hold his child.

He called Angie Segal. There was no point waiting to hear from the Refugee Review Tribunal, he told her, he had made up his mind to go back. Angie said that it was a matter of hanging on. And later, 'So why not wait for them to reject your application? At least you're earning dollars as long as you're here.'

It was Hana, in a way, who had prompted Ravi's call to Angie Segal. Hana, with her transformative schemes, with her list of native plants, instructed by counter-example. Ravi had accompanied her on a history walk that started at a railway station. The guide declared, 'Every Australian should know the work of Henry Lawson.' Lawson had written a poem at the station while waiting for a train. The trains ran once every three hours in his day, and the poem was a long one. The guide kept everyone there on the platform while he read it aloud. The thump-thump of a regular pulse could be discerned; now and then, a rhyme, slotting into place, was a bolt locking up an idea. But most of the poem was rendered unintelligible by arrivals, departures, the broadcast rollcall of destinations. Hana grimaced at Ravi. But she found a pen in her bag and wrote *Henri Lawson* on her palm. There had been plenty like her among the workers at Banksia Gardens, newcomers with their faces set to the future. It was a type, a necessary one. But from the start, Ravi had suspected that he might have more in common with the old people. In his life, too, everything vital had already happened. He felt too tired to start again. Self-invention was poetry written to an energetic beat with rhyme's confidence in endings; in that sense, it resembled love. Ravi thought it likely that when Abebe, Hana and Tarik lived in a house, he would still be only a visitor, hovering. Look at Desmond Patternot: he had spent two-thirds of his life here and still lived in another country. Ravi could see himself ending up like that, his knowledge of Australia as formal as a string of recited stations. He wanted to go back to Sri Lanka, he told Angie

Segal. She made a note on the pad in front of her: *This guy's all over the place*.

She had said as much to Freda Hobson just days earlier. Freda still called, not as often as when Ravi first came to Sydney, but staying in touch; it was one of the things at which she excelled. Why, on hearing Freda's voice, did Angie think of a panther in pursuit of a rabbit? It must have been brought on by the pinch of guilt: she had forgotten her friend's birthday. Work was the usual twenty-five-hours-a-day shambles, Angie was behind with . . . But Freda cut these apologies short. The two women had a long, confiding conversation, in which each agreed with everything the other said. Angie and her husband were considering IVF. Martin, too, wanted children, said Freda, but she was in no rush. She had been in Dhaka for some time now, working for the Sustainable Cities Trust. There was so much to be done! Freda was in charge of Waste Concern, which was going super-brilliantly. 'We had such an inspiring event about dry lavatories—I must send you the photos.' When the talk swung around to Ravi, Freda asked if he was still unable to deal with what had happened. She also said that she knew exactly what Angie was going through with him—hadn't she been there herself? 'It's vital to keep in mind that he's a damaged person.' For ages after Freda rang off, Angie found herself thinking about that word 'still'.

Ravi caught the first ferry that was leaving Circular Quay—he didn't care where he went. He had bought a gelato before boarding; the afternoon, too, was soft, yellow, clean. It said: The hemisphere and you are tipping into light. Once again, Sydney was gift-wrapped and tied with sparkly ribbon, and Ravi was a child hoping his name was on the tag.

In a calm bay, lawns sloped to the water. A boy was guiding a kayak among bobbing white yachts. Ravi realised that he had just been granted a vision of paradise: it was the Saturday afternoon of a boy in a boat on Sydney Harbour. Hana could study the city's past, list its plants, memorise its poems. But it was to Tarik that Sydney would belong. The child's imagination would transform things that were of no significance into touchstones: the swamp of a summer day, the jingle that advertised a theme park, a derelict rollerskating rink seen from a bus. The city would be inseparable from her private myths. For Tarik, marvel and history would amount to the same thing.

A shadow fell across the water, and a cliff slid silently between the ferry and the shore. The boy, the bay, the lawns, the red roofs climbing the hillside vanished. The cruise ship was a large thing seen too close: the victim's view of the predator. The specks caught in its long grin were human faces. From the deck of the ferry Ravi saw, somewhere else on the planet, the other Ravi Mendis and his wife circulating between ports.

When the liner had passed, Ravi's clothes were damp with spray. He looked down, tugging at his windcheater, and saw that his waist had developed a soft little roll of flesh. It came of passionfruit gelato, and delicious white bread that never went stale, it came of boats and trains instead of walking. *You're lucky*, he remembered. There were times when Ravi could almost believe it. He believed, then, that he wanted to stay.

Laura, 2004

A WEEK WENT BY, TEN days, eleven. Another Tuesday, a second Thursday. Now Laura was persuaded that she had blundered on the roof. Paul Hinkel had said *I can't live without you*, but she had been guided by a smell—a thing of no substance. Like any ghost, it might have been a trick of the mind. Ancestral Frasers pointed out that reading should always be confined to the Bible and ledgers: look what came of a diet of fiction. Why not follow the dictates of a ouija board or ask advice of ectoplasm? Laura should have followed their ancestral example: grabbed what she could get, erected a fence, backed up ownership with a gun.

She emailed Paul. Subject: *Editorial error.* Message: *As discussed, this problem is urgent. Please schedule a meeting asap.*

He didn't respond, so she texted him. Again, there was no reply.

More time passed. She crossed to his section of the office. He glanced up, saw her, reddened, fixed his gaze on his screen. She noted coldly, His face is a brick.

They met, by chance, in the kitchen. The designer to whom he was talking smiled at Laura. Paul Hinkel looked, entranced, into his Bushells.

They met, not by chance, in the copying room. A mirage showed her the pale sheen of the skin that stretched between the bones in the small of his back. Without a word, he lowered the lid of the machine and configured its settings. She wanted to say his name, but recognition no longer ran between them. The copier released its flash at his touch. He had already closed his eyes.

Away from Ramsay, she couldn't wait to return. The office was their shared orbit. He would come into view, they might even collide. But at her desk the hours grated. The pettiness of her work overwhelmed her. A cost projection for *Romania*, a meeting about more effective blurbs, what to do about the researcher who had missed his deadline and wasn't answering emails. Rows of tiny Lauras stretched away down the corridors of her mind, all of them trapped under fluorescent lighting in urgent, meaningless labour. If the production of all travel guides ceased on the instant, forever, not a particle of the world's glory would dim. Laura had always known it. But the unremitting busyness of office work obscured its triviality. When Baghdad was burning, what had yanked Laura from sleep was the fear that *Berlin* would be late to the printer.

She botched things: muddled dates and schedules, contrived to lose files from her hard drive. Failure hung around her like a virus that lingers. She attracted bad luck, gave off bad vibes. Even her hairdresser, an old ally, turned adversarial. When he had blow-dried, there were right angles in her hair. The long mirror near the door of the salon gave back a meaty rectangle with pretty hands.

Simple conversations ran onto reefs. An editor called Rhonda Burdett came to tell Laura that she would be resigning; her architect partner had accepted a two-year contract in Dubai. 'The tax rate is unbelievable.' Rhonda held her head like a flower, important with insider knowledge. 'Of course there's the cost of living.'

Laura offered congratulations—on the tax rate, perhaps. And asked, 'But what'll it be like, living there?'

'There's so much prejudice about the emirates.' Rhonda's voice dismissed. 'It's just ignorance. We'll be able to drink at home.'

What no one at Ramsay knew was that in one of youth's unreasoning caprices, Rhonda Burdett had married a Fijian. Fortunately, it hadn't taken long to come to her senses, and she had disposed of the encumbrance with minimal inconvenience to herself. Thereafter she was very alert to racial feeling and often discerned its lurking presence.

'Women can wear whatever they like in Dubai. Within reason, obviously.'

There had never been much warmth between these two. Laura wasn't sorry to see Rhonda go. But she reflected, with a twinge, that in a recent meeting she was one of those who had advised against promoting her.

'What those people have done with the desert is incredible. They've covered it with really modern buildings.'

Before this vision, they were silent.

Laura felt obliged to say, 'Your performance review. I hope that didn't influence your decision. I mean, I'm sure next time . . .'

Rhonda said, 'I'm not in the habit of taking work decisions personally, actually,' so that Laura knew her guess had found its mark. 'This move's been on the cards for ages. Matt's been negotiating the offer.'

'We'll miss you, of course.'

Rhonda inclined her shining topknot in acknowledgment and continued her progress from desk to desk. Later, in the cafe where she was lunching with two or three sympathisers, she confided that Laura had accused her of a lack of professionalism—it was what Rhonda had come to believe. By the time lattes were brought, she was ready to lower her voice and speak of Laura Fraser's *unbelievable attitude towards Arabs*. A version of this was smuggled back to Laura. She accepted the caricature with barely a protest. It was the cost of living. The numbers on the bathroom scale flashed up between her toes, and she cried silently, I am in need of complete renovation! She unhooked a waistband grown so tight it might have been cut from steel.

From the high window at which she spied, she saw Paul leave the office carrying a sports bag. It was Wednesday, therefore the gym with the climbing wall. On Tuesdays and Thursdays he remained at his desk, working through lunch. At least he hadn't replaced her; or only with AutoCad and renewed ambition.

One evening, perched above the harbour, she called his landline. Everywhere the bilious sky that precedes a storm. A woman's faint voice answered: 'Hello?' Under Drummond's contemptuous stare, Paul had confided that his wife had tried to make Ravi Mendis a present of a teaspoon. It had glinted at him from the rubbish bin after Ravi went away. *There was no sense to it*: a phrase he repeated, as if astonished to find this clot of enigma at the heart of his marriage. The teaspoon had propelled him, months later, past convenience stores and into the river of Saturday-night cars flowing over the bridge—at any rate, it was the only domestic scene he offered Laura. 'Hello?' murmured the voice, fainter still.

Laura's own silent caller remained faithful. The next time he woke her, she climbed the stair to the roof. It was icy and moonless up there. Swaddled in polar fleece, slovenly in uggs, she lit the candle in Theo's star. It glowed on the wine she had opened with dinner: Lacryma Christi. But Christ's red tears hadn't killed Theo. The backward gaze travelled beyond the bottle, beyond the vomit in the windpipe and reached a pearly Polish forest. The past had found its way out of the birches and come looking for Theo Newman. Only the dead are perfect, and everyone had left too early.

Laura switched on her laptop and googled *nightingale*. Within minutes, a bird was singing from a Breton wood. Oh, thought Laura, oh. She had imagined that this music, like its associate, romantic love, would be bound to disillusion. In fact, like everything overwhelming, the song could be anticipated but not prepared for. The bird sang on, and Laura acknowledged that she lived in an age of miracles. Critics of the internet pointed out that it trivialised, catered to weakness, misinformed. But it was also a nightingale singing in winter above Sydney Harbour.

All through the drab season, she was granted intervals of grace. At work, it had become a habit to take her mid-morning coffee in the car park. If Ravi Mendis was there, she squeezed between cars to join him. At first her motive had been to peer into the Hinkel ménage. But after a while Laura came to value these interludes for their own sake. The ugly concrete yard held sun, wind, Paul Hinkel's Mazda. Ravi was easy company: a stocky, silent, handsome man.

One morning, the vine along the back fence was hung with brilliant orange. The flowers were trumpets, the buds blunt and tapering at the base. 'Like small orange clubs,' remarked Laura. Ravi inspected the creeper. Then he plucked a bud and stubbed it into the middle of his forehead. It burst with the most satisfying *plop*. Ravi said, 'It was a game when I was small.' Laura had to try it. It didn't always work, but you couldn't help feeling pleased when it did.

RAVI, 2004

THE RAIN THAT WAS FALLING when he came out of the station was the light, needle kind. He put up the hood of his jacket and walked fast. At the block of flats, the Issayases' parking space was vacant; Ravi had calculated that Abebe would be on the evening shift at Banksia Gardens. Tarik would be at home with her mother; that couldn't be helped. Ravi supposed that what he had to say concerned her, too.

Light showed behind the blind in the front room. He could hear a sound like coughing; then a tap ran. Explanations, hesitations, histories could wait. On the doorstep, he said, 'The date for my hearing at the tribunal has been set. I probably won't be allowed to stay in this country. But I don't want to have to go away without saying that I've thought about you every day for a long time now.'

He rang the bell.

'Ravi!' Hana opened the security door. The wire of her heart monitor was showing at her neck. 'Come in, come in, you're getting wet.'

At the table, Tarik sat before an open atlas. She glanced up at Ravi and away. Somehow, imagining this scene, Ravi had failed to place Tarik at the table. The child had been present but removed from the unfolding of events. The room his mind had shown him was expansive. Hana and he had spoken together at the kitchen end of it, while Tarik was several yards away, absorbed in a game or watching a DVD perhaps, in a zone where the light was dim.

'Tarik,' said her mother in a warning tone.

'Hi,' said Tarik, her gaze pasted to a page. She rested an elbow on the table, and her cheek against her palm.

'Just take no notice of this bad child, Ravi.' Hana's voice was severe, but she was looking pleased. 'My daughter is in a mood because I told her no TV tonight. I'm trying to put some sense into her head. Do you know, she thinks Bolivia is a country in Africa! She's as ignorant as a giraffe.'

Tarik laughed loudly and without mirth. A few coins lay on the table. She rattled them, waiting to be told to stop.

'Sit, sit. I'll bring coffee.' At the cooker, Hana looked around. 'You didn't have to make a special trip. And in this weather. You are a good friend to us. But my brother should have told you it's not urgent. Did you speak to him or did he text you?'

It was plain that Ravi had no idea what she meant.

'Didn't my brother call you?' When Ravi shook his head, she sighed. 'He said he would call.' And then, 'So but why did you come?'

On the other side of the table, Tarik stopped playing with the coins.

'I was nearby,' announced Ravi to the air between mother and daughter. 'I had to see someone who lives near here. When I was on my way to the station it started raining and I forgot Abebe would be at work.'

There was silence and the delicious smell of coffee. Ravi said, 'Paul. That was the man I had to see. I work with him.'

Hana came forward with a plastic tray. 'It's good that you came,' she said. 'It's good not to get wet in the rain. And lucky for us. You must have guessed that we needed you.' She placed a cup before Ravi and turned to the child. 'Tarik, you can put that book away and get ready for bed now.'

'But I want to stay here!'

'I have to talk to Ravi about an important matter.' Hana pressed her lips together and stared at her daughter.

Tarik scraped her chair backwards. 'Can I read my library book there?' She pointed to the sofa bed.

'All right.'

The child darted past softly chanting, 'Paul, Paul, pudding and pie.' She gave another loud, mirthless laugh and flung herself on the cushions. Ravi saw that she was taller—older—than his image of her. A small lamp beside the sofa leaked light about her head.

Before Ravi's eyes, the scene had arranged itself as he had imagined it.

Sitting at the table with him, Hana explained. Their computer, bought secondhand by Abebe soon after he came to Australia, was almost ten years old, crashed frequently, was maddeningly slow. 'Even reading about university courses—my brother helped me, but it was so slow, and these days everything is online this, online that. So we have decided to get a new computer.'

The complication was this: her friend Jodie could provide Hana with a Mac at a bargain price. 'Her boyfriend sells them or makes them or I don't know what. He can get us a display model.' But what the family was used to was a PC. 'Even at my daughter's school, that's what they have. So we don't know which one to buy. I told my brother we should ask you, you would know.'

Ravi glanced at the dinosaur on its desk in a corner. 'If you're used to a PC . . .'

'Jodie says Mac is easy to learn. And some people my brother studies with have Macs. They say they are better.'

'People like what they're used to.'

'But what is the difference?'

'There are more programs available for PCs. Especially business software and games. Although it's true that Macs are better for design software.' Ravi recognised that this even-handedness was not helpful, but it was produced by his brain in a secondary, automatic way.

'But which one is better overall?'

Uppermost in Ravi's mind was, How can we stop talking about computers? He wanted to go back to the moment when Hana had spoken of needing him. But it was like trying to run Windows XP on the antique Dell in the corner, it was beyond his capacity. 'Macs have better desktop publishing software,' he said and saw Hana's face go blank. She started to finger the wire at her neck. Inexplicably, he was driven to say, 'But PCs are generally faster.'

Hana stirred her coffee. She remarked that she liked the way Macs looked.

Ravi agreed. But was unable to keep from adding, 'It's easier to upgrade a PC.' Scrabbling for simple words, he mentioned operating systems, UI, megahertz and, at one lunatic limit, *maximum personal customisability*.

Then he had run out of things to say.

The silence that followed was like the silence before the first note sounds at a concert, tense and thickened with expectation. A tea towel, the coins on the table: objects in Ravi's vicinity loomed, receded, loomed. He glanced at Hana and was shocked by what he saw. Her lips looked dry and defenceless. She was leaning forward, very slightly.

On a rush of pity, he began, 'Some people say . . .'—that strange, scaly look to her lips! It compelled him to lick his own—

'. . . that PCs are more likely to get viruses. But they have a lot of advantages.'

Hana folded and refolded the tea towel into a small square. It wasn't as if she had never imagined a version of this scene, but what amuses as a doodle alarms as a blueprint. She unfolded the cloth and smoothed it with the heel of her hand. Made of Irish linen, the tea towel was ugly and indestructible—it must have been a present. It was printed with mushrooms grouped about an open-mouthed fish. The fish led Hana to an evening in Paris. It involved her husband—was that an encouragement or a warning? She thrust the tea towel at Ravi, saying, 'You know, this reminds me of the time . . .' Pierre and Hana had taken his mother, a widow, to a restaurant, where she had scanned the menu and pointed triumphantly: it should be *le* not *la sarde*, she declared. The mistake proved that she had been brought to an inferior establishment; Pierre's mother didn't say so but assumed the pained, virtuous look of a martyr. Her son remarked, in his peaceable way, that he believed the name of the fish was one of those rare nouns that could be either masculine or feminine. At that, the widow grew frenzied and tore off her glasses to display tears. To think that she had produced a son who made elementary errors in his own language! What was worse, she had only herself to blame, for she had knowingly married a man whose mother was a Pole.

Ravi plucked the only thing he understood from this rigmarole: a woman couldn't be too careful in her choice of husband. The tea towel crumpled under his hand. It was too late, he could no longer say what he had come to tell Hana. There was something wrong with his heart—no monitor was required to prove it.

A voice came out of the puddle of light behind Hana. 'Miss Moran at school's got two dogs called Mac and PC. PC is stinky but Mac is soooo cute.'

Ravi saw Hana smile. At once, the agitation between them subsided; an invisible hand, passing over the table, had made everything smooth. She offered more coffee, and he accepted. They drank it, talking of this and that. Like someone in a fog who has discovered, just in time, that the next step forward would take him over a cliff, Ravi was shamefaced and relieved.

On the train home, he replayed everything that had happened, over and over. Each time, he was mortified afresh by how close he had come to making a fool of himself—in the presence of the child, too! By the time his footsteps in the drive set Fair Play barking, he had persuaded himself that he had never meant to go through with his declaration. Unbolting the side gate, he spoke to a dead woman: Did you really think I would leave you?

Laura, 2004

THEY HAD ABANDONED THE KOREANS in favour of the classy new Japanese. Robyn Orr was saying, '. . . so we have another drink, and he asks me if I'd like to go back to his place. And then he goes, "There's just one thing you should know. I'm not gay or anything. But I really like wearing women's underpants." So I ask *why*. And he goes, "My arse looks gorgeous in a G-string!" '

The women spluttered over their sashimi, wiped tears. 'God!' they cried. And sometimes, 'Guys!'

Then it was suddenly over and each was as sombre as if Robyn hadn't told her latest internet dating story.

After a while, Laura asked diffidently if Robyn ever found herself thinking about Ferdy.

Robyn snapped, 'You know that wasn't going anywhere.'

And *going somewhere* was the thing.

Gloomily, they feasted on slivers of raw flesh. Until Robyn said, 'Listen: keep this quiet for now. The general meeting tomorrow? Cliff's going to announce he's taking early retirement.'

'Wow! Really?' Laura put down her chopsticks. 'When?'

'Early next year. It's going to take a little while to find a new CEO.'

Robyn was looking attentively at her friend. Laura Fraser was stacking on the kilos. And she had that caved-in look around the diaphragm that screamed out for Pilates. But she dragged her chin up to say, 'Robyn! Are you going to . . . ?'

Robyn had got wasabi up her nose. She waved a deprecating hand.

'You've got to,' said faithful Laura Fraser. 'You'd be brilliant. Who else could they even consider?'

'Quentin.'

'They couldn't.' Then, less certainly, 'They wouldn't, surely.'

'Or they could go external.'

But Robyn knew that Alan Ramsay would be in favour of promoting someone from the ranks. It looked like sentimentality but was essentially shrewd: internal promotions fostered loyalty to Ramsay and were crucial to motivation. On the other hand, external hires generated loyalty to whoever did the hiring. Cliff Ferrier had hired Robyn. And not because of any fucked-up white guilt either. Robyn Orr scored the top marketing job at Ramsay because she was a marketing genius—Cliff had made a point of telling her so. She'd always felt grateful to Cliff.

That was before the ride home after last year's conference party.

Paddo was on Robyn's way: it had made sense to share a cab with Cliff. In the back seat, leftover aroma of pizza and Friday-night vomit. Robyn fell asleep almost at once.

Minutes later, she woke and saw that Cliff had moved up beside her. 'Was I snoring?' mumbled Robyn. She leaned her head against him. He settled himself more comfortably, his arm slipping around her shoulders. Robyn closed her eyes.

When a hand brushed her breast, Robyn's sleepy thoughts were of Sayyid Jamir from the London office. Fingers kneaded her flesh, and she sighed.

'*When my red, red Robyn comes bob-bob-bobbin*',' wheezed Cliff.

Robyn's eyes flashed open. She pulled away. Cliff's hand followed. Robyn shoved hard, palms against his chest. '*Stop* it. Just fucking *stop* it.'

At first, there was only the sound of their breathing. Then Cliff's hand lunged. But he did no more than run the tip of a finger down her cheek. Robyn's shoulders slumped. Keen to forgive, she turned her smile towards Cliff. A hand clamped itself to her jaw. 'You think you've got it made, don't you?' enquired Cliff pleasantly. He squeezed harder. 'Little girl. Little bitch.' He released her and turned away.

The following day, something that had lasted a minute had acquired the skewed force of hallucination. Robyn's eyes, like the blinds in her bedroom, were closed. Cliff's face was a clown-white balloon under her lids. Her jaw was tender where his fingers had clutched. That was nothing, however, compared to the pulsing in her skull, the milk thistle capsules downed before the party having proved inadequate against vodka. Ferdy came in with a pot of ginger tea, kissed Robyn, straightened the doona, went away.

Robyn knew she had leaned against Cliff in the taxi; he had misunderstood, that was all. A mild eroticism had always vibrated between them. Quite often, aware of Cliff's approval, Robyn had arranged her parts for his inspection: pelvis forward, shoulders back. She could not, with fairness, claim never to have signalled something that might have been encouragement. And in the end nothing had happened. Thus Robyn reasoned, lying in a bath with scented candles set on the rim. Her need to minimise what had happened was strong.

Robyn Orr was neither a fool nor a coward. Refusing to acknowledge trespass was a way of denying Cliff power, as a mother might ignore a child who thrusts himself into her talk. It enabled Robyn to face Monday ready to be flip: Scrub up okay on Saturday? But Cliff hailed her first, between the entrance and the stairs. 'My share of the cab.' The note fluttered as he passed; Robyn grabbed reflexively, missed, looked foolish. But she had yet to feel the force of Cliff's hostility. He conveyed it, simply and devastatingly, by ignoring her. When meetings obliged it, he kept conversation brief and stared at the side of her head.

Robyn's parents, the black one and the pink one, had a mantra in common: *You're in charge of your life*. Robyn Orr reminded herself, Never look back. There was no going forward if the past was a rock around your neck. So Robyn had *moved on*: taken up yoga, devised a brilliant campaign for the new Chinese city guides, laid a last ultimatum before Ferdy. It was just that from time to time, the sense that Cliff Ferrier had got away with something was a sore rubbed raw. His face, whiter and larger than life, hovered in Robyn's dreams. The eyes overflowed their sockets. They were the eyes of a glutton.

On the way back to the office, 'So what's Cliff going to do with himself?' asked Laura.

'Cash in the stock options. Grow bananas on his place behind Byron. Surf. Stay stoned 24/7. Whatever.'

Ever since the global management meeting, Robyn had been running the numbers. Alan would pick Quentin, Cliff wouldn't pick Robyn, either or both might pick someone new. Quentin 1, Robyn 0 and dark horses waiting. Robyn didn't look back, but a pattern of old wrongs flapped at her heel.

Crossing the road, Laura said, 'You have to go for it. Promise?'

'Totally,' said Robyn Orr.

RAVI, 2004

THE MIRROR IN THE LIFT showed Ravi a man in a grey suit and a woman in a blue one. Angie Segal tilted her head. 'You look good—I knew that suit'd fit.' It belonged to her husband. She smiled at reflected Ravi. He would have liked to smile back, but his face was stuck.

Two men, one a skeleton, the other turbaned, were waiting when the lift arrived. Angie spoke briefly to the thin one, afterwards informing Ravi, 'Feverel's the member today. Adrian Feverel. He's new—jury's still out, but signs are he's not one of the total bastards.' She offered Ravi a packet of chocolate-coated sultanas. At a pedestrian crossing on the way to the hearing, she had burst out with, 'Members rake in the loot. They get a flash car and to feel like they're really hot shit. You can bet most of them fall over their arses to toe the line.'

From the window in reception, the view was rowdy with blue and green. At Ravi's shoulder, Angie said, 'Hyde Park.' They examined its trees in silence, and the harbour's unambiguous stare. For the first time, that quick, trilling impression Ravi associated with Angie was absent—she was a phone that was out of credit. She said, 'Feverel's ex-DFAT. That's Foreign Affairs and Trade.'

If that cloud reaches the sun before I count to five. Ravi counted slowly to ten. The cloud had stalled. Spring continued to swagger through every leaf—a plain sign that the tribunal would reject him. Angie Segal was still talking, still untypically spelling everything out. So she, too, expected the worst, Ravi could tell.

The member said, 'Mr Mendis, no one doubts that your wife and son were murdered. But why do you claim that the state was responsible?'

Ravi had rehearsed this with Angie. 'No one was arrested or even detained for the murders, sir member. The police took no credible action. Also, there has been no follow-up to the complaint I lodged with the Human Rights Commission.'

The room in which the hearing was taking place had no window and no shadows. Swearing Ravi in, the attendant's bronze lips had quivered, and she looked no higher than his chin. She checked that the recording equipment was working and left the room. That made sense to Ravi: why sit there listening to what no one wanted to hear?

In the cramped space, the member's desk imposed. Glancing sideways, Ravi could see Angie's blue sleeve moving as she took notes. But he tried to keep his gaze, as she had advised, on Feverel. He saw silver hair cropped close to the skull and a face that had bones behind it. It was saying, '. . . does not, in itself, constitute proof.'

Time passed. At Angie's urging, Ravi had written to Aloysius de Mel and begged. To his amazement, the old tortoise had obliged. A certified copy of his formal statement lay among Feverel's many papers. It repeated what Aloysius had once reported to Carmel: that the police had orders to drop Malini and Hiran's case.

Feverel's pleasant voice asked, 'Why wasn't this statement submitted to Immigration with your original application, Mr Mendis?'

Ravi explained.

'But after your application for asylum was rejected, your friend in Vancouver changed his mind and agreed to put his allegation in writing.'

Angie Segal was allowed to be present but was discouraged from speaking. Ravi felt rather than saw her stir. If only he could pass her something to gnaw, a thumb or a sweet. He said, 'Mr de Mel's sister in Sri Lanka died last year, sir member. He has no need to go back. So he is not afraid to make a statement now.'

'His statement is hearsay, Mr Mendis. It relies on an allegation by an unnamed third party.'

This only added depth to a pattern that was engraving itself on the morning. There was nothing in the dossier to prove that asylum should be granted: a formal order to track down and kill Ravi might have satisfied, or a signed confession that Malini and Hiran had died at official hands. Conversely, what the dossier did contain proved nothing; it might even have been concocted. Absence and presence alike cast a dubious light on Ravi's case.

Angie had been in touch with Freda Hobson, who had added to her original statement at numbing length—the new one went on for pages. But Feverel had passed on to a beautiful, imposing document with a wax seal; from the corner of his eye, Ravi saw Angie turn to the copy in her file. Like Aloysius de Mel, Frog-Face—valiant Frog-Face!—had responded to Ravi's plea.

Feverel said, 'This person.' He was peering at the name at the bottom of Frog-Face's declaration—a venerable, musical, polysyllabic name that easily defeated Feverel. 'Why was this person's first letter typed and left unsigned?'

'He was afraid of being identified, sir member.' Ravi added, 'He was just trying to warn me not to go back to the university.'

'If he was afraid then, why has he made a formal statement now? Unlike your other friend, this one still lives in Sri Lanka.'

'He is a very brave gentleman, sir member.'

The member received this in silence. He turned a page in his file.

A little later, Feverel suggested that the sketch of the vase might represent *a joke in poor taste*. A sullen note began to creep into Ravi's replies. Yes, it was true that when he had no fixed address, he had received no sketches. No, he couldn't account for the failure of whoever was responsible to track him down. What he really wanted to say was, Sir member, you are making the same mistake I did: you are looking for clues and connections. What happened has no plot, it's only true. His eyes strayed from Feverel's—a calm, faint blue behind rimless lenses—to the coat of arms on the wall behind the desk. Ravi told a kangaroo and an emu, How ridiculous you look! Do you have a consistent story?

'Mr Mendis, in your original statement, you claimed that you were afraid when the police were interviewing you in connection with the murders. Why was that?'

'There was a man.'

Feverel offered theatrical patience. 'What kind of man, Mr Mendis? A police officer?'

'Yes.'

'What was his name?'

'No one said.'

'It didn't occur to you to ask?'

'I was afraid.'

'Why?'

'Because they were the police.' Adding silently: You fool, sir member.

'And what did this officer say or do that made you afraid of him?'

'He said there were questions it was better not to ask. He told me I was lucky to know that my wife and son were dead.'

'You chose to interpret these remarks as proof that the police were disinclined to pursue the investigation?'

It went on and on like that. At one point, Ravi's gaze slipped sideways, as if pulled. Angie had angled her notepad towards him: *Keep going, you're doing well.*

'Mr Mendis, you claim that the Sri Lankan authorities were intent on persecuting you. But you were granted the police clearance you needed to obtain your Australian tourist visa. How do you account for that?'

Then: 'Please speak clearly so that the recording equipment can pick you up.'

'A man helped me.'

'Who?'

'I can't say.'

'You will have to do better than that, Mr Mendis.'

'A high-up person,' said Ravi, after some thought.

A wooden bar about six inches high ran across the middle of the member's desk. Describing the set-up at the hearing, Angie had explained that 'the modesty bar' prevented either side from seeing what the other was writing. It had obscured Feverel's hands, but now, as the member raised his glass of water and sipped, Ravi saw that the fingers circling the glass were felted with reddish fur.

His eyes fled to Feverel's face—it remained the face of a spectacled saint. It asked, 'Why did this official intervene on your behalf?'

The kangaroo and emu on the coat of arms had given way to a fox and a goose. When they started cavorting, Ravi's hands jumped to join the jig. Their dance couldn't be seen by Feverel, who said, 'Mr Mendis . . . ?'

'There was payment,' said Ravi.

'Are you claiming that you bribed an official to procure your police clearance?'

'Yes.'

'Was this person a Sri Lankan national?'

He didn't mind the quack, quack, quack, sang Ravi silently. His hands were keeping time.

'What can you tell the tribunal about this official, Mr Mendis?'

'Member, my client—'

But Ravi needed no help—he knew very well what pleased and excited the fox. 'He was frightening,' he said. He tried not to stare at that soft red hand.

'But a minute ago, you asserted that you bribed this official to help you. Is that correct?'

'He helped me, sir member. But he had a frightening face.'

Feverel's eyes moved behind his glasses. He said, 'So this man, like the one at the police interviews, frightened you.'

On the coat of arms, they were singing, *And the legs all dangling down-o!* Ravi would have sung along willingly, but the borrowed tie had him by the throat.

'Was it by any chance the same man?' asked Feverel.

Angie intervened, saying something sharp; Feverel took his time putting her in her place. But his sarcasm had reached Ravi as a revelation. All the devils were one and the same: like happy moments, the devil contained and was amplified by those that had gone before. He might have long ears or wraparound glasses or a borrowed face, he might choose to transfix with pale eyes—what was certain was that he would come. He was everyone's last visitor, a tasteless cosmic joke.

Feverel moved on to his next question. 'Mr Mendis, what do you think would happen to you if you returned to Sri Lanka?'

Crystal was saying, 'Do you remember when there was that fashion for petticoats worn as dresses? That whole inner-becomes-outer thing? I had a blue petticoat with cream lace and a purple one with black lace.'

'Summer ninety-seven ninety-eight,' said Nadine.

This was so amazing that not a mouse clicked in the 'zone.

Eventually: 'I would've said ninety-six ninety-seven?'

But Nadine had finished talking for the day.

'Hang on, I wore my blue petticoat over a black T-shirt that time I went to hear Nick Cave.' Crystal was googling. Then, 'Yeah, you're right: ninety-seven ninety-eight.'

'Was that when razor scooters were everywhere?' asked Will.

'No, that was way later, like maybe 2000.'

On Ravi's screen, Istanbul was the Destination of the Day. A photograph summoned the Hagia Sophia; if he clicked on it, it would transport him to a Grand Bazaar. He remembered that he had once found this effortless travel exhilarating. *Bodies are always local*, whispered Malini the spoilsport. Ravi was meant to be designing an online promotion for a special offer, but where was the call to action? Buy two city guides, get a third free! The task struck him as devoid of all meaning, a busy waste of effort. Still, it would serve to fill up his time sheet. Time was what mattered here, not history—time could be managed. When Hiran's photo appeared in answer to Ravi's summons, he spoke to his son silently: In 2000, someone slit your throat.

After the hearing, when Ravi had changed back into his own clothes and returned the suit to Angie, he had promised her, knowing it was a lie, that he was taking the afternoon off. In the Ramsay car park, he crossed to his usual spot and stood there with the sole of one foot against the fence. Spring had been tranquillised and put to bed under a grey blanket, but it would have been warm there, by the hibiscus, if only the sun had been out. What he had heard in the e-zone had been no more than idle conversation. All it demonstrated was the ability of Crystal, Will, Nadine—lucky people, said Ravi to himself—to connect *then* and *now*. He thought, If I'm allowed to stay, there'll only be *before* and *after*. A hyperlink could replace Sri Lanka with Australia in a flash, but what if you preferred to scroll down a continuous story? Ravi smoked his cigarette to the end. He seemed to be waiting for something.

Before letting him go, Angie had insisted on taking Ravi to lunch. Her small, tortured hands, busy with butter and bread, reproached the immaculate cloth. At the conclusion of the hearing, Feverel had announced that he was *reserving his decision*. That was usual, Angie told Ravi, the decision would be handed down in a few weeks. 'If it goes against you, there's always the Federal Court. But the evidence we offered in corroboration was as solid as it gets in this kind of case.' A red claw rose from a platter of seafood and floated before Ravi's eyes.

Two hours after entering the room, Feverel had picked up the phone on his desk. 'Hearing Officer, could you please return and close this hearing?' Waiting for her, they had sat, Ravi, Angie, Feverel, in a silence that was enormous. Ravi's hands lay quietly in his lap. He stole a look at Feverel: the member's hands, folded under his chin, were only dimly tufted across the knuckles. The fox rearing in Ravi's mind was a brilliantly ruddy animal who frolicked like a male in his prime. Did he answer to the name of Feverel?

The suggestion was far-fetched and the dossier lacked proof; the decision would have to be reserved. The fox had been strong and greedy; beyond that, Ravi knew he couldn't say. Over and over, Angie had impressed on him the need to boost his credibility with details. But memory might preserve only sensations: pain, humiliation, fear rising like a concrete stair. When Ravi thought back to his time with the fox, he saw a scene as dim and unfocused as a botched snapshot. It contained two figures struggling in ecstasy or fear. That was all. But when all the distractions were stripped away, didn't life itself come down to that struggle? Details weren't essential to truth, only to persuasive stories. These days, when he thought of the dripping tap in the fox's den, Ravi couldn't be sure if it was a memory or something borrowed by his brain. It was the kind of detail that turned up in telefilms where an informer sweated in a motel and headlights arced over the wall. 'They do a sensational white chocolate mousse here,' pleaded Angie Segal, but Ravi said that he had had enough.

In the warehouse at Ramsay, an acoustic guitar was tackling 'Hallelujah', complicated by the *beep beep* of a forklift in reverse. Ravi realised that he was waiting for Laura Fraser. Recently, they had discussed iPods. Ravi had confessed that he longed to buy one. 'Oh, you should,' encouraged Laura. 'I love mine.' Then she went quiet. After a while, she said that she missed waiting for a particular song to come on the radio. 'It sounds silly, but because I can listen to any song I want, whenever I want it, I miss hopeful anticipation.'

The fire door opened, and Paul Hinkel came out. He raised a hand at Ravi, then lowered it and pointed at his car. The afternoon was ending, and how did Ravi imagine he was going to fill out his time sheet? Still he put off returning to his desk. Laura Fraser might arrive and say something that changed the look of the day.

LAURA, 2004

CHARLIE MCKENZIE HAD LOST HIS hair and gained a chin. But Laura, looking through a hole in time, saw a faded red quilt. She was eighteen, and *a lovely, sexy man* was attending to her under it. Late one night, Laura had sent an email to Charlie's gallery—like any traveller who has lost her way, she was trying to get back to a landmark she knew.

So here she was facing up to her old love over tom yum and fish cakes in the big Thai place on King Street. Charlie had driven up to the city for the weekend, and was staying with friends nearby.

There was the usual pandemonium at the long tables in the middle. A kindly waiter had placed Laura and Charlie as far away as possible, by the window. Even so, noise crashed about them. Charlie shrieked that Fee was living in Dapto with their three kids and her new partner. It had prompted his own move to Wollongong; he was teaching part time at the university there. 'And you?' he screamed.

She shouted this and that.

She had dressed for the occasion, choosing the grape-green shirt bought to overwhelm Paul Hinkel. Charlie had yelled, on seeing her, that she hadn't changed a bit. 'Nor have you,' said Laura, meaning: Still a liar, still a charmer. She remembered how kind he had been when Hester died. His gallery's website had revealed his latest paintings. There, too, only the surface had altered.

The main courses came. The volume dipped, and Charlie confided that there was 'no give in Fee'. It was a formula Laura recognised. Once, it had applied to her. Decoded, it meant *unwillingness to accept his women*. She smiled at him. He took it as an invitation to touch his knee to hers. The din rose; it was someone's Happy Birthday. Laura and Charlie went on exchanging the occasional shout, but it was easier to empty a bottle, eat red curry of duck, rub up the past under the table.

She would walk him to his friends' place, Laura offered, when they left the restaurant. It was a night filched from summer, although the calendar said spring. There were girls in the street barely dressed in violent hues. A big group of them shoved out of a pub, hooting at something they had left behind. Sydney was doing what Sydney did best, putting on a perfect night for getting shit-faced. Charlie steered Laura into a side street, and the scent of jasmine came staggering out of a yard.

'Ever go back to painting?' he asked.

'Painting!'

'You definitely had something there.'

'No, I didn't. And you saw it, you said I was right to drop out.'

'Really? Can't remember that.' He added, 'Anyway, who's to say I was right?'

She was stunned. Charlie, for all his sweetness, had always been trenchant about art. He would walk through a show: 'Bad, bad, interesting, a copy, a bad copy.'

Across the street was a tall, narrow house. Protected by iron flowers, a man and a woman were dining on the first-floor balcony at a table lit with candles. In the bright room beyond them, the familiar outlines of furniture were blurred and endowed with mystery by the filmy curtain at the window. It was a scene that suggested narrative, progression, symbol. It opened depth and time in the pair at the table. Presently, they would leave the balcony and move from constriction to a brilliant amplitude whose elements remained vague; in a flash, Laura had taken it all in. What she also realised was that Charlie McKenzie was only trying to flatter—with a view to getting his leg over, she supposed. Once, painting had been the one thing about which he had never pretended; he had changed, after all. Laura had gone looking for the past and found a bad copy. She kissed Charlie goodnight at his friends' gate and put him from her.

By the time the taxi dropped her at home, a nor'easter was up. In Sydney, as nowhere else, Laura was conscious of the course of winds; weather here came with compass and map. A nor'easter was the elsewhere wind: its salty fingers scratched up an old itch. I must go away, she thought, fitting her key into the lock.

Since coming home to Sydney, Laura had holidayed in Cuba, Tasmania, northern Italy. Avoiding London—London was Theo—she had met up with Bea in Havana, with Gaby and her children in Venice. These trips, with their satisfactions and disappointments, had been interludes. They were books read and abandoned in hotels, absorbing while they lasted but left behind without regret. Sometimes their contents leaked: a treed slope near Hobart, strewn by a storm with branches and bark, kept sliding into Laura's dreams. But real life was Sydney: an area that covered a few streets of shops and restaurants, a house at McMahons Point, an office in Chippendale, a kinetic blue core. Now Laura felt as if her days were fenced with iron lace. The world waited like a lighted, veiled room: a vague, bright amplitude. *What am I doing here?* she wondered.

There were photographs of Venice, taken by Theo's sister, on Laura's laptop. Each was a tiny, luminous Canaletto: waterways, palaces, tinted skies. Hester had owned a bead like that solid green water—what had become of it? It seemed to Laura that her faith in *away*, too, had been lost. She had mislaid it at Ramsay. There, everything was known about travel. That was true in the same way that a city was Sights, Markets, Itineraries, Eating. Guidebooks lured with the Taj by moonlight, with Machu Picchu at dawn. But the moment that mattered on each journey resisted explanation. It couldn't be looked up under Spoil Yourself because it addressed only the individual heart. It was only an empty Kleenex box, only a dangling wire hanger, only a battered hillside in a cold spring.

Away took on the aspect of a solution. It promised enlargement: glowing, ill defined, a movement away from Paul Hinkel. Laura dreaded and desired it. At work, she went on plotting chance encounters: placing herself in his path, engaged in vivacious chat with a colleague seated conveniently close. Perfect was if she was laughing as his red lips passed. But just before that came the electric moment: she wasn't looking at him, but he couldn't avoid seeing her. A current ran between that moment and all those Tuesdays and Thursdays when, entering the waratah room, he had found her naked. Now, as then, Laura moistened. At her desk afterwards, she was sated and hollow. Nothing had changed. She would begin, almost at once, to plan the next time when she would show Paul Hinkel that she was completely indifferent to him. The clear part of her brain saw this pattern and was sickened by and helpless against it. *A clean break* was called for—it was cleaner. Venice glowed on her screen: space opened in Laura, and movement. She made up her mind that at Christmas, when Ramsay shut down for a week, she would go away.

At home, she was the subject of a quarrel. She learned this, holding her breath, at the top of the stair. Carlo's hip had deteriorated to the point where he could no longer kneel before his vegetables. Would Laura take them over, he had asked. She refused, citing work. 'Work,' repeated Carlo. He had that peering look he wore when trying to find something he needed. But he turned away to fuss over his sauce. And because Laura apologised again, '*Ho capito*. No worries.' The air between them was drunk on garlic. She almost confessed: Carlo, what I want to do is smash everything and pull the world out by its roots. He had known lust, therefore despair; he would understand. But he had his nose to a board on which he was chopping herbs with maddening deliberation. 'Here, let me,' said Laura. She was terribly kind to him all that afternoon.

Opening a noiseless door the following Saturday, she heard voices below. They scraped and ripped but reached Laura, who was tiptoeing forward, too muffled to decipher. In any case, when talking to Rosalba, Carlo used dialect. But Rosalba, coming out of the kitchen, enquired in her pure Italian with its terminal droop: '*E quella grassa di sopra?*' Carlo limped after her, his voice harsh. Their gruesome feet carried the argument along the passage and out of the house. *The fat one upstairs* shrank against a newel. The Whiteley loomed: one of his bulging female landscapes, all rusty buttock and rock. Laura could have vanished into it. She knew what the row was about; it was an old one, inactive for stretches but never extinct. Rosalba wanted Carlo to move to Haberfield. Her house was level and practical. It had big, clean, silent rooms. A long time ago, a crepe myrtle had towered in the garden, dropping untidy pink blossoms. It had been chopped down, and the lawn tiled. 'She sweep everything, always,' Carlo confided. That, however, was not his objection. 'My life here.' What he meant was with Hugo Drummond. Rosalba's tussle was with a dead man. The dead are fearsome opponents, but Drummond couldn't cross the street to avoid her. Laura guessed that she had been brought in when it had seemed that Rosalba was winning. The fat one was a counter-argument, proof that Carlo wasn't risking his neck trying to get up onto the roof, help in the ever-feared emergency, someone in the house at night.

Now he must have admitted about the vegetables. No doubt Rosalba had remarked on a weed or pointed out that the lettuces required thinning.

Laura brought her laptop to lunch that Sunday. Carlo beamed at glossy gardenias, fattened on Organic Life. Such flowers they would bear, Laura assured. He gazed lovingly at oleander, and at the early red flush on the pomegranate. But then he grew anxious: the effect of water restrictions on root systems balled in thirsty terracotta could only bring ruin. Oh, please don't worry, said Laura, she was using that special water-retaining mix, and hand-hosing the regulation three times a week until water brimmed in the pots. She clicked and clicked, summoning creepers before and after the discipline of secateurs, showing soil protected with pea straw. Next thing, he was fretting over a photo in which he had mistaken the speckle of light on a leaf for a fungus. Laura soothed and promised. She laid it on like the pea straw, she moved her hands like snakes. All the photos had been taken the previous year. He was an old man with cataracts, he couldn't tell what he had already been shown. She placed flowers and shining leaves, stolen from other people's gardens, in his vases. She fitted a padlock to the door that led to the roof and worked the tiny key onto her ring.

•

She told Quentin Husker that she would be away at Christmas. 'And a few days either side as well. I'll work out the dates once I've decided where I'm going.'

Quentin scrawled his name obediently on a blank leave form. 'Fill out the details when you know them.' Throughout their meeting, he had turned on Laura the vacant look of a beach house in winter. If he had been asked to picture himself, however, his mind would have called up a public statue surmounted by a pigeon—something like that anyway, lofty and imperilled. Quentin had set himself the task of carrying off a bold, original move, worthy of a CEO, a move that spoke to the *essence of Ramsay*. He remembered that it was Robyn Orr who had first used that phrase; straight away, a tingling in Quentin's groin had acknowledged a masterstroke. The same reverence tinged with fear thrilled in that spot whenever Jenny Williams II, unlacing her corset, revealed a new tattoo or a fresh piercing.

When Laura had gone away, Quentin wrote the Ramsay tag on his whiteboard: *Every traveller is unique.* After contemplating it a while, he circled *traveller*. Then he made a list: *explorer*, *vagabond*, *nomad*, *adventurer*. There was a metallic tang in his mouth; it was often there these days. What would become of Quentin Husker if he didn't make CEO? He could stay on under Robyn, at least for the short term; but losing out would mean everyone, and especially Jenny Williams II, looking at him and thinking, Loser. Moving on was the only real option. But where, where? Whichever way the cards fell, Robyn would be okay: marketing was a content-free career. Any time Robyn Orr tired of Ramsay, she could plug herself into toothpaste or transponders or time-shares and hit play. Editorial was different, it was rooted in the specific. Editorial staff who quit Ramsay either went back to university to reinvent themselves, or drifted around talking about their novel or screenplay before the mortgage drove them to enquire about freelance work. Guidebook experience was too specialised to translate into general publishing; Quentin had no idea how to commission a biography or acquire the local rights to a Swedish bestseller. On the mind map of his future all was wilderness, save for a distant southern peak labelled 'Lonely Planet'.

The following week brought an email from HR. All managers had been rebadged as leaders. *A manager manages, but a leader inspires. A leader has a vision*. The proposal had originated with Paul Hinkel. The sentences were his. HR applauded *Paul's commitment to keeping Ramsay at the cutting edge of corporate philosophy*. From the window where she spied, Laura watched the day's hero—or its leader—setting off at noon with his gym bag. Incy-wincy Hinkel climbing rock by rock.

There was a federal election. Australians were offered a choice between two bullies. 'Enjoy your democratic process,' said the polling official as he handed Laura her papers. In a cardboard booth, she wrote across each one, 'I choose not to vote for any candidate.'

It was October, therefore a gale was blowing. Laura pushed her way up a hill. Jacarandas were throwing out hints about calm blue fireworks to come, and she didn't even lift her head. But she reached over palings to steal mock-orange blossoms from a This Garden Uses Grey Water. In the bay window, a vase of waratahs was a warning red hand.

RAVI, 2004

THE EMAIL FROM NADINE SAID: *what will says.*

The email from Will said: *I can't figure out how many of HR's forty-seven core competencies Ravi ticks. I can't figure out HR full stop. I'd say he's a nice guy, easy to work with, he's smart and takes work seriously. It's been a steep learning curve but his technical and design skills have really improved. But you know how we all spend time doing research online, looking for design inspiration, sussing out cool stuff? Ravi always ends up looking at sites he's found in some archive like the Wayback Machine. He can't stay away. It's not that he lacks concentration or can't work independently but it's like there's a disconnect.*

Crystal Bowles said, 'Have you noticed his jeans? Kmart! At least Nadine's cool in that fugly geek-girl way.'

Uninvited in Tyler Dean's office, Crystal was embroidered all over in a fashion designer's idea of a peasant's smock.

Tyler observed that *cool* wasn't actually a job description.

'Yes it is. Only,' conceded Crystal, 'we don't come right out and say it. But it's what we do in the 'zone. *Deliver practical and stylish travel content*. Stylish means cool.'

Long after he had got rid of her, the cool thing continued to nag Tyler. He was behind it, in a way. When he had first arrived at Ramsay, he had seen at once that digital publishing lacked prestige—that magic element—in a business oriented towards producing solid objects known as books. Tyler Dean, working at the height of his youthful powers, had set about rebranding the unit. There was nothing to be done about Tech: it was guys with bad hair and poor body shapes who installed your new software and couldn't explain how to use it. But digital publishing was a whole other ball game. Straight away, Tyler awarded the web unit a new name: the e-zone. The 'zone was übercool, it was the future of Ramsay. Crucially, it was also the company's past. It was Tyler who first used the phrase *travel content* in a management meeting, explaining that ever since its inception, Ramsay had been *delivering travel content*. The archaic form in which it had been delivered had obscured this, creating the illusion that Ramsay's core business lay in books. It fell to Tyler, effortlessly aligned on his exercise ball, to point out that a guidebook was only a prototype website: an early trace of what the digital era would perfect. It could finally be seen that like any avant-garde, the web was a culmination that threw fresh light on what had gone before. All along, without realising it, the whole of Ramsay had been aspiring to the condition of the 'zone.

Circumstances had changed; Tyler Dean's fortunes had known flux. But with even Cliff Ferrier acknowledging that digital was *now*, the link between cool and the e-zone survived. Tyler had preached it to those who laboured electronically there. The e-zone would transform *travel content*: make it snappier, wittier, less brown rice and more sushi, for a global, net-savvy e-generation. Tyler recalled, with a feeling akin to shame, that he had spoken of *deconstructing Ramsay*. What had he meant, exactly? Somehow, years later, it had brought Crystal Bowles into his office to sneer at Ravi Mendis's jeans.

Now Ravi's contract was almost up, and the question of whether he was to remain at Ramsay couldn't be postponed. Across the globe, travel had bounced back—travel always did, it was only destinations that died. Sales were on the up, and Ramsay was hiring again. Tyler, bidding for two new ongoing positions in the e-zone, was confident of success. But Ravi's official performance review, composed by Will and signed off by Nadine, had been cautious and bland: a sure sign of dissatisfaction. No manager wished to risk coming across as openly negative—that would be inappropriate in a laidback modern workplace like Ramsay. The real assessment made itself known in the casual buzz around an individual. An employee was a Ramsay person or not: like any other essence, it was easy to recognise and hard to describe. It was an aura, it was a vibe. It was Crystal Bowles opening her eyes wide and saying, 'The thing is, I find him a bit creepy. Did I tell you about when I sprang him with this photo of a gorgeous little boy on his screen?'

Ravi Mendis just hadn't worked out quite as Tyler had hoped. He was *a nice guy* but not the right kind of person; could it be that he wasn't the right kind of refugee? His co-workers had welcomed him with little bouquets of compassion. But the films that were screening in their minds had showed long, dangerous journeys and cyclone wire. Invited to *tell us something about yourself* at his first general meeting, Ravi had spoken of working in aged care. The only person older than fifty-five at Ramsay was Alan. The faces turned towards Ravi suggested that while not personally opposed to old people, his colleagues had expected to hear of suffering. It was the first intimation that Tyler had miscalculated again.

Eleven months later, he had appealed to Nadine and Will for a straight-up, off-the-HR-record appraisal of Ravi. Having read Will's response a third time, Tyler stuck his head out of his office and saw that Ravi was on the phone. So Tyler emailed him. Clicking send, he thought, This'll be the end of Damo and me. That was insane! It was also the first glimpse of a country that until that moment had existed only as a legendary, sunless realm, and was now revealed as just another place, stony perhaps, but nothing that couldn't be survived.

On the other end of the phone, Angie Segal said, 'Ravi.' He knew at once: it was the only reason she would have called him at work. Invited to attend the handing down of the tribunal's decision, he had chosen not to go. So now the verdict had been written down and sent to Angie as his authorised representative. Ravi heard her ask whether he wanted her to open the letter, or whether he preferred to come to her office. 'Or I could send a courier over, of course.'

It was one thing to imagine leaving and another to be shown the door. As soon as he had heard Angie's voice, Ravi went to the digital bookmark that brought up Malini's photo. She looked out at him plainly, plainly courageous. He said, 'Please tell me what the letter says.' Tyler's message—a little unopened envelope—appeared at the bottom of Ravi's screen.

That afternoon, he wore his Kmart jeans into Tyler's office. '*Hi*, Ravi,' said Tyler. Leaning from his exercise ball to close the door, he spotted Crystal Bowles. Her eyes watched and smiled. Tyler had once heard Helmut Becker say that a German manager's notion of earning respect was to keep his office door shut. 'You know what is really tragic about this idea? It works.' In Australia, where everyone was equal except for their salaries, managerial doors stood wide. It followed that a closed door switched the office to alert. It was simply amazing, thought Tyler, how often the human factor caused theory to come undone.

'How's it all going out there in the 'zone?' he asked brightly.

Ravi broadened his smile.

'Done any cool stuff today?'

Ravi thought back to the morning—how many centuries had passed since then?—and came up with an online tutorial in wire-frame software.

'Cool!' And as the silence lengthened, 'That's so coo—*great*!'

It was the bit about the Wayback Machine that continued to bother Tyler, as it had bothered Will. A good designer was curious, open-minded, on-trend; Ravi was never going to get there looking over his shoulder. But that morning, Tyler himself had turned to the Wayback Machine and its archived copy of the Sri Lankan website Ravi had developed. If he closed his eyes he could summon it now: clip-arty and ramshackle by today's standards, sure, but Tyler held to his original evaluation. The design was under-the-radar, piratical, it had verve. It radiated 'make' culture—vital in a web designer. Tyler could have sworn that back in the day, Ravi Mendis had been a different person.

He said, 'I'm thinking we should maybe talk directions?'

What Ravi could see was that Tyler, mini-bouncing now and then on his exercise ball, needed something from him. Eager to oblige—he liked Tyler, he liked his loose, booming laugh—he could only hope for guidance. To this end, he stared intently at the tiny silver man with his arms outstretched who adorned the tip of Tyler's ear.

Tyler's nerve went. 'It's HR, dude. Myself, I'm all for flow,' said Tyler Dean, making it up on the hoof—he shone at 'make' culture. 'So the thing is, where do we go from here? When your year with us is up?'

Ravi had made an appointment to see Angie Segal the following week; the delay was her idea, he needed time to take things in and think them over, she had said. He offered Tyler the first thing he had offered Angie: 'I don't want to be a tourist in my own country.' It was all that mattered and made crystal sense to him. 'I'm going back to Sri Lanka,' Ravi explained.

'Dude!' Tyler's dismay was heartfelt. He had envisaged Ravi *moving on*—shifting him painlessly to a call centre, or was Lonely Planet out of the question?—but this was a return, a loop. The cause was obvious. 'They've rejected your application. That's terrible.' The image of a circle persisted behind Tyler's eyes. He blinked to dismiss it, and the circle morphed into a tyre, burning about a man's neck.

'I'm very lucky,' said Ravi. 'I've been granted asylum.'

'But that's awesome! Congratulations!' Tyler paused. 'So then . . . ?'

'I prefer to go back.'

'But isn't it, like, dangerous for you there?'

Ravi might have said, They killed my child and turned my wife into a vase. He might have told Tyler about Varunika and her chipped tooth, adding, I'm like that, frightened of the future, when in fact the worst thing has already happened. Or he might have said, Weren't you listening? What was the first thing I said?

While he remained silent, three things happened. Tyler told Tyler, Don't be evil, tell him to apply for one of the ongoing hires—it could make all the difference. Damo asked Tyler, Didn't you *try* to make him stay? Tell me exactly how this conversation went! And Tyler assured Tyler, Whether he stays in Australia or not, Ravi'll be happier working somewhere else.

'Thing is,' said Tyler, 'what I called you in here to say? You can count on me for a reference if you need one. Any time.'

Ravi seemed to be thinking this over. Then he said, 'Everyone here is very kind. It's a good place. It will be hard for me to leave.' He spoke carefully, as if not to disturb whatever was stirring in his face.

Tyler gave three little bounces to a rhythm: shit, shit, shit. 'Theoretically,' he said, 'it's possible things could be opening up a little in the 'zone? Being mindful that at the end of the day, HR hasn't actually green-lighted anything.'

Tyler couldn't know that Ravi was looking at a picture of himself from the future. It was 4x6 inches and showed a man with a camera marvelling at women grinding chillies, tickled by an ad for soap powder, working out how little to tip. A thought balloon escaped from his baseball cap: *There's no poverty here.* Tyler's broad, anxious face intervened. Off to one side hung a tiny metal man whose death leap was forever imminent and suspended. Ravi might have told him, I'm frightened of going back. But I'm frightened of what will happen if I stay in Australia, too.

'I don't want to be a tourist in my own country,' he repeated.

This time, Tyler remembered an avenue of jacarandas and flame trees. It was getting smaller: all he could do was tilt the rear-vision mirror for a last view. In the back seat, Dean Tyler leaned forward: 'Who are you? You look familiar.' Tyler Dean told someone, 'I know what you mean, dude.'

After that, it was quickly arranged. A new, short-term contract would cover Ravi until he left—Tyler's fingers flashed, composing the email to HR at once. When there was nothing left but for Ravi to go away, Tyler sprang from his shining synthetic ball. 'Dude, thank you for travelling this road with me.' Crystal Bowles, chancing to stroll past, happening to glance in, saw him fold Ravi in his embrace.

RAVI, 2004

LAURA FRASER WHEELED A CHAIR over to his desk and sank down. She produced a guide to Sri Lanka and questioned, underlining passages in green. Her ballpoint might have been a supplementary finger with a coloured claw. Ravi, brought up to look on books as costly, revered objects, didn't like to see even a travel guide disfigured like that. Laura was asking whether he would be back in Sri Lanka by Christmas and whether he was really okay about leaving. With the hibiscus eavesdropping in the car park, Ravi had already assured her that he wanted to go home. The truth was that a light-filled hollow opened inside him at the thought, and he was free to assign it any meaning he chose.

Laura's flight would be getting in two days after his, very early on Christmas Eve. Ravi advised her to get out of Colombo as soon as possible. It was standard wisdom among the foreigners he had met when he was pretending to be a tourist. *Oh yes, there's nothing there, we got out as soon as possible*. The sentiment had puzzled Ravi at the time. What was wrong with Colombo? Travelling south along Galle Road, if you glanced to the right, a gleaming blue ribbon of sea threaded through all the dusty lanes. But Ravi was trained now; he told Laura, 'Colombo is typical and ordinary.' He realised that seeing how local people lived was a myth that lurked like a piece of garden statuary, vaguely ennobling, in the tangle of motives that led to travel. No one on holiday really wanted anything of the kind: ordinary life was what they were on holiday from. That was where RealLanka had erred; its attempt to turn the myth into reality was as mistaken as trying to set marble limbs in motion. He would have to talk all this over with Nimal one day, thought Ravi. To Laura, he spoke of ruins, statues, the beaches of the south, his friend with the internet cafe: 'He will be happy to see you if you go there.' She wrote down everything Ravi suggested on a blank page at the end of her guidebook. In the car park, talking about *getting away* at Christmas, she had clutched a clump of her hair. 'I don't care where I go.' Ravi had remarked that there were plenty of cheap places with great food. Her face told him that he had read her mind.

'I only eat ethical meat,' confided Crystal to her phone. Laura closed her guidebook and went away. A little later, Ravi discovered her pen on his desk. It was Will's rostered day off, and Nadine was in a meeting. Ravi slid the Bic behind his MAD folder. When Crystal left her work station, he dropped the pen into his pack. His furtiveness was merely automatic; the theft of the Bic seemed no worse to him than destroying a plump orange bud, a natural if depraved action.

He had signed out for the day and was heading for the stairs when Paul Hinkel appeared at his elbow. Paul offered him a lift to St Peters station—he always did, if they were leaving at the same time. Ravi thanked him, but explained that he had an appointment in the city.

They had reached the landing when Laura Fraser came into view below, her bag over her shoulder. She seemed to have paused on her way out to exchange a few words with the receptionist, but Ravi had the sense—an almost physical awareness—that the beam of her interest was in fact directed at him. At once he understood that Paul Hinkel and Laura Fraser were colluding in his disgrace. Laura would confront him with his theft while Paul prevented him from running away. He would see the contents of his backpack scattered, his guilt displayed before his colleagues streaming down the stairs.

Paul said, 'You right, mate?'

Ravi muttered that he'd forgotten something and had to go back.

'See you tomorrow, then. Have a good one.'

Ravi went up the stairs as fast as he could, unshouldering his pack, dodging the downward flow. Passing a cluster of deserted work stations, he scrabbled for the Bic. His flight had carried him, instinctively, away from the e-zone. Hedged with room dividers, this unfamiliar part of the office had the look of a maze. At any moment, Laura Fraser's rusty eyes might hook into his spine. It took only a couple of seconds to reach around a door into an empty office, place the pen on a desk and move away.

Angie Segal said, 'I have to show you this.' She had attended a conference at which a Colombian lawyer delivered a talk, she told Ravi. 'It was about the history of human rights abuses in his country. There was a period in Colombia when the military mutilated bodies before dumping them.' A stapled document came across the desk. 'Page four.' Ravi glanced at the diagram—briefly. He had never thought of Angie Segal as a cruel person.

Her mobile was playing the little tune that signalled an incoming text. Angie crumpled a fluted paper cup that had held a chocolate:

Ravi had stopped off to buy her the biggest and most expensive box he could find. She rose and came around to Ravi's side of the desk. Her breath smelled of sugar. 'What was done to your wife—I don't want you to leave here thinking that the way she was killed was personal, that someone who knew about that prediction in her horoscope was behind it. Long before she was born, professional murderers were turning people into vases on the other side of the world. All kinds of knowledge travel. Security forces learn from each other.' Angie Segal squared her narrow shoulders: she was a child preparing to recite a lesson. 'If you go back, I truly believe you'll be at risk.'

Earlier she had said, 'Going back frightens you. I can see it does.' That was true, so there was no answering it. Ravi knew that everything Angie said was said for the best—it wasn't her fault that to him the best no longer meant a place where he would be safe. A grave, too, is free of danger. Like Freda, Angie had done whatever she could to help him, and he had behaved badly with both women. Ravi acknowledged it not as self-reproach but as proof that he couldn't be helped.

He apologised again for wasting Angie's time. 'What about this?' she said. She might have been selecting a chocolate from the assortment, determined to come up with one he would enjoy. 'Why don't you stay long enough to get your residency? You could go home afterwards, see how you find things there, come back if you have concerns.' Ravi saw himself strapped to a seat inside a silver capsule, wafted back and forth across sunsets; a connoisseur of clouds, he belonged nowhere. The suggestion was rational, kind and made no sense. For a start, there was the cost. A child in his country could have told Angie Segal that.

She walked him to the lift. She placed her small, bitten hand in his and produced a last violet-stuck praline. 'You might have children one day. The right to live here could be something they'd appreciate.' What Angie hadn't understood was that some sweets are flavoured with ashes.

In the street, sacred ibis were high-stepping through the day's discards like aristocrats picking their way through filth. When Ravi had called Varunika, she listened to him in silence before saying, 'I hope you're not imagining I'll cook and clean for you. I'm not coming back to be anyone's servant.' But Priya, whose reaction to his news Ravi had dreaded, was elated. One of her stepsons had recently announced that he intended to emigrate to Malaysia. Priya, radiating maturity and kindly concern, would now be able to draw his wife aside and say, 'You know I never interfere, Sharmala, but I wonder if you have considered every angle? You see, my brother . . .'

At Circular Quay, the deep blue evening was as large as temptation. Ravi went into the station and up the stairs; a train was just pulling out. What remained was the bridge, the ferries, the opera house: the harbour was a casket lidded with light. How could he have chosen history over that marvel? He asked Malini, Will you be waiting? How will I live? No one answered. Ravi dragged his gaze from the view and saw that he was alone on *the marvellous platform*. But overhead a promise appeared: quite soon now, the train that he needed would arrive.

LAURA, 2004

ROBYN LOOKED UP AT LAURA and said, 'Two secs? Just have to finish off these cards.' There were dozens on her desk, sorted into piles marked Authors, Booksellers, Media, and so on. Produced by a famous aid organisation, the midnight-blue cards showed a dove hovering over the word *Peace*. The 2003 card had featured a golden star and a scroll that wished *Happy Christmas*. An uprising spearheaded by HR had judged it *inappropriate to a multi-ethnic, non-denominational workplace*. There had been emails and meetings; the guilty one in Publicity had been identified and reduced to tears. More people than usual wound up not speaking to each other. That was why Peace reigned in 2004. Peace was up there with dolphins and Nelson Mandela, what was not to like?

Before reaching Robyn, the cards had already been signed by some of her colleagues. There were those who had chosen to scribble a brief message, but Robyn noticed that Quentin had just signed his name. Robyn didn't offer a message either—who had the time? not a senior leader, that was for sure—but she followed her name with a big blue *X*. That was so her: distinctive, efficient, warm.

Laura examined a book called *Managing Brand Me*.

'Great, that's out of the way.' Robyn put down her pen. She cast a cautious glance at the open door and lowered her voice. 'Get this: Paul Hinkel's going for CEO.'

Laura returned the book to its place. She was able to ask, with just the right amount of casual interest, whether Robyn was sure.

'He emailed me and Quentin. He thought it was'—Robyn's fingers made scare quotes—'*right to let us know*. He thinks the experience of the interview will *help him grow professionally*.'

Laura observed that if Paul wanted to waste his time, why not? 'From senior cartographer to CEO? I don't think so.' She produced a little laugh marinated in scorn.

'Who knows how the mindset works around here?' Robyn said grimly, 'Paul's got all the right accessories. Wife, two kids, mortgage in the burbs.'

'One kid. He's got one kid.'

'Well, he's about to have another. Didn't you know? Due any day.'

A cold part of Laura's brain informed her that it was November. Nine from eleven made February. February was Bali. Bali had been budgeted for: seven *nuits d'amour.* No one had mentioned a baby.

'Anyway, let's go eat. I'm starving,' said Robyn. And because Laura Fraser was just standing there looking vague, 'You coming?'

Laura's mind swooped slowly back into the office. It perched on Robyn's desk and looked around. It noted a blue felt-tip and a black one, a Wite-Out pen, three fluorescent markers, a stubby pencil, a green Derwent with a broken point and—

'Is that my pen?' asked Laura. She crossed to the desk. Her fingers closed around the plump plastic casing of a four-colour Bic.

Robyn stared. A memory stirred: something to do with the Bic. But the sudden swerve of the conversation had confused her.

artist, Laura had pushed a stolen pink frangipani into her hair. Her laptop came to life on the kitchen table, and Carlo sat before it, ready for enchantment. Quite calmly, Laura noted the date in a corner of her screen: Rafael Hinkel had completed his first week in the world.

After lunch, Carlo joined Caruso in a duet: *O dolce Napoli, o suol beato*. There were Camels and *babàs*; the liquid in the shot glasses was sticky and foully green. They were knocking it back when Carlo said, 'Why you sad?' Laura opened her mouth to deny, but Santa Chiara fixed her with a cold blue plaster stare. So Laura said that she had decided not to come back to McMahons Point after her holiday. 'I'm going to look for somewhere closer to work, I've been thinking maybe Surry Hills.'

By Christmas, Carlo would have his artificial hip and be in rehab; after that, he would recuperate in Haberfield until Rosalba could be persuaded to let him go. Alice Merton had already agreed to water upstairs and down while Laura was on holiday; it would fall to her to expose the dereliction on the roof. If Carlo forgave, Rosalba would not. There would be no coming back for Laura, no more nightingale above the harbour, no more garlic and lilies and rosy afternoons. In the bay window, dolce Napoli, supine in a sea-blue shirt, was blowing a smoke ring. On the mantel, the peacock feathers were all eyes. Oh God, how could I have ruined his garden? thought Laura. This had become a recurrent theme. But the anguish that bit at intervals, sharpening its teeth on the presence of Carlo, was velvet-mouthed as soon as she stepped onto the roof. There she only surveyed, justified, conjured fresh deceits. The two states of mind flourished in her like plants that grow peaceably side by side and have no bearing on each other; her ongoing inertia fed both. The house was her accomplice, with its discrete geographies of downstairs and roof.

Guilt rushed to assure Carlo that she wasn't deserting him. 'You won't need me next year. Your new hip will have you powering up those stairs.'

All he offered was an equable, '*Sí, certo*.'

'You don't mind that I'm going?' She was just a tad piqued.

'You no happy, no good you stay.' He remarked, 'Long time, you no happy.'

'Work gets me down,' said Laura eventually. 'It's nothing to do with you or this house, you know I love it here.'

'*Sí, certo*.' The terminal droop was Rosalba's best. Carlo Ferri was vain, sentimental, pig-headed, capable of cruelty, but he was never ironic. In a preposterous future, Laura knelt before him on a roof crying, I'm sorry, Carlo, I'm sorry.

She ate the last *babà*, swallowing misery.

Wiping her fingers on her skirt, she rose to find their record. 'No,' he said. 'Is not necessary. Is okay—you go.'

'But I would like to. Please.'

It was true. She wanted to. She undressed slowly, slowly displayed her luxuriant flesh. The afternoon thickened, the record stuck, Carlo gasped, it was all as usual. But: *You go. You go*. This time, Laura hadn't mistaken his meaning. No one was asking her to stay.

Ravi, 2004

THE CHRISTMAS PARTY, HELD BY tradition on the second Friday in December, was raging through the office. Even the Ramsays were present, fresh from their yoga break on Mustique. *He* loomed in silent gravitas over the turbulence; at six foot four, Alan Ramsay was used to flying above the weather. *She*, clad briefly in silver, spoke only to senior leaders but showed her tiny teeth to all. The back of her skull was as square and flat as any Balkan war criminal's, but the back of Jelena Ramsay's head was the last place anyone looked. The photograph taken when she was crowned Miss Croatia Underwear had been widely circulated at Ramsay. At seasons of workplace angst, when pay wasn't reviewed, say, the unkind drove pins into her paper eyes. Others, no less savage but more technologically proficient, turned to Photoshop for relief.

Jelena Ramsay was never in Ravi's vicinity. A crowd always swirled between them, so he glimpsed her, like a goddess, in distant flashes. Laura Fraser, on the other hand, came and went like the music pumping out from Sales. Ravi had spotted her there earlier on, in the space that had been cleared for dancing; she was gyrating with Robyn Orr. Laura's white arms rose and fell—they were contained in black netting. It gave her the look of something dragged from the sea.

Materialising afresh beside Ravi, she shrieked her *plans for Sri Lanka* into his ear. She was doing everything he had suggested, going from Colombo to the south coast, where she promised to visit Nimal's internet cafe, then travelling to an ancient capital and a fortress carved from rock. Crystal Bowles, slithering past in an emerald-green caftan with a drink to match, flicked her hair and her eyes; Ravi wondered if he would have the nerve to ask her to dance. Laura bellowed of frescos and ayurvedic massage. Ravi had no interest in her holiday beyond a vague native pride in her choice of destination, but she continued to shout at him. Then there was a lull in the music, and she muttered, 'Your hometown—it's near the airport, isn't it?' She had yet to finalise her bookings, she said, and could easily alter her plans. 'We could meet up. If you'd like to, of course.'

Ravi answered at once that the beaches in the south were far superior to those on the west coast.

'That doesn't matter,' said Laura. 'To tell the truth, I don't care where I go.'

Pride gave way in Ravi to an equally vague rage. He had a vision of a horde. It ate, loved, frolicked, trampled unthinkingly; at its head strode Laura Fraser. He saw the rooms of childhood forced open, despoiled, laid bare to the light. She loomed over him, sly and suggestive, and—I'd like to kill you, he thought.

She was saying hastily that of course a visit wouldn't be convenient. 'How silly of me. It'll be Christmas, you'll be busy with your family, you must be longing to see them.'

Laura ended on a screech because the music had started up again. To hear her more clearly, Ravi looked into her face. Having imagined her triumphant, he now saw that the multitude she led was in flight. *Pray for them, child*, commanded Brother Ignatius. *Going here and there, far from home*. Like many another victor troubled by instant capitulation, Ravi felt he had behaved badly. The red ring spluttered on Laura Fraser's finger. Netted in black, she was a tower besieged.

Ravi wasn't finishing up at work until the following Friday. But many of his colleagues seemed to think that this was his last day. Throughout the party, people came up to him, hugged him, asked for his email address, urged him to stay in touch. How lucky I am, thought Ravi, and found himself shivering. In Sales, one track ended and another began. It crept out from Ravi's bones. The last time he had heard it, it was playing on Freda Hobson's Discman. The remembered texture of those days received him like a pillow: a cottony compound of grief, music, fear. When he opened his eyes, Crystal Bowles was before him. 'Would monsieur care to dance?' He followed her turquoise patent-leather slingbacks past the mobile bar in reception. Under the mirror ball, she lifted her shoulders and made boneless passes with her arms. '*La* la, la la la la, *la* la,' sang Crystal, while Ravi's feet tried to follow the rhythm of her hips. Her palms were slipping down her thighs: '*Dance* me, la la la la, *dance* me.' His obedient hands reached, but the music broke off. Crystal slid away.

People were massing at the foot of the stairs; the Ramsays waited on the landing. Switches were being hit. When only the staircase hung in light, Alan Ramsay began to speak—a phenomenon that disturbed, as if an Easter Island statue had come to life. But Alan brought the glad tidings that the global upturn in sales meant Christmas bonuses for all. There were cheers, although some of those present, occupied with trying to squint up his wife's skirt, missed the moment. As for Jelena, she had long been in the habit, when men made speeches, of looking divinely blank while noting the lie of the land. In another century, there had been a mountain village where the wine, like the bread, was black. What remained of that was a dream in which Jelena opened her wardrobe to discover that she owned no shoes. But recently her husband had made her watch a documentary about North Korea. She had been struck by the twin portraits that oversaw everything there: the Great Leader and the Beloved Leader. From her vantage point on the landing, Jelena had spotted a wall in reception that would be perfect. Gilt frames, or would a nice veneer with beading be more elegant?

When Alan, applauded, had reverted to stone, Tyler Dean leapt lightly up to the landing. His big shorts flapped about his knees. Jelena Ramsay took a step back to accommodate them, but her smile didn't move an inch.

He would be quick, promised Tyler. 'I know there's serious partying to be done. But I totally had to say—Ravi! Where are you? Come on up!'

The crowd parted. Willing hands shoved Ravi up the shining stair. When he arrived at the landing, 'Dude, it's been stellar working with you,' said Tyler. 'We're all sorry you're leaving, even though we're stoked because we have a place to crash in Sri Lanka now.' This caused much merriment below. 'Anyway, this is from all of us to say we'll miss you and thanks for having been part of our story.' He handed Ravi a bag.

Ravi drew out a box and saw, in wonder, that it contained an iPod. Far away, the mirror moon glittered in Sales. Closer at hand, Jelena Ramsay was giving off violent twinkles; Ravi turned to her, half dazed. It was a casual occasion so Jelena was wearing only a single strand of diamonds, but Ravi had the impression he should kneel. Jelena widened her smile but lifted her chin to show that none of this had anything to do with her. So she had stood when they were herding her brothers, even the little one, into the trees.

Demands were floating upwards, and, 'Speech, dude,' said Tyler. He touched Ravi on the elbow, turning him towards the crowd. Ravi said thank you, more than once, and told his colleagues that he would miss them. 'I have been very happy in Australia and working with you.' It was okay as an exit speech, but a joke would have been better or a complete breakdown. Pale masks, friendly and avid, gleamed up at Ravi from the darkness. They wished him no harm but wouldn't have minded him making a little bit of an arse of himself: it was Christmas after all!

The iPod had been Damo's idea; Tyler had contributed a fifth of the cost. An outrageous private whisper continued to inform him that he had failed Ravi Mendis. It was outrageous because the truth was the other way around: it was Ravi who had failed to rescue Tyler's career from the straight, flat highway to Loserville. In the end, rescue had come from Tyler's old webmaster. Restructured out of Ramsay, Dave Horden now worked for an awesome outfit that made video games. The interview for creative director was scheduled for Monday, and Tyler had been assured that all he had to do was show up. So he really couldn't have said why the last thing he felt like was a party. He punched Ravi's shoulder in a kindly sort of way and started clapping. Gripping a paper bag, descending into obscurity, Ravi wanted to howl, Please keep me from making a terrible mistake.

When he had recovered, he was standing at the back of the crowd and Cliff Ferrier had ascended the stairs. Pineapples and hula girls frolicked on Cliff's shirt. Jelena had disappeared, and Alan was informing a distant horizon that Cliff's resignation was a great loss. 'I'm sure you all feel that Cliff's irreplaceable. I certainly do. So we'll be replacing him as soon as we can.'

This was received with dutiful titters, while Alan observed that it was a matter of prioritising the priorities now. 'Over the next few days, Cliff and I'll be meeting with all the candidates for CEO, and we hope to have news for you about that before too long. But as it happens, this week marks a very special anniversary. Twenty years ago, when Ramsay wasn't much more than a stapler and a photocopier in my attic in Glebe, Cliff signed up for the ride. We'll be sending you off in style when you go next February, Cliff, but what we have for you tonight is a special trophy to honour your two decades at Ramsay.'

Jelena Ramsay was now perceived to be wending her way down from the floor above. Her shapely ankles appeared, stepping stiffly in their silver shoes. She was moving with care, encumbered by a bulky form. When she rounded the bend, it was visible to all: a china vase moulded and painted to resemble a naked female torso. Jelena came to a halt, shielded by rosy nipples and golden fronds: a lifesize parody of the glories they obscured.

There were wolf-whistles and screams of delight. Crying, 'My favourite hobby—ikebana!' Cliff seized his prize. Ravi's hands, too, had shot out: they were warding off something. 'For he's a jolly good fellow,' came the roar. Fleeing from it, Ravi almost collided with a chair. But a monolith grabbed his wrists. Laura Fraser steadied him. He thought he would throw up on her, but her flesh smothered him just in time.

Netted arms waltzed him past the mobile bar and through Design. There was singing above Ravi's head: '*La* la, la la la la, *la* la.' The mirror ball menaced, but Laura whizzed him through Finance, steering between a room divider and a tank of orange fish. Off to his left, the stationery cupboard undulated and vanished. A filing cabinet could easily have finished them off, but she twirled him to safety through the downstairs tea room. '*Dance* me, la la la la, *dance* me.' They swept past This Month's Top Ten, but it was a near thing with Returns. At a fire door, she released one of his hands and fumbled. Then they were through and into the car park. It was empty: responsibly mindful of their intention to end the night rat-arsed, no one had driven to work that day. '*La* la, la la la la, *la* la.' Rain must have fallen because the concrete was shining. The moon had been left behind in Sales, but the security lights snapped like stars. They swirled across the car park on a loose diagonal until the hibiscus fence put an end to it. 'Dance me to the edge of love,' sang Laura Fraser. There was something wrong with that, but Ravi couldn't remember what it was.

The trumpet vine, in luxuriant leaf, was no longer in flower, and Laura had stopped singing. Still her netted arms clutched.

She was unused to exertion. Her flesh moved in slow waves.

Ravi farted.

It just popped out: a little odourless explosion. A bodily full stop, it put an end to a bodily conversation. What can two people who are more or less strangers say to each other after a fart? It provoked humiliation in one and embarrassment in the other. The night was rather chilly, after all; they noticed it at the same time. Thank goodness Laura could cry, 'Ravi! Where's your iPod?' and loosen her hold. An absence was something to talk about and pursue. He must have dropped the paper bag as he fled. The fire door had swung shut, so they had to retreat up the side of the building. The smokers sheltering under the awning at the entrance hailed them. 'Think I'll stay here and bot a ciggie,' announced Laura. 'Sing out if you need a hand to find your iPod.' Ravi could picture her creaking down to peer under workstations. But they weren't after the same thing.

LAURA, 2004

ALL WEEK, SHE HAD BEEN bringing flattened boxes home from work; also a roll of masking tape nicked from the stationery cupboard. As it turned out, there were more boxes than she needed. She was giving away the silks, the pintucked cottons, the vintage Indian blockprints, stuffing them, some still on the hanger, into garbage bags she would lug to the charity bin. Many of her prettiest clothes no longer fitted, and all had been bought for Paul Hinkel. What an idiotic compulsion, she thought, eyeing a lacy shirt: all that money on finery he had stripped from her without delay. A buttonhole in the shirt was ripped. Laura remembered, *I couldn't wait*. At the sight of the torn shirt, the Goth receptionist had blushed, turning before Laura's eyes into a child. Then she had produced a pin.

Boxes were stacked on the landing. Robyn would store them at her flat, which Laura was going to share until she found a place of her own. 'There's heaps of space,' Robyn had said. 'It used to be Ferdy's synthesisers.' Laura taped up a last box and added it to the stack.

The house struck silent, secretive, large. Laura had never been there alone on a Sunday afternoon. She made a mug of tea and carried it, on impulse, to the big front bedroom. No harm in gazing, one last time, on Drummond and his works. In the gloom, as she passed him, his eyes were judge and hangman. But when she had got the blind up and turned around, he was only a genius with a green face.

Downstairs, a bell insisted. Robyn Orr, come earlier than planned to collect the boxes—so Laura guessed. But on the doorstep: 'Darl! We couldn't let you slip away without a bon voyage!' Tracy Lacey kissed and kissed, while peering down the hall. A black-haired sprite held out a parcel tied with gold string and labelled *Chocolate Panforte*; and Laura crouched and enfolded, smitten, as always, by the child. Destiny accepted the embrace but didn't return it. Something compelled her to keep her eyes open, yet close-ups of adult faces disgusted her: the slabs of pocked flesh, the giant black nostrils! But by the end of her first week at school, she had learned the uses of deception. Her expression remained compliant and sweet.

In the hall, Tracy explained, exclaimed, lingered and wondered. For where was the old man? It was Tracy's last chance, because Laura Fraser, always inclined to think only of herself, had suddenly announced that she was moving out. Yet at the gallery they believed that Tracy was the vessel into which Carlo Ferri decanted moods, secrets, whims. How had this come about? Tracy had no idea, although she might have said something like, 'He's an absolute sweetie, darl. It's a matter of pushing the right buttons.' Or she might have smiled and looked as if there was no end to what she could tell. None of this was exaggeration: Tracy knew that Carlo and she would get on like a horse on fire as soon as they met. But he was never at home when Laura invited, and anyway of late the invitations had grown rare. Whenever Tracy proposed, Laura countered with a tale of work or a virus, or suggested lunch in Newtown. So if anyone was to blame for the situation with Carlo, it was Laura Fraser. But Torquil's star had risen to deputy director, and he seemed to think that Tracy had promised to set up *an exploratory meeting* with Carlo Ferri. Torquil could be really unreasonable, he could sink his teeth into an idea and shake until something snapped.

Laura was leading Destiny into a room off the far end of the hall. Tracy followed and found herself in a kitchen. There was an oilcloth on the table—was oilcloth retro now or still ethnic in the wrong way?—but no old man. Through an archway, Tracy saw a room that hadn't been aired in years. The walls were a faded red, but the rose on the ceiling was nicotine yellow. Tracy always tried to maintain positive energy—it was the keystroke of Stew's philosophy—but she could feel a headache coming on, the close-fitting, all-over kind like a swimming cap made of lead.

When she turned around, it was just in time to prevent Laura from poisoning Destiny with almond-milk cordial. 'Sugar is death, darl! Nothing but fresh juice, *n'est-ce pas*? Or organic spring water.' There was only tap, but Tracy put slices of lemon in the jug to counteract the toxins and rinsed Destiny's glass herself. When she suggested that they go up to the roof, Laura muttered that everything there was a mess because she was packing. But no way were Tracy and Destiny staying in that kitchen, who could say what damage the passive smoking had already done?

On the landing, Tracy paused. She had noticed a door, usually shut, that today stood ajar. Of course: *la siesta*! It transported her at once to the Tuscan farmhouse, Tracy, Stew and Destiny all snoring lightly in shuttered rooms after an *insalata del pastore*. Not a trill issued from the room, so the old man hadn't dropped off yet. Calling to Destiny, who had gone ahead with Laura, Tracy set off. Laura said something that might have been 'No!', but Laura hadn't driven all the way from Paddo with Destiny and a panforte because Italians lose their heads over children and sweets.

When Tracy saw what was in the room—well, as she would tell Torquil, it was nothing less than an epitome. Laura buzzed at her elbow saying, 'But Carlo.' Tracy came out of the vision in which she lowered her gaze when Torquil got to the bit in his speech about her *invaluable service to our cultural heritage*. It emboldened her to enquire where *was* Carlo? 'Haberfield,' said Laura. 'He's having an operation on his hip first thing tomorrow. His cousin's driving him to hospital this evening. So we shouldn't—' 'I'm sure he won't mind, darl,' said Tracy. 'I'm a trained professional, *n'est-ce pas*?' She had been examining the canvases stacked on the bed but was overcome by the need to document. She took her phone from her bag and aimed. 'Mum,' wailed Destiny, '*Muuum*.' Destiny Lacey-Buck was bored but was not allowed to be. Bored is childhood's name for the formless, treeless, weatherless place from whence it comes: a memory and a presage. But *the b word* was banned in Paddo. What were piano lessons and *conversazione* and swimming classes and Free Expressive Movement for if not to maintain positive energy? As the flash went off, 'Would you take Destiny up to the roof, darl?' asked Tracy. 'Go and look at the boats, gorgeous, big hug, Mummy's working.'

Contemplating the vegetable ruins around her, Destiny remarked, 'Everything here is very old, isn't it?' She was still holding the panforte by its golden loop. Laura said, 'Shall we have some of that, do you think?' She took the parcel into Drummond's studio to find a knife, while Destiny wandered hither and thither among the devastation. She had soft dark eyes and a rosy-dark pansy face. In a woody tangle of summer jasmine high above her head, she saw what no human eye had seen, a pale blue egg. It was out of reach but was magically connected to a plant at home from which small pink and purple ballerinas dangled. Their name was fuchsia and they were a sign, like the egg, that Destiny's wish for a dog would come true. Stew said, 'For God's sake, don't start,' and Tracy said, 'Think of picking up the poo.' Destiny looked on as tiny Tracy and tiny Stew plunged from the roof and were lost in blue. At her silent whistle, Hotdog cleared the bridge in a bound. He swam and flew.

In the studio, Laura had been diverted from her purpose by the sight of the red glass star. The red rug waited in a roll on the landing, but she had forgotten to take down the star. That year, while the merry-go-round in her skull revolved to things Paul Hinkel and she liked to do to each other, she had let Theo's deathday pass unnoticed. *Forgetting was the real meaning of death*: she had realised that on a cold street in Prague. She addressed the star: But you haven't gone yet, not while I'm still here. Theo would live on as long as he was remembered: even humanly and imperfectly. She would leave the red star for Carlo, decided Laura. Not as an olive branch or an apology but as *a tiny object in the night*. He would understand or not, but she didn't want to leave only darkness behind when she went.

She had carved out two chunks of panforte and brushed the leaves from the table under the frangipani when she looked up to see Destiny making free expressive movements on a chair she had dragged to the edge of the roof. There was the protective wall, but the child already had one foot on it. Laura exclaimed and commanded. Destiny was perfectly safe because of Hotdog, but she came obediently when called. 'Have you seen a little dog around here?' she asked, startling Laura, whose thoughts had strayed to Paul Hinkel. 'Oooh, he's gorgeous,' went on Destiny. 'Shiny brown—no, I mean black, about this size.' She measured with her hands, described. All the while, she was trying to decide if she was crazy about panforte. When Laura came to Paddo, she would say, Have a squiz in my bag,

Destiny. There would be a book or a toy or a bracelet. But there was no bag here, only dead sticks and sour water. Laura was asking one of the dumb questions grown-ups ask about school. There were only three that mattered: What must you not show? Who is the leader? Where can you hide?

A long time later, when Tracy and Destiny were leaving, the child went unbidden to Laura. She pretended to kiss but placed her mouth very close to the large ear. Very softly and very distinctly, in her light, childish voice, she said, 'Everyone says you're ugly.' Destiny's best friend had said this to her on the last day of school, and Destiny knew its power. At the gate, she turned her flower-face to Laura and waved.

When her mobile rang that night, Laura didn't hear it. She was keeping watch on the roof, and the phone was in her bedroom below. After she had packed Robyn's car with boxes and seen her off, Laura had gone upstairs and done brutal things with secateurs. She had watered until everything on the roof looked soaked and wild. Halfway through laying into the bougainvillea, she had thought, What's the point? So she lit a last candle in Theo's star and settled down to see it out. The bridge was a rhinestone-studded handcuff finished with a ruby; its missing twin had closed around Laura's heart and was squeezing. The phone beseeched in a muffled way, but a child spoke plainly: Everyone says you're ugly. All evening, it was the only thing Laura had heard.

On a Blue Mountain far to the west, Donald Fraser dropped his phone into the pocket of his dressing-gown. Why was the runt sulking tonight? He hated it when she wouldn't talk to him. Still, she always came round in the end, he could count on her cheery hello. She was the true child of his true wife. The imposter had tried to feed him to a silver-skinned beast. But Donald wasn't fooled. She could call it *your car* all she liked, but he could see the snarling cat and read the label: *Jaguar*. Not long after that, Cameron had come. He asked, 'Do you know the prime minister's name, Dad?' Had the boy lost his wits? The prime minister's name was always Opportunist. Then Donald realised what had happened: the imposter had dug out Cameron's eyes and replaced them with the stones from her hand. The sparkles spelled, *A ring of thieves!* Together they had delivered him here, repeating that it was a lovely place, just like a hotel really, Donald was going to love it. That was quite true: Donald did. The carpets were so kind to his corns after the parquet, and in five weeks? eighteen months? eleven centuries? no one had once said, 'Pull yourself together, Don.' Sometimes the Rottie rested his heavy head on the arm of a chair, but the imposter had pushed her orange face close to Donald's going *mwa, mwa* and vanished forever. The food was excellent, exactly as she had promised, and every night the stars held a party. His wife usually dazzled there. By day, the telescope showed her backcombing her hair in a tear stain called a waterfall. The long window didn't open, but Donald could always hear her calling across the valley. Tonight she had prompted, 'Isn't there something you have to say to Laura?' Donald explained that he had been trying to get through to the runt for years. But whenever her voice greeted at the other end of the line, Donald would realise that it was too late to call.

Ravi, 2004

THE PEOPLE WALKING TOWARDS THE lights were making better progress than the cars. In the back seat, Hana clicked her tongue. 'We should have parked near the main road.' It was what she had proposed, but Abebe had said that it would mean a fifteen-minute walk. The evening was chilly, and it was drizzling on and off—they might have done better to postpone the trip. But on discovering that Ravi had never seen the Christmas lights, all three—Hana, Abebe, even Tarik—had insisted that he couldn't leave Sydney without doing so. 'We go to a different place every year.'

Light spiralled around the trunk of a palm tree in a garden. When Ravi remarked on it, Tarik said, 'Just wait.' A family strolled past the stationary car, the three young children in dressing-gowns over pyjamas. They were followed by a woman wearing a lilac jacket, denim skirt and short boots. Ravi had noticed her further back, when the car had overtaken her; she had caught up with them now. Hana was saying, 'It's like a different country, all these people out in the street at night.' There were dogs, babies in slings and strollers, a man with a walking stick. Something eased ahead, and the traffic slipped forward. Abebe was looking for a side street, but there were none, and soon they were at a standstill again. The lilac jacket drew level with the car, the woman walking briskly past Ravi's window. This happened two or three times. She was dark-haired, dark-skinned. Under a streetlamp, her jacket shone fluorescent blue about the shoulders. A group of teenagers carrying pizza boxes filled up the pavement, and when Ravi next saw the woman, she was a long way ahead.

At last they reached a roundabout and turned left. Their luck had changed: just in front of them, a Pajero was pulling out. In an undertone that couldn't be heard in the back seat, Abebe said, 'You know what *pajero* means in Spanish?' His hand at his crotch made a universal gesture.

When they had joined the people flowing uphill towards the roundabout, Ravi saw something wonderful: in the distance, a ship of light floated above the massed darkness of trees. The others looked where he pointed. But: 'Wait,' said Hana and Abebe together, and Tarik said, 'Wait.'

Hours later, they dropped Ravi off at Hazel's. It was his second-last night there. The following evening, Hazel and the boys were taking him out to dinner; Damo would drive him to the airport the day after that. Ravi couldn't know it, but that offer of a lift represented the outcome of a struggle. On learning that Ravi was going back, Damo had choked on incredulity, anger, hurt, disappointment, loss—in other words, rejection. Savaging a sausage in the sunroom, with his brothers and Hazel around the table, he came out with, 'So that's it, is it? He waltzes in here, when there are people literally dying to get into this country, and then decides he's going back?' For a while, there was only the sound of knives. Then Russ, blanketing a T-bone with tomato sauce, was compelled to say, 'Who spent two years pulling pints in Dublin when he finished uni? Can't see how this is different.' Russ had always been thick *as*, it was completely different, you couldn't compare a working holiday to . . . Damo chewed and chewed. He was remembering an afternoon of strict, clean light when he had taken Ravi to the plague cemetery at La Perouse. They had looked at the graves of nurses, girls in their twenties, who had caught the contagion from their patients. Damo's father had taken him there—it was one of Damo's special places. Why had he shown it to Ravi? Fair Play chose that moment to whine at the back door. Damo decided silently, You can just stay out there.

Hazel's present to Ravi was a photograph album. She had given it to him in advance, so that if she'd forgotten anything important, there'd be time to take a photo of it before he left. Night after night now, Hazel came to stand in the sunroom. She was looking for Ravi's light. On the dresser, her babies smiled and faded daily, trapped behind glass. Sometimes Hazel was still there, holding her elbows, when dawn broke in the plumbago; Blue Heaven, her mother had called that flower. Two questions jousted for supremacy during these vigils. Why must everyone go away in the end? When will it be my turn?

Sitting on his bed, Ravi turned the pages of the album. There was the sleep-out: in summer with pumpkins encroaching; in winter, with Ravi grinning in the doorway, hands shoved into his fleece. Passionflowers were a red riot over the dunny. There was the shed, and the view over the river, and the lane clotted with jasmine. Fair Play appeared with her legs braced for attack, chewing Lefty's face. On the next page, she stood over a freshly limp mynah with her tail straight up. But it was the third photo that made Ravi pause.

It showed Fair Play regal on her throne, one ear tucked back, head held high. What was striking was the spread of white on her muzzle. 'Fair Play!' said Ravi. The little dog stared with unsparing clarity from his pillow, and he saw that she had aged before his eyes. The photo had shown him a change to which he had been blind in life.

When Abebe was driving away from the lights, Ravi had spotted the lilac woman again. She was on the driver's side of the car this time, moving at the same steady pace, looking straight ahead. So ghosts are said to walk through walls. The car drew level for a moment. Then they had left her behind.

In the back seat, Tarik asked, 'Which one was your favourite?' Hana voted for the house where every row of rooftop tiles was roped in light. 'I loved the reindeer,' said Tarik, alluding to the giant shining beast that had galloped across a lawn. 'And the Baby Jesus scene.' 'You only liked the Baby Jesus scene because Mr Whippy was parked outside.' 'That is so not fair, I loved the little lamb and the donkey and the angels,' said Tarik in an excited voice. Abebe looked in the mirror and said, 'It's okay to like both, Mr Whippy always parks outside the best lights.' 'When we live in a house, can we have a reindeer?'

No one asked what Ravi had liked. He had been transfixed by it all: the stars and flowers and waterfalls of light, the good-natured, festive crowd ambling past the illuminated houses, the children waving neon wands, the emblazoned night. But among all the surfing Santas and inflatable snowmen and electric Nativities come to kindle silent Australia, what had truly moved Ravi was the ship: a simple outline like a child's drawing in light. *The Christmas houses*—Tarik's phrase—stood along four or five streets that climbed and twisted and dipped. As soon as the ship of light loomed, a bend in the street would take Ravi away from it. Then it would appear again, floating above the trees.

Eventually, he realised that he would get no closer. He found that he didn't mind. The ship would remain with him, a radiant prospect. Close up, it might have failed to enchant. So that's what I've become, thought Ravi, a man whose best hope of happiness is avoidance. He remembered when the whole world had floated before him, a ship of possibility.

Hana, Abebe and Tarik had reacted each in their own way to the news that Ravi was returning to Sri Lanka. As usual, the child said nothing direct, but her expression declared that she had always known he was a fool. Abebe was dismayed, but it was not in Abebe to oppose what anyone wanted. Before long, he was of the opinion that Ravi was right to go back: the ceasefire was holding, there would be all kinds of opportunities for someone like Ravi. 'With your IT skills and English.' *Politics* hovered, an unspoken question to which Ravi didn't have the answer. But Abebe and Hana didn't pursue it: they were occupied with plans. Abebe had passed his final exams and was looking for work as an accountant. Hana had applied to two universities to study social sciences part time. Her attention had swung away from Ravi: he felt it, like an absence of breeze. She remained sharp and scornful but only impersonally so, saying of his decision to leave, 'Nothing will ever drag me back.' On their outing to see the lights, she had walked ahead with Tarik, leaving Abebe and Ravi to follow. At one point, Ravi had fallen behind, distracted by a flashing green kangaroo on a golden surfboard. When he turned around, he saw that the other three had crossed the street and were walking together, hand in hand, Abebe saying something to his sister over the head of the tall child. Earlier that evening, Ravi had shared their meal. Abebe Issayas had torn off a piece of bread, dipped it in spicy stew and placed it between Ravi's lips. Across the table, Hana smiled faintly. Ravi pictured her long fingers busy at the sleek new keyboard behind her. When she said goodbye outside Hazel's, her cheek against his was smooth and cool. He saw that she had never been available anyway: she belonged to that winner, the future. Tarik, kneeling to face the wrong way on the back seat, waved with both hands as Abebe accelerated. Ravi lowered his arm when the tail-lights had disappeared around the corner. There was a glint in the corner of his eye. He looked down and saw that the verge was scattered with broken glass.

More than an hour had passed since then and Ravi still hadn't started packing. Once again, he turned the album's pages. The boys lifted their stubbies to him around a barbecue, Kev in a plastic apron brandishing the tongs. Hazel beamed from her latest chair. One of its arms was patched with a coffee sack, but Ravi didn't notice. He was thinking of the lilac woman. He had seen her quite clearly, but trying to call her up now, he produced a composite, Hana, Malini, the lilac woman herself: a figure who looked to neither left nor right but steadily ahead. For a little while her life had kept pace with his, but they were moving at different speeds.

In her hotel room near Central, Mona Fleurie, née Mohan Dabrera, had taken off her lilac jacket and gone out onto her balcony. She had come to Sydney to see the son she had fathered when she was still Mohan. The boy was in trouble at school for truancy and bullying. Mona knew, because he had told her so, that everything wrong with his life was her fault. He had set the place and time of their meeting, but when Mona rang the doorbell, he wouldn't leave his room. His red backpack hung like a promise in the hall, but her son refused to see her. Variations on this theme had been going on for three years. His mother had dinner guests, and Mona wasn't invited. There was nothing to do in the end but turn around and walk all the way back to the station. Mona had taken planes, taxis and an upstairs train to reach the child who didn't want to see her; however you looked at it, she had travelled a long way. Now, seven storeys below her balcony, the wet street was a black mirror. Mona Fleurie had trained herself to keep her gaze on where she was going. But you couldn't outdistance the past. It drew level eventually, whether or not you recognised it, and then it overtook you.

His mother's grey suitcase lay on the carpet. When Ravi opened it, Fair Play jumped off the bed and scratched at the door—she knew what an empty suitcase meant, and she was wasting no more time here. A second case stood by, because Ravi was returning with more than he had brought. Priya had sent a detailed list of requirements, which she updated almost daily. In addition to these gifts, Ravi was taking home things like memory sticks, packets of soup, T-shirts with logos, Kmart jeans.

He began with the photograph album, trying to fit it into the inner pocket of the case. But it encountered an obstruction. Ravi slipped his hand behind the ruched satin and drew out a yellow viewfinder shaped like a TV. He placed the little toy to his eye and clicked. Nothing happened: long ago, the mechanism had broken. Sitting there on his heels, Ravi could see that the picture wasn't going to change. But he went on clicking for quite a long time.

LAURA, 2004

ON HER FIRST DAY IN Sri Lanka, she was to have breakfasted on the terrace of a famous hotel in Colombo, gazing at the Indian Ocean. But her connecting flight from Bangkok had set off only to turn back after an hour. The engine trouble wasn't serious, the pilot announced, while the passengers looked at each other. How strange—they had never expected to die in the company of a bald man in tracksuit pants and a child vomiting on his mother's shoes. Regulations required the flight to return to its port of origin. The next hour was one of those that contains—oh, more minutes than anyone can count, certainly not sixty. Time stretched, sagged, snapped, sang. Afterwards, an endless day passed to the tinkle of electronic carols in gate lounges, and then Laura was boarding her connection again. By the time she had reclaimed her case and cleared Customs, 'Merry Christmas, madam,' said the Sri Lankan official who exchanged her dollars for rupees. A whole day of her holiday had vanished. Laura thought, Why not go straight to the southern beaches? In Bangkok there had been an email from Ravi Mendis inviting her to spend New Year's Day with his family. She would be able to tell him that she'd skipped Colombo altogether; that was even better than *get out as soon as possible*. She looked for the rental car sign.

When Laura woke the next day, it was to the thought that she would have to rearrange her itinerary to take in the visit to Ravi's family on the west coast. There would be fresh bookings to make, more deposits sacrificed, new hassles. The previous evening, the rental car had carried her from one southern hotel to another until, at last, in a decrepit establishment facing away from the sea, a vacancy was found. Here there was no pool, no air-conditioning, no complimentary cocktail on arrival: only the whisk of a rat along a beam. But what did it matter? She had a booking at a flash place up the coast the following day; meanwhile there were coconut palms at her window. Surrounded by concrete, Laura pointed her toes at the ceiling fan that had expired some hours before dawn. It was the unforeseen that returned tourism to travel. Ramsay was dedicated to the reverse. That was the real message of the letters and emails that arrived by the thousand there. Prices had rocketed, beggars had menaced, sunsets had disappointed, but it was the soul that bled and composed accusations. It had learned that it was a tourist—not an explorer, vagabond, nomad or adventurer. And if it sent compliments because the advice had been awesome and the trip really amazing, what did that mean? *Exactly the same thing*. The true guidebook would advise: 'Pay attention, be kind, think twice, shut up.' Laura informed the fan, I'm hitting Jobsearch as soon as I get back. But what was she fitted for? And what would change? What could she do that wouldn't stun with busyness, lull with routine, infect with compromise like a slow, fatal blight?

But tourism existed to postpone such questions. It was the first day of Laura's holiday, the country unknown, the morning pure potential. Rising to meet it, she was conscious of joy. The magic land existed. It had to—hadn't Laura always known it? She would find it yet: in the depths of a wardrobe, at the top of a faraway tree.

Her lightness of being persisted as she made her way along the beach; she was heading towards the internet cafe run by Ravi's friend. Lightness had kept her company throughout her dip in the warm, glassy bay, throughout breakfast, where she had considered pineapple jam, then spread hard, cold toast with a fiery sambol. Doing things differently was the point of leaving home. It wasn't until she was under the shower that Paul Hinkel showed up—at home, he was waiting as soon as she woke. *Getting away was starting over*. The old dream of renewal gathered Laura up; Alan Ramsay had founded a fortune on it. A holiday was as good as a change, it was green growth on the twig.

At that, Carlo was with her. On Laura's last day in Sydney, Rosalba had answered the phone by his hospital bed. The operation had gone well, Laura heard. The voice was mascarpone: triple cream, with never a hint of denaturing acid. It thanked Laura for her concern, and informed her that talking tired the patient; it was sure Laura would understand. What Laura understood was that Rosalba had been sitting by Carlo's bed for half a century, waiting for him to come round. The voice claimed to be grateful 'for everything you have done for my cousin'. The very faint emphasis on 'everything' notified the fat one upstairs that *Rosalba knew*—knew or guessed about rose-red Sundays. But you don't know what I didn't do, thought Laura, after she had broken the connection. She picked up a sealed envelope and placed it with the rest of Carlo's mail. It contained the greater part of her savings: enough, she hoped, for new plants for the roof. It had seemed the least she could do. But thinking of that envelope now, Laura remembered the cheques that had arrived over the years bearing her father's signature and was ashamed. What Fraserish reflex had persuaded her that damage could be wiped out with dollars? Carlo knew better, he left without a backward glance. Rosalba wept in the Spanish Quarters; in her strawberry-pink villa, a *principessa* raged. The betrayer had moved on: *that was the meaning of betrayal*. Tracy Lacey's flash went off in Drummond's face. That was another discovery in store for Carlo: among the envelopes waiting for him had been one printed with the gallery's name. A breathy whisper assured Laura, Everyone says you're ugly. She vowed to write to Carlo, neither requesting nor expecting forgiveness, as soon as she got back. She would change her life, she would start over.

It was not quite nine o'clock, but the beach was crowded. Tourists and locals were sunbathing, breakfasting on hotel terraces, breaststroking in the calm bay. The perfect, cloudless morning had summoned vendors of batik and greeting cards and a depressing lace tablecloth. Laura no thank you-ed, no thank you-ed. She came to a cluster of fishing shacks thatched with coconut. A wave of children poured from them and into the sea—only the boys, noted Laura; the girls stood in the shallows with their skirts bunched.

There were more boys further along, playing beach cricket with a tennis ball. While Laura was still some way off, one of them lunged for a catch, missed, went running after the ball. A fielder at the far edge of the group, hands on hips, had a shock of black hair. In four seconds, Laura thought: first, It's that boy. Next: But taller. Then: Well, he would have grown over the years. Finally: But it can't be the same boy! He had turned to watch the fate of the ball. Then, as Laura looked on, he strolled away. She realised that he had nothing to do with the game, after all—he was only a bystander. A horn startled, and, glancing around, Laura saw a blue Mercedes pull off the road and park. The driver got out. Behind his wraparound sunglasses, he appeared to be scanning the beach. But it was a sign nailed to a tree that caught Laura's eye: an arrow pointed along a sandy path on the far side of the road to *Network Cafe*. When she looked back along the beach, a quartet of English teenagers was approaching, and the boy was splashing into the bay.

Robyn had emailed from her parents' place in Townsville: . . . *told us that gina'll be taking over from cliff. quentin and i didn't even know gina was going for ceo. she's got experience running an office and we don't—that's the party line anyway. i've already talked to the headhunters and we've lined up a meeting in january. i'm also thinking i should maybe talk to alan about taking over from gina in london. a few years there could be pretty cool* . . .

Turning a dull red stone on his finger, Nimal Corea was studying the back of Laura Fraser's head. She had agreed, readily, to have a cup of tea with him when she had checked her email. 'No breakfast for madam?' She had already breakfasted, she said. But then she smiled. 'I can have a second breakfast, can't I? I'm on holiday!' Nimal suggested an omelette made with green chilli, and she agreed to that, too. She said, 'Call me Laura—please.' A vista opened as if activated by remote control, and Nimal strolled hand in hand with Laura over the Harbour Bridge in a deep mauve dusk.

A cry drifted from the beach: 'Run! Run!' Absorbed in Robyn's news, Laura didn't hear it. In any case, she wouldn't have understood. Nimal, who did, assumed that the shouts sprang from the game of cricket. Laura closed Robyn's message, and her inbox reappeared. It now contained a second email. There was no subject line and, when she opened it, no message. But the sender was Paul Hinkel. Was it a truce, carte blanche, a summary of what she had meant to him? Laura could read his blank letter any way she chose.

As she pondered its intent, there came a great shuddering sigh, as if the whole planet were sorrowing. It was about 9.20 on the 26th of December, and a tsunami had just struck. On the veranda that served as a kitchen, an omelette stiffened in its pan, the cook's attention claimed by a blue car surfing a black wave. Nimal had only to glance that way to witness the marvel but he was slow to emerge from the vision in which he lay entwined with Laura Fraser on a buttery leather couch. The power cut out, but not before Nimal had seen every detail of their harbourside mansion. It was white and storeyed with a view of water from every room.

Permissions

ACKNOWLEDGMENTS

Thank you to the Literature Fund of the Australia Council.

Thank you to Devika and Michael Anthonisz, Penelope Asselineau, Sophie Cunningham, Robert Dessaix, Robert Dixon, Clara Finlay, Goolbai Gunasekera, Philip Hoare, Ayalew Hundessa, Gail Jones, Sharmalie Joseph, Chris Mander, Michael Meyler, Sue Mitra, Peter Morris, Christa Munns, Virginia Murdoch, Jane Nethercote, Maria Psihogios-Billington, Varunika Ruwanpura, Sanjaya Senaweera, Glenda Sluga, Lachlan Strahan, Maithree Wickramasinghe and Charlotte Wood.

Thank you to Victor Melder and the Victor Melder Library in Melbourne. Thank you to Maureen Seneviratne, in whose *Dark Nights of the Moon* I read of a children's game about bombs.

A special thank you to Sarah Lutyens, Clare Drysdale, Ali Lavau, Jane Palfreyman and Pat Strachan. Also to Vita Giordano, Kerry Murphy, Joseph Pearson, Nicholas Poynder, Sally Webster and particularly Walter Perera.

Last and first, I thank Chris Andrews.